The
Daisy
Children

Center Point
Large Print

The Daisy Children

SOFIA GRANT

CENTER POINT LARGE PRINT
THORNDIKE, MAINE

The text of this Large Print edition is unabridged.
In other aspects, this book may vary
from the original edition.
Printed in the United States of America
on permanent paper.
Set in 16-point Times New Roman type.

ISBN: 978-1-64358-046-3

Library of Congress Cataloging-in-Publication Data

Names: Grant, Sofia, author.
Title: The daisy children / Sofia Grant.
Description: Center Point Large Print edition. | Thorndike, Maine :
    Center Point Large Print, 2019.
Identifiers: LCCN 2018045334 | ISBN 9781643580463
    (hardcover : alk. paper)
Subjects: LCSH: Texas—Fiction. | Family secrets. | Large type books.
Classification: LCC PS3612.I882 D35 2019 | DDC [Fic]— dc23
LC record available at https://lccn.loc.gov/2018045334

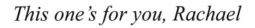

This one's for you, Rachael

AUTHOR'S NOTE

The explosion that ripped through the New London School in 1937 was all too real, as was the devastation it left in its aftermath. The Daisy Children, however, exist only in my imagination. I created these mothers and their "replacement" children to both honor all those who found a way to go on in the face of unimaginable loss, and to keep bright the memory of all those who perished.

PROLOGUE

ARCHER DAILY TRIBUNE

HUNDREDS OF CHILDREN PERISH IN NEW LONDON SCHOOL EXPLOSION

New London, Tex., March 18, 1937—

At 3:20 this afternoon, as nearly seven hundred children and teachers finished the school day before what was to be a long weekend, an explosion ripped through the new Consolidated School, reducing one entire wing to rubble. Fire immediately erupted, the roof caved in, walls tumbled down, and the ground shook for miles around. Those close to the school at the time of the disaster mistakenly believed that a bomb had gone off, and within moments, dozens of bystanders had rushed to the aid of the injured and dying.

At the time of this writing, over four hundred bodies have been counted, and fewer than one hundred injured survivors have been accounted for. Many others are still missing.

Help continues to pour in from Texas, Louisiana, and beyond. Hundreds of workers rushed from the busy East Texas oil fields to lend assistance, armed with torches and tools. They are joined by doctors, nurses, coroners, and undertakers who continue to arrive by automobile and train and seemingly every other form of conveyance. National Guardsmen have established martial law at the order of Gov. James V. Allred.

The cause of the disaster has yet to be determined. Had the explosion been delayed but a few hours, the school would have stood silent and empty, and hundreds of souls would have been saved.

Chapter One

Katie Garrett's hopes were dashed right after the arrival of the ridiculous trousers. It wasn't the fault of the trousers, of course, but it was tempting to blame them nonetheless.

Her morning had already been off to a bad start. Yesterday, Katie's boss had unceremoniously announced that Nickell, March & Co. would no longer be requiring her services. This was unexpected news—her performance reviews had always indicated that she was a perfectly satisfactory Designer II of Structural and Graphic Solutions (in other words, a packaging designer)—but apparently "market realities" had come to bear and *blah, blah, blah*. Katie stopped listening and focused on her boss's puffy, creased neck flesh while willing herself not to cry. When it was over, and with her face burning, she'd cleared out her cubicle and come home in a daze, trying to figure out how to break the news to Liam as the twilight leeched from the cramped rooms of their tiny apartment.

At nearly eight he'd burst breathlessly through the door, arms full of flowers, already apologizing—the wretched Sanders account, sucking the life from his poor overworked soul, had demanded yet another eleven-hour day—and when he finally wound down, she couldn't bring herself to burden him further. She put the flowers (a dozen dazzling gerberas, bright and gaudy and ungodly expensive) in a vase and called their favorite Thai place, and when Liam went out to pick up the *mee krob*, she allowed herself a quick cry before blowing her nose and taking off her ruined mascara.

She'd fallen asleep on the couch and woke several hours later to discover that Liam had turned out the lights and gone to bed. She shuffled groggily to the bedroom and collapsed. In the morning, she woke after Liam had already showered and gone. As she squeezed past the ancient bathroom sink to the toilet, she caught a glimpse of herself in the mirror and noticed that a noodle was stuck in her hair. So this was how unemployment was going to be.

She had intended to use her first full day of unemployment to plan how to deliver the bad news, and also to bring up the subject of finding a bigger apartment. She'd let Liam talk her into this minuscule one-bedroom after they got married because it was right smack on Beacon Street, in the pulsing heart of the Back Bay; but the prospect of wedging herself past the sink to reach the toilet for as long as she was unemployed was simply too depressing. That, and they'd soon be needing more room, with any luck.

She opened up her laptop and created a document called Moving Pros and Cons, but by ten-thirty in the morning she'd gotten no further than the kitchen counter, where she was eating cold leftover noodles from the takeout carton when the doorbell buzzed.

"Oh, *hell,*" Katie blurted. She was still wearing Liam's old Celtics T-shirt that she slept in, with nothing but panties underneath. People often pushed buttons at random until someone in the building let them in, but Katie dashed to the bedroom to pull on her sweatpants anyway, then rushed down the two flights of stairs and caught the delivery man just as he was turning to go.

She felt a twinge of something—indigestion, perhaps—as she accepted the box with its plain brown wrapping and Seamless logo (raised-print topstitching, very expensive) and signed the little keypad before heading back up the stairs. Liam had been eagerly anticipating this package ever since he'd visited the Seamless shop on Boylston, where a man redolent of aftershave spent half an hour taking measurements in a dressing room tricked out like a nineteenth-century haberdashery before charging Liam two hundred forty dollars and reminding him that "the pants of a lifetime" couldn't be made overnight, but that in three weeks' time a pair of trousers as unique as Liam himself would arrive at his door.

The pants could not be returned, of course,

which was most unfortunate, since Katie was about to break it to Liam that their household income had just been cut in half. Back upstairs in the foyer of their tiny apartment, she bent over to set the box down next to the spittoon that Liam had insisted on buying on their honeymoon and now used to toss his keys in, when the twinge became something else and, with utter and immediate clarity, she knew.

Her period had trumpeted its arrival with the twinge, the gut twist, the sudden gush.

Which meant that, once again, they had failed to make a baby this month. No adorable precious goddamn baby for Liam and Katie, the couple who had everything, the couple everyone envied.

Katie put her back against the wall and slid slowly down. They'd been here before—six times in a row, in fact. And of course, as disappointing as this was, it wasn't nearly as bad as her miscarriage last fall. Liam had been wonderful then, taking time off work to take care of her, binge watching three seasons of *Shameless* next to her on the couch. Since then, as the months ticked by, he'd grown less enchanted with the idea of "trying," had even balked a few times when the ovulation tracker called them to act, and while it was tempting to wonder if they'd missed their chance while he'd fallen asleep in front of the Patriots game, she could hardly blame him: their grim couplings no longer held much joy.

Still, they'd try again. Or they could have that conversation they'd danced around, about other possible sources of babies—there were lots of options, loads of them. But just for the moment, Katie was glad that Liam wasn't home, because she needed to be alone to let go of the little stash of forbidden hopes she'd been stockpiling: the starfish-shaped hands, the crisp eyelet of the christening gown Liam's sister was saving for them, that exquisite shade of aquamarine she'd snipped from the color chart and taped to the bottom of her desk drawer because it was *perfect* for the baby's room, boy or girl.

The cramps got a little sharper. Katie had always had miserable periods, accompanied with lower back pain and bloating and irritability and nausea. She might as well just curl up on the couch with the remote until Liam got home. Maybe he would bring her sizzling rice soup and shortbread from Flourhouse, like last month—although he'd been working so much overtime lately that she probably shouldn't ask.

Katie's phone, sitting on the floor next to her, trilled. Her mother. Katie rolled her eyes out of habit, then reconsidered; maybe—just maybe—this was one of those rare moments when Georgina would prove to be exactly what she needed.

She picked the phone up and tapped the screen. "Mom?" she croaked.

"What's the matter?" Instantly on alert, Georgina's voice drew up tight as the neck of a burlap sack. "Katie, honey, what is it?"

"It's—it's—" Katie snuffled into her sleeve.

"Oh, honey. Got your period again?"

You had to give Georgina that—not much got by her. Even during the two years during college when Katie quit speaking to her, Georgina had a knack for intuiting what was going on.

Katie mumbled a yes.

"You want me to come out for a visit?"

"No," Katie gasped. "Definitely not."

"Oh, well." Georgina clucked matter-of-factly. "I'd probably just make things worse. And I'm going to have my hands full."

"With what?" Katie asked, resigned to changing the subject, as every conversation with Georgina was about Georgina, no matter what else was happening. News of her unemployment would have to wait, which suited her just fine.

"Well—the nursing home called, and Margaret passed last night. Plus I'm supposed to host book club tonight, though I suppose I ought to cancel. Which is a shame, because—"

"Margaret?" Katie interrupted. "As in, *Grandma* Margaret?"

"Katie." Georgina sighed. "You've never called her Grandma."

"She signed her name that way when she wrote to me."

"Which was what, all of two times? Listen, I refuse to pretend to be devastated by this. She was barely more than a stale piece of toast in a wheelchair after her stroke, anyway. At least now I don't have to drive two hours to sit around watching them all drooling on their cardigans."

"Oh, Mom," Katie said. After a beat, she added, "Are you maybe a little bit sadder than you think?" *Deep inside, where you've stuffed all your feelings behind all those bourbon sours and plastic surgery?*

"No, pretty sure not," Georgina said briskly. "I did all my mourning years ago. Like when I was six and she locked me in the basement because she didn't want to listen to me *sneeze*. Listen, how about I send something nice? Maybe a case of wine?"

"Well, that would be a step up from last time," Katie said drily. After her miscarriage, a package from the Dallas Neiman Marcus had arrived, containing a lace push-up bra and an enormous bottle of Clé de Peau, along with a computer-generated note on the invoice that said "Feel Better Love Georgina." "I mean . . . thanks, Mom."

She was about to say "I love you," something that still felt very unnatural, when her mother said thoughtfully, "It *is* strange, though, isn't it? I mean, if my mother had died on the day a baby was *born,* the symbolism would be obvious. But I can't quite figure out what to make of this."

"It doesn't mean anything at all," Katie said shortly. She started to get up, going slow, helping herself with a hand on the wall. "Women get their periods every day. It hasn't really even been all that long—our doctor won't even discuss it until we've been trying a whole year."

"Honey girl," Georgina said, so tenderly that Katie started crying again. "Oh, my pretty little girl. I *do* love you, you know. More than you'll ever know, until your own baby comes. Which she will. She *will,* darling. The next one's going to stick."

Katie smiled through her tears. "What about you? You sure you're all right?"

"I'm fine," Georgina said crisply, "other than I have no idea what I'm going to do with two dozen gorgonzola mini quiches and two pounds of shrimp."

CHAPTER TWO

November 1948
New London, Texas

Margaret Pierson was hiding in the coat closet, so close to the Daisy Club mothers gathering their coats and gloves that she could smell their perfumes. She was here to collect secrets—secrets she would record in her diary for further consideration, because if there was one thing that Margaret had learned in her eleven years on earth, it was that everyone had something they were hiding.

She was meant to be in the sunroom, saying goodbye to the other children, but three of them were boys and lately she had found their company unappealing. Boys were loud and reckless and often dirty, and worst of all, they seemed indifferent to her. Margaret had been accustomed to being the center of attention since—well, since as far back as she could remember, which was a sunny afternoon with all of these very same children.

Her mother, Caroline, insisted it wasn't possible for Margaret to recall something that happened so long ago, but she distinctly remembered being set on her back on her parents' bed in a row with the others, their infant arms and legs waving in the air. She remembered being unable to move, to walk or even crawl, and having to depend on her mother to pick her up and move her about the house. She remembered dust motes dancing in the sunlight and watching the others, her fellow Daisy babies, though she did not know that name yet, grasping at the sparkling flecks.

And—on this point her mother burst into laughter—Margaret remembered thinking that the other babies were rather stupid to believe they could ever catch one.

Even then, her mother's amusement annoyed her. Margaret knew that there were certain unbreachable principles in the world, and sunlight illuminating specks that would other-wise be invisible was simply a fact. The babies had been lined up on the bed that day so that their photograph could be taken, the earliest group photo of the Daisy Club children. The photograph was now in a silver frame on the little curvy-legged table in the living room, and Caroline Pierson insisted that Margaret believed she remembered that day only because she'd grown up looking at the photograph.

So Margaret had stopped taking her mother into her confidence. Instead, she had turned her keen eye on the other adults in her life. She'd hidden herself in the coat closet when the luncheon started breaking up, and now she had a view of the foyer around the folds of Alelia's patched woolen coat, which she hung every morning when she came to work. Alelia had taken the ladies' coats upstairs to the sewing room, as there wasn't room in the closet for all of them, and brought them back downstairs after the luncheon and even remembered which belonged to whom. Margaret watched the women huddle close together, whispering while they waited.

"I wish they'd just stop having it," Mrs. Sowell said. "It's been more than ten years now. Isn't it time?"

"Never," Mrs. Dial said fiercely. Her face, usually powdered and rouged to perfection, was mottled with rage. Her fingers were wrapped so tightly around the handle of her purse that the skin had turned white. "As long as I'm alive, no one is going to forget what happened that day."

Caroline Pierson made a clucking sound that Margaret knew well; she employed it to end arguments with her father. "There's lots of time to decide," she said in an overly bright voice. "Alice, don't forget to write down your deviled egg recipe. Hugh can't stop talking about them."

"If you don't want to be on the committee, you can always quit," Mrs. Dial snapped at Mrs. Sowell, unmollified. *That* was certainly interesting. People rarely ignored her mother.

Her mother stiffened for a moment, then put her hand firmly on Mrs. Sowell's shoulder and steered her toward the door. Once she was gone, Caroline closed the door a little more firmly than necessary and turned back to the others with a pained smile on her face.

"Don't give this another thought," Caroline told Mrs. Dial soothingly. She stood only inches away from the closet door, close enough that Margaret could count the houndstooth checks on her skirt. "Of course there will be a Remembrance Day, and the Daisies will attend, as always. But you must remember that Alice lost more than most. She's . . . vulnerable."

"I don't care," Mrs. Dial retorted in a strangled voice. "I lost Ralph that day, she lost her three—what does it matter? We both lost our children. And now she wants to just sweep them all under the rug like they were nothing—nothing but—"

She broke off in muffled sobs, and Caroline patted her shoulder uncomfortably. Margaret knew that her mother despised public displays of emotion, and she felt ashamed for poor Mrs. Dial.

"What we must do," Caroline said confidently once Mrs. Dial had composed herself, "is focus on the planning and not worry about our detractors. We have lots to do in the next few months. I could certainly use your help on the publicity committee, how does that sound? The others will come around—we'll just work on making this Remembrance Day the best ever."

"The best ever," Mrs. Dial repeated, her face bearing the dazed expression of cattle in the railcars headed for the Fort Worth stockyards.

Margaret knew why Mrs. Dial was so sad. Her son Ralph had burned up in the same school explosion that had killed Margaret's own sister, Ruby, along with hundreds of other children, when natural gas leaked out of the pipeline and built up in the school basement. Helene Dial had told Margaret that sometimes her mother stayed in bed all afternoon clutching a dirty, ragged old baby blanket that had belonged to Ralph.

Margaret and Helene—and all of the other Daisy children—had been born to make their parents happy again. They arrived in the world as the new school was being constructed, and there was a newspaper picture of them, lined up in their mothers' arms, at the ribbon cutting ceremony when it opened.

In the photograph, all of the mothers were smiling at once—something that, as far as Margaret could tell, had never happened again.

CHAPTER THREE

After hanging up with her mother, Katie called Liam at work and got his voice mail. In truth, she was relieved not to have to speak to him in person, not yet. "Oh, hey," she said breezily, clutching the hem of her sweatshirt for dear life. "My grandmother died. I mean, not that I even ever knew her or anything, but . . . and also, I got my period today, so, you know, guess you're off the hook for a while." *Ha, ha.* Their sex life served up as gallows humor. "Anyway, just thought—I don't know, if you don't have to work late tonight we could . . . but yeah, I know, the Sanders thing. So. Okay, see you when you get home."

Cripes! If it was that hard to leave a voice mail, how was she ever going to bring up the rest of it? The layoff—moving—adoption. Long ago, when they'd first met, as undergrads at Columbia, it had seemed like they were perfectly aligned by fate and luck. They agreed on everything from late-night noshing (onion rings at Bernheim & Schwartz) to running (up Riverside Drive to the public track at 138th Street, avoiding the throngs circling the reservoir). But now there was a distance between them, a coolness, that seemed to go beyond the awkwardness of ovulation tracking, beyond Liam's long hours and Katie's dissatisfaction at her dead-end (and now dead) job. No question, they'd grown apart, but didn't everyone—

Her phone rang in her hand, the caller ID flashing "Laura Rabinowitz." Lolly! As if she'd read Katie's mind. Rex and Lolly—Liam's best friend and his beautiful artist wife—were abundantly, disgustingly happy together. Lolly called her at least twice a month to get together for matinees and whiskey tastings and window-shopping and gallery-crawling in the South End, and Katie—who'd never had a proper girlfriend in her life, having switched schools nearly every year since the third grade and having met Liam a few weeks into their freshman year—couldn't quite figure out why Lolly bothered.

"Hi," she said brightly—then burst into tears. *Again.* Stupid period hormones.

"What's wrong?" Lolly asked in alarm. "Are you all right?"

"I'm—I'm fine," Katie sniffled. "Just, I got my period, and, well . . ."

"Aw, hell," Lolly said with feeling. Katie had surprised herself by telling Lolly about her and Liam's struggles a few months ago, drinking mulled wine in front of a fire in the living room of their beautiful brownstone while fat snowflakes drifted past the windows.

25

"*And* I got laid off yesterday."

"No!"

"Yes! And—and Liam bought pants that cost more than any dress I've ever owned." An exaggeration, but not that much of one.

"That *bastard,*" Lolly fumed, despite the fact that she had inherited gobs of money that they didn't even need because Rex did something clever with hedge funds or bonds or something. "Let me grab the Tito's and I'll come right over."

Katie giggled despite herself. She considered mentioning Margaret's death too, but that one was harder to explain; most people had at least met their grandparents more than once. "Thanks, Lols," she said, "but I think Liam's going to try to get out of work early."

"If you're sure," Lolly said solemnly. "But only if you let me take you to tea at the Reserve soon. We can get dressed up and act like ladies."

"That sounds wonderful," Katie sighed.

"Can you hang in there until then? You know all you have to do is call and I'll come over, right?"

"Right," Katie said, but after she hung up she stared at the phone with a sense of wonderment. Too-good-to-be-true Lolly, who had singled out Katie from all the other women in her large and glamorous circle, for reasons she didn't really understand. Next to Lolly, with her wild curls and thrift-shop dresses and moonstone rings,

26

and paintbrushes stuck in Baccarat vases and an honest-to-god Rothko in the dining room, Katie felt about as interesting as a club sandwich.

Though it had been wishful thinking when Katie told Lolly that Liam would be coming home early, he showed up well before dinnertime with another plastic-wrapped bouquet and a carton of the potato salad that Katie liked. He seemed oddly buoyant, but Katie reminded herself that he was probably forcing himself to be cheerful for her benefit.

She'd taken some of the extra-strength ibuprofen that was left over from her miscarriage and was fuzzily numb, lying on the living room couch in a nest of blankets and imagining that she was in a canoe being carried down a lazy river, when Liam came into the living room with a plate in one hand and her cell phone in the other.

"Your mother's on the line," he said, setting the plate on the coffee table.

Katie struggled to sit up and stared at the phone in his outstretched hand. "Tell her I'm asleep," she mouthed, then took the phone anyway, because Georgina delayed would only gather more steam.

"Hi, Mom, I'm fine," she said.

"Of course you are. Listen. Interesting news. Margaret's lawyer called. You've apparently been named in her will."

"She had a will?"

"Well, of course she did. Don't get excited, though; anything of value got sold off years ago."

"Yes, you've told me," Katie said, but any attempt at sarcasm was lost on Georgina, who plowed on as though she hadn't complained dozens of times over the years that Margaret had never worked a day in her life, preferring to drain the dregs of the family fortune until there was nothing left but the moldering old house on a quarter acre. Georgina herself had never had a full-time job either, unless you counted the pursuit of men, which she worked hard to monetize while Katie was growing up. A series of boyfriends had generously supplemented Georgina's income until, as her crowning achievement, she met a moderately wealthy podiatrist a month shy of her fiftieth birthday, who expired from a heart attack on their honeymoon, leaving her enough to live rather nicely and date strictly for pleasure.

"She didn't leave *me* a thin dime, of course," Georgina continued. Katie was pretty sure she could hear the rattle of ice in the background.

"Well, I'm sorry to hear that," Katie said. "You can have half of whatever she left me." It was a safe offer to make, because other than a few antiques and a pile of mismatched silver, her grandmother had owned nothing of even dubious value, according to Georgina.

"I'll hold you to that. Word is that the house might actually be worth something now."

Katie sat up straighter on the sofa, clutching the blankets up under her armpits. Outside, snow fell gently onto Beacon Street, creating the Currier & Ives–like tableau that Liam loved to gloat about to their friends.

"What do you mean?"

"Industry has come to New London. In the form of an Amazon fulfillment center. They're getting ready to break ground somewhere near town—they say it's going to be hundreds of thousands of square feet and create tons of jobs. Now there's a rumor that they're going to build a new hospital next."

"How do you know this?"

"Katie," Georgina said witheringly. "We have NextDoor down here, for your information. Nell Klaspaugh forwarded the post to me."

"So?" Katie said, although if pressed she'd have to admit that she was surprised. New London, where her mother had grown up and which she had visited exactly once, was frozen in her memory as the sleepiest town on earth. Its only distinguishing landmark was a memorial to the children who had perished in some sort of local disaster in the thirties. She couldn't picture the town having a chain coffee shop, much less a bustling warehouse, and she doubted her mother had set foot in Rusk County in years—at least, until she'd had to move Margaret to a nursing home six months ago after her stroke.

"They're having all kinds of town meetings, apparently," Georgina continued, ignoring her. "Some people are talking about a protest, even. But that ship has sailed. Once they get Amazon in—oh, and an industrial park. Though that one's a little iffy. Anyway, Margaret's house may well be right smack in the middle of the biggest building boom in East Texas."

"Like what are we talking?" Katie said, keeping her voice low. "I mean, I assume there's a lot of deferred maintenance . . . ?"

"I'm sure I don't know," Georgina huffed. "I guess you'll have to come down here to find out. Assuming that ad agency can get by without you for a day or two."

Katie pressed her lips together tightly. The barb was an old, familiar one; according to Georgina, the expensive art history degree from Columbia was being completely wasted at Nickell, March. At another time, she might have made the point—again!—that she worked in design, not advertising, but the distinction was lost on her mother.

"But even if it turns out to be worth something, you don't have to share it with me," Georgina said, in a more conciliatory tone. "You kids can use it to buy a bigger place where you are. You're going to need more room when my granddaughter comes along. Which she will, I promise."

And just like that, Katie's irritation melted

away. Never mind that on her last visit, her mother had pronounced their current apartment unlivable and asked Katie how she could stand sharing their one closet with Liam. In her own way, Georgina was trying.

And Katie could try too. "Tell you what," she said. "If she really left me a fortune, I'll take you to Vegas. Just the two of us. We can eat at Le Cirque and ride the roller coaster."

"Now you're talking," Georgina crowed. "Tell Liam to take good care of you."

Katie hung up and snuggled back down into her pile of blankets, letting the drowsiness overtake her. She was almost back to sleep when Liam plopped down on the couch next to her and began eating her untouched food.

"How's Georgina? They have a date for the funeral yet?"

"Fine," Katie said, yawning. "And there isn't going to be a funeral. They're just going to put her in the ground and call it a day."

"That's terrible," Liam protested. He came from a sprawling Boston clan, with dozens of nieces and nephews and aunts and uncles. Katie had attended two family funerals with Liam, multiday events that seemed more festive than their wedding had.

Katie sighed. "It's not terrible. It's just—the way my family is. There's no law that says you have to stay close to your blood relatives. You don't even have to like them." Words taken almost verbatim from her mother. "Besides, I have a family. A family of choice. You, and your sisters, and Rex and Lolly, and—"

"It's still not right," Liam mumbled around a mouthful of potato salad.

"I'm in her will," Katie ventured. "Kind of a shock."

"What? I thought she was penniless."

"She is. Was. I mean, she had some kind of trust that she lived on, but there wasn't even enough to keep up the house. She was kind of a hermit, anyway—never went anywhere, didn't have people over, so she didn't need much."

"So what did she leave you?"

"I'm not sure. I mean . . . there's the house." Katie decided not to repeat her mother's claim about the land's value, since Georgina tended to exaggerate and she didn't want to get her hopes up. "And maybe some old family stuff. Silver and china and whatnot."

She'd been to Margaret's house exactly once, on her eleventh birthday. For some reason, Margaret had invited them that year, and Georgina had agreed to make the four-hour round-trip drive. There had been a luncheon in the dining room, some sort of casserole and a bakery sheet cake with her name spelled out in frosting. The only guests were her mother and grandmother, who maintained a chilly silence through most of the visit. All Katie remembered about the house was that it was crowded with old furniture and knickknacks everywhere, none of them interesting to an eleven-year-old. When Georgina announced that it was time to leave, Margaret had snatched a china cup off a shelf and presented it to Katie as a gift. Georgina had tossed it into the trash as soon as they walked in their door.

"A house in Texas," Liam mused. "We could become ranchers."

Katie rolled her eyes. "I should make you come with me, just so you could see for yourself how miserable it is down there."

"So you *are* going."

Was she? She wasn't really considering it until the words were out of her mouth.

"I got laid off on Wednesday," she confessed. "I didn't tell you because . . . I was *going* to tell you, and then, you know." She gestured at the nest of blankets, the crumpled tissues, the *Vanity Fair* that she hadn't even opened.

Liam's expression went from shock to dismay to a hopeful little smile with comical speed. "That's awful," he said, "but you hated Nickell, March and they didn't appreciate you, and now you can take all the time you need to be with your mom."

That was Liam at his best . . . finding a silver lining in the cloud that seemed to have parked

33

over Katie's head. He took her hand, and she squeezed back. He'd been suckered by her mother, who specialized in misleading men to believe she was charming, but that was all right—the fact that they got along forced Katie to be civil to her.

"I'm only going so I can make sure Mom's okay," she warned him. If it turned out that there really was any value to her inheritance, she could surprise him when she got back. "Do we have enough miles?"

"I'll check," Liam said, brightening now that he had a task to keep him busy. "Or maybe we can get you a bereavement fare."

Ah, right. She was supposed to be bereaved. Katie turned the word over in her mind— it sounded old-fashioned, like *pinafore* or *scullion*—and decided she would do her best to honor the grandmother she never really knew. Experimentally, she dabbed at her eyes, but for what felt like the first time in days, she discovered that they were perfectly dry.

CHAPTER FOUR

1949

The second Sunday in March dawned crisp and clear, streaked with pretty white clouds as whisper-fine as the cotton balls her mother used to put witch hazel on Margaret's shoulders when she stayed too long in the sun. Margaret woke up early, but she stayed in her bed quiet as a mouse to listen to the sounds of the household coming to life.

Today was a day to savor—a day that, like frustratingly few lately, would feature her at its center. Not just her, of course—she would have to share it with the other Daisies—and with the dead ones, of course, but they weren't here to hog all the attention. All that was expected in return was that the Daisies look sad all day long and accept the attention that was lavished on them humbly, without making a fuss.

Looking sad and pretending to be humble were two things that Margaret was exceptionally good at and, truth be told, that she very much enjoyed. Unlike Helene Dial, who was arguably the prettiest of the Daisies, Margaret knew that pretending to cry and letting her lower lip wobble and her eyelashes flutter delicately would bring her lots more nice things, in the end, than the shrill displays of pique that were Helene's specialty.

Oh, Helene. With thoughts of her rival intruding unpleasantly on her anticipation of the day ahead, Margaret pushed off her bedspread and sat up in her bed, because Helene was a problem she would have to deal with rather soon. Ever since Mrs. Dial had joined Mother's publicity committee, she and Helene had been coming over to the house an awful lot. While Mrs. Dial and Mother sipped their coffee in the dining room and bent over their plans and notes, Margaret was expected to play nicely with Helene.

Just last week, Helene had been sitting on the floor in this very room, playing with Margaret's Rose O'Neill Kewpie dolls. Margaret had tried to make her play with her new army nurse kit, but Helene had balked at being the patient, especially when Margaret told her to pretend that her leg had been blown clean off at the knee— like Clifford Aiken, who had to sit on the porch with a blanket over his stump since he came back from the war.

"Your mother sure comes over here a lot," Margaret said, lazily wrapping her ankle in one of the play bandages. "It's because our house is so much nicer."

Helene said nothing, pursing her mouth in a quivering little rosebud, and working diligently to prop one of the little dolls into the toy baby carriage.

"But that's all right," Margaret went on generously. "My daddy owns the wells and your daddy works for him. That means my daddy is the boss and your daddy is a worker. But the oil business wouldn't be what it is without the workers." This was a good line, one Margaret had remembered from the Pierson Production Company picnic last summer. She had been hiding under the cake table at the time, watching the speakers up on the bandstand while the other children were over in the baseball field participating in the games led by Mr. Cheek, the physical education teacher. Margaret had no desire to lope along with her ankle bound to another child's with twine in the three-legged race, or to get her braids wet in the apple bobbing barrel, and besides, watching her father address his workers and their wives gave her a special, fizzy feeling in her stomach. Her daddy was the most important man in New London every day of the year, of course, but on picnic day, everyone gathered around to honor him and his family.

"My daddy is handsome," Helene whispered. Margaret pursed her lips: this was undeniably true. All the ladies said so—at least they did when Mrs. Dial and Mother were out of the room.

She had heard Mr. Dial discussed on two separate occasions: once when spying at her mother's meetings, and another time at the Pierson Production Company Christmas party, when the children were meant to be in the basement, and the ladies were gathered in the kitchen washing the glasses while the men smoked cigars.

It was impossible for Margaret to say if Mr. Dial was all that handsome, because he was a grown-up, with a *mustache* no less, and big, hairy forearms. But she had to admit that her own father was not very handsome at all. Hugh Pierson was barely taller than his wife by a smidge, which meant that Mother had to wear tiny flat heels, and that made her cross. Daddy's face was pink and veined with tiny blue lines, and his chin swelled above his collar. His nose was too dainty for his face, and his hair—long, pale strands of it plastered to his gleaming skull with Brylcreem—was not adequate to cover his head.

This, then, was a topic to be avoided. Margaret sighed and tossed the bandage on the floor. "But my daddy's *rich*. That's better. Ladies have to be pretty, and men ought to be rich. That's just the way it is."

That had been enough to silence Helene that day, but today posed a fresh challenge. By virtue of the many hours that Mrs. Dial and her mother had spent together on the publicity committee in the months leading up to Remembrance Day, the two girls had been cast together as a pair, and Margaret would be expected to entertain Helene during the Mothers' Breakfast that kicked off the day's events.

The breakfast had taken place in the Piersons' dining room since the very first Remembrance Day, when the Daisies were all still babies, or not even born yet. After, the Daisy families walked together to the site of the new school, the one that Margaret and Helene and all the other children had attended their whole lives. It was hard to imagine a time when the school wasn't there, but Margaret had seen the pictures herself: reporters had come from all over Texas, and even all over the entire country, to interview the families in front of the building site.

When the Daisies were babies, their families had done everything together. "Not everyone was happy for us," her mother had explained primly. "You would have thought we were raising little demons instead of babies." But instead of letting that hurt their feelings, the Daisy mothers had worked very hard to make Remembrance Day special for everyone, a party to which the entire town was invited.

All these years later, the breakfast would be followed by a solemn parade down the main streets of town to the park. Along the way, others would join them, until it seemed like half the town was walking together, dressed in their best, men with photographs of their lost children pinned to their lapels, ladies with carnations tied with ribbons. Eventually, someone would start humming a hymn, which would be picked up by the whole parade, even people who never sang at church—and Margaret secretly believed it must be like being on the inside of God, inside his breast, while all around him the angels sang in praise. Holding her parents' hands, she would close her eyes and allow them to lead her along, enveloped in the hymn, and she would feel almost as though she herself was an angel.

But when the parade reached the park, everything would change. There was no signal, no specific moment that the group dispersed, but when the bandstand came into view, festooned with bunting and balloons by the decorations committee, there was a collective gasp and then the spell was broken and everyone began talking at once and children broke away from their parents and ran to see.

The speakers selected by the program committee would find their places in the folding chairs arranged in neat rows, and the ladies of the refreshments committee would take their posts behind the long tables covered with bright cloths and pitchers of lemonade and platters of sandwiches and cookies. Mr. Cheek would corral the children, along with several of the other teachers recruited to help, and the reporters who still came—fewer of them every year—would mill around with their notebooks and the pop and flash of their cameras.

"And then we'll be off the hook for the rest of the day," Margaret had overheard her mother saying recently to her father, as they talked in their bed before turning out the lights. Nighttime roaming was a new habit of Margaret's, now that she was nearly twelve and judged herself ready to stay up later than her parents believed she should. "We won't even have to help with cleanup this year."

"I shouldn't think so," Daddy said irritably. He did not enjoy Remembrance Day; he was of the same opinion as Mrs. Sowell, who thought that the event had gone on long enough, that after more than a decade they should let all the dead children rest in peace without reminding themselves and everyone else of the tragedy every year. He'd only said so once—and Mother had told him in no uncertain terms that she didn't want to hear it again. After that, he'd borne the flurry of preparations in gloomy silence, and they knew to stay out of his way each year until the day was finally over.

Margaret had a secret about Daddy. A long time ago, a few days before her eleventh birthday, she had come upon him one afternoon in the garage. Daddy did not spend a lot of time in the garage,

41

not like other fathers who had all kinds of tools and worked on their own automobiles and made furniture and fixed things. Daddy had men to do those things for him, so their garage was neat as a pin and held only Daddy's car and the workbench that he never used and an area where he kept his golfing equipment.

Margaret had been looking for her birthday gift. She had asked for a children's portable electric phonograph, and she was not at all sure she was going to get it, because her mother thought she should just listen to the real one in the living room with the rest of the family, and her father said she should wait until she was older. The phonograph was large and came with six real records and would probably arrive in a big crate that would be hard to hide; but if it had come while she was at school, her mother might have had the deliveryman carry it to the garage, the only place besides the basement where it could have conceivably been hidden. Margaret had already checked the basement, and if she didn't find a large box in the garage, then she was likely to be very cross indeed.

When she let herself in the side door that afternoon while her mother was preparing the supper that Alelia had cooked before leaving for the day, she was surprised to discover that the lights were on, and she was confronted by a strange sound—like Ferdinand the bull from the story, she thought, lowing and snorting. It didn't occur to her to be frightened, but she moved carefully and quietly because she was curious, edging around the big dark Packard and being careful not to brush against the rakes and shovels hung along the wall.

It wasn't a bull at all. It was her father—still dressed in his work shirt and suspenders, his sleeves rolled up his pale forearms—hunched over the workbench, his big body spilling over the stool and his head cradled in his arms. And he was sobbing—huge, racking sobs that shook his shoulders and sounded both ethereal and heartbreaking.

Margaret moved forward without thinking. Years later, she would think often about how her father had carried this remarkable emotion around with him, hidden away so that no one ever saw it, and what a feat of determination that must have been to keep it from being discovered—but that day, she was merely awestruck and curious: What on earth could make her taciturn father cry?

"Daddy?" she ventured, when she got close— just as her gaze fell on the object lying on the workbench next to his head. It was a small, oval silver frame, and inside the frame was a photograph of a girl.

Margaret knew who it was right away, even though she had only briefly glimpsed any like- ness of her dead sister, Ruby, other than the fourth-grade school picture from the year she died, which was used at every Remembrance Day. Any other photographs and mementos of Ruby that her parents had kept were stored in her mother's curved-front armoire in the mysterious locked top drawer. Margaret very much wanted to pick up the photograph and study Ruby's features, to look for similarities, for proof that—as Miss Pellingham said at Sunday school—Ruby was watching over her from up in heaven.

But when she spoke his name, her father froze, his shoulders instantly going rigid and still, his keening ending on a hiccup of grief, and closed his fist over the little frame. He palmed it into his shirt pocket, and when he turned around to face Margaret, his hands were empty and his expression guilty.

"Margaret, I was, uh . . . What are you doing in here?" he asked, swiping at his eyes.

"Looking for nails." Margaret lied without thinking, marveling at how disheveled her father looked. His eyes were puffy and red, and a smear of snot glistened along his upper lip.

"Oh. Nails." Her father dug for a handkerchief with shaking hands, then blew his nose on it noisily. When he was finished, the snot was thankfully gone from his lip and he seemed to have composed himself. "Well, there aren't any, I'm afraid. I was just in here, ah, working on my speech for the Lions Club."

"But why were you crying?"

At that point, Margaret hadn't actually made the obvious connection, something that would puzzle her in the years to come. Even though she knew that other Daisy families missed their dead children very much, and even though her mother always created elaborate displays for Remembrance Day in which Ruby's name was surrounded by hearts and ribbons and pictures of flowers and kittens and dolls and other nice things, she would have been hard-pressed to say that Ruby featured very prominently in her parents' lives and minds. For instance, when anyone inquired about Ruby, her mother would answer vaguely and quickly change the subject. Her father would barely seem to notice at all, focusing on tamping down the tobacco in his pipe, or taking a sudden interest in the newspaper lying on the table, as though the subject bored him.

"I was, ah . . . ." Daddy picked up an empty coffee mug that was resting on top of a calendar from Morty's Auto Service, then set it down again. "See here, Margaret, I was thinking about dinner. I'm awful hungry, aren't you? I wonder if we should go see what Alelia fixed for us."

Now the memory made Margaret feel mean-spirited and sneaky—but on its heels came an idea. "I forgot," she told Helene. "We're supposed to be getting a bag of flour for Alelia."

"We are?"

Stupid cow, Margaret thought, looking into Helene's trusting, relieved face, happy to have something other than her father's secret to focus on. Margaret led the way down the back stairs to the larder, a place that had often come in handy for hiding when she wanted to eavesdrop on goings-on in the kitchen, where now and then Alelia would visit with one of the neighbors' maids during the long afternoons when the bread was rising or the laundry had been hung on the line.

Margaret had been there last week, in fact, when the coal man came, pressed uncomfortably between the bins of onions and potatoes while she waited for them to finish visiting. And there she'd spied the rip in one of the sacks of flour on the shelf, the tiny white avalanche spilling over the side.

She went first into the dim interior of the larder, and hooked the edges of the small rip with her fingers. To cover the sound of fabric tearing, she pretended to sneeze—not the easiest thing to fake, but Margaret was a born actress, everyone said so.

"It's so heavy," she sighed, turning around to face Helene. "Can you please help me?"

She picked up the sack and clutched it in front of her, and when Helene reached to help, Margaret executed the perfectly timed stumble on which her plan hinged.

Helene fell backward, the bag toppling forward with a little extra shove from Margaret so that it landed right on top of Helene. It split open, and flour went everywhere—great drifts of it billowing onto Helene's dress and face and hair and arms, a cloud of it wafting upward through the air like the newsreels of German submarines sinking the HMS *Barham*. Helene squealed and batted at the flour, flapping her hands helplessly.

Margaret had to stifle a grin.

"Oh, no—what have you *done?*" she demanded sternly.

"But it was an accident," Helene gasped. "I think the sack must have ripped!"

"Mother's going to be furious," Margaret said. "Now Alelia won't be able to make any more biscuits today." Alelia had actually been in the kitchen before dawn taking fragrant trays of her flaky biscuits out of the oven, but Helene didn't know that. "Tell you what—stay here, and I'll go get a rag to clean you up. Maybe we can hide what happened so you don't get in trouble."

When Margaret returned a few moments later with a rag dampened in the powder room sink, Helene was on her knees, frantically trying to sweep the flour into a pail with her hands. "Here, let me," Margaret said. She took the wet rag and wiped it across the front of Helene's pink organdy dress, and the dusting of flour turned into a sticky paste.

"Don't—you're making it worse!" Helene cried, trying to push Margaret's hands away.

"Stop it—I'm helping," Margaret said. A noise behind her made both girls turn, and Margaret's heart skipped in alarm.

But it wasn't Alelia standing there, or either of their mothers. It was Helene's brother, Hank.

Hank had been a fourth-grader on the morning of the explosion, which had sent him through a window like a stone tossed through a waterfall. The only lingering proof that he'd been there at all was a small half-moon-shaped scar on his forehead and burn scars on the backs of his hands, from when he'd tried to crawl back into the rubble to rescue his little brother, Ralph, who'd been in the second grade. Twenty-one now, Hank had a habit of keeping his hands in his pockets, so the ridged, shiny pink scars were out of sight.

"Mom's looking for you," he told Helene, and then—almost as an afterthought—"Hello, Mags."

He knelt down and took the rag from her without asking, and Margaret tried to think of something to say. Hank Dial was an honest-to-God hero, the closest thing to an angel that she had ever seen. He had not been able to save his brother that day, and maybe it was that failure that shaded the depths of his beautiful blue eyes and roughened his deep voice. Not only was he as devastatingly handsome as his father, with thick brown hair that fell over the sculpted planes of his face, but he was famously reckless, and he'd wrecked a car that didn't even belong to him and won an airplane in a game of cards and was setting up his own business taking oilmen to look at the fields from up in the sky, and he sassed his mother and had gotten in a fistfight with three men in a bar (so they said) and talked back to the policeman who'd come to break it up.

But he was always nice to Helene and Margaret.

"I don't know what you were thinking, Helly," he said mildly, tossing the rag into the bucket. "That'll just make it worse. Mags, I bet you've got a pretty dress Helene can borrow, don't you? Oh now, don't cry, sis. You'll break my heart right in half."

He picked Helene up and set her on his shoulders and Margaret's plan was ruined, but there was nothing for it but to lead them up the back stairs to her room and offer Helene her best dress—yellow dotted swiss with a wide white sash—just because it made Hank smile. He made a great show of waiting outside the door while Margaret helped Helene change out of the ruined dress, and then, when he was allowed back into the room, he whooped.

"You're the prettiest girl in East Texas," he assured Helene, while Margaret burned with envy.

CHAPTER FIVE

It turned out that Katie *could* get a bereavement fare, but it was still so expensive that Liam hunkered down over his laptop with a furious expression on his face, muttering, and spent the evening searching until he figured out how to save a hundred bucks on a flight with a three-hour layover in Charlotte. Katie left him to it while she packed, already fairly sure how the exercise would turn out, but grateful to have Liam kept occupied. He seemed to think of Texas as an exciting new ride at Disneyland, and Katie as the gatekeeper who refused to honor his Park Hopper pass.

Luckily, Margaret's death prevented him from suggesting, as he had on a couple of occasions, that it would be *really fun* to rent a convertible and *make a week of it,* driving from one end of the state to another, from San Antonio to Houston to Dallas before ending up in New London.

While he searched and cursed the airlines' lack of compassion, Katie moved her hangers from one end of the closet rod to the other and back, trying to figure out what to take. She was packing for two weeks, to be safe; the first to do whatever one had to do to claim an inheritance, and the second to loll poolside at Georgina's town house complex. Ordinarily she tried to limit her rare visits to Georgina to long weekends, but the events of the last few days had left Katie feeling vulnerable and raw, as though someone had taken a paring knife to her outermost layers, leaving her nerves and emotions and maybe her very heart exposed.

Under her mother's wing she would be smothered—literally, by the Jo Malone orange blossom candles her mother favored, and also by the attentions of her many friends in Pecan Ridge Estates, a luxury town house complex billed as an endless pleasure romp for the fifty-five-plus set. Katie could never be sure what her mother would have told her friends, and on various occasions in the past she'd discovered that she'd been offered a modeling contract (after a photographer at the mall had tried to sell Georgina on an expensive set of head shots) and that she had outwitted an armed attacker while waiting for the T (her mother had confused public transportation, which she considered uncivilized, with the shuttle Katie's company had hired to transport her group to an off-site in Amherst; her laptop bag had been pulled off her arm as she exited, but luckily, all that was in it were dirty gym clothes that Katie kept forgetting to take out at home). Georgina's friends, most of them widowed or divorced, fawned over Katie; they plied her with bottles of seltzer and visors to protect her face from the sun and copies of *Harper's Bazaar*, and told her she was much too thin and left lipstick kisses on her cheeks.

The attention sounded rather nice, to be honest. Katie would let her mother take her out to lunch every day, and mist her face with her mother's cucumber-scented hydration spray, and wear her expensive sandals and swimsuit cover-ups. Maybe, after two or three or seven days together, she'd be ready to cry it all out.

In the end Katie settled on her good black pants, mid-heeled ankle boots, and tweedy Rag & Bone blazer for the reading of the will, or whatever they called it—and for any fancy dinners her mother might take her to. She added two sports bras and two pairs of spandex capris and her sneakers, and then she got stuck. She hedged, carefully rolling her panties and bras and a tasteful navy one-piece swimsuit while she tried to decide what was appropriate for a thirty-one-year-old professional woman to wear in New London, and finally settled on two pairs of jeans, two skirts, and six sleeveless tops. Her ivory cashmere wrap, a splurge purchased on her honeymoon (by Liam, to atone for the spittoon). A T-shirt a coworker had given her in the Secret Santa exchange, to sleep in, which inexplicably showed a cartoon mound of noodles wearing a pained expression and the legend "Big Eat Now."

She moved everything from her black leather satchel into a floral tote that had been a gift from Georgina, put it with the suitcase by the front door, and joined Liam on the bed.

"You were right," he sighed. "Fucking blood-thirsty airlines. I got you on Southwest for three-twenty one way. I'll book your return once you figure out when you're coming back."

"And no connections, right?"

"And no connections. Even though I could have knocked off almost a hundred bucks if you'd been willing to go through LAX on a red-eye."

"Liam—"

"Kidding!" Liam yawned and slithered down under the blankets. "Better get some sleep. That alarm's going off early."

"I could take an Uber," Katie said halfheartedly.

"Yeah, no. I'll drop you off and get to the gym early."

Don't fall asleep yet, Katie thought. She wanted to talk about how this trip was bringing up the divide between her Life Before—before Columbia, before she learned that most girls didn't receive a brow wax on their twelfth birthday from their mothers, before she discovered that the slight gap between her front teeth was actually an asset—and her Life with Liam. But the subject seemed as unbroachable as ever.

"I'll be fine," she said pertly. "I'll bring you a souvenir. What time do we need to leave?"

"Flight's at six," Liam said. "Sorry—the eight o'clock was eighty dollars more."

Or one-third the price of your new pants. Katie banished the thought—Liam's occasional vanities weren't worth arguing over. "Okay," she said, grabbing her phone. "I'm setting the alarm for three-thirty, but you can sleep until four if you promise to get up when I tell you to."

"I promise." Liam took her phone from her and set it on the bedside table. They only had one, because their bedroom was so narrow, and he leaned over and turned out their one lamp, then tunneled back down into the covers. In the dark, Katie finally let her features relax, suddenly aware of how much effort she had been putting into staying positive.

She burrowed against Liam, trying to mask her tears. *No baby. Unemployment. Texas.*

"You okay?" Liam mumbled.

"Yeah . . . hiccups."

In a little while, his breathing grew regular and Katie clutched her pillow tightly.

They'd keep trying, or they'd do something else. She'd have a baby when she was meant to. She'd get to New London and discover she'd inherited a fortune, or a pittance; she'd go to Dallas and bond with her mother, or argue with her. All of it would be fine.

54

The thing she really ought to be worrying about was that Texas would seep into her pores and take root, and that when she came back to Boston, she wouldn't be able to shake it off as easily as she had when she was eighteen.

The alarm jarred her from a deep sleep. "Okay, okay!" she said aloud before she was all the way awake, already swinging her legs over the side of the bed.

Only when Liam grunted and tugged the covers back over his head did Katie remember. She glanced at her phone and grimaced; there were two texts from her mother that she'd sent around midnight.

The first was a photo with no accompanying caption—Georgina and two of her friends, obviously a tipsy selfie, as their faces were blurred and someone's thumb covered a corner of the picture.

The second, twenty minutes later, a guilty after-thought:

Book club girls just left thinking of you LOVE YOU fly safe call me

Katie trudged to the shower and turned the water on as hot as it got, which wasn't all that hot. That was something to look forward to—her mother kept her town house sealed up three seasons of the year with the air-conditioning set to frigid, and she had lovely strong water pressure and plenty of hot water, and Katie began all of her days there with a long shower under the steaming, stinging spray using all of her mother's expensive bath products and luxurious fluffy towels.

Here, though, the landlord had rigged the heat not to kick in until six o'clock every morning, and so it was a race to finish and dress before her fingers got so cold she couldn't work zippers and buttons. Some mornings, Katie resorted to push-ups just to get her blood moving, and often her teeth were chattering when she brushed them. She put on her traveling clothes—the dark-washed jeans and a white blouse and her cashmere wrap, which she would drape over herself like a blanket the minute she got on the plane. She dabbed on concealer and eyeliner and lip gloss and then she went to wake Liam, only to find him dressed and ready to go.

They were silent as they went down the stairs, Liam carrying her suitcase and huffing softly from the effort. Through the lobby doors, the street was uncharacteristically still, with a single Lyft sedan cruising slowly by in the dark.

"Forty-nine," Liam intoned somberly, because it was his job to check the weather every morning and let her know the temperature. Chilly, for May, but it had been drizzly and dreary for days. They each took a breath and then they were out in it, the fine mist settling onto her face and into her hair, ruining the effort she had made to straighten it.

They paid $165 a month to park in a tiny space squeezed next to the Dumpster in the lot behind an apartment building two blocks away, an arrangement that required the skills of a professional driver with a physics degree— or Liam, who seemed to have a sixth sense for maneuvering his prized Peugeot around the various obstacles and angles. Katie rarely drove, and when she did she had to call Liam to come park for her when she got home.

There was no one on the street, and they walked in silence. Katie peered up into bay windows lit with the soft glow of lamps left on by people who'd spent more to decorate their living rooms than Katie made in a year. For once, she wasn't beset with the burn of chronic envy; her mind was spinning ahead, over the nation's sprawling middle all the way to Texas, which she imagined waiting for her with the saved-up affront from the snub of her departure over a decade ago. Like a hostess who greets you at the door with a brittle smile to let you know that she knew you didn't include her at *your* last dinner party.

The mist seemed to seep through to her bones, haloing around the streetlight and making the street glisten. Katie pulled her wrap tighter, and walked a couple of paces behind Liam. When he stopped abruptly as they rounded the corner into the parking lot, she ran right into him.

"Oof," she said, surprised.

"Fuck," Liam said.

"Let's make this easy," a strange voice said. Appearing from nowhere—or, more likely, from the alley perpendicular to the building, which was narrow and blocked by the same Dumpsters that boxed in their space—was a skinny short guy in a hoodie right out of central casting. It overshadowed his face, so that all Katie could make out was a chin with a wispy blond beard and an acne scab. And a gun. A gun in his hand, pointing at Liam, not two feet away.

Katie grabbed Liam's sleeve and yanked him backward, and he dropped the handle to her suitcase and it flopped over with a plasticky clatter. Their mugger shook his head, almost sorrowfully.

"I'll take that off your hands, but you go ahead and pick it up for me." He had a nasally accent that didn't sound all that authentic, like one of the secondary characters in *Mystic River*. Katie didn't think anyone in Boston actually talked like that anymore.

He pointed. "Your purse, okay? Your wallet, dude. Just drop them on the ground. Rings and watches, please, and then turn around and walk away, like normal. Calm. No need to run. *Don't* run."

Katie and Liam looked at each other. Katie would have said that there was no way this kid—he probably weighed less than she did, and she noticed that he bit his fingernails—would possibly shoot them, except that his hands were twitching slightly and his nose was running, in a drug way. Not that she would know, but he was probably, definitely high . . . crack, heroin, both, probably things she hadn't even heard of, and so who knew what he would do?

"Give it to him," she said, and poked Liam in the side with her knuckle. "Give him your wallet."

"Look," Liam said, opening his hands wide, palms up. "Her grandmother died. She's flying to Texas. I know that sounds like BS, but if you let her show you her flight confirmation—"

The guy smashed the gun against Liam's face, cutting him off. Katie gasped, but Liam just staggered back with his hand to his cheek, then stepped forward with his hands in fists. Good for Liam—Katie felt a surge of pride in her husband; she'd never thought of him as her protector before, but it was kind of nice—though now he was going to get his ass beat, or worse.

"Give him what he wants, honey, please!"

"Honey, please!" their mugger echoed in a singsongy voice. "Look, asshole, I don't care who died, just give me your fucking wallet."

Katie watched in horror, suddenly certain that

59

Liam was going to be shot, that he was going to die in her arms. She jumped in front of him with her arms out, only belatedly wondering if a bullet at such close range would go through her and hit Liam and kill them both, and then it occurred to her that this was *exactly* like the opening of practically every *Law & Order* episode she'd ever watched. All those bodies found in dark alleys—all that terrible dialogue. Chris Meloni's awful quips and Mariska Hargitay stepping daintily over the pooling blood in her high, high heels.

"Shut up already," the guy said. "Look. Give me your wallet and your phone now and maybe I'll let her keep the ticket."

"I don't have a ticket," Katie said. Hadn't this guy taken a flight in the last decade? But maybe he hadn't. He probably grew up in the projects. "I just need my credit card and my driver's license," she said, speaking slowly and calmly. "They won't let me on without them. But I'll just take my AmEx, it's almost at the limit anyway. Keep the Visa."

Liam gawped at her; she hadn't exactly told him about the AmEx. "And twenty bucks," he said, recovering himself enough to peel a bill from his wallet. "Come on, man, you can have my watch and my credit cards, but let her get a goddamn cup of coffee. Her grandmother—"

The mugger grabbed the wallet and phone

and plucked the twenty from Liam's hand. Very cautiously, Katie bent down and set her purse on the ground. Her laptop was in it, and her Vuitton cosmetic case, a gift from Georgina. She took out her wallet and straightened slowly while showing him the credit cards lined up neatly in their slots. She took out the license and AmEx and gave a last sad, fond glance at the buttery soft pink leather with solid brass trim—another Georgina gift—and dropped it onto the pavement.

"Okay? We're good?" Liam snapped. "Or do you want to hit me again just to make your point?"

What do you know—there was Liam's recklessly brave streak again. Katie pocketed the plastic cards and linked her arm with her husband's. She felt somehow lighter.

"Rings."

Liam hadn't worn his regularly since they returned from their honeymoon. As Katie took hers off and dropped them in the mugger's palm, she thought of Liam's simple gold band, sitting in the soap dish. It didn't seem fair that he got to keep his, but she could ponder that later, when there wasn't a gun in her face.

"Get the fuck out of here," the guy said. After they'd turned away and gone a few steps, she heard the wheels of her suitcase skittering on the broken asphalt as it was being rolled away.

Despite the heart-pounding rush of adrenaline

that coursed through her, Katie followed Liam calmly, almost sedately until they were out of sight around the corner, and then she threw her arms around him and hugged him so hard the breath whooshed out of him.

"Jesus," he muttered, his voice shaking. "He could have—that was—"

"It's fine," Katie said, cutting him off. "We're fine, we're alive, how's your face?" She brushed his cheek tenderly with her fingertips and kissed the purpling welt. "You were amazing, by the way, Mr. Garrett."

A warm little tendril unwound inside Katie, and she thought: *Bless your heart.*

CHAPTER SIX

The speeches were over and the choir began singing "Peace in the Valley," the cue for the Daisies to get up from their seats and file down off the bandstand.

"Careful, *careful,*" Mrs. Briggs hissed up at all of them, but most especially at Johnny, her son, who had been seated next to Margaret in the boy-girl-boy-girl arrangement of the chairs, and so was walking in front of her.

"Jeez," he muttered.

Margaret felt sorry for Johnny, because his mother was bonkers. Her own mother had explained that some people had gone a little crazy after the explosion and would likely never get better. After losing Johnny's older brother Bill, who had lingered for four days before dying in a hospital in Kilgore, Mr. Briggs had called up the parents of several of Bill's surviving classmates and threatened to set fire to their houses. The sheriff had had to talk to him.

That was all gossip, and the Piersons didn't trade in hearsay (according to Caroline, though Margaret had seen her do it oodles of times, when she didn't know Margaret was listening), but what wasn't gossip was the fact that Mrs. Briggs was forever running after Johnny and pleading with him to be careful. Every bruise, scratch, or sniffle was cause for alarm. Every Daisy Club event had to be vetted for potential dangers. Mrs. Briggs's picnic dishes never had mayonnaise in them lest they go bad in the sun, Johnny had to wear a jacket when the temperature dipped below sixty, and he was not allowed to go on any field trips unless she came along to chaperone.

Thankfully, Margaret's own parents were considerably more lax. Now that she'd endured the ceremony, she would be free to do as she liked until late afternoon, when she would be required to help pick up the litter and take down the decorations.

Margaret helped herself to a slice of chiffon cake and, spotting Hank talking to some of the men over by the memorial boards, sauntered casually over, ducking behind them so she could listen.

"How're the lessons going, son?" Mr. Gaston, an elderly farmer, asked him.

"Great, sir. I'll have my forty hours by the fourth of July. After that I've just got the written test and the check ride."

Through Helene, Margaret knew that Hank had spent most of his air force stint working as a flight mechanic, first at Pounds Field outside of Tyler and later at Las Vegas AFB. During high school, he'd watched the war on newsreels like everybody else and set his sights on becoming a pilot, but he hadn't done well enough on the test.

Now he was making up for lost time at Elders Field up near Kilgore, trading side jobs for flight hours.

"We sure could use you around here," another of the old-timers said. "Fella I hired last spring didn't know what he was doing. Sprayed a couple of my fields, but the drift was so bad I think most of it ended up on my neighbor's land. Top it off, he nearly hit one of my standpipes. You get that license, I'll have work for you."

"Me too," Mr. Gaston said. "You'll do us proud, boy!"

Well, that was interesting! Margaret needed a little time to think about this news. Helene had been boasting that Hank was going to become an airline pilot and fly around the world, which was a terrible thought, because it would take him away from Texas—and her. All she needed was time to grow up, so that Hank would realize that she was so much more than just his kid sister's friend.

But if he became a crop duster—why, she'd be able to look up at lunchtime and wave at him as he buzzed the fields near town.

Margaret got a cold bottle of Texas Punch from the cooler and went around the backside of the big cedar elm under which they'd set up the refreshments. She shimmied up and settled herself in the crotch of the tree and took a sip of her soda. From here she could watch nearly everyone, undetected.

There was her mother, not ten feet away, chatting with Mrs. Baker. "These are just so clever!" Caroline was saying, holding up one of the centerpieces Mrs. Baker's committee had made by gluing yarn round and round empty coffee cans before filling them up with blue-bonnets and roses from the committee members' gardens. Mrs. Baker was beaming, but as Margaret watched, her expression slipped.

"Caroline," she said warningly, and they both looked out toward the street.

A man dressed in dirty rags was walking toward them—lurching, really—drinking from a bottle and spitting on the sidewalk. He was wearing a stained cap and shoes so worn that one of the soles was flapping with every step. And he seemed to be coming straight toward their table.

"Do you think he's hungry?" Mrs. Baker asked. "Should I get Pete?"

"I'll handle this," Caroline said, her voice sounding strained and funny.

"There you are," the man croaked. He stopped a few feet away from the ladies, swaying on his feet. "Look at you."

"Do you *know* him, Caroline?" Mrs. Baker asked.

"I—no—of course not. You know what, why

don't you see if you can find Pete after all. I'll handle this until you get back."

"But he could be . . ."

Margaret, perched high above them, couldn't hear the rest of Mrs. Baker's sentence. The two women conferred in whispers for a moment and then Mrs. Baker said, "All right—but do be careful."

This was exciting. Margaret had been dragged briskly down the street by her mother often enough to know that Caroline could easily get away, if need be, but the man didn't look like he could chase a sick dog. He was *drunk,* a condition that her parents had warned her about, and a distinction her father was careful to make between his nightly glass of whiskey and the kind of thing that could turn you into a bum.

Which was what this man apparently was. New London had a few bums already, mostly war veterans who couldn't work on account of being shot up, but Margaret had never seen this stranger before.

"Big day, huh, Caroline?" he said, and Margaret gasped—he really did know her mother. But how could that be?

"Now listen here," Caroline said, taking two steps forward and brandishing the coffee can full of flowers, her hands shaking. Margaret couldn't tell if she was frightened or only very angry. "You turn around and go. You're not fit for public."

"Not fit," the man echoed, and burst into laughter that ended in coughing. He worked up a gobbet of brownish spit and hawked it on the ground between them. "Ha. You're the one who's not fit, Caroline. You and Hugh."

"That's a lie and you know it."

"You belong in hell for what you did."

"You had your say," Caroline said. "It was all settled a long time ago. You're just trying to blame your troubles on someone else. You're nothing but a lazy drunk."

Across the grass, Margaret could see Mrs. Baker hurrying back with Pete DeLong, the brawny owner of DeLong's tavern. "What's going on here?" he bellowed.

The bum looked at Caroline bleakly and started to speak, then muttered something indistinct and turned to go.

"If you ever come back here, I'll kill you myself," Margaret thought she heard Caroline say—but surely she'd been mistaken, because the Piersons had everything, and the man had nothing, and why would it even be worth her mother's trouble?

CHAPTER SEVEN

Growing up in Dallas, Katie had learned that the phrase *Bless your heart* could be a stand-in for all kinds of sentiments. It had once been a staple of Katie's vocabulary, handy not just for expressing affection but also for pity and condescension and even contempt.

Hearing it come out of her own mouth after all these years was a surprise, and as Katie stood in the security line, she replayed the events of the last hour and wondered what to make of them—whether her words had been an omen. Because at some point between the mad dash to Rex and Lolly's brownstone—where a very sleepy Rex eventually answered the buzzer and called an Uber and gave Katie seventeen dollars, which was all the cash he could find—and arriving here in the crowded terminal, the warm glow of admiration for her husband's moment of heroism had faded.

The Uber had showed up in what seemed like thirty seconds and Katie gave Liam a careful kiss, avoiding the welt from the gun. Rex wished her luck from the foyer as he stood shivering in his bare feet. Inside the Prius it was warm and smelled like incense, and once they were on their way, Katie realized that being in an Uber without her phone was a strange experience, as foreign as if she found herself riding on a camel. Blessedly, her driver didn't speak except to ask her which airline, and when he pulled to the curb she made the dash to the terminal and felt, for the second time that morning, the strange lightness of traveling with virtually nothing.

It felt unexpectedly indulgent, like a vacation— more like a vacation than their vacations felt. Their last trip—Vineyard, house share with people they didn't like all that much, beach bonfires and rainy days browsing in the overpriced boutiques—had required a suitcase and a duffel and Katie had still felt like she had nothing to wear.

Now, she literally had only the clothes on her back and Rex's crumpled bills and loose change.

She couldn't help feeling a little smug when it was finally her turn with the screener. Whenever she traveled lately, it seemed that carry-ons had become a sort of battleground, her fellow travelers packing them with military precision and guarding overhead bin space zealously. She'd been one of them—she'd paid a small fortune for the suitcase that had been stolen that morning, for its cleverly engineered innards that promised precious extra cubic inches of packing space. No, ma'am, she had *not* checked a bag like some kid going to summer camp; but the sour TSA officer with her hair pulled back so hard it stretched her eyebrows was not impressed. She barely glanced at Katie's license and scrawled a loopy orange squiggle onto the boarding pass that Katie had printed at a kiosk.

At the Starbucks, Katie scanned the menu and wondered how long she would have to make her seventeen dollars last. Liam had promised to wire money just as soon as he figured out how, and to pay down her AmEx so she could use it again, all of which seemed like it might take a long time. Wow—a small coffee was almost three dollars. Seventeen minus three . . . left less than the price of an arugula salad at Thymes Square.

Reluctantly, Katie stepped out of the line.

She felt ridiculous buying a newspaper that was actually printed on paper, as though she was attacking an old-growth forest with a chain saw, but no one appeared to notice. But two dollars for a newspaper—when had that happened?

By the time Katie boarded and got to her seat—aisle, blessedly, though two-thirds of the way back—the sense of adventure and lightness had evaporated. It took forever for the flight attendant to come with the beverage cart, and when Katie asked for *two* cups of coffee—because they were very small and who knew when the flight attendants would return—she was rewarded with a frosty glare.

Katie drank both cups of coffee, skimmed the headlines, spotted a sale at Lord & Taylor and forgot for a moment that she didn't have any money currently, considered putting on the free headphones and watching the movie, and then fell like a stone into a deep sleep.

Georgina had agreed it would be silly for Katie to come to her condo before driving to New London, because Pecan Ridge Estates was half an hour out of her way in the wrong direction, and after a perfunctory half-hour visit Katie would have to get in the car and go the *other* way, which would mean that she might not get to New London by dark, and *oh my God why did old people think that if you drove in the dark the gates of hell would open up and swallow you forever?*

"I need to calm down," Katie murmured, out loud, but very softly. She was next in line at the Hertz counter, but the man in front of her was taking a long time, or maybe it was the clerk, who had extraordinarily long fake nails that made typing practically performance art. Eventually the clerk handed the man his sheaf of papers; he snatched them as though she might change her mind and drove his suitcase to the exit like a bat out of hell.

"Next."

Katie proffered her license, her AmEx (*thank you, mugger*), and her best, patient smile to show that she wasn't like that *other* guy, who was clearly a dick, a businessman with no patience for what the rest of us go through every day, but the clerk did not seem impressed. Tapping, tapping, silently tapping with those long nails (a tiny diamond appeared to be glued to the tip of each), and then a speculative, distrustful stare.

"Decline."

Katie waited, confused. "Umm . . ."

"De-*cline*," she enunciated in a voice laced with irritation. "Your card, it's declined. You got another maybe?"

"But my rental should already be paid for. My husband—"

"It's *paid* for, but not the authorization hold. You got to have two hundred dollars for the authorization hold. You near your limit?"

Well, of course she was near her limit, Katie thought, feeling her face get hot. But only because she put all her secret—her *discretionary*—purchases on it, and only because she had been planning to put her entire bonus toward paying it down. A bonus which she would not be receiving now, unfortunately, due to circumstances (fucking Arthur Salisbury and his fucking *rightsizing!*) beyond her control.

"Oh," she said meekly. "I mean, yeah, but—"

" 'Cause we need another card with at least two hundred dollars' credit on it before I can give you this . . ." She tapped some more. "Jetta."

"I can call my husband," Katie said. "I mean, can I borrow your phone? He can read you off the credit card information for another card. I was—we were mugged this morning. It was . . ." She swallowed, dangerously close to tears. "It was terrifying. He had a gun."

The clerk looked at her with renewed interest. "How did you get on the plane? If he mugged you and all?"

"He let me keep my license and this card," Katie admitted uncomfortably, knowing how unlikely it sounded. "I mean, he took the cards that had room on them." *Obviously.*

"Uh-huh," the clerk said, drawing out the syllables so that they seemed to encapsulate an entire conversation. "Well, I'd have to *see* that card. Like, in your *hand*. And there's folks waiting behind you, so . . ."

Katie whipped around, mortified to see that a line had formed while she'd been talking to the clerk: three hostile and impatient-looking fellow travelers.

And yeah . . . if it had been her, she'd be pissed too.

"Okay," she sighed, taking back her license and useless, no-good, embarrassing credit card. "I'll go and, and, make some calls."

"Mmmm-hmmm," the clerk said, her eyes already on the next person in line.

Katie walked away from the counter with

her head down and searched for a bench, but of course there was no bench, because they designed the whole place to keep people moving like docile cattle into the trough-like food courts and the pen-like waiting areas, and God help you if you had an actual human problem and needed help. There were signs for the medic and the airport police, but Katie's problem didn't really fall into those parameters and all of a sudden she found herself noticing, as she had never really done before, the families huddled together on the floor, surrounded by luggage, speaking a dozen different languages and glancing uneasily up at the tide of travelers swarming around them. *I am like them,* she thought, and immediately felt even worse, because they were refugees fleeing real problems like genital mutilation and water-borne bacteria and being silenced by murderous regimes.

She was going to cry if she didn't get her shit together.

"Okay," she said out loud. "Okay!"

She took several deep breaths and considered the shops lining the aisle. There was a massage business (never, *ever* would Katie allow a stranger to touch her in public view like that) and a cheap jewelry shop and a Genuine Texas Souvenirs shop with rows of China-manufactured gimcracks lining the display shelves, and after considering each she settled on the jewelry shop because the young female clerk with the painstaking winged eyeliner looked, if not *nice* exactly, at least not cruel.

"Excuse me," she said, approaching the counter with what she hoped was an engaging smile. "Is there, I mean, could I use your phone? Mine was stolen and I need to call someone."

"Oh," the girl said. Her upper lip was pierced by a delicate, tiny gold stud. "Like, there isn't one. I mean, I'm not allowed to use mine while I'm working? And like, I *literally* can only call my boss or, like, the headquarters on the store one."

Literally. A faint, shrill buzz had started somewhere behind Katie's temples—as though her brain had been invaded by a horde of tiny, angry insects.

"Thank you," Katie whispered; whispering seemed safer than trying to speak.

"You can use mine."

The voice was very close to her ear; someone was speaking very close behind her. The clerk's eyes widened and she shook her head almost imperceptibly. Katie turned and sure enough, the man offering his phone was wearing the outfit (stained Hanes T-shirt, fishing vest, plaid shorts, knee socks and sandals) and haircut (bowl, with bangs) and expression (just this side of voracious; mouth breather; roving eyes) of a serial murderer. Also: he smelled—like Listerine and body odor.

"Wow," Katie said. "I just—I just remembered something."

She ignored the phone (camouflage case) the man was holding out to her and dashed past him, into the throngs.

She didn't have it in her to try again, to speak to another stranger. Her stomach growled, but the thought of food nauseated her. She trudged toward the baggage claim, searching for an information desk. Surely, someone there would allow her to use a phone; they had to keep one in the airport for—for old people, for children, for emergencies like hers. But by the time she'd walked the entire length of the baggage claim area, all she'd seen was an unmanned desk with a broken phone receiver dangling under a poster of a smiling woman riding a DART train, her eyes and teeth blacked out and enormous breasts inked over her sweater.

There was no way around it: Katie was going to have to find a way to ask her mother for help. She staggered over to a row of seats and collapsed into the only empty one. In a minute, after she'd collected herself, she would try again. The nice, grandmotherly woman to her left—or maybe the young mother with a toddler to her right—one of them would let her use their phone, would tell her that it would all be all right, would perhaps even laugh and offer an anecdote of her own. *Oh goodness, that happened to me once, there I was,*

77

stranded without my purse or any way to call anyone . . .

The grandmotherly woman got up and joined two other elderly women making their way slowly to the exit. The mother scolded and the toddler began to wail. A man took the older woman's place, flopping into the seat with a smile and a cheery apology.

"Hope you don't mind," he said. He was dressed in a suit—not a very nice one, shiny and too tight. His shirt was a bit gray at the collar from being washed too often. This was not a man who could afford to send his shirts out. Also, his accent was New York. Maybe even Queens. "There weren't any tables free down at the food court."

He held up a sandwich wrapped in waxed paper as evidence. Something fried—fried chicken, fried fish, fried shoe leather for all Katie knew, but it smelled delicious. Her mouth watered and her stomach started up the growling again.

"Oh," she said, embarrassed. "I, um, didn't eat on the plane."

Without asking he tore the sandwich down the middle and handed her half. "I shouldn't even be eating this," he admitted, and it was true that he was a bit doughy and his shirt was straining across the gut. He couldn't have been more than thirty, thirty-five tops, but he had the dissipated air of a man who'd been climbing the middle management ladder for decades: florid complexion, blond hair already receding halfway back his skull, neck squeezed unflatteringly by his yellow tie.

"I shouldn't," Katie said, then took a bite. It *was* chicken, with some sort of tangy, piquant sauce and slices of lovely ripe tomatoes. She moaned with pleasure.

"Almost worth flying through Dallas for that sandwich," he chuckled. "Don't tell my doctor, but I had a sausage biscuit for breakfast this morning in Henderson."

"Henderson? Really?" She managed to get the words out between bites. "That's near where I'm going. What were you doing there?"

He dabbed at his fingertips with a napkin. "Setting up shop, basically," he said. "My company's opening a branch there in a few weeks."

"Are you with Amazon?"

"Naw, but I ought to thank them, I guess." He dug in his jacket for a card and offered it to her with a little bow. "We're in the waste hauling business. Construction sites, oil rigs, entertainment venues. 'Course, in New London it's all going to be construction until that Amazon vein of gold dries up."

Katie polished off the last of her sandwich while reading his card. "Well, Dan Daschauer, I'm Katie Garrett. Nice to meet you. And thank you—I might have starved without you."

They shook hands formally, but Dan's eyes

sparked with interest. "Can't have that," he said. "Lady as pretty as you—it would be a shame to let you starve. Are you from New London?"

"Oh no—Boston. I'm just—well, I'm here for a funeral. My grandmother. We weren't close."

"Ah, that's too bad," he said. "I would have liked to watch you tackle a rack of ribs next. Or maybe a side of beef. Your appetite is . . . well, let's just call it refreshing."

Katie laughed. It felt good—not just to let go of some of the tension of the day, but to have grease on her fingers and not worry about the number of calories she'd consumed. She'd been watching her weight ever since she and Liam started trying for a baby, a prophylactic measure recommended by friends who'd already given birth. "Less to lose later," they advised.

Dan smiled. "Listen, I don't know how long you'll be in town, but I'll be back Thursday night. How about I give you a call?"

"Oh," Katie said, unprepared. "I'm, I just—I'm sorry. I don't think that will work."

Because I'm married, was the obvious conclusion to that sentence, but somehow it didn't come out of her mouth. This sweet, rumpled, homely man was flirting with her, and God bless him for trying—it wasn't his fault that her wedding rings were probably in some back-alley pawnshop right now, paving the way for her mugger to buy whatever his drug of choice

80

was. Liam's grandmother's 1.8-carat rose-cut stone nestled between twin sapphires, traded for a mound of heroin that would be gone in days. Or weeks. Katie wasn't actually all that clear on the details of the heroin epidemic.

Dan's smile slipped a little. "No problem. Hey, I had to give it a shot, right? I mean, it's not every day that a gorgeous woman mainlines a Chester's Chicken Deluxe right in front of me. That smudge of barbecue sauce on your chin—a man would have to be made of *ice*."

Katie's hand flew self-consciously to her chin.

"No, no," Dan laughed. "Kidding about the sauce."

"Ha," Katie said. "Listen, I was wondering— I've lost my phone. And my ride, actually. I mean, there's lots of people I could call, I'm just trying to decide who."

"Use mine," Dan said instantly, handing her his phone.

Something occurred to Katie. "Damn. I have no idea what my mother's phone number is."

"Ah, yes," Dan said philosophically. "Who knows any numbers these days? But maybe she's listed? Personal information isn't all that personal anymore."

"I could try . . ." Katie tapped her mother's full name in: Georgina Dial Hunt. Images of her— at the Pecan Ridge Estates clubhouse, with her girlfriends, in a golf cart, on a safari bus—flooded

81

the screen, but no phone numbers. "I guess I could Facebook message her. Could I . . ."

"Be my guest."

In moments her mother's profile picture popped up. Dan, watching over her shoulder, cleared his throat.

"Maybe your mother would give me her number," he said. "Since she must have given birth to you when she was nine. And she's almost as, um, attractive as you are."

"Oh God, don't ever let Georgina hear that," Katie said. If this man found her attractive in her current state—slept-in clothes, unwashed body, wrecked hair and smudged makeup—then he was more pathetic than he appeared. "She'd suck the blood right out of you. And besides, this photo is, let's say, heavily staged."

Her mother had been posing on a bouldered trail at Canyon Ranch at sunset, a filmy scarf drifting on the breeze and concealing the faint suggestion of neck wrinkles that her plastic surgeon had been unable to completely erase. Her smile was predatory, though people often mistook it for simply carefree. Only Katie knew that Georgina had had her fangs filed down to conceal her true nature . . .

"Not really," she mumbled to herself, tapping out a message.

"Excuse me?"

"Oh, nothing . . ."

DM me! ASAP—got mugged, no phone, no $$$. Pick me up at airport?

It was nearly noon on a Tuesday morning, a time when her mother was usually shopping or golfing or meeting girlfriends for lunch, but almost immediately, the dots appeared on the screen indicating that her mother was messaging back.

Oh no!!!!!
Katie so sorry I can't
Long story
Not in Dallas not back until tomorrow night

Katie stared at the series of messages, an uneasy numbness settling in. Where could her mother have gone, the day after her own mother died?

"No luck?" Dan asked gently. He was probably beginning to piece together a narrative that was unflattering, to say the least—in which Katie figured as unbalanced or perhaps on the run.

No worries

Katie typed quickly. She gazed at her mother's brittle smile, then tapped "21 Mutual Friends" out of curiosity. Up popped the list, a veritable ghoul register of their shared past: several of the men Georgina had dated and discarded, including Katie's orthodontist and the man whose wife had taught her piano lessons before their divorce. A few friends from their old neighborhood in Dallas.

And Scarlett Jesse Ragsdale.

Katie's fingertip hovered over her cousin's name. She didn't remember ever accepting her friend request, but there she was—a photo taken in a restaurant, with an absurdly large margarita in front of her and her long, dark hair piled messily on top of her head. The photo was blurry, and the light wasn't good, but even so Katie could see that her cousin had a pleasantly heart-shaped face with long dark eyelashes and a shy smile.

On impulse Katie Google-searched Scarlett. Up popped a white-pages listing on Canterbury Court in Archer, Texas. Before she could change her mind, Katie tapped "Call."

The phone rang twice before it was answered. There was a clatter, someone yelped *shit,* and a male voice shouted, "Digger, you can just fuck off if you can't come up with that ham or ten bucks by suppertime!"

And then someone hung up on her.

CHAPTER EIGHT

June 1954

Margaret felt Ernest Drake's hand slip a little lower on her back and knew it was time to do something drastic. He and his friends had been into the punch, which had been liberally spiked at some point in the evening and tasted a little like Lavoris. She waited until Ernest had waltzed her into the corner of the dance floor, where they were semi-hidden by the edge of the small stage, and ground the heel of her satin pump into his instep.

"Ow ow ow!" Ernest yelped, releasing her. Margaret smiled.

"Oh, how terribly clumsy of me," she said. "I'm so sorry. Let me get you some more punch."

She didn't wait for Ernest's answer but hurried off toward the coatroom that had been carved out of one of the salons on the mansion's sprawling first floor. She needed a moment of privacy to gather herself. It was nearly nine-thirty, and the rumor was that the happy couple was going to slip away for their wedding trip at ten o'clock. Which meant that she didn't have much time.

She'd planned for this moment all week, writing out her plan in her diary, complete with sample dialogue; how she would gaze adoringly at Hank Dial's bride, and tell her how beautiful she looked—and then she would turn to Hank and allow her gaze to flutter down. It was a trick she had perfected over the last year as part of the repertoire that went with her newly lush figure and the startling revelation that, at sixteen, strangers judged her a fully grown woman. Not Hank, though; she was counting on Hank to hook his arm around her neck the way he'd done to her and Helene for years, gruff and good-natured hugs for his "best girls."

But this time would be different. This time, in that exquisite space of a second or two when her cheek was pressed up against his, she meant to show him her heart. "You're too good for her," she would whisper, and she was counting on it to be true, so that in the years ahead, when his wife disappointed him, when she turned into a nag and a bore and a fat nursing cow, he would remember how pretty she looked tonight, in the petal-pink peau de soie gown that she'd begged her mother for.

Margaret ducked between the rows of coats, damp from the earlier rain and lending a musty, woolly scent to the cramped room, and took her lipstick and her mother's silver compact from her little evening bag. She dabbed on a bit of lipstick and checked her teeth, pinched her cheeks to make them rosy, and touched the waves in her hair that she had worked so hard over, which were beginning to wilt from the dancing and humidity in the air from the recent rains.

Satisfied that—wilting or no—she was still one of the prettiest girls at the wedding (some might say *the* prettiest, but Margaret prided herself on being realistic about herself), she adjusted her bodice so that the swell of her bosom showed above the ruched sweetheart neckline and glided out into the ballroom with her head held high. As she was scouring the room for the bridal couple, her mother appeared at her elbow, her brittle "public" smile fixed on her face. Caroline Pierson took her daughter's arm in a grip that was stronger than one might have imagined: Margaret was trapped.

"Margaret, darling, come and meet your cousins."

"Levander and Audrey are here?" Margaret asked, surprised. Her father's sister Ruth had married a preacher who did not allow his wife or children to attend any events where there would be dancing or alcohol. Besides, they lived almost six hours away, in Oklahoma. And, of course, there was the fact that Aunt Ruth would have barely known the bridegroom, who had been just a child when she'd met her husband and moved away.

"No. Not them. Your cousins on the Wooley side."

Margaret's eyes widened with surprise; she knew these cousins existed the way she was aware that they had recently added two new elements to the periodic table: they were exotic, but unlikely to have any impact on her life, and never discussed in her house. According to Caroline, on the few occasions when Margaret had been curious enough to ask her mother about her family, her sister, Euda, had squandered every opportunity and advantage God had visited on her to marry a heathen criminal and give birth to a squalling horde of brats, one after another. Euda apparently had failed out of school and took AFDC money from the government and had called Caroline something so egregious and unforgivable that the sisters had vowed never to speak to each other again. So complete was their estrangement that Margaret didn't even know how many children there were, and whether they were boys or girls, and how old they were. In Margaret's mind, they were all toddlers, dressed in dirty diapers with knotted and tangled hair, sitting in a dirt yard with a mangy dog to watch over them.

But as her mother fussed with an invisible speck on her gloves and avoided her gaze, Margaret did a quick calculation and realized that her cousins would be in their twenties now—just like the bridal couple.

As if reading her mind, Caroline said, "Tansy knew the girls from the WAVES."

Ah, yes, perfect Tansy Monroe, youngest child and only daughter of the Tyler Monroes, whose wedding she was here to celebrate. Tansy had spent the war years volunteering with the Red Cross, and famously missed only one day, when her brother was killed in the Pacific. Tansy was known to be beautiful and kind and generous, which made her marriage to Hank all the more galling.

Her mother was tugging Margaret toward the wide French doors leading out to a veranda onto which the guests repaired when they grew overheated from the dancing. "Let's just get this over with," Caroline muttered, giving her wrist a pinch.

Margaret, long accustomed to these corrective pinches, reflexively straightened her spine and fixed a pleasant smile on her face as she followed her mother to a small, round table at the far end of the veranda at which four women were seated: two elderly dowagers who were shouting into each other's ears, and two skinny girls with owlish eyes and weak chins who were pushing bits of cake around on their plates. The girls' gowns—one pale blue and the other leaf green— had obviously been sewn by someone unfamiliar with the art of tailoring, and the shoulders gapped and the hems buckled with uneven stitches.

"Girls," Caroline said stiffly. "Allow me to present my daughter Margaret."

"It's very nice to meet you," Margaret said with the slight curtsy that she'd learned at the age of seven so she could properly greet the Daisy mothers in the parlor, and which she supposed she would never be able to shake. And then, when it seemed neither girl was going to do more than smile shyly, she added, "Isn't it a lovely wedding?"

"Oh yes," said the one in the blue, staring down at the table.

"I like your dress," the other said. "Did you make it?"

Margaret blinked: the dress had cost nearly seventy dollars at Neiman Marcus in Dallas, and had been worked on by not one but two separate tailors, one of them French. "No—I don't have that talent, unfortunately."

"Please give your mother my best," Caroline said, her fingernails—she was still clutching Margaret's wrist—digging deeper. Margaret wondered if she realized that she had forgotten to introduce the cousins by name—or if she perhaps didn't know their names.

"Oh, we will, ma'am. She's doing a bit better lately."

"Was she ailing?" Margaret asked politely. The girls looked at each other, turning an identical shade of pink that unfortunately did nothing for their complexions. Some girls were improved by a bit of a blush, and some weren't, and Margaret was finding it surprising that she was even distantly related to these two.

"She, um . . ." said the one in blue.

"Female troubles," the other mumbled. "She took to her bed near upon a month ago. But just yesterday she ate a bowl of stew and walked to the mailbox and back. Lassiter's rigged her up a rail so she can get in and out of her chair."

"She been living with Lassiter and Bess since she took ill," Blue Dress piped up, encouraged by her sister's loquacity. "They got the spare room."

"Yes," Caroline said briskly. "Well, we all have our burdens, don't we? Now we must let you two get back to enjoying the party."

Margaret was practically spun around and dragged away, released the moment they entered the ballroom and the crowd swallowed them. Her mother sagged against the wall, closing her eyes and pressing the back of her hand to her forehead as though she'd just fought her way through a horde.

"Mother," Margaret said, piqued. "What was the purpose of that? Since we've been acting like we don't know them for my whole life?"

"Because apparently Joan Dial failed to explain the situation to the bride's mother." She shrugged. "And *someone* let it slip that Tansy used to play with those two dimwits, and since she was already throwing this gauche *circus,* she just added them to the list. And now everyone knows that we are related."

Margaret allowed herself a small smile: now it was all clear. Joan Dial had played second fiddle to her mother for years, but the marriage of her son to a girl from a family that was even more well-to-do and socially prominent than the Piersons had given her an unexpected opportunity for comeuppance. It would take a bold woman to go up against Caroline Pierson in public, but in private, Mrs. Dial must have been relishing her role as mother of the groom at the wedding that would overshadow every other social event that year. She could just imagine Mrs. Dial explaining to the bride's mother that yes, the Piersons were blood kin of those poor, unfortunate Wooley girls to whom Tansy had shown such kindness.

Still, the distance between the Piersons and even the next-most-wealthy family in New London was so vast that her mother rarely gave such rebellions any notice. The fact that she was visibly unsettled was surprising and intriguing.

"What exactly is wrong with my cousins?" Margaret asked, reaching for a flute of champagne from a passing waiter's tray. "I mean, other than those *dresses*."

Her mother gave her an automatic frown of disapproval, then sighed. "Everything, frankly. First of all, there are so many of them that one can't possibly remember them all."

"Wait," Margaret said. "How many, exactly? And are they boys or girls? And how old are they?"

"Three of them. Boy, girl, girl."

"Three is hardly a lot. The Temples have four, and the Kelleys have *five,* and the—"

"Well, perhaps, but Euda was always so dramatic about it. Every time she was expecting, we all had to hear about it, as if she'd invented the entire process."

"Hmmm," Margaret said, realizing that she'd unintentionally hit upon one of her mother's sore spots. Depending on Caroline's mood, she sometimes seemed regretful about not having more children—which would be understandable, considering that she'd lost her first child in the school disaster. But at other times she could be downright cold toward women with large families, criticizing everything from their squandered figures ("if her bosom falls any further, she'll have to pick it up off the floor") to their fortunes ("three daughters, three weddings, there goes any hope she's got of a vacation in the next decade").

In Caroline's sister Euda's case, however, there had been no fortune to squander. Caroline and Euda had been raised in tiny Archer, where Euda still lived. Their parents had eked out a spare existence and died penniless. Caroline did not like to talk about how she'd gone from the edge of ruin to the height of New London society, but Margaret had managed to fill in the details missing from her mother's account by listening closely when the ladies gossiped: at sixteen, Caroline hitched a ride to Henderson, where she lied about her age and got a job tutoring the children of a wealthy family that had made its fortune in timber. When the ungainly young nephew of her employer came for a visit, Caroline had turned on the charm, and the young man had been dazzled—dazzled enough to overlook her poverty and family history. Within a matter of months they were married, and Caroline was pregnant when her homely groom announced that his father and uncles were sending him thirty miles east to the tiny town of New London to invest in drilling rights for the newly discovered East Texas oil field.

Back in Archer, Euda did not fare nearly so well. Caroline had been sharp-witted enough to win academic prizes at school, and that in turn caught the attention of her teachers, who gave her extra guidance, so that by the time she graduated from the eighth grade she was at the top of her class. Euda was plain in both looks and spirit, so her intelligence was overlooked, and she managed to escape the attention of nearly everyone. She dropped out of sixth grade to take a job in a laundry, and when the boy who delivered the cleaned and pressed bundles asked her to marry him, she said yes.

Caroline had little patience for Euda's misfortune: "poor as church mice and dumb as dirt," she'd said of her sister and brother-in-law. Any charity she might have felt for her sister had been, Margaret suspected, scoured away by Caroline's social aspirations. Margaret was insightful enough to realize that her mother's ambitions were probably fueled by insecurity and a fear of being found out—but poor Euda had paid the price, cut off from her only family.

"Well," she said drily, as she sipped the last of her champagne, "not everyone has your thirst for success, Mother."

Caroline sniffed. "Those girls may seem harmless now, but they were dreadful when they were little—colicky, and they caught every little illness that came along, because Euda couldn't keep them fed or washed. She and her husband wouldn't let the boy go to school after third grade, either. They're unmanageable."

"Where is the boy now?" Margaret asked.

Caroline sniffed and shrugged her shoulders. "Prison? An early grave? Really, Margaret, had I known you were so curious about your extended family, I would have invited Audrey to spend the summer with us. I'm sure you would enjoy sharing your bed with her and joining her for morning prayers on your knees. Now if you'll excuse me, I see Martha Briggs over there, and I really must talk to her about the garden club luncheon."

She hurried off, stepping impatiently around the guests who were in her way. Margaret waited until her mother was out of sight to take a half-full glass of champagne that had been left on the long table nearby, and drank it in a single swallow. She dabbed daintily at her lips, wondered where she could get another, spied the bride and groom descending the curved staircase, and promptly forgot all about her cousins.

The bride looked fresh and pretty in a trim little yellow traveling suit, and the groom was carrying her train case and holding her elbow. Margaret's heart was in her throat as she tried to fight her way through the crowd gathering to say goodbye, and she didn't even stop to apologize when she jostled an elderly man and nearly knocked him down.

But she was too late. Her little speech died on her lips as the couple waved and the crowd threw rice and cheered—and then they were gone, dashing for the convertible that Tansy's parents had given them for a wedding present, Hank never even knowing how hot the flame of Margaret's love for him burned.

CHAPTER NINE

"You heard that, I guess," Katie said, mortified.

Dan seemed to have finally exhausted his seemingly bottomless well of goodwill. He had taken back his phone and was polishing it nervously on his shirt. "Well," he said, then cleared his throat. "Whoever you were calling, he does have the sort of voice that carries, doesn't he?"

The phone rang and Dan nearly dropped it. Then he recovered and answered with more dignity than Katie would have expected.

"I'm *sorry,* okay, but he thought you were Digger," a female voice said, loud enough for Katie to hear. "Who *is* this, anyway?"

Dan handed her the phone like it was on fire.

"Scarlett? This is Katie Garrett. Katie, um, Dial? Your cousin?"

"Oh! Oh, Katie, it's just awful, isn't it?" The voice changed timbre and lost a few decibels. "About Gomma?"

Gomma.

"Um, yes, yes, it is. So sad!" Katie clutched the edge of her vinyl seat with her free hand and avoided Dan's gaze. "I haven't talked to you in—

97

well, I guess about twenty years, now that I think about it."

"Wait, you mean we actually met? I met you?" Scarlett sounded unaccountably pleased. "That's so cool! When was it?"

Katie chastised herself—maybe she shouldn't have mentioned that. "You were four," she said. "Or maybe five. Your dad brought you over to our house one time when he had business in Dallas."

"Heh," Scarlett said, considerably more quietly. "If I was five, that wasn't my dad. He took off before I was even born. It was probably just one of Mom's boyfriends. How old were *you?*"

So they had something in common after all. Katie thought back to that afternoon; all she remembered was Scarlett splashing all the water out of the plastic swimming pool and then sitting in it holding a damp jam sandwich, while the neighbor's tiny schnauzer barked its head off and tried to climb in.

"Nine or ten, I guess."

"You live in Boston now, right?" This, spoken with a sense of awe, as if Katie had decamped for the rings of Saturn.

"I do, actually—but I'm, um, well, I just landed in Dallas. I'm coming for the, um." There wasn't going to be a funeral or a service, according to her mother—Margaret had expressly forbidden it. She had been cremated and her ashes interred next to her long-dead husband's grave.

"The *will* thing?" Scarlett said incredulously. "For real? Oh my gosh. I told Merritt there wasn't any way—I figured it would be just us. That's so great! Where are you staying?"

Katie took a deep, careful breath. "Uh, well, I haven't quite figured that out yet."

"Oh *gosh,* I'm so sorry, Katie, I wish I could ask you to stay with us but it just isn't the best time here but I can—but I'll *totally* come to you," she stammered. "I mean, I can't wait to see you. I could like come over to get ready first?"

Ready for what, Katie wondered—the meeting with the attorney? But surely not. "When's the, um, will thing?"

"It's tomorrow afternoon. I have to check what time. Is your mom coming too?"

"Look, Scarlett . . ." The buzzing in Katie's head was growing louder; the growling of her stomach had turned into a dull ache. For a moment Katie wondered if she might pass out right here in front of the endlessly spinning, screeching baggage carousels.

It would simplify some things . . . like trying to explain to her estranged cousin that her mother didn't give a shit. That she and Georgina were bad relatives, selfish ones, who'd never even bothered to Facebook stalk her cousin until she had no other possible alternative because she *didn't care*.

Scarlett was notable for only two things in the

family lore—at least, what passed for family lore with Georgina, who had disowned her few relatives years ago. (Twice, in fact; once when she first managed to escape New London at the age of eighteen and then again at twenty-seven, after getting knocked up in Paris. The second time, she stayed just long enough to have a fight with her mother, before hitchhiking to Dallas and giving birth two days later in a church-run shelter.) The first notable thing about Scarlett was that her father had been Mexican.

The second was that she was the last living descendant of the Willems family besides Katie and Georgina, now that Margaret was dead.

Katie had had to do a family history project in the fourth grade, so she knew that Espen Willems and his young bride, Griseldis, had come all the way from Holland to the Gulf of Mexico in 1904 to grow rice, which had struck her as a really dumb thing to do. But apparently lots of other Dutch people had the same idea, because a few years later there were so many of them that overproduction wiped out the coastal Texas rice industry. Many of these poor immigrants simply turned around and went home, but not stubborn Espen Willems, who moved two hundred miles north to the tiny town of Archer and opened a general store.

Espen and Griseldis had two daughters before succumbing to overwork when the girls had barely reached adulthood. From there, the two branches of the Willems family tree had gone in different directions. The only thing that the sisters and their descendants had in common, as Katie learned by reading through the lines, was a propensity among the girls to give birth before carefully considering the provenance and character of the father. Generation after generation of women found themselves abandoned, widowed, or simply unloved and uncherished, until it seemed as though any romantic inclinations ought to have been bred out of their blood.

Georgina liked to imply that her own out-of-wedlock pregnancy was the result of a mysterious serendipity, a bohemian sense of adventure; but when Scarlett—daughter of Georgina's cousin Heather—came out of the womb caramel brown with no father to claim paternity, it was something entirely different: *trash,* in Georgina's words, *doing what trash does.* By the time Katie realized how hypocritical and cruel her mother's assessment had been, it was much too late to offer any sort of olive branch to her cousin. When Scarlett's mother had died a few years earlier in an accident that twisted her Hyundai like a pretzel between a semi and a guardrail, Katie had sent no card, no flowers . . . not even a sad-face emoji on Facebook.

Katie couldn't very well make amends now— *Say, sorry about your mom, by the way.*

Instead, she blurted, "I got mugged, Scarlett. I'm at the airport with no money and no way to rent a car and—and—I don't know what I'm going to do."

Scarlett's gasp was audible. "Are you hurt? Did they hurt you?"

"No, no—nothing like that. I mean, it didn't even happen here. It's, well, a long story."

"Well, you just sit tight," Scarlett said, her voice suddenly edged with steel. "My car's out of gas, but I'll see if I can borrow Merritt's truck, okay? I'll be there in, like, well, I don't actually know how long 'cause I got to find him first. I'll call when—oh wait, I can't call you, can I?"

"No, no, that's fine," Katie said, suddenly weak with relief. She was being *rescued*. "I'll just stay right here. I'm at D31 in arrivals. I won't go anywhere. Take your time."

"I'll try to hurry. What do you have on?"

Katie looked down at herself. "White blouse, jeans, black boots."

"Okay," Scarlett said doubtfully. Katie couldn't blame her—half the women in her office wore the exact same thing on their days off, though the style didn't appear to be quite as prevalent here. "Tell you what, keep your eyes peeled for a red Dodge truck with tires up to your tits. Oh, Katie, this is going to be great!"

"Well, I'd better get going if I'm going to make my flight," Dan said. "Thank you for making the airport a little less soul-sucking today."

102

"And thank *you* for, well, saving me. I don't know what I would have done without you."

"You would have done just fine." Dan rose, stretching; his shirttails had pulled out of his slacks, revealing a slice of pale, rounded stomach. "I can tell—you're a survivor. You would have figured it out."

He gave a little bow, then a smart salute, before turning and striding purposefully away from her. He checked his watch, then broke into an awkward jog, pulling his carry-on along behind him. It fishtailed, nearly taking out a woman with a stroller.

Katie watched him go. No one had ever called her a survivor before—which probably spoke to Dan's poor judgment (well, of course: he was the sort of guy who talked to strangers in airports). Georgina was the tough one in the family—some might say ruthless—and Katie had been blessed with luck. And genes, of course. Very good genes that had been her ticket out of more than a few difficult situations, like the one she'd just found herself in—pretty enough to capture a man's attention, if that man was Dan.

Katie sighed. She'd traded on her looks ever since she saw the way her mother smiled at the man at the deli to make him add a few extra slices of turkey onto her order. By the time she left for college, it was as natural as breathing.

But maybe it was time to stop.

After all, this was turning into a journey of discovery, wasn't it? A few days to figure out who she really was, and what she really wanted. Maybe the first step was to strip off all of the trappings of tony Boston—especially since it was being done for her. Looking around the airport, she was reminded of how far she'd come since she left Texas, putting behind her the teased and highlighted hairstyle that she'd learned at her mother's knee; the wardrobe of "cute tops" (Georgina's words) designed to show off her cleavage, her bare shoulders, her midriff; the acrylic nails and the logo purses and a hundred other details of the illusion Georgina worked so hard to create. What a revelation it had been, on her first date with Liam, when he told her that he'd noticed her for the first time in their freshman psych class because she'd overslept and rushed over in no makeup and an old sweatshirt: "I could finally *see* you," he'd said in a husky voice, and then he'd changed the emphasis slightly: "I could finally see *you*."

But that first blush of wonderment had quickly turned, as it must for all insecure girls, into studying and decoding what this new man in her life had really meant. "No makeup" turned into learning to contour and highlight and shade until she looked natural under as much makeup as she'd worn before. The bright-colored sun-dresses and camisoles were traded for simple but expensive pieces that she worked two off-campus jobs to pay for, jeans with no bling and boots with no heel and sweaters with no synthetic fibers.

More than a decade later, it suddenly dawned on Katie that this was a costume too, just harder to recognize. She brushed at a smudge on her white pinpoint shirt cuff and headed off to find a ladies' room.

She checked the time on a departure screen and did the math. It would be midafternoon by the time Scarlett arrived, and that was if she drove the maximum speed the whole way.

In the bathroom, she used one of her precious dollars to buy a couple of tampons and then, after considering, bought two more to be safe, stuffing the extras in her back pocket. She took care of business and then gave herself a long, hard look in the mirror as she washed up. The flight had taken its toll; her eyeliner was smudged, her lipstick chewed off; her nose was shiny and there were dark hollows under her eyes. Her cashmere wrap hung like a dirty rag around her shoulders, her blouse had a mysterious stain on the front, and her face looked puffy from the flight. She dampened a wad of hand towels under the faucet and scrubbed off as much of the remaining makeup as she could.

There—better. Already, she was feeling like she'd shed a few layers that were weighing her down. Maybe it was the period hormones gone haywire and the lack of sleep, but Katie was feeling . . . something. The start of a second wind, maybe. Giddy, almost.

She dug in her jeans pocket to make sure that her remaining ten dollars were still there as she left the bathroom. It wasn't even enough for a paperback—not the kind Katie liked, anyway, the beautiful matte-finished novels with soft-focus watercolor covers and titles like *The* —— *of* —— or *All the* —— *We* ——. Lately, they had all run together, and she hadn't even minded; she had used her pregnancy as an excuse to go to bed early with her orange blossom tea and lose herself in the stories that blended into each other.

She couldn't buy, but browsing was free. Katie found the biggest bookstore in the airport—a real one, not a souvenir shop with a few titles shelved next to the packaged peanuts and granola bars—and tried to make the experience last. She read each title on the shelves, picked up half a dozen and read random pages as though she was trying to find the perfect choice, squinted at the magazine titles. Finally, when she couldn't keep up the ruse any longer, she squared her shoulders and marched out with her head held high, the way Georgina had taught her all those years ago.

Make them think they have nothing to offer you, her mother counseled her at thirteen, when she took young Katie window shopping at Highland Park Village. *Act like nothing in the store meets your standards*. And it had worked. Salesclerks had fawned over Georgina, bearing her disdainful dismissals with equanimity, even humility.

But Katie didn't have her mother's confidence. She walked slowly up and down the terminal, making a deal with herself that she wouldn't check the time on the arrivals and departures screens again until she had completed a circuit, and still the time crawled. Eleven o'clock came and went. Eleven-thirty . . . noon . . . twelve-fifteen. Her stomach was angry, growling mutinously, and her brief burst of energy dwindled like a jet turned down on a stove. The aromas from the Cinnabon were torture; even the greasy burnt smell wafting from Manchu Wok made her salivate. She spotted an abandoned newspaper and picked it up discreetly, squaring the pages and tucking it under her arm, thinking she could find a quiet gate and read stale news.

But then she spotted something even better.

A *People* magazine with Kate Middleton on the cover, slightly worn and wrinkled from something being spilled on it, left on a seat at the end of a row. Katie glanced around, but no one was nearby. She picked up the magazine and hurried to the exit. It was almost one o'clock— really, she ought to be waiting outside anyway, in case Scarlett made excellent time. In the midst of the arrivals, the honking of the horns and the tweeting whistles of the security staff, she found a bench next to the crosswalk, sat down, and flipped through the magazine until she found the glossy photos of the beautiful princess, regal even in an ugly blouse and awful hat. One could do worse for company. Glancing around every so often to make sure that she didn't miss the arrival of a monster truck with wheels up to her tits, Katie dug deeper, looking for clues into the princess's beautiful yet inscrutable life.

CHAPTER TEN

1958

"Wait a minute," the gangly young man in the houndstooth vest said. "You're one of *those?* The Daisy children?"

The boy, whose name Margaret had instantly forgotten, was intoxicated, but then again, so were most of the boys in the Withnalls' backyard. Half of them were Tripp's fraternity brothers, familiar from two years of Phi Psi dances and parties, but the rest were boys he'd gone to St. Stephens with and boys from his baseball days and boys who'd grown up in the same tony Austin neighborhood. The engagement party was to be tomorrow night—an elegant affair that Mrs. Withnall had been planning for months—and she'd made it known that she expected all of Tripp's guests to be on their best behavior. By way of a bribe, she and Mr. Withnall had offered them the use of the pool and cabana this evening for a much more casual party.

"I'm surprised you've heard of us," Margaret said, favoring the drunk boy with a modest smile. She was stretched out on a chaise longue, her yellow patent sandals on the pool deck next to her. Earlier today, she and Tripp's sisters had gone to the salon to have their hair and nails done. She wasn't quite sure about the set that Mrs. Withnall's hairdresser had given her: for one thing, the curls piled on her crown added a good two inches to her height, which made her perilously close to Tripp's five feet nine inches and meant that she wouldn't be able to wear her silk pumps tomorrow night; for another, she could still smell hairspray even over her perfume, and it was stiff as a board to the touch. Thank goodness Mother was going to have Mr. Jaffrey, her Tyler hairdresser, stay in the guesthouse for the wedding weekend, so he could make sure that the bride and her mother looked nothing short of perfect all weekend long.

Tripp wandered over with a drink in his hand and plopped down on the chaise next to Margaret. Now they were a proper foursome, as the drunken boy was sharing a chaise with Margaret's roommate, Gert. Tripp was still wet from having been thrown, along with several other boys, into the pool half an hour earlier after they'd lost some sort of bet, and Margaret shifted away from him to avoid brushing his clammy thigh with hers.

"We were just talking about the Daisy children," the boy said. "You didn't tell me she was one of them."

"Yes, Everett, I did," Tripp said, tipsily affronted. "I'm writing the article about them, remember?"

"Her mother's the *president* of the Daisy Club," Gert chimed in. Gert had come home with Margaret to New London over the Thanksgiving holiday, since she was from Ohio and it was too far to travel. She'd been fascinated by Margaret's family—annoyingly so, asking dozens of questions and asking to see her mother's scrapbooks—and thought that story of the explosion was *ever so sad.* By the end of the weekend, as Gert trailed Caroline around the house helping her mother arrange flowers for the dining room table or bringing in the mail, Margaret was thoroughly sick of her.

But Margaret had few female friends—a lack that she hardly considered a deficit, given how melodramatic and time-consuming friendship with other girls seemed to be—and she would need at least five to serve as bridesmaids, so she had put up with Gert all through the winter and spring. She'd suggested to Tripp that an earlier engagement would allow them to be married right after graduation, which seemed expedient, but his mother had been adamant that they wait so that she could hold the engagement party when her garden was in bloom and would photograph its best. By the time Tripp had finally produced the two-carat emerald-cut diamond and platinum ring, Mrs. Withnall had already met with the caterers, the florist, and the society editors of the *Statesman*, whose favor she had curried for decades to make sure that her parties received the proper attention.

In Marilyn Withnall, Margaret had met her mother's match, and she was both amused and a bit apprehensive to imagine the two of them squaring off during the wedding weekend. But as all of the planning was the domain of the bride and her mother, Mrs. Withnall would be able to do little more than follow orders and seethe. Margaret had half a mind to put her in a salmon-pink gown, which would clash with her future mother-in-law's sallow complexion—but she'd known since she was a little girl that her colors would be robin's egg blue and pale yellow. Daddy had promised that no expense would be spared, and when Margaret tested that notion by suggesting that he buy a matched pair of swans to swim in the little pond out back during the reception, he'd barely flinched.

Despite the fact that they were sitting inches apart, Everett barely seemed to have registered Gert's presence, even though she was leaning forward so that her breasts were practically spilling into his lap. With only a week to go before their graduation from UT, Gert was understandably panicked; her boyfriend had broken up with her back in March, and there had been no suitable prospects since. She was planning to make the most of Margaret's wedding to meet Tripp's single friends, and Margaret couldn't blame her: if their roles were reversed, she'd be doing the same.

"Now, I understand that you're going to be a dentist," Gert said brightly, attempting to steer the conversation. Margaret felt a familiar spike of annoyance: it was all simply too dull for words.

"A funny thing about being a Daisy," she said, pretending not to have heard Gert. "All of our birthdays were within a few weeks of each other. It's as though, following all the funerals, our parents went directly home to screw."

She held Everett's gaze as she said it, fully aware of the effect she had on the majority of men. Next to him, Gert tittered nervously, a hand to her mouth.

"People always screw after disasters," a nearby voice said. A tall man had separated from the hazy edge of the crowd of young people, many of whom were attempting the Bop dangerously close to the edge of the pool. He was wearing a brown bomber jacket and blue jeans, and he had a cigarette and lighter in hand; as the four of them squinted in the darkness he lit the cigarette, took a single puff, and then handed it to Margaret.

She took it automatically, then nearly dropped it as she realized who he was: her entire body seemed to shift with the knowledge, heat flooding the places inside of her that she hadn't known had gone cold.

"Heh," Tripp said, scowling. "Hello, Lucky. I suppose Mother sent you down here to break up the party."

"Hank," Margaret whispered.

The last Margaret had heard, Hank had been working in one of Tansy's father's bank branches. She'd lost touch with Helene, who'd married and moved away after her father's death. At least, that's what Caroline had reported offhandedly, never knowing how hungry Margaret was for these occasional bits of news, which she recorded in the diary that she kept hidden behind her textbooks in her room at the sorority house.

As she watched Hank shake a second cigarette from the pack and light it for Gert, never taking his eyes off Margaret, she wondered: What would he make of the fact that he featured prominently in all of the diaries that she had kept, from childhood on? That writing his name had kept him close to her all of these years?

"Miss," he said, and Gert, who never smoked, nonetheless put it to her lips and immediately convulsed in a fit of coughing. She jumped off the chaise and barely managed an "excuse me" before hurrying away.

"Nervous girl," Hank said mildly. "You don't even remember me, do you, Mags?"

Margaret shrugged and let the cigarette dangle from her fingertips, fluttering ash onto the pool deck. Her skirt had somehow skimmed up over her knee, and she stared down at the long, smooth expanse of her calves, shimmering in the light of the tiki torches. Her heart seemed to pause for a moment before beginning to beat again with what felt like renewed purpose—and she knew that her life was finally changing. "Perhaps," she said. "Have you done anything memorable lately?"

Tripp and Everett goggled. Hank laughed and pulled up a chair.

"You know each other?" Tripp demanded.

"Hank's sister—I'm sorry," Margaret said, recovering herself. "*Lucky's* sister was my best friend when we were children." An exaggeration, but Helene wasn't here to argue.

"You're from New London?" Everett asked. "Tripp's doing a magazine story about the school disaster."

Hank's smile didn't slip, but something shifted around his eyes. "No kidding. What's the angle?"

"It's, ah. Well, you know, it'll be a long piece. Think Joe Mitchell in the *New Yorker*," Tripp said.

Joe? Margaret thought. Tripp had made her read the man's pieces—endless long, boring column inches by Joseph Mitchell and other writers, whose talent Tripp felt his own equaled and sometimes exceeded. Margaret was no critic and not much of a reader, but even she could tell the difference between the published stuff and the pieces—the fragments of pieces, actually, because as far as Margaret knew Tripp had never finished anything that wasn't required for a class—that Tripp was convinced would launch his literary career and eventually make him famous.

To be fair, she had rather thought she might like to be the wife of a famous author—living in a New York City apartment, rubbing elbows with glamorous people—and that, combined with the knowledge that Tripp's parents would fund the literary life for a while even if it didn't work out, had been enough to keep her enthusiasm adequately stoked.

Until now, anyway. The way Hank was looking at her—and where he'd picked up such an undignified and absurd nickname, she couldn't begin to imagine—she actually felt a little . . . soiled by Tripp. A tiny bit ashamed, even.

And there was something else. Something worse. The story of the Daisies . . . she'd given it to Tripp like feeding steak to a dog, knowing he wouldn't be able to resist, knowing he'd swallow it whole, a morsel of shock and horror with a larding of infamy and a taut crust of pain. She'd offered it up to him to see herself reflected back in his eyes, to give him a project with herself as its center, a way to make sure he never looked away.

Except that it wasn't her story to give. There, sprawled in the pool chair with his dark core of unknowability under a disguise of insouciance and swagger, was one who truly could claim it. To her parents, his parents, all the parents and siblings of the lost, the story of what happened on that long-ago afternoon—once you stripped away the headlines, the reporters from all over the world—was sacred. And she'd bartered it like a cheap bauble.

"Tripp," she said warningly—almost pleadingly.

But Tripp had taken a long slug from his tumbler and fortified himself. "It's been two decades," he said. "How old were you when it happened? Five or six?"

"Nine."

"Nine, then. Still too young to know what it all meant. You were, what, sick that day? I read that there were a few kids who were absent. Talk about *luck*."

"I was there." Hank held out his hands; even in the light of the tiki torches, or maybe because of it, the scars stood out in high relief, ridged and shiny and still shocking.

"You were there? Aw, this is fantastic. I mean, God, you know what I mean, I'm sorry, hell, all that suffering, all that loss. Your parents, I mean, I can't even imagine how relieved they must have been that you survived—"

"They might have been, if they weren't busy burying my brother," Hank said—and still the only sign of emotion in his languid, placid voice was the hard flash in his eyes and that twitch of his jaw. If anything, he seemed to relax even further in the chair, and his fingers trailed lazily in the pool. "He was eight. He went in the coffin in pieces, what was left of him after he burned up."

"Uh." Finally, Tripp seemed to have realized that he was in over his head. Everett had sobered up fast, and swung his legs over the edge of the chaise—he was sitting very straight, his mouth hanging open. "Look, I'm sorry, Luck—Hank. I didn't know."

"Yeah, that's okay. I mean, I'm just the guy who takes your dad up to check on his rigs. No reason for you to know my life story."

"The piece is going to be sensitive," Tripp said earnestly, and Margaret thought *shut up, shut up, shut up*.

"You're still flying, then," she said brightly. "You've got your own business?"

"Don't, Mags," Hank said heavily.

"Wait," Tripp said. "The lady was just trying to be polite."

Hank raised one eyebrow and stared at Tripp, then at Margaret. His eyes took her in, coming to rest on the diamond glittering on her left hand. Finally he said, "You know, you're right—here she's gone and grown up. A regular lady," he added, almost to himself.

Then he stood and yanked Tripp off his chaise as though he was picking up a bag of autumn leaves, and threw him into the pool. This time, when Tripp came up sputtering and coughing, the party guests looked on in shocked silence.

"What the hell—" Everett said.

"I'll show myself out," Hank said. "You can tell your dad not to worry about my last check."

"Fuck you, flyboy," Tripp said, water streaming in his eyes. "Get the fuck off our property!"

Hank shook his head, chuckling mirthlessly. "All right. Sorry to crash your party, folks. Good to see you again, Mags." He paused next to her, so close she could see the frayed seam of his jeans. "You really marrying him?"

Before she could answer, he shook his head. "Never mind, forget I asked. I guess that's a mistake we all have to make on our own."

"I barely knew him," Margaret pleaded an hour later, when the last of the guests were either gone or passed out in the pool house. Margaret had arranged the pillows under the bedcovers in the guest room, just in case anyone was nosy enough to look in on her, and snuck down the stairs to meet Tripp.

She had a vague plan to mollify and distract him, but it turned out that Tripp was in no mood to pursue his campaign up her thighs and under the elastic of her underwear, a battle he'd been waging for months now. Instead, she found him waiting for her in the swing hanging from an old oak near the end of the drive, in an unfamiliar and dangerous mood.

"Mags?" Tripp demanded, incredulously. "You told me you hated nicknames."

She'd actually told him she hated *his* nickname—who would stand for being known as the *third* of something?—but no matter. "I never told him to call me that. We were kids."

"When did you last see him?"

"Must you interrogate me? Like some—some criminal? It was at his wedding, if you must know."

"He's not married," Tripp said. "He rents a room from a rancher."

Something stirred inside Margaret. This wasn't news, of course; the annulment had been scandalous, awash as it was in rumors that her parents had secured it with a sizable donation to the Church. The public version of the story was shifting and vague; no one seemed to be quite sure who left whom, and why. Tansy was in Europe with her mother, or maybe she was back by now. If she was lucky, she'd soon be married again—swiftly, without fanfare—to a widower or a friend of the family. If she was smart, she'd produce a baby within a year and never speak of her first marriage again.

These were things that girls from good families knew. Margaret bit her lip, frustrated with herself: now was not the time to indulge in idle speculation. Rather, Margaret needed to do what she did best, which was to go on the offensive.

"It was completely callous of you to talk about your article like that," she chided. "He lost his brother. He got those scars trying to save him from the fire. He received a letter from the governor, did you know that? He risked his life. And that was before he ever served in the armed forces."

"God*damn* it," Tripp snapped, pushing up from the swing and pacing in front of her. "I knew that's what this was about. You know I would have fought. I would have been the first one to sign up."

But I was only nine years old on V-J day. His words echoed in Margaret's memory—she'd heard it all at least twice before, the bravado of boasts that could never be proved. Lots of boys said things like that when they were drunk. She couldn't really blame them.

But then again, that was the problem. Compared to Hank—and wouldn't she have liked to look at him in the light of day, to see if there were lines around his eyes, grooves from sorrow, gray in his hair—Tripp was lesser and always would be.

"Something else," Tripp fumed, stopping his pacing to shake his finger at her. "He's been to jail, did you know that?"

"What for?"

"I don't know, does it matter? He probably came to Austin to get out of hot water."

"How do you even know it's true?"

"Dad told me, that's how. Dad knows a judge—talked him into giving him a chance."

"Listen," Margaret said. She needed time to think. She dreaded the party tomorrow—she needed to get to bed soon or it was going to be horrid, and Mrs. Withnall sent the girl up at an atrociously early hour every morning to announce breakfast. "I'm sorry that he spoiled the party"—though of course he hadn't; Tripp's temper tantrum had done that—"and I probably won't ever see him again, and we're going to laugh about this later, but right now I think we should just go up to bed."

"And *you* egged him on," Tripp said, without any indication that he had heard her. "Talking about his *business,* as though he owned a bank or something!"

"I did no such thing!" Margaret said. She had had enough. She got up from the swing and put her hands on her hips. "You're being ridiculous. What if I created a scene every time I met some girl who came to your birthday party when you were nine? No, don't answer that," she snipped, already picking her way across the brick driveway. "Good night."

"Margaret," Tripp called after her, but she didn't turn around.

A letter arrived the next morning. The girl brought it up on a square silver tray. "Thank you," Margaret said regally, even though the envelope was cheap and her name appeared to have been written with a carpenter's pencil. She caught her breath and closed her eyes and waited for the door to close behind the girl, all the while her mind tumbling like diamonds spilled into a chasm.

Mags—you can't be serious. I'm staying at the Pratt Ranch, come here once you've come to your senses. I'll fly you home, you can be there by supper.

Margaret dressed quickly and summoned the girl with the little electric intercom by her bed. When she arrived moments later, her eyes swept over the neatly made bed, the suitcase standing by the door—the ring resting on the little silver tray. She met Margaret's gaze and her brown eyes flashed with some emotion that belied the rest of her carefully neutral expression.

"Miss?"

"I'll need a car. I'm sorry, I don't know your name."

"It's Poppy."

"Poppy, then. Is there someone who can drive me? I'm going to see a friend who's staying at the Pratt Ranch, and I'd prefer not to disturb the family. Perhaps I could wait by the carriage house?"

Poppy looked over her shoulder, into the empty upstairs hallway. "I didn't see nothing," she said. "But I expect Magnus might be out there polishing up the Cadillac."

Margaret smiled. "I can carry my own suitcase."

She had ten crisp dollar bills that her father had given her when he came to the sorority house to take her things back home to New London. She gave the driver six of them. He didn't look at them when he closed his large hand over them, but he carried her suitcase up onto the porch of the dusty long bunkhouse.

"You want me to wait, Miss?"

"Thank you, but that won't be necessary."

She waited until the shiny maroon Cadillac had disappeared in a cloud of dust back the way they'd come before knocking on the door. When no one came, she tried the handle and the door swung open.

There were four plain, spare rooms in a row. Three of them were empty, save the battered dressers and empty bed frames. In the one on the end, there was little more—shirts hanging from a rail, a cracked mirror the size of her palm on the wall, a dun-colored wool blanket folded at the foot of the bed.

A photo in a small tarnished frame: two boys, hair like straw, the younger one missing his front teeth, laughing into the sun.

"Well, well."

She turned fast, knocking her hip against the dresser, jostling the photo so that it toppled over. She righted it with care, suddenly more nervous than she had ever been.

"I got your note."

"So I gathered." Hank watched her from the doorframe, leaning against it, arms crossed. Many years later, this was the way she would remember him—his eyes a faded blue, hair in need of a cut, shirt streaked with dirt and grease and sleeves rolled up over tanned and corded arms. Time, now that she had a proper look at him, had aged him. It was as though every hard moment had left its imprint, every searing memory its scar.

"Well, you were right." Suddenly she was frustrated. Why hadn't he stopped her sooner? Why hadn't anyone? Twenty years of indulgence, her whole life, a thread loose on the spool, a feather released on a breeze. Someone should have tethered her.

But maybe it wasn't too late.

"All right." He walked into the room, passing within inches. Her skin seemed to register his presence. He smelled of hard work in the warm early hours of the day, sweat and oil and dirt.

He went to the dresser and opened the top

drawer; took out a clean white cotton shirt, held it loosely in his hand. "Would you like to wait outside? I'll just be a minute."

"Well." Her heart beat like a bird's, much too fast. "I'm not . . . I don't want to go."

"You're afraid of what they'll say? Come on, Mags. You're better than that."

"No, it isn't that."

He waited, and she had the dizzying sense of the ground rushing up. "It isn't that I'm afraid to go home," she finally managed, little more than a whisper. "It's that I want to stay here. *Here,*" she said for emphasis, pointing at the bunkhouse floor. "With you."

His hands stilled, clutching the shirt tight. He did not look away. If anything, he seemed to look deeper inside her. His mouth tightened and for a moment she thought he was going to order her out of the room.

Instead he moved toward her. A step, another, until he was close enough that she could see the faint crescent-shaped scar bisecting his eyebrow.

"Are you sure you know what you're asking, Mags? Because there ain't a soul alive who'd give their blessing."

"I'm not going back." She managed to hold his gaze, even as she seemed to be melting from within. "I won't. I'm staying with you."

He reached for her, his work-scarred fingers brushing her jawline, then hooking up her chin.

Not gently. "You're making a mistake big enough for both of us."

She took a shuddering breath and found her voice. "I don't care."

Then she found her courage. She put her hand on his chest and felt the beating of his heart, steady as the tides, and that was the end of his objections.

CHAPTER ELEVEN

Two o'clock had come and gone, then three, and Katie had to face the facts: her cousin had not made excellent time. Had not, perhaps, made the trip at all. A thousand things could have gone wrong—a flat tire, a wrong turn, a change of heart—and she couldn't do anything about any of it.

She'd read the entire issue of *People*, slowly, making it last. Of particular interest was a feature about a young starlet who'd gained eighty-five pounds and lapsed into obscurity after losing a baby to SIDS. Now, two years later—flush with health and photographed on a rooftop garden wearing a gauzy off-the-shoulder sundress— the actress discussed her upcoming film and theorized that she'd entered a twilight realm in the months following her loss, during which her mind and soul had been gently hijacked by a guiding spirit while her body did its best to stumble along on a diet of fried chicken, celibacy, and fourteen hours of daily sleep.

Katie closed the magazine and laid it gently down next to her on the bench. Was that what she was doing—was this trip to New London an effort to keep her body occupied while her subconscious mind adjusted to a new, childless reality? Was she even now giving up on that dream? And had she needed to get away from Liam to do it? And if *that* was true—what did it mean for the two of them in the future?

Why, a tiny voice inside her wondered, had she been so eager to leave him behind?

So engrossed was Katie in her thoughts that when the truck rumbled to a loud, exhaust-belching stop in front of her, she jumped up from the bench in alarm, dropping the magazine, and found herself staring at bright red fenders rising up above huge tires. They weren't really at the level of her tits—more like her rib cage. The engine revved one last time and sputtered out with a ground-trembling cough. The driver's side door opened and out of the corner of her eye, Katie saw security guards converge from both directions, already blowing their whistles, but her cousin didn't pay them any mind. She came barreling around the front of the truck and threw her arms around Katie—a blur of wild hair and warm skin and skinny limbs that smelled like watermelon and hairspray—and lifted her off the ground.

Literally.

"Oh my God, oh my *God!!*" Scarlett squealed. "Where's your stuff? Oh, listen to me, you don't *have* any stuff, obviously. I mean, shit, sorry, that's probably the last thing you want to think about. Okay, upsy daisy! Get on in there before they set the dogs on us. Fuck off," she added cheerfully, flipping off both guards on her way around the truck.

Katie opened the passenger door and hoisted herself up to the step, a gap of at least two feet that took a gymnastic effort. Her cousin was a surprisingly tall girl, close to six feet in flat sandals, and as thin as a rail. She had no curves at all, no hips or breasts or tummy or calves. Her hair started out dark brown at the roots and gradually faded to white blond at the tips, except for chunks that were dyed a mesmerizing green, and a tattoo of monkeys—*monkeys*—looking exactly like the ones in the plastic Barrel of Monkeys set that Georgina had bought her once, then inexplicably never let her play with—linked by their tails, frolicked across her collar bones, the outermost disappearing into her tank top at the armholes.

But that was not the most remarkable thing about Scarlett Jesse Ragsdale. As she put the truck in drive and moved aggressively into traffic, earning a horn tap and a rude gesture from the cars she'd cut off, she turned and regarded Katie thoughtfully, and Katie wondered if they were thinking the same thing: each had the Griseldis Nose.

Oh, that nose! A perfect clone of the one that adorned the center of Griseldis Willems's pinched, unsmiling face in the only surviving photograph of her great-great-grandmother, it had been the bane of Katie's thirteenth year, a year in which a few of the girls at the Heckinger School (Georgina had strategically dated a member of the school board to get Katie not just admitted but granted a full scholarship) had had a variety of cosmetic procedures—but Katie had been flatly denied. Georgina said it wasn't the money; in her heart of hearts, Katie thought she might be telling the truth. Georgina, after all, had been made to suffer through adolescence with the same nose, and perhaps she felt it had given her the grit she needed to survive.

It wasn't the *worst* nose in the world, or even in the eighth grade. It wasn't, in the grand scheme of things, even all that bad. But it was distinctive, and no girl wanted to be distinctive in 2000, when Britney Spears hadn't yet lost her mind and was still setting the pretty-minx beauty standard for a generation. The Griseldis Nose was narrow, with incongruously wide nostrils that flared when Katie was experiencing any strong emotion, and there was a ski-slope shape to it—a gentle angle that suddenly took a sharp dive half an inch down the bridge. Head on, it wasn't particularly noticeable, but from the side it looked—well, a kindly teacher had told Katie at the start of eighth grade that it looked "Roman," unwittingly cementing her loathing of it.

Now Katie was staring at that same nose in profile. A dead ringer, though Scarlett's was the same gorgeous caramel shade as the rest of her. Other than the nose, Scarlett's features were quite different from Katie's: a high forehead and a bit of a widow's peak visible under the tumbling mass of curls that Scarlett had secured with the sort of plastic barrettes one generally only sees on toddlers. A dainty little chin and a rosebud mouth slicked with clear gloss; big, white, slightly crooked teeth. She was a knockout—maybe she'd never even given the nose a thought.

"You hungry?" Scarlett asked, suddenly more subdued. She wrenched the wheel, narrowly fitting into a gap in the traffic.

"Oh God yes," Katie said, weak with relief.

"Reach down there on the floor—'less Merritt got to it, which I wouldn't put past him."

In a wadded Target bag, Katie found a half-empty sack of Flamin' Hot Cheetos, an unopened can of Men's Health Nuts, and a package of bright orange cheese 'n' peanut butter crackers. She settled on the nuts, popping off the top of the can and digging in.

Scarlett nodded approvingly. "Go for the healthy shit, good idea. Plus, you know what, I don't think there's really any difference between the men's and the regular. Except maybe the pistachios. Like, are we supposed to believe pistachios are good for dick health or something?" She shook her head in disgust. "Marketing, right? So tell me about getting mugged. Were you scared?"

"I was . . ." Katie thought, chewing. "Actually, you know what, I wasn't really. I guess I was more surprised. And—and annoyed, because I thought I'd miss my flight. If Liam hadn't been there, I might have put up more of a fight." She remembered now that the mugger had a little mustache, which she'd barely registered at the time; was it supposed to be ironic? Some sort of defiant nod to the coffeehouse poet look that Johnny Depp and Justin Timberlake had affected? And following quickly on that thought was another one: Were her references dated? Had she officially become . . . *not young?*

"Damn," Scarlett said admiringly. "You got the family stubborn streak. I would have been like, *shit,* please don't kill me, you know? What did he get?"

"Well, my suitcase, obviously . . . my bag, which had my laptop and my phone. My wallet." She looked down at her hand. "Liam's wallet. And our rings."

"Your *wedding* rings?"

"Mmm." At least the diamond was insured; there was their rent money, anyway, for the next few months.

"Aw," Scarlett said. "That's just fucked-up. I mean, take my purse, take my car, but when I get

133

married I'm not taking my ring off for *anyone*."

"Is, um, Merritt, is he your boyfriend?" Fiancé, husband . . . Katie should have known these details. She was a terrible cousin.

"Yeah, well, that's a little complicated," Scarlett said in a rush. "See, we broke up, but our lease isn't out until September, and we can't get out of it early, and I don't have anywhere else to live, so . . . Plus we'll probably get back together. He's a little crazy. I mean, but not in a bad way. Like an artistic way. He's a musician? When he's not doing carpet cleaning?"

She glanced over at Katie, as if for agreement, and Katie was thinking no, no, no, *artistic* wasn't good for anyone, especially not a girl like Scarlett. Not that she knew her cousin, not really. But she was . . . sweet, that was the word that came to mind, despite the tattoos and the sandals with the heels practically worn off and the sad little sequin detail on her shorts pocket, grimy and crusted, the black nail polish flaking off, that *hair,* the thin orange straps of a bra visible under a practically transparent tank top.

Sweet enough to drive two and a half hours to pick her up and another two and a half hours back.

"I need to pay you for gas," Katie blurted. "I'll get money—Liam's wiring it to me. I just need to go to the bank or something. He's figuring it out."

"Don't worry about that," Scarlett said, waving her hand breezily. "I mean, after this week, we're going to be rich, right?"

Katie fell asleep about ten miles out of Dallas.

She didn't mean to; Scarlett had been telling her a complicated story about how she and Merritt had somehow missed each other at a show he was supposed to play in Tyler, which led to the fight that turned into a breakup. When the story finally hit a lull, Katie had asked to borrow Scarlett's phone to look up Liam's number, but it was an old clunky thing with no Internet. Luckily, it turned out that directory assistance was still a thing.

Liam wasn't listed, but his company was, and Katie got to him fairly quickly through the automatic directory system. He picked up on the second ring, and to Katie's surprise, he sounded . . . annoyed.

"It's me," she said. "I'm all right."

"Katie, shit, it's crazy. I mean, the cops said they'd come to my office and it's been like, what, seven hours already?"

Katie blinked. "I'm with Scarlett. She picked me up," she said slowly, enunciating carefully. "At the airport. We're driving to New London now, but we won't be there until after dinner."

"Oh, good that she was able to come." Liam sounded distracted. His voice was muffled as he called something to someone and Katie knew he'd covered the receiver with his hand. "I'm working on the bank thing. Can she float you until tomorrow? Because the wait for customer service is like forever."

Katie's heart sank. She peeked at Scarlett, who was spinning the honest-to-God dials on the radio, country music coming through the static on low. Scarlett didn't look like she could float *herself* until tomorrow, much less Katie, who hadn't yet broached the topic of where she would stay tonight if she didn't get her hands on some money.

"Can you call again?" she said.

"Yeah, okay, but shit, Katie, I mean, I've got to file a police report, and Rex is picking me up after work so I can meet the locksmith at the car."

"What? Why?"

"Because that shithead got your keys, and because, okay, and I really don't need you to come down on me about it, but I lost mine again, okay? I mean, I know they're somewhere in the apartment."

Katie clamped her mouth shut and inhaled, let it out slowly. How Liam, who'd graduated cum laude from Columbia, could lose critical objects on a weekly basis was an enduring mystery in their home, one that she had once found adorable.

"Oh" was all she said.

"But shit—how are you, Goldilocks?" he

added, his tone softening. "I mean, jeez, let's start this conversation all over. Duh. God. Katie. Are you okay? How do you feel?"

Katie shook her head and sighed. There wasn't anything he could do for her right now—it would have been better not to call. "I'm okay, really. I mean, cramps and whatever but I'm fine. Mostly I think I need a shower and something to eat and to sleep for like twelve hours straight."

"Yeah, I know what you mean," Liam said with feeling, and Katie thought—*no, no, this doesn't get to be about you.* Then she chastised herself: Liam was allowed to be freaked out about the mugging. After all, the guy had pointed—no, worse, he'd *hit* Liam with the gun. Metal to skin, to his face, where a bullet would have gone straight into his brain and killed him.

When Katie and Liam fought, which wasn't often—not as often as, say, his sister Cat and her partner—he often accused her of being stubborn, as if her stubbornness was standing in the way of the resolution of whatever issue had come up.

You're so damn stubborn, he had said, when she'd raised her concerns about the apartment, when she'd begged him to keep looking until they found something a bit bigger. *Don't be so stubborn,* he'd implored, when she balked at going to Antigua with his parents for their anniversary. *Maybe if you weren't so stubborn,* he'd counseled, when Katie refused to sit by and let Arthur

Salisbury take credit for her work in department meetings, something that had undoubtedly played a part in his decision to let her go.

But Scarlett had said it with admiration—*the family stubborn streak*. And maybe now, in these particular circumstances, it was an asset.

"I need to go," she said suddenly and decisively, cutting Liam off in the middle of his sentence. "I need to figure out the rest of the day. Don't forget to call the bank again, okay?"

"Yeah, of course," Liam said, peevishness battling with concern. "Call me when you get settled, okay?"

"He's cute," Scarlett said, once Katie had hung up and set the phone back in the drink holder in the console. "I looked you guys up on Facebook. I couldn't find yours, though. Only his. Liam Garrett—it's not like a super common name but there were still like ten others."

"Listen, Scarlett . . . I was wondering." Katie took a breath. "Is there any way I could stay with you tonight? Just for one night—Liam's wiring me money, so I'll be fine by tomorrow. I can buy a new phone and check into a motel and rent a car and—well, everything. But right now I just . . . I mean, you never realize how cut off you are without your credit cards."

Scarlett's smile faltered, and she stared straight ahead. Her hands clenched the wheel more tightly.

"Oh! Gosh!" she said, her voice overly bright. "That would be so fun! But, Katie . . . God, I feel so shitty even saying this, because you coming here is, like, the *best,* and I'm so excited we're finally going to get to know each other, but . . . I just, I can't. It's super complicated."

She looked like she was going to cry.

"It's absolutely no problem," Katie said automatically, the reassurance slipping out of her like air from a balloon, before she even had a chance to remind herself that she *really needed* this. She didn't know another soul in Texas, besides her mother and a few old friends who undoubtedly thought she was a bitch because she—well, had acted like a bitch, cutting ties with everyone she knew.

Scarlett was probably embarrassed by her home, but there had to be some way for Katie to reassure her that whatever the problem with the place—too small, too humble, too messy—she wasn't above it. She wished she hadn't worn the cashmere, the fine leather boots. Heck, at this point she would be happy to sleep in the truck bed.

"No," Scarlett said softly. "No, it's not right. I'm so sorry. I'll make it up to you, I swear. I promise. You'll see. And for tonight, you can just stay at Gomma's. I've got the keys."

"Oh," Katie said, brightening. Why hadn't she thought of that? Even better—she could finally relax, after the long, crazy day she'd had, without having to make conversation. Margaret's house would be run-down and shabby, but it would do.

"And she didn't *die* in there or anything like that," Scarlett added. "I'll come in for a bit and help you get settled. And I'll be back first thing tomorrow. I'll bring you breakfast."

"You don't have to work?"

"I quit my job," Scarlett said. "When I found out Gomma left me the house. It was a shitty job anyway, I was on the line at the elastic plant, and they were only giving me like thirty hours a week because they didn't want to give me the benefits and—"

"Scarlett," Katie interrupted delicately, having got stuck on the *left me the house* part of the conversation—the whole reason she was here. "Did you just say . . . I'm sorry, but—I thought that the contents of the will were . . . unknown?"

"Oh, well, yeah," Scarlet said. "But Gomma always said she was leaving it to me. Like, for the last five years or whatever."

Stars were beginning to swarm in front of Katie's eyeballs, and not in a fun way. She was exhausted, starving, perhaps hallucinating slightly. The scenery rolling by outside her window—fields dotted with wildflowers, white clouds scudding overhead—was almost garishly beautiful, the colors as lurid as a tinted photograph from the fifties.

This was going to potentially get really awkward, if Scarlett thought she was inheriting everything. Unless . . .

"Georgina said I was named in the will too," Katie ventured, trying to ignore the awful possibility that had just popped into her head. That Margaret had left her, say, a moldy bureau; a few gaudy trinkets; a family Bible. Some token of disaffection, a final "fuck you" to the grandchild who'd never sought her out. Or maybe the snub would be meant for Georgina, for the daughter who'd made it her life's goal to move as far away, in every way, as she could.

"I mean, I was totally shocked, of course," Katie said, a bit more forcefully. "I don't expect anything. It's exciting just to be part of, the um, the historic nature of—"

"I bet she left you the cups," Scarlett said reassuringly. "She told me once that she had always wanted to start you a collection. Or maybe the silver dimes. Do you know she had every year going all the way back to 1946?"

"I thought . . ." The dream of wealth, an enormous payoff from a house that some Amazon exec would kill for, was beginning to recede rapidly, like a wave skittering back to sea. But Katie was getting ahead of herself. She didn't know—neither of them did. Georgina said Margaret was flighty and unpredictable. Who knew what she might have done?

A thought occurred to her—a thought that was desperate and mean and low: that perhaps she could offer to buy Scarlett out, explain that she could offer her cash now, perhaps with a loan from Liam's family, so Scarlett could avoid the hassle of trying to list and sell the house. Then Katie could turn around and fix it up a little and flip it for far more. She could even give a percentage of the proceeds to Scarlett, who probably would have no idea of the value she was sitting on—who might feel like she'd gotten a perfectly fair deal.

But no. Katie felt ashamed of even having the thought. Scarlett was vulnerable; Scarlett needed some help in looking after her own interests. Let the chips—or the clauses of the will—fall where they may; Katie would accept them with grace, and if the entire inheritance went to Scarlett, she would try to be happy for her cousin. Katie would prove to herself that Boston hadn't changed her, hadn't turned her into her mother, striving and voracious.

"But who knows?" Scarlett said, grinning again. She tapped the steering wheel in time with the radio. "Maybe she left us each half! Wouldn't that be *fun?* We could maybe open up a day care. That's my dream," she added. "To own my own child care center."

"Sure," Katie said. Who was this impossibly cheerful creature who shared her DNA, no matter how distantly, as evidenced by the Nose? Who on earth dreamed of owning a *day care?*

"Dang, I nearly missed our exit," Scarlett said, swerving over two lanes and nearly clipping a decrepit old pickup half the size of hers. The startled driver gave a tiny wave—or maybe she was having a heart attack. "Can you believe we're officially a two-stoplight town now, what with all the new development? Used to be there wasn't nothing off this exit but the Methodist church and the old Esso. And now look."

This last was spoken with an indignant edge, and Katie quickly saw why. Coasting onto the two-lane road freshly gouged from the earth alongside the broken asphalt it had replaced, they passed a field so newly turned that slaughtered cornstalks protruded from the ruts, baby ears still suspended from the withering fronds. On the other side of the field, the foundation of an enormous edifice had been poured, its concrete surface pristine, earthmoving equipment huddled at the edges, shut down for the day.

"It just simply kills me," Scarlett sighed. "That used to be the prettiest little field—cowslip in the spring, and bluebonnets everywhere, and we had a fort over there once. All of it's gone now. And for what? Do we really need a Walgreens when we got a perfectly good drugstore already?"

"How awful," Katie said. She could certainly use a Walgreens right about now, with its shelves full of feminine hygiene products and lovely bins of travel-size products. Shampoo and conditioner and those tiny containers of dental floss, towelettes in individual packets and little cubes of bath salts. And she'd buy the biggest bag of Lay's potato chips in the store—her stomach growled at the thought. She sniffed discreetly at her underarms and decided that deodorant would be her first priority.

But she could wait just a little longer; soon she'd be alone in Margaret's house. For one night, at least, she'd be free to comb through her grandmother's possessions, look through her closets, page through her scrapbooks . . . and try to piece together her story from the artifacts.

"I just need to run home and . . . and take care of a few things," Scarlett was saying. "I'll come back tonight if I can, but definitely tomorrow. For sure. And I'll bring you a change of clothes. Do you mind sleeping in what you're wearing, just for tonight?"

"It's fine."

As they drove, the freshly turned fields gave way to modest houses with wide yards. Red brick, white clapboard, pitched roofs; tubs of geraniums and wash hung on lines in backyards; cats perched on porch rails. Scarlett turned onto the main street, and a long-ago memory came back to Katie: there had been an ice cream shop with a sign shaped like a cone, and she'd begged her mother to stop and buy her a scoop of rainbow sherbet, but Georgina couldn't get out of that town fast enough. She'd waved at two little boys eating their cones out front, and they'd stared solemnly at her.

The teacup wrapped in paper towels, tossed into the backseat.

The tight set of Georgina's mouth, the lipstick wearing thin as she drove ten miles over the speed limit back to Dallas.

Up ahead, a tall stone obelisk came into view, in front of the sprawling high school. As they neared, Katie could make out the figures of children and teachers carved from the granite at the top. "The dead children," Katie said. "I remember driving by it with my mom."

Scarlett shuddered. "It's so sad," she said. "I mean, you grow up around here, it's kind of just part of life when you're little. You don't realize until you get older what it all meant, you know, to the families and all."

"What exactly happened again?"

"Well, that school, it's just the high school now, it was built on the site of the old London school. Back in 1937 it was this big, new expensive school, only five years old—that was back during the oil boom, and there was all this oil money, and the school was all tricked out. Originally it was supposed to have steam heat, but with raw gas being free, they went with that instead, and—"

"Raw gas?"

"You know, natural gas. When you drill for oil, the gas comes up first. You know how a lot of times you see the orange glow on a rig, that's the flare-off, but you can also install a residue line to carry it away, and they, the oil companies back then, basically let whoever wanted to tap into it because it wasn't worth anything to them anyway."

"Wait, I don't get it. They were giving away gas?"

"Yeah. They only wanted the oil. So the people in town, a lot of them worked for the oil companies anyway, they'd just tap into the line and use it. It's kind of like when you hook up to the neighbor's cable, right? Except the oil companies knew about it and they didn't care. So when they were finishing the school they figured they'd just do the same thing. And it worked for a few years, but what they didn't know was there was a leak in the line, and it was slowly filling up the crawl space under the school."

"And no one noticed?"

"Well, back then, natural gas had no smell to it. It was the New London explosion that gave people the idea to add the sulfur to it as a warning, but without it, no one knew it was building up down there. Kids were getting headaches and stuff and I guess a lot of them had complained, but nobody had thought to check down in the

146

crawl space. Anyway, the day it happened, a shop teacher plugged in an electric sander and all it took was just this one little spark, and the entire school blew up. All that was standing in the main building afterward was one wall."

"That's—I can't even imagine—how many children died?"

"Almost three hundred. Plus teachers and visitors. At first they thought it was even more— some of the news accounts said as much as seven hundred. And they'll never know the exact count because all the school records burned up. Plus they took the kids, the hurt ones, all over the place trying to get medical help—every hospital for miles around. And some people just took the bodies of their children home with them. It wasn't like now. Obviously." Scarlett's voice had gone hoarse, and she glanced at Katie and quickly away. "Some of the migrant families? They just picked up and left. It was like they weren't ever even there. The Mexican kids were allowed to go to the school, but that was almost worse, because no one wanted them there. They got beat up and made fun of. So it wasn't like anyone was looking for them after the explosion."

"Oh," Katie said, horrified. "Are you . . . I mean, did your dad's family . . ."

"My dad?" Scarlett's tone changed instantly. "No. I mean, not that I know of. The only person our family lost was Gomma's sister."

"Her *sister?*" Katie asked, surprised. "Do you mean Margaret?"

"Yeah. You didn't know about that?" Another glance, this one incredulous.

Katie craned her head around to see the twin granite columns of the cenotaph disappearing behind them. "I had no idea. My mom never said anything."

"Well, Gomma didn't like to talk about it. And she said her mother—Caroline—when she got older she didn't like to talk about it at *all*. I guess when Gomma was growing up they were in this club, the kids who were born right after the explosion . . . I mean, I know how weird it sounds, but a bunch of families had babies right away. To kind of replace the ones that died."

"Is that what Margaret was? A . . . replacement?"

"Yes, she was born like nine months afterward. And these kids, these babies, I guess their moms stuck together. I mean, think about it—they had these brand-new babies, but the whole town was in mourning . . . the kids grew up together. But Gomma said she always felt like she was on display. You would have thought those kids would have been super close, but I think instead it was just . . . painful."

"My mom said that Margaret was, um, solitary." What Georgina had actually said was that no one could stand to be around her mother, that Margaret was cold, and imperious, and basically a friendless bitch who brought on her own misery.

"Yeah, she didn't have an easy time of it, that's for sure," Scarlett said wistfully, and Katie felt guilty for believing her mother's version. "Anyway, getting her to talk about it was like pulling teeth. I remember back a few years ago they wanted to interview her for this documentary they were doing and Gomma was all, just leave it be. She didn't see the sense in stirring it all up again, sensationalizing it, I guess."

"But . . . her *sister*. I had no idea." Why hadn't Georgina ever mentioned this? "What was her name?"

"Ruby. Ruby Pierson. She was eleven. Her name's on the memorial. I can show you if you want." Scarlett took a lazy turn onto a tree-lined street, her face shadowed and melancholy. "I saw a picture once, by accident. I'd gotten into Gomma's dresser. She took that picture out of my hand and wouldn't talk about it. I guess . . . I mean, it's complicated because she never even knew her sister. I always thought maybe Caroline made Gomma feel like they'd loved Ruby best, like she'd never be good enough, like that's maybe why it was such a sore subject."

"Did you ever meet Caroline?"

"No, she actually died before I was born. And that side of the family was completely estranged from ours. Right up until one day Gomma came to my house and knocked on the door." A smile returned to Scarlett's face. "My mom didn't even recognize her! She introduced herself and asked if she could babysit me sometimes, because I was only five or six and she knew my mom didn't have any help."

That didn't sound like the selfish, callous woman that Georgina had always painted her mother to be. "And . . . your mom said yes?"

Scarlett laughed. "Oh hell yes. Mom was working two jobs—she was a file clerk during the week and she bartended on the weekend, so she was super grateful. And Gomma used to bring groceries over and take me shopping for school clothes and stuff. She used to put everything away before Mom came home so she wouldn't find it until later. You know, so Mom wouldn't have to feel like it was charity."

"Wow. This is all . . . I don't even know." Katie was going to have a conversation with her mother, that was for sure. She felt oddly gypped, deprived of both the story and the chance to know the people in it. It was her family history too, after all.

Scarlett waved at an elderly woman with a walker as they cruised slowly down the street, passing old houses and gardens bursting with spring flowers. Most of the homes were modest, four-square construction with tidy porches and garages set back, but a few were grander. They approached the largest one as Katie tried to remember what her grandmother's had looked like, but her impressions of the day were of squinting into the sun, two dogs chasing each other down the street, her mother's hand gripping hers too hard. The smell of starch in her blouse and the shine of new shoes, her socks' scratchy lace around her ankles.

Scarlett pulled to a stop in front of the imposing old two-story stucco house with a Juliet balcony and a stone arch over the door. If it hadn't been so run-down it would have qualified as a mansion, but as it was, the stucco was broken and flaking and stained black near the ground, paint peeled from the trim and window frames, and a section of gutter had broken off and leaned against the house. The yard was full of weeds and crabgrass, and one of a pair of redbud trees had been hit by lightning and grew lopsided.

"We're here!" Scarlett said. "Do you remember it?"

"I'm . . . I'm not sure. Maybe once I'm inside."

Scarlett's smile slipped a little. "I know it's gotten kind of run-down. I should have probably tried to help keep it up more. I mean, I tried to help clean whenever I came over, but . . . anyway, let's get you inside." But she didn't get out of the truck immediately, gazing up at the house and biting her lip. "I haven't come here since . . . you know. I'm glad you're with me. I don't think I could go in there alone."

Together, they stared at the house, cast in the purpling shadow of its much more modest neighbor, the sun slipping down behind the trees. Near the end of the block, kids played in a sprinkler arcing lazily back and forth onto a bright green lawn. The house had obviously once been the grandest on the street, a showplace. On either side were considerably newer houses, seventies-era boxes with ugly angled roofs, which made Katie think that this house had once anchored an enormous lot, maybe even the whole block, lording its stature over everyone in the neighborhood. But now it seemed to sag under its own defeat, as though it was only a matter of time before the timbers rotted and it collapsed in on itself. To say it had seen better days was putting a lot of faith in its history: cobwebs crusted every corner, an upstairs window was broken, the mailbox had been shot at several times, and the greatest insult of all had been worked by someone wielding a can of spray paint: a loopy purple design three feet high along the side of the house.

Someone knocked on Scarlett's window, and they both jumped.

"Oh, hi, Mrs. Oglesby," Scarlett said sheepishly as she rolled down the window. Humid air wafted into the cab of the truck and a short, redheaded woman peered past Scarlett at Katie.

"Is this your cousin? Just look at her!" she exclaimed.

"Hello," Katie said politely. "I'm Katie Garrett. It's a pleasure to meet you."

"You're the one from Boston," the woman said. "Well, I'll let you girls get to visiting."

"Thanks, Mrs. Oglesby, we will," Scarlett said. But when the woman was safely out of hearing, she sighed audibly. "Got to watch that one; she likes to look in the windows. All right. Guess we best get to it."

Scarlett lifted a corner of the ancient rubber welcome mat and picked up a key attached to a mini replica of a bottle of Big Red soda. The door took a little jiggling and coaxing, but eventually she got it open; the scent of decay and rosewater wafted out of the house. Inside, the twilight filtered through the ancient lace curtains onto a scene that suddenly came back to Katie. Until now, her memories consisted mostly of a vague impression of old, musty-smelling furniture and every surface covered with junk—but look, she remembered that tottering little round table with the curved legs; and that oil painting of a girl in a white dress with her hand on the back of a yellow dog. Even the afghans, folded on the back of the couch, sparked a memory; eleven-year-old Katie had run her fingers over the nubby crochet stitches, tracing the alternating bands of yellow and pink in the granny squares.

And there was the rack of teacups from which Margaret had plucked the one she gave to Katie for her birthday. In fact, there was the empty hook on the end, anchoring the rows of delicate cups painted with blowsy cabbage roses and stiff-stemmed zinnias, delicate forget-me-nots and bowing lilies of the valley.

Margaret had tapped each cup and ticked off the names of the flowers in a voice that sounded a bit like a threat. "Someday," she'd added, "I'll be dead and these will be yours." Her hand had hovered over the cups until it came to rest on the one decorated with lilies of the valley, tiny dots of gold adorning the tiny frilled bell-shaped blossoms, while Georgina rolled her eyes and looked pointedly at her watch.

"Gomma was a collector, all right," Scarlett said, without a trace of irony. She handed Katie the key. "Here, you'll want this. We usually always just leave it under the mat, but I guess we should probably make a copy now."

She led the way through the house, straightening the antennas of the ancient television and picking up an overturned picture frame.

In the kitchen, there was a faint but unpleasant smell, and a horde of flies buzzed around the sink. All of the surfaces were coated with a thin layer of grayish dust. Curtains embroidered with teakettles hung in the windows, their ruffles flattened and drooping. A yellow box of baking soda sat out on the counter, the only thing that looked like it had been acquired in the last few years. Scarlett picked it up and sighed, then set it back down again.

"Yikes! Well, we've got our work cut out for us, huh?" she said.

Katie picked up a hot pad from the counter; it had a faded design of a crab wearing a chef's hat and the caption "I got crabs at Captain Don's" printed underneath. Long ago, someone her grandmother knew well enough to be on souvenir terms with had gone to a place called Captain Don's, had seen the silly hot pad and thought of Margaret—but why? This was a detail that had died along with her grandmother, and for a moment Katie had to resist the urge to press the hot pad to her face, to breathe in the memory of long-ago casseroles, looking for clues, and her eyes pricked with tears.

Probably just the flood of emotions released by her hormones.

Scarlett was already heading up the stairs to the second floor, raising dust from the ancient, threadbare carpet on the treads. "There's five bedrooms up here," she called over her shoulder. "You can take your pick."

One of the rooms was so tiny that Katie wondered if it had been a bedroom at all, the size of a decent walk-in closet. The "master bedroom" held a double bed with a fussy carved headboard and matching nightstands, a visible shallow in the mattress under the candlewick bedspread. It seemed too tiny to have been made by an adult, but Margaret had been shorter than Georgina, and thin and hard-angled in her high-collared dress that day. Katie shuddered, thinking about climbing into that bed, and hoped there was another alternative.

"Look, I need to probably get going," Scarlett said abruptly. "Let me just . . ." She grabbed the tarnished brass handles of the window sash and jimmied it up, grunting from the effort. The breeze wafted into the room, scented with charcoal and cut grass.

"I can do that," Katie said. "I'll open up the house. Give me something to do."

"The bathroom's down the hall," Scarlett said. "There's just the one up here. The lawyer sent me an email and said he paid the bills so they won't turn off the water or electric. He said something about hiring a cleaning service, but . . . well, I figured we could do it ourselves and save the money."

Katie trailed after her back down the stairs. "Heaven knows what-all is in the medicine cabinet," Scarlett continued. "You'll probably want to get one of those little travel-size toothpastes 'cause lord knows how long Gomma's things have been here. Let me show you how to get to the market, and tomorrow I'll bring you some things when I come."

"Yeah, I need to get some tampons too."

"I'll bring you some!" Scarlett seemed thrilled to be able to help. In the kitchen, she opened the screen door that led to the backyard. "I'll go out the back way. If you come out here, mind you don't put your foot through the boards."

A fat moon was rising up over the tops of the trees, bathing the overgrown yard in a silvery glow. The grass was ankle-high, and the brick path was choked with weeds, but black-eyed Susans and spiky canna and Indian paintbrush lined the flower beds. An overturned watering can next to an old webbed lawn chair made it seem as though Margaret had just gone inside for a glass of lemonade, and would soon be back to finish weeding.

"It's—it's amazing," Katie breathed, a memory dancing at the edges of her mind. There—over there, under the graceful branches of an old willow—there was a tiny pond, with shiny bits of mother-of-pearl inlaid into the concrete. At the end of the ill-fated birthday luncheon, while Georgina insisted on helping Margaret carry the plates to the kitchen, Katie had wandered back here to shut out their angry whispers, and bent down to trail her fingers in the cool water. A silver-green winged dragonfly had settled on her wrist.

"The very best part of the house," Scarlett agreed. "You should have seen it, back when Gomma could still take care of it."

"I remember it."

"You do?"

"From that one time I was here. There was still water in the pond."

"Oh, I loved that pond. I used to play Barbie deep-sea diving. She'd always have an accident and then Bubble Angel Barbie would have to rescue her."

"Bubble Angel?"

"Yeah, she had these like bubble wings that I pretended were like a seaplane so she could float."

Katie laughed. "That's pretty badass, Scarlett."

"Can you imagine the fun we could have had here? I always hated being an only child . . . did you? I always wished for a sister." Scarlett gave a shy little laugh. "Never mind—we'll have ages to catch up tomorrow. Okay—"

Katie found herself enveloped in a hug that was all elbows and bony shoulders, that left her awkwardly patting her cousin. Katie wasn't much of a hugger—Georgina showed her affection by shopping, and her in-laws were more of the brisk cheek-kiss type.

Scarlett finally released her and gave a little wave as she disappeared through the vine-draped garden gate. Moments later, Katie heard the monster truck rumbling to life, and then it too was gone, and she was all alone.

She stood in the darkness for a while longer, letting her eyes adjust, gazing at the houses on either side. Lights were on; inside, families went about their business. Had they been friendly with Margaret? Had they pitched in when she got old, brought in her mail, made sure she had groceries, gone to the pharmacy for her? Next door, a pale face appeared in the window, and then a curtain was dropped and it disappeared from view. What must they think of her—the granddaughter who only showed up when it was time to collect her inheritance?

Nearby, there was a rustling in the overgrown brush, and Katie jumped. It could be a cat—or maybe a bird, or more likely rats. Katie went back up the stairs and into the house, and when she closed the door she turned the lock and then slid the dead bolt.

She might be back in Texas—but she was a city girl now, one who didn't fancy getting robbed twice in one day.

CHAPTER TWELVE

"Don't look at me," Margaret yelped, slamming the bedroom door.

She stood in front of the scrap-bin mirror Hank had rigged for her almost two months ago, when they'd moved from the bunkhouse to the cottage out past the creek, on land that the rancher had bought when the neighbor died with no sons to take over. The cottage had been empty for several years, so Margaret had spent the first week of her marriage clearing cobwebs and washing windows and scrubbing the old floors until the paint came off in long strips, revealing the old pine boards underneath.

Now she couldn't bend over without feeling dizzy. Since last week, bilious spells had come on her so fast that she'd had to run to the tiny bathroom and wedge herself under the sink so that she could throw up into the toilet. By her best estimate, she might well have become pregnant that very first night—but no one need ever know, because they'd gone down to the Travis County courthouse four days later and tied the knot.

Margaret had worn the dress she'd bought for the engagement party, a powder-blue chiffon with miles of skirt stitched to a tightly fitted hip yoke, and a wide boatneck that showed off her neck and shoulders. She'd told her mother, in the salon at Neiman Marcus, that the dress made her feel like a princess; when she said her vows in the bare, hot judge's chambers, she felt like a woman for the first time. Hank had worn a clean shirt and the black eye that Tripp had given him.

"I'll give you one hit," Hank had told Tripp when he showed up, drunk, on the front porch of the bunkhouse two days after Margaret left, "so you'd better make it a good one." Margaret had been expecting Tripp; she knew she couldn't count on the old chauffeur to keep her secret forever.

Tripp had taken his hit and Hank had barely flinched, though the blow knocked him against the rail—Margaret was watching from inside with a handkerchief pressed to her mouth and a strange flutter in her heart—but then Hank caught Tripp's wrist in his hand and twisted it somehow so that the next thing she knew, Tripp was on his knees, howling.

(When Margaret asked Hank that night, still breathless from the things they'd skipped their supper to do in his narrow bed, how he knew to do that, he hadn't answered. Or rather, he'd answered by kissing her to silence and then doing other things that she'd never known were possible, and she forgot all about her question.)

"You can't stay shut in there all day," Hank

said patiently from the other side of the door.

"I'm not. I'm only staying here until Mary Beth comes. And you have to be gone by then."

"Mags, I've seen pregnant women before. I know how this stuff works. I changed Helene's diapers, remember?"

Margaret grimaced, glad he couldn't see her face. A package from Helene had arrived last week—a pair of inexpensive cut-glass candlesticks with a note in her familiar, careful handwriting, in which she'd congratulated Margaret on her marriage to Hank as though they were perfect strangers. Above her return address, she'd written "Mrs. William Slope." Margaret had held the candlesticks in her hand, feeling the lightness of them; if she'd married Tripp she'd have had a whole breakfront full of heavy crystal, not to mention silver and china. And she certainly wouldn't be assembling a maternity wardrobe from her neighbor's castoffs.

"Well, that will come in handy," she said lightly, determined to stay cheerful despite the heat of the day, the nausea that chased her all through the mornings. "If we keep you busy, maybe you won't notice how enormous I'm getting."

"Listen, Tubby, you can gain a hundred pounds and I'll still think you're beautiful."

"Stop it, Hank, what if I don't get my figure back after he's born?" Margaret fretted, slapping at his hands covering the small bulge in her stomach.

She had taken her waist measurement every week since discovering that she was carrying a baby, recording the figures in a neat column in her diary, determined not to let herself balloon to grotesque proportions. Mary Beth, who was expecting her third child in a month's time, complained that each pregnancy caused her breasts to sag and flatten more after the baby came, the pouch of her stomach to droop. She'd already outgrown most of her maternity clothes, which was why she was loaning them to Margaret.

"Well then, I'll just go to seed too," Hank said. "I'll grow a big gut and jowls like a turkey. I'll be the ugliest mug in town and you'll have to hide me away from your friends."

The sound of the doorbell—literally a cowbell that Hank had found in a field and fixed to a hook—made Margaret push him away. "Go entertain Mary Beth while I get dressed. I won't be a minute."

But as she buttoned her blouse and struggled to zip up her skirt, the voices she heard in the living room were both male. One of Hank's clients, then, come to schedule a flyover of the rigs and fields, or to ferry some bigwig from Galveston or Houston to the capital. Margaret dabbed on lipstick, as her mother had done all through her childhood whenever anyone came to call.

She blotted her mouth on a bit of tissue and touched her hair, which had recently grown increasingly lustrous and glossy (Mary Beth said that was evidence of a boy) and swanned out of the bathroom with everything she was worth, because it had been a long time since she'd had anyone to impress but her husband.

But there, sitting on the sofa that Hank had bought secondhand for a few dollars, hat in hand and wearing a look of misery on his face, was her father.

"You know your mother," Hugh Pierson pleaded for the third or fourth time, the refrain to which the conversation kept returning after their initial embrace and Margaret's tearful joy at seeing him and Hank's awkward leave-taking, off to see to an engine problem that Margaret was fairly sure he'd invented as an excuse to escape. As a first meeting between the two men since the elopement, Margaret supposed it had gone well enough, but it wasn't Hank whom her father had come to see.

"Yes, I know my mother well," Margaret parroted. "I know that she sent you to do her dirty work because she couldn't be bothered to do it herself."

"We were worried, pumpkin," Hugh protested. "And—and you must see how hurtful it was that she had to find out about the baby from a letter."

"But she didn't have to, Daddy. Hank invited you both to come visit. I wanted to tell you in person." Hank had done more than just invite them, actually; he'd offered to fly her home himself, but pride and no small measure of apprehension had held her back.

"Well, but you didn't invite us until after you were already married. Your mother thought—and I must say I do see her point—that you might have waited to have a proper ceremony. You know how much work your mother put into planning your wedding, and she was looking forward to—"

"—to me spending the rest of my life with a man who bored me to tears? I'd rather *die!*" Margaret exclaimed, regretting the words as soon as she'd said them. "Oh, Daddy."

"No, no," he sighed, not looking at her. "I would never want you to be unhappy."

"I didn't mean— Daddy, I'm such an awful pill. I never wanted to hurt Mother. I know I put her in a terrible position." All those wedding gifts to return, the notes to write, the pained smiles Caroline would have to produce when she ran into her friends—her embarrassment would last for years. In this one reckless act, Margaret had managed to threaten her mother's established place at the top of the social hierarchy.

But Margaret did not care for the uncomfortable weight of guilt, so she tossed her hair and willed it away. "Think of it this way—with all the money you saved on the wedding, you can finally take Mother to visit New York City. She'll forget all about me when she sees Fifth Avenue."

"Margaret," her father said quietly, and she saw that he was not to be jollied out of his mission. She picked up her glass of iced tea—the glass was one of a pair that she'd found abandoned in a high cupboard in the kitchen, printed with the Pearl beer logo—and then set it down again without drinking.

"I'm sorry, Daddy. I really, truly *am*."

"It's not what you think, though. That's what I came here to say. It's not the dresses and the flowers and the band, even though it cost a king's ransom to cancel all that. Your mother . . . she has a heart. Don't look at me that way, sweetheart, she does. I know your mother can be . . . difficult, sometimes. But she's cried every night since you—since it . . . *every* night."

Hugh had been staring fixedly at the handkerchief that he was twisting in his hands, but he looked up now with such genuine anguish that Margaret thought immediately of that other time, back in the garage behind their house, when he'd swept the little frame holding the photograph of her dead sister into his pocket. *Love,* she suddenly realized—this was what her father's love looked like, all bound up in loss and grief. How desperately sad he must be, and how beastly she was to make it worse. Tentatively, she laid a hand on his arm.

"What can I do?" she asked. "How can I make it up to her?"

"Well." Her father cleared his throat. "See here—just promise me that you'll try. That you'll try your best, Margaret."

"Daddy, of course I'll try—what do I have to do?"

"She's here. In Austin. We're staying at the Vandeveer Hotel."

It was decided that Margaret would take her father's car back to the hotel and have tea with her mother, while her father stayed behind, with a plan to walk over to the barn that Hank was using as a makeshift hangar. Hugh had joked that maybe he'd even pick up a wrench and pitch in, and that had broken Margaret's heart a little, because how could two men like them ever find common ground—especially when the one thing they had in common, other than her, could never be spoken of?

(The tiny frame in her father's pocket. The crisscrossed scars on Hank's hands.)

She changed into her dove-gray sateen, which was much too formal for afternoon but was her only dress that still fit over her growing belly, dabbed on a bit of perfume and tucked an extra handkerchief in her purse, and set off.

Her father had taught her to drive the summer before she went to college, but the automatic transmission in his new Bel Air took some getting used to, especially since its eye-popping turquoise color and miles of chrome trim drew stares and double takes. She crept along the road into town and had to circle the block twice looking for a parking spot that she could navigate, before giving up and pulling up in front of the valet stand. A year ago she wouldn't have given it a thought, but Hank was so very conscientious about money that she couldn't help but think about the charge to her parents' bill, the tip someone was going to have to press into the boy's gloved hand—and it wouldn't be her, because she had thirty-eight cents in her pocketbook and she needed it to buy starch and baking powder and milk.

She'd become a housewife with a grocery list—that was the thought that followed her into the grand lobby of the Vandeveer, appointed with thick carpets and marble columns and coffered ceilings that only increased her self-consciousness. The vastness of her own transformation dawned fully upon her in the time it took to pass the gauntlet of bellboys, the haughty concierge behind his grand desk.

"Room two-eleven," she told the elevator operator sternly, but he leered as he pulled the lever: even he seemed to know she was only playacting now.

Standing in front of the door to her parents' room, her hand raised to knock, Margaret was hit with a wave of panic. She lowered her hand and closed her eyes, and thought about Hank, coming in from an afternoon of flying, his face ruddy from the wind and his lips tasting of the whiskey he'd stopped for on the way home. Hank, picking her up and spinning her around their tiny living room and making her squeal—his strong hands in her hair at night, his weight on her, his hot breath at her neck forcing her worries away like dandelion silk on a breeze. If only they could be together always, every moment of the day—if she could hide herself in him like a tortoise in his shell. But right now he was miles away and it might as well be an ocean that separated them, because she was feeling dangerously like herself again.

She choked back a sob and knocked hard enough to sting her knuckles and her mother opened the door so quickly it was as if she'd been standing on the other side, waiting.

"Margaret Anne Pierson!"

Her mother was wearing an unforgiving slate-blue day dress with a stiff white collar, and her face was a tight-wound rictus of fury. For a moment they simply gaped at each other, and then Caroline seized Margaret's upper arms in a painfully tight grip and pulled her close, so that Margaret felt more than heard the shuddering exhalation of a breath that her mother might have been holding for a century. And just as quickly Caroline pushed her away.

"Well, you may as well come in," she said, and the moment had passed. Margaret followed meekly into the suite, took in the heavy brocade drapes and the peonies in the round crystal bowl on an inlaid ebony console. Such luxury—how she'd taken it for granted, how she missed it now: but acknowledging the ache felt like a betrayal.

"Sit," Caroline said, pointing at a matched pair of emerald-green velvet settees that faced each other over a dainty oval coffee table in front of the tall windows overlooking downtown Austin. "I'll have tea sent up."

While her mother spoke to the room service operator, Margaret gazed out at the view. Piercing the searingly blue sky was the thin white line of a jet's contrail, and Margaret thought of the afternoons when she heard the plane's engine high above and went out onto the porch and found Hank in the sky, buzzing her on his return from wherever it was he'd gone that day. He'd told her he always blew her a kiss, and she always blew one back to him.

Her mother hung up the telephone and walked stiffly to the same window, staring out of it as though she were alone in the room, back as straight as a ruler.

"All right," she finally said, and sat down on the other settee, her legs crossed primly at the ankle and her hands folded in her lap. "Please don't say anything until I've finished, Margaret. I've given this a lot of thought and I would appreciate it if you would hear me out. There is a way to make this right. It's not going to be easy, but I've spoken to your father about it and he agrees that it must be done."

"Mother, I—"

"*Stop!*" Caroline roared, slamming her fist down on the coffee table, rattling a potted African violet and a tray of candies. Margaret drew back against the scratchy velvet, her heart in her throat. "You *listen* to me, for once. You have no idea—no idea!—what sacrifices I've made for you. The things I've done for you. It's time for you to stop thinking only of yourself now, just like I—like your father and I—did the day you were born."

Margaret felt dangerously close to crying, more from shock than any genuine affront. She'd expected her mother to be angry, but not like this—the woman across from her was barely recognizable. Margaret had only seen Caroline lose her composure once before, on the day of the long-ago picnic when the hobo had come looking for her—but even then her mother had managed to quickly restore a sense of outraged decorum.

But now angry spots of red showed through her mother's powder. A tiny bubble of spittle was lodged in the corner of her mouth, and one tail of her blouse had come free of her skirt. Also, she'd become old. But how was that possible? Margaret had seen her only six months earlier, when Caroline had come to UT for the Alpha Chi Omega Mothers' Weekend, carrying a heavy satchel full of fabric samples and menus and registry lists. Caroline had been positively radiant then, as she debated the merits of Wallace sterling versus Towle, Heisey goblets versus Tiffin, in the sorority's parlor.

Margaret focused on the lines bracketing her mother's mouth and cleaving the space between her brows and calculated her age: she was twenty, so that made her mother . . . fifty-three. *Fifty-three!* An unpleasant roil of guilt crowded out her other emotions; her mother's birthday was in April, and Margaret had meant to call, meant to send flowers . . . and in the end had done neither. Her father could always be counted on to see to that sort of thing, and Margaret had been caught up in the final days of her senior year. How long ago that seemed now!

"Mother!" Margaret barked, determined to arrest her mother's fury before things spun further out of control. "It can't be undone. I'm *married* and I'm going to have a *baby*. And that's all there is to it."

"I've spoken to Mrs. Withnall," Caroline continued doggedly. "They are willing to . . . cooperate, on several conditions."

"You *spoke* to her?" Margaret cringed inwardly; she'd started several letters to Tripp's mother, but was stymied by the memory of Tripp lurching down the stairs of their cottage after Hank had punched him.

"The marriage will be annulled," Caroline

plowed on shrilly. "I've made a number of calls, and a very sizable donation to their parish building fund. Our position will be, and the Withnalls will support this, though of course not in public, but everyone will be made to understand that there was . . . coercion. That you were not in your right mind."

"Wait—"

"Your father is prepared to make Hank understand his options, if necessary." Caroline looked down at her hands, examining her perfectly filed nails. Then she looked up at Margaret with an inscrutable expression. "You'll go to Dallas until it's all over."

It took a moment for Margaret to take her mother's meaning. Her hands went to her stomach, protecting the tiny swell. "I will *not*."

Her mother exhaled angrily. "There is no reason for you to throw your life away like this, Margaret! If you'd just take a moment to think about this—about *Hank,* for God's sake, about the life he could provide for you—well, it's all well and good now, when you're in your little fairy-tale cottage and Hank hasn't seen you haggard from being up all night with a baby, and too tired to fix his breakfast. How do you think it's going to be then? Do you think you'll still be his little darling when you've lost your figure and you're nagging him for egg money?"

"You don't *know* him." Margaret hurled the

words back at her mother, but buried in her anger was a snag, a splinter of doubt. "He's *good* and he's hardworking and he'd do anything for me. He *loves* me."

Caroline laughed, an ugly sound, harsh and unfamiliar. "He loves you? Let me tell you what they say about him, Margaret. Hank Dial loves his liquor and he loves to fly his plane. And that's the whole story. I'm sure he's fond of you, and every man wants a girl who's above his station—a prize he can show off, especially after he took you away from Tripp Withnall. But in the end, he's headed for ruin and he'll take you down with him. You forget that I've known him his whole life—even before that day. I knew him when he was just a boy, I saw him fly kites on your father's land. I saw him cry when his dog got run over—just think about that for a minute, Margaret, I saw Hank Dial *cry*."

Margaret sucked in her breath. Because she knew what her mother was insinuating. Just as Caroline always described the disaster only as "that day," she'd never come out and say what she really meant: that Hank had been damaged beyond repair by surviving the explosion that took his brother, that something in his soul had been left behind in the flames when he emerged, burnt and out of his mind with grief.

No, Hank was not a man who cried—nor did he laugh unguardedly, or tell jokes, or sing drinking ditties like Tripp and his friends did. The range of his emotions hung heavily on the dark end of the spectrum; he was a brooder, a man who kept his thoughts to himself.

But there was another side of that coin, one that Margaret couldn't possibly share with her mother. When Hank walked through the door, windburned from a day in the sky, there was a hunger in his eyes that stirred something in her every time. When he drove himself deep inside her so hard their little bed shuddered and knocked against the wall, she was as ready for him as if it was the only use for which God had made her. When she brought him his coffee, he closed his scarred fingers over her wrist and even the look that passed between them could undo her.

He called her his angel. He told her nearly every day she was too good for him, and it only made her want to work harder to deserve him. He laid his head in her lap when the dark thoughts became too much—anyone could see when that happened, anyone who loved him—and she stroked his hair until he fell asleep, his eyelids twitching with the dreams that chased him.

Margaret was healing him, she was sure of it. Slowly, yes, but they would have a lifetime together. And what could Tripp have offered her that could compare to the intoxication of being needed like that? What good were the rows of crystal goblets, the silver engraved with a monogram that would never be hers, the dress that had been ordered from New York?

"You don't know the first thing about him," Margaret snapped. "Or about love. Look at you—you married Daddy, just because he was rich. I don't believe you ever loved him at all, you just *pretended* to so he'd buy you nice things."

"How dare you," Caroline gasped. "I've worked my entire life so you could have this chance! You want to be like your cousins, with a dirt yard and babies they can't afford to keep in shoes?"

"Better than tricking a man into marrying you just so you could live in a big house," Margaret shot back. "Better than ordering Alelia around because you're too lazy to fix lunch. Better than having your husband hide in the garage because he can't bear to listen to you anymore."

The impact caught her by surprise: her mother launched herself off the sofa and slapped her face. Margaret put her hand to her cheek, felt the burn, the tears pricking her eyes. She couldn't believe her mother had done it—but mixed in with her shock was a strange, thrilling shiver. Caroline stumbled backward, collapsing onto the settee, her expression aghast.

"I won't be told what to do, Mother," Margaret said coolly; the balance had somehow shifted. "Hank and I make our own decisions now."

"You won't convince me that baby was one of your decisions. It was—it was reckless."

"We didn't plan to have a baby so soon," Margaret allowed, "but we're certainly going to have more. Three or four or—I don't know, but we want a big family."

In truth, she and Hank had had no such discussion; Margaret wasn't all that certain how he might feel about more children, despite the reverent way he placed his hand on her stomach. She hadn't found the courage to bring up the subject yet.

But her mother's interference had to be stopped, and now, when she held this unexpected advantage, was the time. "Is that all you wanted to discuss?" Margaret asked. "Because I find that I'm feeling a bit indisposed."

"I'm going to give you one more chance," her mother said, regaining her own composure. "But before I do, there's something you should know. This family you've married into—they don't even want you."

Margaret blinked: other than the note and gift from Helene, there had been only a single letter from Hank's mother, from up in Wichita Falls, where she'd moved with her new husband after Mr. Dial's death. In two misspelling-addled paragraphs in a tight, miserly hand, Mrs. Dial had promised a visit "once Mr. Weathers gets the crop in"; she had signed it "your devoted Mother," and Margaret had tried not to be affronted by the exclusion. For Mrs. Dial—now Mrs. Weathers—

would never be her mother, and given the way Margaret and Caroline had treated her and Helene all those years ago, she was smart enough not to pretend.

"We were never that close before, as I recall," she said haughtily. "I suppose I'll simply have to carry on without their approval."

"It's not just them," her mother snapped. "Do you know what I overheard Dessie Webb saying the other night after dinner at the club?"

"I can't imagine."

"That after what you did to your fiancé, you deserve what you get."

Margaret felt her face heat with shame; it was all very well to pretend the snubs didn't bother her, but this one hit too close to home. She'd been cruel, but she wasn't—despite what everyone thought—intentionally cruel by nature. Selfish, yes, though she blamed her mother's example; spoiled, certainly, but loads of girls in her sorority were spoiled. And she'd been a crafty and occasionally unkind child, but children were often unkind, if the impulse went unchecked—it was simply part of growing up.

Even now she couldn't think of Tripp—of that ring on the silver tray, of her covert escape down the back stairs—without a measure of guilt and the suspicion that she was going to be made to pay.

"I don't care," she said grimly, as much to

remind herself of the need to be resolute as to defy her mother.

"Well, maybe you'll care about this." Her mother stood and went to the little inlaid writing desk along the wall, and picked up a piece of notepaper.

No, not notepaper but a check, Margaret realized, as her mother marched back and held it up just out of reach. The figure Caroline had written out nearly made Margaret's eyes pop.

"This is my final offer. I won't beg, Margaret. Do the right thing, and your father and I are prepared to make sure that you are more than comfortable once you return from Dallas. You can have your own house; you'll never need to worry about money. If you're clever, you'll find someone else to marry—this will certainly help convince him."

Margaret held her chin high. "I don't want your money."

The second the words were out of her mouth, she thought of all the things she and Hank could not afford: a bigger house with a room for the baby, a bassinet. A car, a vacuum cleaner, a washing machine. Even a trip to the salon—Margaret had been forced to trim her own hair as well as Hank's, and while she made light of it as she wrapped toilet paper around his neck to catch the snipped bits, she missed the smells of hairspray and setting lotion so much it made her want to cry.

She'd secretly assumed that her parents would begin sending her a little to help, once the baby came, and it was with alarm that she understood that was not going to happen now. Everything she needed, from bobby pins to baking powder, she would have to beg money for from Hank. And she could not count on him to understand. Money coming in from her parents, to be spent on fripperies and follies, would be easy to hide for the simple reason that a man like Hank was unlikely to notice a new dress or lipstick; but the unfortunate truth was that she had no hope of explaining why she *needed* them.

And that was if there truly was to be extra, if the money wasn't needed for something else. It sounded so romantic, when Hank had first explained that he worked for whom he wanted, when he wanted; these three months later, she had come to understand that Hank had a temper that did at least some of the deciding for him. She'd once answered the door to a man who claimed that Hank had cheated him—and another time, Hank had left without telling her where he was going, leaving instructions that "if anyone shows up, tell 'em I'm not working today."

The unfortunate but perhaps unsurprising fact was that at least some of the time, liquor was behind Hank's rash actions. But there was no way Margaret would confess *that* to her mother. Besides, she had a plan. She was going to talk to Hank about it, when the baby was a little closer to being born. She'd remind him of the sacrifices that they both had made—him his first marriage, her a fiancé who'd once seemed quite good enough—and convince him that it was time to settle down for good. He'd come home in the evenings, he'd start keeping more regular work hours, he'd quit playing cards and frequenting taverns and start looking for a house that he could fix up on the weekends.

Reminding herself of these plans did the trick. Margaret smiled, not very nicely, and moved forward so that she was mere inches from the check her mother was still holding. She snatched it out of her mother's hands, tore it in half, then tore the pieces in half twice more and let them flutter down onto the exquisite rug.

"You stupid, stupid girl," her mother said tonelessly. "I should have known."

The words stung, but Margaret did her best to hide it. "Known what?" she asked loftily. "Known that I was capable of making my own decisions? That I'd never settle for a life like yours?"

Her mother's face drew in on itself, her eyes narrowing into glittering slits, her lips compressed until they were devoid of color. Margaret was almost to the door when she finally spoke.

"That no good deed goes unpunished," Caroline called after her. "Though I imagine you'll figure that out for yourself soon enough."

Chapter Thirteen

The little supermarket smelled faintly of American cheese and Windex, and there was no one in it besides Katie except for the clerk, a bored-looking young man with a mop of jet-black hair that hung in his face. Katie wandered the aisles, her hand closed tightly around the bills in her pocket. What she really wanted was a bottle of the moderately expensive cab that she and Liam bought for date night, with its pretty scrolled label and the pinkish foil cap. But even if she used all her money, there wouldn't be enough for a single glass.

She settled for a toothbrush and tiny tube of Crest, an apple, a Clif Bar. She deliberated over the Lunchables, which were on sale for a dollar off, but the pink circle of lunch meat made her feel slightly nauseous. The tinny country music playing in the background seemed like it had come from another era, all fiddle and twang. It was as though all of New London had been frozen in 1998, when she'd last come to visit.

The young man at the register cleared his throat. "Fried chicken's half off," he called. "After six o'clock, when my boss figures she can't sell it.

I think there's a couple of thighs left, over in the fridge there."

Katie thanked him and went over to the refrigerator case, and sure enough, wrapped in plastic and labeled with a strip of tape and "1/2" written in a shaking hand were two plump, golden-brown thighs. Even through the plastic Katie could see that they had been perfectly fried, the breading crisp and cratered. She imagined the first bite, the icebox-cool crunch and the meat flavored with sage and buttermilk, the way she remembered it from a dozen family dinners at friends' houses, made by Texas housewives who'd learned from their mothers. She thought about telling the clerk that a wildly popular fried chicken restaurant had opened up near her apartment in Boston, an outpost of the original location in Brooklyn, where a two-piece combo cost almost fifteen dollars, and left a ring of grease on the waxed paper and a feeling of lead in her stomach.

"How much?" she said, hoping she could afford both pieces.

"It's, ah . . ." The young man looked toward the door, then down at the floor. When he looked up, he had a shy, pained expression on his face. "I forgot—when it gets close to eight, well, we just give it away. Saves us from having to throw it out."

Katie waited, uncertain she'd heard correctly,

until understanding dawned on her. They didn't give it away—he was lying and he wasn't a very skilled liar. He felt sorry for her. Katie looked down at her blouse and discovered that in addition to the coffee stain it now bore several huge streaks of dirt, probably from the dusty house. She touched her hair; it was a greasy, knotted tangle. She hadn't looked in a mirror since the airport, but after sleeping in the truck, her mascara probably ringed her eyes like those women she saw poking around the Dumpsters late at night. The heroin addicts.

Oh my God—the boy thought she was a heroin addict.

"That is just extremely nice of you," she said in a quivery voice, laying her things down on the old rubber conveyer belt. She wasn't about to challenge him, not after he'd overcome his embarrassment to make the offer in the first place. Up close, she could see that he'd dyed his hair himself—a telltale grayish band still ringed his hairline—and he was fighting a precarious battle with a ridge of acne along his jaw. His ears were pierced with six or seven cheap silver rings. A name tag pinned crookedly to his T-shirt said "Kyle."

Katie desperately wanted to explain—to make him understand that she'd been a victim of a crime, of bad luck, of circumstance, of Liam's inadequate efforts to help—but as she unfolded the sweaty, damp bills and tried to smooth them

184

out, Kyle carefully averted his eyes, pretending to be fascinated by a business card from a towing company taped to the cash register, all in an effort to preserve her dignity.

Her heart broke a little and she thought of little Bomber, the nickname she'd privately given the baby she'd mistakenly believed she'd conceived, who she'd imagined playing lacrosse and taking immersion language lessons and having playdates with the delightful children of the nice moms she always saw in the park, with their fancy strollers and their sleek designer diaper bags. She'd wager that Kyle's childhood had included none of those things—and yet somehow, a mother in New London had managed to raise an incredibly decent human.

"Thank you, Kyle," she said after he had placed her purchases carefully in a plain brown paper bag and folded the top over twice.

He looked at her in surprise, then touched his name tag. "Oh yeah," he said. "Thank you, ma'am. Have a nice evening. We could sure use a little rain, couldn't we?"

She was almost out the door when he called after her. "Don't forget," he said. "Come as close to eight as you can when you come back. Tomorrow's brisket."

It wasn't until Katie got back to the house that she remembered the key on its soda-bottle keychain . . . lying on the kitchen table, where she had left it.

"Fuck!" she exclaimed. *Fuck, fuck, fuck.* Was this no-good, terrible day ever going to end? She tried the doorknob—old, bronze, heavy and warm under her hand—and naturally, it didn't budge.

She felt tears threatening and swiped at them angrily with the back of her hand. The tiny spark of hope that had come to life in the grocery store sputtered out. She was thousands of miles from home and had just been mistaken for a vagrant, her only kin had no room at the inn, and now she'd managed to lock herself out of the only shelter she was going to find, at least until tomorrow. The exhaustion she'd been staving off hit her like a wall, and suddenly Katie wanted nothing more than to lie down and sleep until it was a new day, until she could start over again. She looked around the empty street in despair; with the way things were going, one of the neighbors would probably report her for trying to break into the house.

The two windows flanking the front door were filthy and painted shut; she wasn't getting in that way unless she broke the glass. If only she'd finished opening up the house as she'd planned, she could shimmy up and crawl over the sill. Maybe, just maybe, she could get in through a window in the back.

In the dark, the shapes in the backyard looked menacing. The moonlight that had seemed so romantic earlier reflected off the mottled old glass of the kitchen window, distorting the view of the inside of the house. Katie gave the handle an experimental tug, but it didn't budge.

A movement out of the corner of her eye startled her, and she let out an involuntary yelp: a man was standing on the porch, setting something on the top step. He looked up and, in a surprising display of physical prowess, leaped over all three steps to land in a combat-ready stance, coiled and ready to attack. Just as quickly, his body relaxed and he stood.

"Who the hell are you?" he demanded, in a voice that was as bitter as poison and as rough as burlap. Katie couldn't make out his face in the dark; he was tall and solidly built and dressed in jeans and an old plaid shirt over a T-shirt, which, if Katie wasn't mistaken, was wet, and clinging to his muscular torso.

"Who are *you?*" she shot back. "This is my grandmother's house."

"No it's not," he said. "I know Scarlett. You're not her. What kind of bullshit is that?"

"I didn't say I was Scarlett," Katie said, adrenaline draining out of her body, leaving her limp and light-headed. "Also, Margaret wasn't Scarlett's grandmother. She was her . . ." She tried to mentally untangle the relationship. "Her great-great-aunt or something."

She glanced at the object that he'd left on the porch; it looked like a bowl of dirt. The fact that he knew Scarlett did seem to make it unlikely that he was there to murder her. And at this point, Katie didn't have the energy to muster a lot of suspicion. "Look, I haven't eaten in hours, I didn't get much sleep last night, and it has been one of the longest days of my life. I'm locked out of this house. Margaret really was my grandmother, and so Scarlett is my, uh, some sort of cousin—you can ask her next time you see her. You can call the cops if you want, or you can just go away and leave me alone." She walked past him, giving him a wide berth, and sank down onto the top step of the porch. Up close, it looked like the metal bowl he'd left was full of the leftovers from a dinner of meatloaf and mashed potatoes, and she almost wondered if she should eat it herself.

When the man didn't budge, Katie unrolled the paper sack and said, "I'm going to eat my fried chicken now. I'd offer to share, but I'm pretty sure I need it worse than you do."

"Hold up," he said. "Are you the one who was shoplifting down at the market?"

Katie paused in the middle of unwrapping the plastic from a chicken thigh. "I was *not* shoplifting!"

"Sorry." He didn't sound sorry. He came closer, looming over her, his torso at eye level. This close, she could smell him—stale sweat, which might also explain the damp shirt. "Kyle texted me that you were casing the place. Guess he caught you before you could rip them off."

Katie sighed. She hadn't thought things could get worse, but even the one person she'd mistakenly thought was being friendly had only been checking her out because he thought she was a criminal.

"Are you a cop?"

He laughed. "No. More like . . . I caught Kyle tagging your grandmother's house. Told him he could either get a job and buy some paint and fix it right, or deal with me. After that he, ah . . . well, he comes around sometimes. What can I say? Weird kid."

"I saw that," Katie said, remembering the strange purple design. "What's it supposed to be?"

"I guess you could ask him, next time you get sticky fingers."

Katie rolled her eyes. There was nothing left to do but eat her chicken before some new disaster came along.

"Oh God," she moaned. It was perfect: delicately seasoned, the skin crispy and the texture perfect. She wished the hipster chef from the Brooklyn chain could be here now, with his spice rubs and ancho paste and Italian rotisserie, to see how it was really done. "So good," she mumbled as she swallowed.

"Kyle *gave* you that, didn't he," the man said indignantly.

Katie shrugged. "Why are you still here? Can't you just wander off the way you came and go make someone else miserable?"

The man didn't answer. His shoulders sagged, and he looked around. "In a minute," he said.

Then he whistled.

Three notes—if Katie remembered correctly from her music theory class at Columbia, a perfect fifth. A compact, fast blur came shooting out of the shrubs bordering the yard and flew straight up the steps, then began wolfing down the food in the bowl. A *dog,* of unknowable lineage, perhaps thirty pounds of short legs and flopping ears and a blunt tail and a barrel chest and a coat that was sort of striped and sort of spotted. After it had taken a few gulps, it glared at Katie and snarled, its lips pulled back over its teeth, then resumed eating.

"Wait—is that your dog?" Katie said, scooting away from it. She didn't like dogs; she was more of a cat person, but had never owned one because she couldn't bear the thought of sharing their tiny apartment with a litter box. "You feed your dog on my grandmother's back porch?"

The man shook his head in disgust. "If she really was your grandmother, you'd know."

Katie had almost polished off the first piece of chicken. She gnawed the last bit of meat from the bone and picked up the second piece, wishing she had a tall, cold glass of milk. "Know what?" she said with her mouth full.

"Know that she was always feeding strays. She'd take care of them until they were healthy and then drive them to a no-kill shelter in Henderson." After a moment he added, "This one only started coming around right before she had her stroke, so I had to take over."

Katie mulled that over for a moment. She doubted that he "had" to take over; any sane person would take this dog, who was emaciated and mangy, straight to the animal shelter—and not the no-kill one, either. It was probably diseased, and definitely a menace; if it did bite her, she'd probably spend the entire night being treated for rabies—if the doctor would even agree to treat her with no insurance card.

"Who are you, anyway?" Katie asked.

The man hooked his thumb over his shoulder at the house next door, a plain little white-sided cottage. "Neighbor. Jam Mifflin."

"Excuse me . . . *Jam?*"

"Yeah." His tone challenged her to make an issue of it.

"Well, I'm Katie Garrett. My mother is Margaret's daughter, Georgina."

"You're the one from Boston?" He sounded

skeptical. "No one thought you'd bother to come."

"Em, yes," she admitted, stung. "You were friends with Margaret?"

"Friends?" He laughed again, a clipped, humorless bark. "Not sure about that. Your grandmother was mean as a wasp and tough as stewed skunk—except with Scarlett. She adored Scarlett."

"Well, then why are you feeding her dog?"

"That ain't anybody's dog," he said with feeling. After a moment he added, "But it needs to eat, and I'm a dog trainer, and dumb enough not to pass up a challenge. Though if I was to make a bet on who was going to out-stubborn the other, I'd bet on Royal."

"Royal?"

"Mutt can thank Margaret for that. How the hell she came up with that . . ." He ran his hand through his hair. "Look, if you're really locked out, I guess I could let you in. I mean, it'll be just one more bad decision in a series, I guess. Though it's hard for me to believe you're descended from Margaret if a little thing like that lock's going to stop you."

Katie let that pass. "Listen, um, Jam, I'd be really, really grateful if you'd help me get in. You have a key?"

He didn't even bother to answer, but took his wallet out of his pocket and removed a credit card. He stepped over the dog, who stopped eating only long enough to snarl and snap, and jiggled the handle while he slipped the card between the door and the frame. A second later, he had it open.

"Well, that was impressive," Katie said. "Although one does wonder where you picked up that skill."

"Don't bother inviting me in," he said, ignoring her comment. "Royal and I were just leaving. And do yourself a favor—after you're done robbing Margaret blind, keep on going and don't even think about coming after me next—I'm armed, and I'll shoot an intruder faster than you'll know what hit you."

With that, he turned and jogged around the house at an easy clip. The dog took a last, hopeful lick at the bowl, growled one last time, and slunk off into the bushes.

Chapter Fourteen

August 1963

"Give me that," Margaret said, holding out her hand and holding in her temper. Georgina gazed up at her with enormous cornflower-blue eyes and not an ounce of guile, and then she ran out of the room, tottering barefoot on her chubby legs out the open screen door.

Margaret leaned against the doorframe for support. She was tired—more tired than she'd ever been. When she'd finally gone to the doctor, giving in to Hank's pleas after trying for months to convince herself that her fatigue would go away on its own, he'd given her a painful injection and instructed her to eat liver three times a week. He'd promised she'd be feeling better soon.

But that was nearly a month ago.

There was something worse than her exhaustion, something worse than her loneliness in this wretched cottage that they still, after nearly four and a half years, had not managed to escape; something even worse than trying to get from one week to the next on the handfuls of bills that

Hank handed over, sometimes still smelling of motor oil and cigarettes from his pockets.

The terrible secret that was weighing Margaret down was that she wished she had never had a child.

Not always, certainly. Not even most of the time. But on afternoons like this—the mercury in the thermometer that some former tenant of the cottage had mounted on the window frame in the kitchen had risen steadily all morning and now hovered around ninety-five after lunch—all she wanted was a swim in the pool at her parents' club and a cool glass of lemonade and a beautiful dress to change into for dinner. She longed for the days when babies belonged to other girls, when they were tucked neatly into carriages to be admired and cooed over, and then taken away when they fussed.

Georgina had been a happy infant, sleeping through the night at three months, smiling for both her mama and her daddy. At eighteen months, she'd turned into a spectacular flirt, apt to peek between her hands at strangers in the market, or pull up her skirt shyly at church. She copied everything Margaret did, pretending to read the newspaper or put on lipstick or cook in the kitchen, stacking pots on top of each other on the floor that Margaret could never quite get clean.

On her second birthday, however, when Margaret put a wedge of buttermilk cake on a saucer and set it in front of her, Georgina had smiled merrily, picked up the plate, and dropped it on the floor, to the accompaniment of gales of laughter. When Margaret had scolded her, she had screamed for her daddy in a shrill volume that Margaret had never heard before. Hank, in a rare good mood, asked Margaret if she'd pinched their daughter and then paraded her around the house on his shoulders while Margaret cleaned up the mess.

"The terrible twos," the other mothers told her at the park on days when Hank drove her into town, rolling their eyes when Margaret swore that Georgina had always been an angel. But Margaret had seen them with her own eyes, the little scamps who put mud pies down each other's shirt and teased their siblings and pulled the tails of dogs and cried, cried, cried at the slightest provocation. It was different with Georgina: for reasons entirely her own, she seemed to have simply decided one day to wage a war on her mother, one that was going on its third year. She threw her toys on the floor, smeared her dinner in her hair, pulled Margaret's dresses off the hangers when she tried to take a bath. As she got older, she sassed back and refused to do as she was told and invented new forms of mischief seemingly every day. Today, she'd gotten into Margaret's jewelry box and taken the brooch her parents had given her for her eighteenth birthday, one of the only good pieces she still owned after selling off most of them one by one when there wasn't enough money to pay the bills.

And now Georgina was running through the backyard to the edge of the sorghum field. If she dropped the brooch among the feathery orange stalks, Margaret would never be able to find it. The thought made her nearly hysterical with anger and frustration.

She yanked off her apron and went running after her daughter, but Georgina was moving with incredible speed, dashing over the tricycle she'd upended on the lawn, heading straight for the plants, which were taller than she was.

Margaret let out an inhuman roar and launched herself at her daughter, managing to snatch the hem of her sundress. Georgina went down hard, Margaret twisting her ankle and nearly falling on top of her; out of the corner of her eye she saw the flash of gold as the brooch went spinning through the air and fell into the grass.

Georgina started screaming, incomprehensible angry shrieks, and Margaret smacked her.

She hadn't meant to; it hadn't felt like her palm that smacked against Georgina's plump, smooth cheek, whipping her head to the side and leaving an angry red mark. She was shocked into silence—or no, her head lolled listlessly, like a doll's, and Margaret gasped: Had she knocked her unconscious? Broken her neck?

"Baby," she cried, getting to her knees and crawling to where Georgina lay sprawled. The bodice of her dress was streaked with a grass stain that would never come out of the yellow broadcloth, and bits of cut grass stuck to her sweaty neck, but Margaret gathered her into her arms, her heart in her throat. *Please, please, please,* she thought, then realized she was saying the words out loud. "Don't be hurt, darling, Mama is so sorry, please."

A figure came striding toward her on long legs, blocking the sun. Hank—Hank, who was supposed to be gone all day taking a pair of brothers from Oklahoma to see some land that a rancher was selling. He shouldn't be home so early—but that's how it went with Hank these days: sure things fell through for reasons he never bothered to elucidate; repeat business evaporated, cold calls somehow ended up with him at the tavern until his supper was burnt or cold or both and Georgina was put to bed yet again without saying good night to her daddy.

But at least he hadn't seen Margaret hit their child. She hoped he hadn't, anyway; she was pretty sure he'd come around the corner of the house only after she'd already fallen.

"What happened here?" he said cheerfully, and she was relieved—even as she was trying to make sure that Georgina was all right, she was still gauging her reaction by how Hank responded.

"She fell," Margaret said, wincing at the lie. "I was just—she had my brooch. She was running toward the field. I didn't want—"

Georgina stirred in her arms, blinking in the sun that slanted past her father, touching a pudgy hand to her cheek. She started to cry, but it was her fake cry, big breathless sobs accompanied by crafty peering through her thick eyelashes to see if her audience was convinced.

"Mama hit me, Daddy," she announced.

"That's not—Georgina!" Margaret snapped. "Don't lie to Daddy. You took my nice brooch out of my jewelry box. That was very bad."

Georgina pouted and sniffled and reached for Hank, and for once Margaret was glad when he picked her up and swung her into the air.

"Take her inside, won't you? I need to find my brooch."

Hank laughingly obliged, and she could hear their voices as they went back to the house. It wouldn't last—afternoons at the tavern usually meant brooding evenings on the back porch, no help with the baby's bath, fights picked at bedtime—but at least Margaret had a few moments to get herself together.

She found the brooch in a matter of moments. The spray of garnets set in gold reflected the sunlight so brilliantly that it caused spots to appear in her eyes as she closed her fingers gratefully around it, almost too hot to touch. It was, she realized with a sob, the most beautiful thing in her world—other than her daughter, she reminded herself furiously, *her own child*— too fine to wear with anything in her closet. The years—and a pregnancy and long months of nursing—had reduced her wardrobe to a stained and worn mess. Few of her dresses even fit anymore, and she'd taken to wearing Mary Beth's castoffs most days, housedresses with no waist, baggy trousers from her days in the WAC, kerchiefs in her hair.

In fact, she was wearing one of Mary Beth's blouses now, a thin seersucker that gapped over her bosom. She pinned the brooch to its collar for safekeeping and wiped her hands on her skirt and stared longingly down the road toward town. Earlier today she'd calculated that she needed eleven dollars for groceries and the electric bill, but she didn't have the energy to ask Hank for it now.

Across the lane and up the gentle hill, the windows in the rancher's house were open, but no one peered out past the curtains; no one would come over later to make sure everything was okay. That was because Mrs. Pratt, the rancher's wife, was dying. Every morning her husband came out of the house a little more stooped, his face a little more lined, and headed for the barn. Soon it would be over—Mr. Pratt and Hank had shared a flask at sunset last week, walking the perimeter of the field; he'd confided that once his wife was dead and buried, he was moving to town, where his sister and her husband had an extra room.

Margaret sat on her haunches, delaying the inevitable, the fraught hours between now and when she would finally be able to convince Georgina to sleep. Then she would have a bit of time to herself, half an hour to read the book she'd gotten at the library or write a letter to one of her old sorority sisters, who didn't seem nearly as boring now as they had in college. Only, a few moments into a new chapter or halfway down the piece of notepaper, she was bound to be overcome with such exhaustion that she'd fall asleep practically before her head hit the pillow.

Was this how Mrs. Pratt had felt, thirty years ago, when her young husband had brought her home to this land? They weren't particularly friendly people, but from their few conversations Margaret knew that they had two grown sons, both of whom had moved out of state. Until she'd gotten too weak last fall, Mrs. Pratt had moved steadfastly through her chores each day, unsmiling and serious, the loose skin of her bare arms jiggling as she hung the laundry and beat the rugs and washed the windows. Margaret had seen her once on the porch, silhouetted against the morning sun, her sheer housedress revealing the sagging breasts, the loose skin of her stomach, and she'd had to turn away in disgust. But would the decades wreak their sly havoc on Margaret, as they had on Mrs. Pratt, until she would find herself on this very porch one day, Georgina grown and gone, and realize that she'd traded her entire life away?

"I can't," she whispered, flicking bits of grass from her skirt. Slowly, she got to her feet. Her ankle throbbed, but at least it wasn't sprained; she limped slowly back to the house. She dragged herself up the porch stairs and held the railing for support.

Inside, she found Hank reclining on the sofa with Georgina on his lap and the Burpee seed catalog in his hands. Georgina was laughing and poking her finger at the cover illustration of impossibly bright, perfect dahlias, singing nonsense words the way she only did for Hank.

"You were at Hemphills," Margaret said. These were not the words she had planned to say, but they tumbled out on a wave of bitterness.

Hank peered over Georgina's shiny pale curls, frowning. "One drink, for God's sake. I had *one drink* with a fellow who may well hire me. Is that a crime these days?" When she didn't answer, he sighed, and set Georgina gently on the floor with the catalog. That would be the end of it—Margaret had been looking forward to paging through it before bed, admiring all the lovely drawings of asters and zinnias and bluebonnets, choosing a few packets of seeds as a special treat to buy with the money she'd saved over the winter in a coffee can in the back of a cupboard behind the yeast and the baking powder. But now its pages would be torn and wrinkled, reduced to trash, like everything else that spent any time in their home.

"Come here, baby," Hank said.

Margaret folded her arms over her chest and refused to look at him. This was a familiar ploy, and one she rarely resisted, because as hard as her life had become, as tarnished as her dreams and diminished her hopes, Hank could still, always, make her forget all that. He'd gather her into his arms and she'd inhale his whiskey-scented breath and then he'd kiss her and she'd taste that wicked reminder on his lips. He'd run his hands over her hips and growl deep in his throat and she'd be lost to him, all over again. She'd protest that she hadn't bathed and her hands were rough and raw from the laundry and her hair was awful from the humidity and he'd stop her with a deeper kiss, and they'd settle Georgina in her room and sneak away to the bedroom and make love with their hands over each other's mouth, laughing until they couldn't help themselves, until their lives fell away from them and it was just the desperate holding on, ascending and crashing, forgetting everything else.

But not today.

"Sweetheart," Hank pleaded, holding his arms out wide, willing her to come to him. "I'm sorry I didn't come straight home. But this might be a steady job. Big as the Yates field, they're saying, and just imagine what it'll take to get it up and running. Look, I'll take you to the quarries this weekend, I'll buy you a new dress—*please, baby.*"

"I can't do this anymore," Margaret said quietly. A big fat hot tear spilled over and splashed on her cheek, but how could that be? She wasn't sad, exactly, she was just—tired.

"Can't do what?" Hank said warily, letting his arms fall.

"Let's move back to New London. Please. Daddy will give you a job, you know he will." (He'd been offering, in fact, since the week after her parents' disastrous visit to Austin; a letter had arrived on his company letterhead, smelling like his tobacco and written in his blocky hand. Since then he'd written every month, slipping in a few dollars now and then.) "And you can still fly," Margaret added hastily. "On the weekends and— and maybe after, you know, you and Daddy work things out. We can live in the garage apartment until we find a place, we won't have to pay rent or—we can finally get ahead, like you always say you want to."

And her father would smooth things over with her mother, if there was any grace in this world, and maybe, just maybe, Caroline would watch Georgina now and then and Margaret could finally rest. Blessed, delicious sleep, in the dark back room of the old groundskeeper's apartment where she had once played. It was shaded by overgrown cherry laurel and the windows were hung with heavy plain brown oilcloth curtains, and there was a darling little pint-size stove and painted cupboards and hooks for pots and pans. It was small, but it wouldn't be like here, because Hank would be working and Georgina could start nursery school and surely Caroline would soften when she saw that Margaret was . . . well, that Margaret was sorry. Sorry for the nasty spoiled girl she'd been, sorry for the way she'd treated her parents, sorry for the boys she'd strung along and the girls she'd snubbed and for never caring enough about the events that had taken place before her birth to let her mother tell her about them.

Hank's face had drained of color and he was leaning back against the couch as though she'd shot him. "Mags," he said in a strained voice. "I'll do better. Look, I know it's been hard for you, stuck out here with no one to talk to. I remember what I promised you, baby, I do. But I can't go back to New London. I can't."

He stared out the window, but his eyes were blank. "Name another place. We can go west, if you want, there's work in Abilene and San

Angelo. I can ask around . . . or I can get rig work. It pays, it's steady."

"No," Margaret said. "It'll be the same, wherever we go." She couldn't bear to tell him that she knew more about his promises than he did—that no matter how many fresh starts and second chances he got, they'd all end up the same: tempers boiling over, handshake deals falling apart, too little rest and too many meals of beans and corn bread. Somehow, Hank managed to keep believing that it would be different.

Margaret played her ace, the lie she'd been holding back. "I miss my family. It's different for you, but it doesn't have to be—all we have to do is apologize to my mother. You can do that, for me, can't you? Sweetheart? It doesn't mean she's right, it doesn't mean I love them more than you, darling. You know that, right? You know I love you more than . . ."

Than anything, she was about to say, but that would mean that she loved him more than her own child, and only monsters felt that way, women too brittle to nurture their offspring, too selfish to care for their families.

And besides, it was different with him, an entirely different kind of love. Margaret was still astonished by her love for her husband, but it had been there always, as long ago as she could remember, until it had become as much a part of her as her bones or blood. At those early

Daisy meetings—there was Hank, age thirteen, fourteen, careering across her mother's backyard with his BB gun and his baseball glove, smoking his father's cigarettes and pulling the girls' pigtails, pilfering the cupcakes that were meant for the ladies and dancing jeeringly away from his own mother when she threatened to warm his bottom with a paddle. Margaret had loved him then and it was her first love, the pure one, the best one; and as she got older, he only grew in her estimation until she arrived at adulthood with a particular notion of what it meant to be heroic. Just out of reach—always running—untamed and ungovernable: that was her Hank.

"Forever," she finally settled on, whispering the word and tracing his hard jaw with her fingertips. Often this worked; her touch could soothe him when nothing else did.

But Hank put his face in his hands and for a moment Margaret wondered if he was crying, a possibility so frightening that she wished she'd never said anything at all. But he merely rubbed his eyes and took a few deep breaths, the sharp planes of his shoulder blades rising and falling, before looking up at her bleakly.

"Don't ask me for this," he said. "Because I won't live in your parents' house and I won't apologize. Do you hear me, Mags? I'll never apologize. When I left, I promised myself I'd never go back. I didn't ask to get blown up and

I didn't ask for my brother to die, and I didn't ask for my mom to wake up in the middle of the night screaming all the time, waking Helene up, so I was the one who had to get her and walk her around until she went back to sleep. You understand me?"

Margaret nodded, afraid to say anything. He'd told her parts of the story before, and she wasn't at all sure she wanted to hear any more. Besides, it would only make him dig in further. It remained to be seen if Hank meant what he said, about refusing to come home with her. He didn't seem that drunk, at least not blackout drunk, and despite everything he was still a proud man; if she gave him some time to get used to the idea, he might come around.

"I saw him, you know," he said, laying his head on her shoulder so his words were muffled against her neck. "That day. When, when I got burned. He was under a piece of the ceiling. I saw his legs—I knew his shoes, see, because they used to be mine. It was his pants. His shirt sleeves. Only I couldn't see his face. The ceiling fell right on him. I got hold of his ankles and I was—I was—and it was so hot, it was like—you've never seen anything— but I thought if I could just—"

"Oh, Hank," Margaret whispered, and something opened up inside her. A bloom like a spent rose, lovely but doomed. She would do anything to heal his hurt. And: she couldn't.

He caught her fingers in his and nearly crushed them. He put his weight against her and she struggled to support him. She knew he got his strength from her. And the giving of what he needed, that was what gave her strength.

"Come with me," she said, and he released her hands and followed her meekly to the bedroom. But once they were inside he was no longer meek. He shut the door carefully, quietly, so as not to wake Georgina. He looked at her, taking his time, and she stood tall and still and felt the uneven ends of her home-cut hair grazing her shoulders, and she put her fingers to the pearly buttons of her blouse. The blouse was cheap, not good enough even for the plain, crooked-toothed wife of a deliveryman, but Margaret pretended it was scarlet satin, and she imagined her breasts spilling from it as if they were as firm and inviting as they had been when she first came to him. She begged Hank to see her as she was on the inside, blazing with want and need and her passionate devotion.

He pushed her hands away so that he could attend to the task himself, his impatient fingers callused from work, clumsy. Finally the blouse fell away and she unhooked her brassiere, and with his needful hands on her, she forgot that she was worn and tired and found that other version of herself, the one who flaunted her beauty and gambled with everything that mattered.

• • •

At four forty-five the next morning, Margaret slipped out the front door with a satchel over her shoulder and Georgina heavy in her arms. She'd been up for nearly an hour, gathering what she needed as quietly as she could, her last task to write the note now laid out on the counter and held down with a jar of peach preserves that Mary Beth had dropped off.

"My darling, please don't make me beg. It's only for a while until we find our own place. Mother will understand. I promise. Don't break my heart, for I won't last a day without you. Your love always."

The walk to town was only half a mile, but with a sleeping child in her arms and her bag over her shoulder containing apples and bread and cheese and a change of clothes for Georgina, it seemed five times as long. The kerchief she'd tied over her hair quickly became too warm, her forehead dampening with sweat. When she arrived at the bus station, the sun was breaking over the trees. Men stood waiting, their weariness in the hunch of their shoulders, the thin streams of smoke from their cigarettes. These were men accustomed to waiting, in shabby coats and worn-out shoes, their eyes downcast. They glanced at her, at Georgina, with no expression at all.

The bus waited, belching and stinking. Finally, the driver emerged from around the corner of the building and hoisted himself into his seat. The men parted, allowing her to board first.

"Ma'am," the one closest to the door said, holding out his hand for her satchel. Gratefully, she let him take it, but when he followed her up into the bus, she set Georgina down in the first empty seat and took her bag back with a curt nod. She did not intend to start a conversation with him or with any of her fellow travelers: despite appearances, she was no drifter, no unmoored unfortunate like the rest of them.

Margaret was going home.

CHAPTER FIFTEEN

Katie had eaten the fried chicken and apple and Clif Bar awfully fast—maybe too fast. Now she felt a bit queasy. After washing her hands at the sink and drying them on a threadbare towel embroidered with a cluster of cherries and the word "Tuesday" in a curving scroll, she decided to call it a day, head to bed, and put off any further explorations until morning.

Katie turned off the downstairs lights and checked the locks twice, though after seeing how quickly Jam dispatched the lock with his credit card, it was difficult not to imagine all manner of ambulance-chasing thugs breaking in to steal the remaining detritus of her grandmother's life. She padded upstairs in her socks, carrying her toothbrush and toothpaste, and surveyed the old bathroom. A thin yellow towel was hung over the tarnished towel rack, and a cracked plastic shower cap hung on the knob of the cabinet. Katie touched it with her fingertip, imagining the last time her grandmother had pulled it over her head.

She opened the door of the medicine cabinet and peered inside. The shelves were filled with toiletries of a dubious vintage: a tin of talcum powder, a bottle of Jean Naté body splash, roll-on deodorant and Pond's cold cream and Vaseline and tweezers and nail clippers. There were two Estée Lauder lipsticks with the gold trim faded from the tubes; she twisted off the caps and found them worn down to chalky nubs, one a lurid pink and the other an orangey red. A cake of rouge was dried out and cracked, the brush losing its bristles. Katie shut the medicine cabinet door guiltily, feeling as though she had violated the old woman's private sanctuary.

She ran the sink taps for a while to flush out anything that might have collected in the pipes, then rinsed off her face and brushed her teeth.

Then it was time for bed.

If the old house had ghosts, Katie meant to seal them out, at least for tonight. By tomorrow night, she'd have a nice antiseptic room at the Days Inn, clean clothes, a proper meal. The old braided rug felt soft under her bare feet, and the evening had cooled off comfortably. Katie patted the mattress experimentally and it didn't seem too terrible. The mattress pad was yellowed with age but otherwise looked as though it had barely been used. Well, that made sense; according to Georgina, Margaret had no friends and had alienated everyone she ever knew, so who would there have been to stay in the guest bed?

(But Georgina hadn't known about Scarlett,

213

about the fact that she'd been visiting Margaret all along, a thought that nagged at Katie. Unless Georgina had known but decided to keep it to herself for some reason. What else might her mother have kept from her?)

Katie went in search of linens. A single blanket was all she needed; she could sleep in her dirty clothes. In the linen closet in the hall, she found stacks of folded quilts, boxes of incontinence pads, an old humidifier.

And a shoe box marked "Letters."

Something smelled wonderful.

Katie yawned and slowly opened her eyes, to find—not Liam sliding an omelet from the pan to a plate, one of the two dishes he knew how to cook flawlessly—but her cousin Scarlett sitting cross-legged on the other bed and digging into a Taco Bueno bag.

"Well, good morning!" she said, grinning. "Did I wake you up? I've been trying to be quiet—I figured you were probably beat after yesterday."

"I was—I didn't even hear you come in." The events of the day before came back with a dizzying rush. Katie sat up against the headboard, and something crinkled under the sheets. She dug through the covers and there were the thin pale blue sheets of airmail paper that she'd been reading before she fell asleep.

"What's that?"

"It's . . ." Katie felt suddenly shy. "Uh, something I found in the hall closet. A box of letters. They go back to when Margaret was in college . . . There were a few that my mother sent to Margaret when she lived in Europe."

"Aunt Georgina?"

Katie paused, having never heard that phrase before. *Aunt Georgina.* "Did you ever meet my mom? I mean, other than that one time you visited when you were little?"

"Almost. This one time I went to see Gomma at the convalescent home, and she had just left." Scarlett's smile turned pensive. "I would have liked to, you know, but Mom always said . . ."

Her voice petered out and Katie felt embarrassed. "Look, Scarlett, I'm sorry we never made more of an effort. I mean, I know my mom and, uh, Grandma didn't get along. But now it seems kind of silly that Mom never brought me around to get to know you. I mean, not that it's all her fault. I should have, I don't know, tried harder."

It felt so strange to say the word "Grandma." All of Katie's life, her mother had referred to her as "Margaret," on the rare occasions when she deigned to say her name at all.

"Gomma told me your mom lived in France. Is that where Aunt Georgina sent those letters from?"

Katie looked down at the thin sheets, at her

215

mother's familiar loopy handwriting. "France, Switzerland, one from Lake Como in Italy. Well, that one was a postcard. Here." She handed over the postcards, touristy photos of fishing boats in Italy and a Swiss mountainside dotted with wildflowers.

"Wow, she went all those places? I've barely been out of Texas."

"Yes, she ran off to New York City right after she graduated from high school, and then after that she went to France. She's always pretty vague about how exactly she got by, but if I know my mom, some generous boyfriends were probably involved." Katie smiled at the thought. "She used to say that she went to the school of life instead of college."

"Wait, so she didn't even work??"

"That's a good question. I know she waitressed for a while, and she had some sort of job at a gallery. The thing is . . ." Katie hesitated, not sure she ought to confide in someone she just met, even if it was her cousin.

"Yeah?"

"Well, it's just— Mom always made it sound like Margaret threw her out of the house. Like she disowned her or something. But I don't know . . . if Margaret saved these letters all this time, well, I feel like she must have missed her. Worried about her."

"Well, of course she missed her," Scarlett said.

"She was still her mom, even if they didn't talk much. You said you found these in a closet?"

"I wasn't snooping—I was trying to find a blanket."

"Upstairs in the hallway? That closet?" Scarlett seemed surprised. "Were they underneath something?"

"No, just sitting there in a box. Here." She picked up the empty box from the floor, where it had fallen.

"That's weird. I've never seen it before. It was just on a shelf?"

"Um, yes, right in the middle. Next to a stack of towels."

"It's just that I *know* I looked through that closet before Gomma had her stroke. She used to ask me to get things down from high shelves." She stared at the box; it was labeled "Spring Step Comfort, Size 7.5." "I just feel like I would have noticed it. Oh! I brought you coffee, here."

Scarlett jumped up and went to get a Styrofoam cup from the dresser top. She was wearing a pair of cutoff shorts that barely covered her crotch and a tiny white sleeveless turtleneck that revealed enough of her midriff for Katie to see that a pink stone winked from her navel. Long, feathery silver earrings twisted through her colorful hair.

"Oh God, I think I might cry," Katie gasped, accepting the cup, which was still blessedly hot. "Remind me to buy you a really, really nice lunch. With cocktails."

"I didn't know what-all you take in your coffee," Scarlett said. "Mine's got sugar and creamer, if you want to trade."

"No, this is perfect," Katie said. She sipped, sighing contentedly.

"I would have made you some here, but Gomma quit drinking coffee because it didn't agree with her, and she gave her machine away. Oh, and I got you a sausage quesadilla too. Can I look through those while you're eating?"

She handed over the bag of food, and Katie handed her the box. She unwrapped the layers of waxy paper, inhaling gratefully. The first bite was pure greasy cheesy heaven.

"That's unbelievably good," she managed around a second bite, washing it down with another belt of coffee. "Sorry, I barely ate yesterday. I mean, I went down to the store and some guy mistook me for a homeless person, which, I guess I can't blame him, and he gave me some fried chicken that was amazing."

"Wow," Scarlett said reverently, examining each envelope and laying them carefully on the bed. "Did you read all of these?"

"Honestly, just the ones from my mom, and then I fell asleep. Do you recognize any of the other names?"

"Uh-uh." She picked up a square white

envelope, examined the return address, and carefully removed a folded sheet of paper. "This one's the oldest. 'Gertrude Bell.' Want me to read to you?"

"Sure," Katie mumbled around a mouthful.

"Dear Margaret, I hope this finds you well. As I write this, it's eleven degrees outside and Pop has his card club over so I'm holed up in my room, hiding. Christmas here was nice but I can't wait to get back to campus. You don't know how lucky you are to be in New London, they say it's going to snow every day next week!

"I'm still dreaming about that chestnut stuffing from Thanksgiving! Your mother was so gracious to me. I was just telling my friend Beth from high school about her and about the Tragedy she endured. I practically started crying just thinking about it. To think that she somehow found the strength not just to carry on but to care for your beautiful home and be involved in so many worthy causes.

("Wow," Scarlett said, looking up from the letter, "what a kiss-ass!")

"I've been thinking about the spring formal, Margaret, and I wondered if you might do me a small favor. Now that Carter and I have broken up, I wonder if Tripp might know a boy who might like to go to the dance with me. I've got a few fellows I'm thinking about but Tripp is so clever and kind. Once we get back to school we'll be so busy, I thought I would 'put a bug in your ear' now.

"Please give your parents my best, and see you soon! With Lyres and Pearls, we're the Greatest of Girls! Love, Gert."

Scarlett laid down the paper. "Lyres and pearls?"

"It's a sorority thing," Katie explained, feeling a bit embarrassed. "I think it's A Chi O. I had a friend who was a member. The lyre's their symbol, it's like a harp."

Scarlett raided an eyebrow doubtfully. "Honestly? She sounds like all she wanted was for Margaret to set her up."

"Was Tripp the guy she ended up marrying?" Katie asked, trying to remember if Georgina had ever told her the first name of her father, who had died when she was only a small child.

"No, that was Hank. Hank Dial. You didn't know your own grandfather's name?"

Katie sighed. "You'd have to know my mom. Or . . . well, you already know she didn't keep up with her relatives. She just didn't care much about family. I mean, I know that sounds terrible . . ." She trailed off, wondering how to explain without besmirching Margaret's memory. She couldn't exactly tell Scarlett that her beloved Gomma had—according to Georgina, anyway—been neglectful and borderline abusive, that she'd turned her back on her only child when Georgina

220

was broke and desperate. "I guess they just didn't get along."

Scarlett nodded. "I know it made Gomma sad. She didn't hardly talk about it, but every once in a while she'd say, 'I wonder what Georgie's up to these days,' or she'd see something in the Dallas news about a shooting or something and fret all week over whether your mom was safe."

"She did?"

"Uh-huh. Oh look, here's one from the museum." She smoothed out a typewritten page.

"That little building across from the school?"

"Mmm, they started it back when I was a little kid. It used to be a drugstore. This is from 1990. 'Dear Mrs. Dial, We are putting together a special exhibit about the Daisy children and their families and are looking for any memorabilia, photographs, or other materials you might be able to loan to the museum. In addition, we are soliciting first-person accounts and would be honored to include yours. Please contact us at the number below if you are interested.' Wow, I'm surprised Gomma even kept this—she didn't want anything to do with those folks."

"Who, the museum people? But why?"

Scarlett shrugged. "I don't know, really. I guess she just didn't like to think about it. With Gomma, she'd let you know if there was something she didn't want to talk about. Listen, can I read the rest of these after you're done with them?"

"Of course," Katie said, but her mind was on what Jam had said the night before: that Margaret had been "mean as a wasp and tough as stewed skunk." And yet, if she wasn't mistaken, he'd been fond of her. "By the way, Scarlett, do you know some guy named Jam that lives next door?"

"You met Jam?" Scarlett peered at her with interest, putting the letters back in the box before digging in the paper bag and pulling out a second quesadilla.

"Well, if you can call having him help me break into the house, and then him threatening me, meeting, then . . . yeah, I guess we met. Though it was dark—I don't think I'd know him from Adam in daylight."

"Well, he's . . ." Scarlett trailed off thoughtfully. She took a bite of her own quesadilla, chewed and swallowed, and dabbed at her lips with a napkin before finally saying, "Jam's interesting, that's for sure. He's had a hard life."

Katie turned that over in her head, wondering what would qualify as a *hard life* from the perspective of her cousin, who lived with a jerk boyfriend and had lost her only parent in a horrific accident and until last week had been working on the line in a factory.

"So listen," Scarlett continued, changing the subject. "I brought you some clothes and stuff. The lawyer thing's not until three o'clock, so what do you want to do until then? And also, like—do you know what people wear to see a lawyer? I mean, is a dress okay, or I have a suit—well, it's not really a suit, more of a jacket and skirt thing I wear for interviews . . ." She trailed off, peeking up at Katie uncertainly. "Honestly? The only lawyer I think I ever met was from when Merritt had to go to small claims court."

Katie had now let so many mentions of Merritt pass that it felt awkward to ask more about him. There was the casual way Scarlett had let slip the details she knew about Liam—she'd obviously cared more about the delicate thread of blood kinship that bound them than Katie did. Katie had never liked feeling socially unbalanced this way. She wished she'd asked Georgina a few more questions about her cousin while she had her on the phone.

"Well, I need to get to the bank," she said. "As soon as Liam lets me know which one, though . . ." She realized that she had no idea what time it was, and had no phone to check. But the sun was high in the sky, and besides, it was an hour later there, which meant that Liam would surely be at his desk by now. "Did he happen to text you?"

"My phone doesn't really do texts," Scarlett said. "I mean, not very well, anyway. Sometimes I get them, sometimes they're like hours late—that's the first thing I'm going to buy, I think."

"A new phone?"

"Yeah!" Scarlett's eyes lit up. "With texting and streaming and all that. I *had* an iPhone for a while—Jody, he was my boyfriend before Merritt, he gave me his old one. But I upgraded the operating system and then it wouldn't do shit." She shrugged. "This time I'm going to be like, put everything on that thing. All the memory, all the data, the . . . well, whatever they put on phones."

"That's really wonderful," Katie said, sincerely. She couldn't imagine getting by without her phone—the last twenty-four hours had been unnerving, to say the least. She—and everyone she knew in Boston—was tethered to her phone. She'd read somewhere about a study that revealed that women would go without sex before going without a phone and men would trade an inch of height before giving theirs up.

By now, on an ordinary day back home, she would have checked her schedule and caught up on her Instagram feed and taken at least a first pass at her email; she would have exchanged half a dozen texts with Liam and Lolly and sometimes Liam's sisters. She might have scheduled her wax (the salon had a convenient app for that), and at nine o'clock on the dot her thumb would be poised over the SisterCycle schedule, because that was when they opened up the classes for the next day, and if you didn't nail it right away the five-thirty after-work class would be gone.

By the time she left work at five-twenty with her gym bag slung over her arm, walking the two blocks from the office to the SisterCycle studio, her digital tracks would have taken her through four social media apps and dozens of texts and several laps around the work calendar and a Yelp review or two and—her secret indulgence—a round of SpellTower while in the bathroom, and she might have even used the thing to make or answer a call, though she and Liam and pretty much everyone she knew, with the exception of Georgina, did better texting.

"Hey," she said, overcome with a rush of generosity toward her cousin. "How about as soon as I get my new credit card, let's both go get new phones. You can put the plan on your credit card, but the setup and all will be my treat." She grinned, feeling pleased at this idea: the few hundred dollars it would take to set up the plan and get a phone in her cousin's hands would be a fitting gesture of gratitude, considering the ready kindness Scarlett had shown her.

"Oh," Scarlett said, and her face went through an odd series of subtle tics. "I mean, yeah, that's so great. Except I, um . . . well, I don't have a credit card anymore. Because of some things that happened . . . I mean, that's the *other* first thing I want to do, is get a new Visa. I probably have to get like one of those secured cards where you put the money on it up front—my friend did that.

After a year they let her have a thousand dollars in actual credit. But I mean, to start with, I'm probably just going to have to pay cash for the whole thing."

"Oh," Katie said, embarrassed. She did the calculations in her head—prepaying for the iPhone and service was more than she really ought to be spending. Especially if she really had come all the way down here only to score a few old teacups. "Well, tell you what, let's see where we are tomorrow, after the, um, lawyer and everything."

Except, *shit!* That meant that she couldn't very well go and get a phone of her own after having made the halfhearted offer to Scarlett. This was all getting so complicated, as though Katie had taken a wrong turn on a twisting path and found herself in another dimension.

"I really have to pee," she said instead, buying herself a little time to think. What she really needed to do was talk to Liam, and break it to him that she probably wasn't inheriting any life-changing sums of money. "And honestly, I badly need a shower. Would you mind . . ."

Scarlett unpretzeled her legs with the grace of a cat. "Go ahead! I'll just poke around. I only came here one time after she went in the home, to get her sweaters, but then some of the other patients stole them all. I mean, they didn't *mean* to steal them, they were just all so absentminded, with

226

the dementia and all." She sniffed delicately at the air. "Anyway, she definitely isn't here. She's moved on."

Katie resisted the urge to smile at the notion of the old woman haunting her home.

"Here's clothes," Scarlett said, offering Katie a lumpy white trash bag. "I brought a few things so you could pick. And there's some toiletries and stuff."

She dug into the bag and pulled out a cosmetic case, the kind that comes as a gift with purchase at the Clinique counter.

"Thank you." Katie accepted the bounty, touched. "This really means so much to me."

Maybe she ought to just take the plunge and buy the phone. Definitely, as soon as she got cleaned up and they went by the bank—and maybe she'd take them out to a nice lunch too. Even the nicest restaurant here probably cost less than a salad and a glass of chenin blanc at home.

CHAPTER SIXTEEN

September 1963

"Thursday," Margaret said, trying in vain to get Georgina to stay still enough to wipe the smudges of syrup from her cheeks. "Or maybe Friday, depending on whether it rains. He can't take them up in the rain."

Margaret had held out as long as she could before finally telling this lie, making it nearly all the way through breakfast before Caroline finally forced the issue, asking when precisely she could expect her son-in-law to join the rest of the family.

For nearly a month now, Margaret had been living in the groundskeeper's apartment with Georgina, sharing the one room, bathing her by making her sit on the counter with her feet in the sink and using a sponge. When her mother went to her weekly bridge game, Margaret took Georgina into the house and took a long soak in the tub with her, making sure that everything was clean and there was no evidence of their visit before she left. Her mother certainly wouldn't have minded if Margaret had asked—but Margaret was unwilling to ask for anything that wasn't absolutely necessary, and so they snuck around instead.

In this, she had an ally: Lucille, her mother's housekeeper, had been unfailingly kind since their arrival. Margaret knew that it couldn't be just because she was Alelia's niece; Margaret was fully aware that she had tested and tried Alelia's patience during her childhood and stormy adolescence. In retrospect, Margaret was astonished that Alelia had held her tongue as often as she had.

Mortifyingly, Margaret suspected that Lucille felt sorry for her, returning home without her husband and as poor as a church mouse. It was Lucille who had cleaned and prepared the apartment for her; when she climbed the stairs and opened the door with its tiny leaded-glass window, she was greeted with the scents of Ajax and vinegar, and every surface gleamed, even the old wobbly wooden table and the shaving mirror that hung from a nail. She opened the closet door and discovered, hanging from the rod, the clothes she hadn't liked well enough to take to college with her nearly a decade earlier: girlish full skirts and prim cardigans, dresses with outmoded, fussy details that wouldn't fit her anymore.

The second afternoon, wearing a sleeveless poplin that was too small and cut her cruelly around the middle, Margaret came to her room to find the dress she'd worn the day before washed, mended, and ironed and laid out on the bed. The other clothes had vanished, replaced by what were clearly her mother's castoffs: large enough to fit her, but unquestionably matronly.

"It certainly has taken him long enough to put his affairs in order," Caroline observed, as Lucille cleared the dishes from the table in the morning room. "I thought you said he'd found a buyer for the plane?"

This too was a lie, but at least one based on a shred of truth. Last week, Margaret had been convinced she'd finally talked some sense into Hank. He walked almost a mile every other night to borrow the neighbor's phone after dinner, and on Friday evening he reluctantly admitted that a man was coming out from the city to make an offer on the plane.

"It'd be like cutting off my own arm," Hank said morosely. "I only feel like myself anymore when I'm up there."

The words had stung, but Margaret was sure that if she could just get him to come, she could help tame the dark mood from which he'd had no relief since she left. "Your place is with us," she pleaded. "Georgie asks after you every day. She misses you so much."

"Goddamn it, Mags, you know that's not the issue. Hell, I miss you so much it's like I'm—I can barely stand it. I'm *starving* for you. But I can't—that place."

"It isn't forever," Margaret said. They'd had

230

this argument many times, but this time she was better prepared. "I went with Mrs. Alford to see a little place out past the Bradens' land. It's small but it's only ninety dollars a month. I know Daddy would give me the money for the first month. We don't even have to come visit here if you don't want to—we could move there right away and you won't have to spend a single night in Mother and Daddy's house."

"It isn't the house!" he snapped. "Do you think I care about that goddamn house? And your parents—they've got nothing to say to me. I'm a grown man. I won't take a cent from your father, but I have no quarrel with him."

"Then . . . what is it?"

The silence stretched so long that Margaret wondered if he'd set the phone down. "Hank . . . ?" she finally ventured.

"The school," he mumbled in a hollow voice. "I can't—I can't just walk by it every day as though—as though—I can't *forget,* Mags."

"The school? But it's not even the same school. It doesn't look anything like the old one. Besides, you passed by there every day for years."

For a moment he said nothing, but Margaret could hear him breathing. "It was different when I came home from the service. I couldn't— I had to get out. That's all Tansy was—a ticket out of there. You think I ever really wanted to work in her daddy's bank?"

"I *thought*," Margaret said hotly, "that you loved her. Most people do, you know, when they get married."

They'd rarely spoken about his first marriage; on the rare occasions when Tansy's name came up, Hank became oddly formal and unusually polite. Margaret had always assumed he felt guilty about the ignominious end of the marriage.

"Tansy was a nice girl," he retorted. "Sweet. When I got back home, she was just *there* . . . And she was easy on the eyes and never gave me any guff."

"Oh, I see," Margaret snapped. "Like me, I suppose you mean. Well, she never had a baby to look after, did she? And she never had to ask you for money, either. I'd like to see her try taking care of a house all by herself, to try stretching what you call a paycheck to take care of every little thing, with no help." The frustration and loneliness of the past weeks welled up in her with nowhere else to go. "But since she was so wonderful, I guess you could always call her up and see if she'll take you back."

"Shut up, Mags! You think I could have *loved* that girl? She was nothing to me. I tried, but— nothing means anything to me. Christ."

The desperation in his voice made Margaret wish she'd never brought Tansy up, never said anything at all to upset him. "Hank," she blurted. "I went to see Daddy's friend Dr. Galbo. He says that they have new medicines now, for, for moods. There's one called diazepam that, I mean, soldiers who came back from the war, with, when they're having trouble sleeping, or, or all the terrible things that happened—"

"You calling me *crazy,* Mags?" Hank's voice instantly hardened; if she'd been in the same room with him she would have instinctively ducked. Hank had never struck her, but he'd come close once, last year when he'd come home late in a terrible mood and she'd told him he could get his own supper; he'd drawn back his hand and stopped himself with a visible force of will. He'd brought her a bouquet the next day, but ever since then, there was a part of her that was always on alert.

"I never used the word *crazy,*" she protested. "It's just, the nightmares, the bad dreams—"

"I don't have nightmares!"

Margaret bit her lip; she'd tried to talk to him about his night terrors once before, but Hank grew angry when she told him that she'd woken him because he'd been crying out in his sleep, thrashing, his pillow damp with sweat.

"I have dreams," he conceded, in a calmer tone, after a moment. "There's times when I can't sleep. Me and every other man in this country."

"Well, there's help for that," Margaret said. Dr. Galbo, who lectured at Baylor in addition to his private practice, had listened carefully when

Margaret described the symptoms and suggested that Hank might be experiencing "psychoneurotic disorder." "The doctor says you just need some time to rest. And you can do that here."

She didn't share with Hank the other things Dr. Galbo had said—that his psychological issues were the result of infantile anxiety and hostility that had been buried until the air force years unleashed them; that his emotional defects had been present all along. Margaret had listened with a growing sense of despair, but also a kernel of outrage—how dare the sanctimonious Dr. Galbo, with his wall of diplomas and honors but not one moment in the armed service, call into question the deepest reaches of the man she loved?

She knew there were other men, those who'd come back missing arms and legs and pieces of their faces, with bullets embedded so far that they could never come out; and others who spent their days hunched in wheelchairs with hollow eyes and voices silenced forever. But that wasn't Hank. Her husband was always just slightly out of reach, there but not there, slipping achingly away the moment he left the house in the mornings or rolled off her at night.

There was one thing that Margaret had made sure that Dr. Galbo understood: she wasn't about to abandon hope. Hank was the turning point of her life—not just because he'd turned her from a silly rich girl to a woman in the lush bloom of passionate love; from an ingénue who rarely thought past what she would wear the next day to a wife and mother who put the needs of her husband and child ahead of her own. In the blink of an eye, loving Hank had made her believe that what they were together mattered more than anything they could ever accomplish alone.

It was true that Margaret had loved Hank since the first time he'd chased her and Helene down the back stairs of her house, earning a swat from Alelia. At four, Margaret had memorized teenage Hank's sunburnt, freckle-dusted face; had found it fascinating when he swaggered to the edge of the diving board at the pool, glancing slyly at his audience before cannonballing into the water. At six, she begged a ride in his parents' car when he got his driver's license.

When her bosoms seemed to swell overnight a number of years later, Margaret's first thought was to wonder whether Hank would notice. When she pilfered her mother's Folie Rose lipstick from her purse before a pancake breakfast hosted by the Lions Club, it was Hank she imagined kissing when she blotted on a square of toilet paper, just as she'd seen her mother do. And when Hank had driven away on his wedding night with Tansy's small blond head on his shoulder, a piece of Margaret's heart had broken off and drifted free.

But the years between sixteen and twenty-five had brought no shortage of changes of their own.

Now, Margaret understood, her soul (bruised by Hank, stunted by the strange tension between her father's generosity and his devotion—never spoken of—to her dead sister; between her mother's hovering scrutiny and the brittle distance she kept) had been lured by the promise of relief in the form of sorority dances, Saturday-night dates, autumn football games, summer crushes. She tended the fragile shoots of her own identity that her mother had planted and the Alpha Chi Omegas had nurtured, allowing herself to be feted and chased, toying with both boys and girls alike, ever bored and longing for something out of reach. Eventually it had been easiest to simply allow herself to be chosen, pinned, engaged, a prize won by the boy whom everyone around her had acknowledged to be the best.

And so she'd found herself on her mother's path—but Margaret, with no other outlet for the hunger and fire inside her, blazed bright enough to eclipse everyone around her. Caroline had had to carve out a life from the scraps that fell from the table of her wealthy employers, but Margaret—unfettered by her mother's humble beginnings—would settle for none other than the best to be had at UT. Her mother had landed the grandest home in New London, but Margaret would take her place among Austin's elite. If her mother—and here it grew complicated, because there was a murkiness in the past that Margaret could never understand (Why just the one child? Especially when her father had so clearly longed for more, and they could more than afford them.)—but anyway, if her mother had had one perfect little girl, the spoiled and celebrated and beloved Ruby, Margaret would have three or four: boys first, girls to follow, all of them smart and precocious and destined for charmed lives.

When she thought of Hank in those years (which she did, more often than she ever confessed to anyone), she felt almost ill with bitterness that Tansy had captured his heart first. She imagined him working near his father-in-law, perhaps by now the youngest vice president at the bank; imagined Tansy arranging flowers for the table in their home, waiting at the door for his kiss. (These notions had been naïve, but of course back then Margaret had known little about the practical aspects of marriage outside her parents' incomprehensible union.)

When word came that Hank and Tansy had split up (and it came through none other than Helene Dial, whom Margaret ran into on a visit home during the winter of her junior year), Margaret surprised herself by feeling, of all things, betrayed. Because if Hank could leave Tansy, who was perfect in every way, then what chance would Margaret have had with him?

She'd been in Linden's Pharmacy with a list of things her mother had asked her to pick up, and didn't recognize the thin woman dragging a snuffling little boy by the hand, clutching a bottle of calamine. Margaret had gotten in line behind her and been mildly repulsed by the angry red bumps of poison ivy on the little boy.

But after the clerk gave the stranger her change, and she turned to go, she spotted Margaret and her eyes widened. It took several seconds for Margaret to recognize her, and then it was too late to pretend not to have and escape without a conversation.

Helene forced a thin smile and looked her up and down. "Well, college agrees with you."

"And marriage agrees with you!" Margaret exclaimed. She made a few desultory comments about the little boy (named Billy after his father, who must have had an enormous forehead and a pronounced underbite if his little boy resembled him at all) and then couldn't resist asking.

"And how are Hank and Tansy?"

Helene regarded her through narrowed eyes, and it suddenly occurred to Margaret that the secret she thought she had guarded so carefully all those years, of her love for Hank, had not been a secret at all.

Helene tipped her head slightly to the side and said, "Actually, I wouldn't know. Hank hasn't been in touch lately, I'm afraid. Which means that I really must get home to Father, since there's no one but me and Mother to look after him."

And with that she cut their chance encounter short, leaving Margaret to goggle after her.

Of course, Helene had given her the entrée she needed with her own mother, for now she could say, "You'll never guess who I saw at Linden's—and what she told me!"

When she did, Caroline—who was tugging at a loose thread in her coat at the time, lamenting the purchase of an American designer recommended to her by her girl at Neiman's, a mistake she did not intend to repeat—rolled her eyes and said, "Oh, that. People really ought to mind their own business."

"But . . . why did he leave her?" Margaret asked innocently. "Surely she was faithful . . . ?"

"Margaret Anne!" Caroline reproved, tossing down the coat and whipping off her glasses. "Where on earth you get these notions, I've no idea!"

This conversation had often come back to Margaret during the eternal weeks since she'd returned home, because Caroline looked at her with precisely the same thin disgust that she had back then. Hank's ignominious annulment had been beneath her consideration then; now she was being made to endure the insult of having him as her son-in-law. Occasionally Margaret almost felt sorry for her mother: she could hear the pain and shame in the brittle, cheery comments Caroline made to her friends, as she tried to put the best face on an untenable domestic situation.

But this would be too much. In the matter of Hank's continued absence, as in so many things, her parents kept secrets from each other. The trip to see Dr. Galbo was framed, by her father, as a trip to see "a fellow who could use an ambitious young man like Margaret's Hank." If Caroline knew that they'd actually gone to discuss his psychological issues, it might be the last straw— Caroline might bar the gates to the family and forbid Hank entry. And while Margaret often fantasized about telling her mother off once and for all, she couldn't do so until she was sure that she and Hank were set up for whatever was to come next for them.

"No one needs to know," Margaret repeated, twisting the telephone cord around her fingers. "Dr. Galbo has an office in Tyler. We can say you're there for—for an injury sustained in the service. A training accident."

"Margaret, I swear to God that I'll never go see this quack or anyone else." She could hear Hank's breathing, heavy and labored—and something else, the slight slurring of the voice that signaled he'd been drinking. "Besides, you're barking up the wrong tree."

"What do you mean?"

"I never dream about the service. Come on, Mags, I told you that I loved flying. I *loved* it. Working on planes was the second-best thing to flying them."

"But I hear you, at night—"

"Stop!" Hank bellowed. Margaret cringed, imagining Hank in the neighbors' kitchen, as the rancher and his wife tried to pretend not to listen. After a moment he mumbled, "It's Ralphie—all right? It's always Ralphie."

Ralphie, the brother they never talked about, the lost boy, the child Helene was meant to replace. Ralphie, whom Hank knew he couldn't possibly have saved, but blamed himself nonetheless. Ralphie, whom time had gilded until he'd become as perfect in Hank's mind as Ruby was in her parents'.

"Hank," Margaret whispered, his pain mixing up with her own dull resentment. Wouldn't she ever be enough, for anyone?

"Never mind. Just—never mind. Look, I've got to go, the Martins need to get to their supper."

"Just promise me that you'll be here on time on Friday, won't you, dear?" Margaret said, trying to inject a note of cheer into her voice, reluctant to end the call on such a contentious note. "Mother's having Lucille make a roast, and Daddy wants to take you for a ride in his new car." When he said nothing, she plunged on. "And Georgie will be just deliriously happy. But most of all it's me, darling. I miss you. I *need* you. Don't make me wait another minute."

Another pause, one that ended with a cough that Margaret suspected he'd faked. "Sure, baby,"

Hank said. "You know I love you too. Always, and forever. Just—kiss Georgie for me. Tell her she's my best girl. Her and you—my best girls."

He hung up, leaving Margaret to remember that he'd said the same thing all those years ago on that sunny morning when she'd doused Helene with flour in the larder. "My best girls." Then, she'd been an afterthought, his kid sister's pal. And now Margaret felt like an afterthought once again—because Hank loved their daughter best of all.

The question echoed in her head. *Wouldn't she ever be enough?*

The next day, Margaret distracted herself with a rash of cleaning that was entirely unnecessary, as Lucille had scrubbed the apartment only the day before, changing the sheets and dusting and polishing every surface. Caroline had taken Georgina to lunch at the club after promising her a taffy apple if she promised to be good.

When Lucille came hurrying up the stairs without knocking, Margaret assumed it was for some last-minute detail in preparation for Hank's arrival: to inquire which side dishes he preferred, or to ask if he would expect breakfast or prefer to sleep in.

But when she saw the girl's stricken face, Margaret's heart slammed against her chest. "What?"

Then she was shaking the girl, her hands on her thin shoulders, snapping her head back and forth. *"What?"*

"It—it—there's a call for you. It's Mr. Dial. He's—there's been—his plane—an accident—"

Margaret released her and stumbled backward, hitting her ankle on the table leg. "Is he dead? Tell me—is he dead?"

Lucille was crying so hard that she could only nod.

CHAPTER SEVENTEEN

Katie came out of the bathroom feeling like a new person.

A person who smelled like mothballs and had a synthetic-lace wedgie and the makings of a blister between her toes from the platform wedge sandals with the little plastic flower clusters on the straps.

"Thanks so much for letting me borrow all of this," she said, wondering if she should have opted for dirty underwear over the thong Scarlett had supplied. Putting her jeans and boots back on was out of the question, given the fact that the day was turning unseasonably warm—and besides, the fringed white shorts did fit her pretty well, as she'd confirmed by checking out her ass in the full-length mirror on the back of the bathroom door.

"That top is perfect on you!" Scarlett gasped, rushing over to tug the peekaboo shoulders a little lower, frowning with concentration. "You have got the *nicest* tits. I'd give my right leg for them, I really would." She slapped a hand to her mouth. "Oh gosh, I'm sorry. That was really insensitive."

"Um . . . I mean, thanks, Scarlett," Katie said. "I thought it was kind of a nice compliment, actually."

"Yeah, but—" She pointed out the window at the house next door. "You know, with Jam and all."

"Sorry . . . I'm confused."

"Because of his *leg*." Scarlett tapped her knee for emphasis. "Oh come on, you didn't *notice?*"

"Didn't notice what?"

"That he's missing his right leg?"

Katie thought back to the night before, to the figure of a man standing under the eaves of the back porch, arms folded on his chest, watching the mangy dog eat. She certainly hadn't noticed anything amiss. "It was dark, and he was wearing pants, but—"

"Pants? He must have had an appointment with a new client," Scarlett said. "That's the only time he wears pants. And he hardly ever takes new clients, which means he must have been having a good day."

"That was him on a *good* day? Could've fooled me," Katie said with feeling. "He was awfully rude."

"Oh, that don't mean nothing. He was like that even before he went to Afghanistan."

Oh, Katie thought.

"But check this out, you have to see what I found." She picked up an old, threadbare scrapbook and opened it to a faded, sepia-tinted photograph. "This must have been Caroline's. I'd swear it was you."

Katie accepted the book, sitting down on the edge of the bed and opening it onto her lap. There, staring up at her, was . . . herself. Her unruly blond hair coming out of its bun, her wide-set pale eyes, her broad forehead and strong jaw, that nose . . . the long, lean shins and slightly chubby knees. Even the same smattering of freckles across her nose.

And in her arms: a perfect cherub of a chortling infant with darling fat little hands and feet and an eyelet romper.

Katie let out a sound, a cross between a sob and a gasp. Without thinking she reached out and touched the baby's cheek in the photograph.

"I know, it's amazing, isn't it?" Scarlett said. "It's got to be Gomma when she was a baby, with Caroline. You look so much like her."

"It's—it's really remarkable," Katie said. She took a breath and forced the thought of her own lost baby out of her mind. "Where is this taken?"

"You can't tell? That's the courthouse in the background—we drove right past it on the way into town." Scarlett wrinkled her nose. "Good thing they moved the fulfillment center, it was going to completely ruin the town."

"Wait. They moved it? Where?"

"Out of town a couple miles, halfway to Leverett's Chapel." She looked smug. "There's nothing out there but dirt and cows and a few rigs, so even if they want to bulldoze it and put in some huge parking lot, at least the rest of us won't have to look at it."

"But . . ." Katie tried to hide her dismay. Any premium the house might have fetched by being practically next door to the fulfillment center disappeared in the blink of an eye. "Wasn't the town worried about losing the extra revenue?"

"That's the beauty of it! They're still going to honor the deal they made—they're giving money for a new middle school and fixing up the hospital, but now they won't mess up the town with traffic and stuff. We shut down this housing development they had planned too; they finally gave up and moved it to Henderson." She grinned. "I guess the protestors there didn't get their shit together in time. Their loss!"

"But, Scarlett—this house would be worth a lot more money if the fulfillment center moved *here*."

"Yeah, I guess. But then some Amazon employee would be living here instead of us." She shrugged. "I mean, I know we can't keep the world out forever. Once people see how pretty it is here, it's just a matter of time. I guess I'm just old-fashioned."

This coming from a girl with red monkeys tattooed across her chest and a fake diamond in her nose.

As Scarlett set the scrapbook on the dresser, a paper fell out and fluttered to the floor. Katie picked it up: a hand-drawn invitation, with graceful floral boughs surrounding the year 1940 and the words *Daisy Club First Annual Benefit Dinner*. Underneath, in smaller script: *Proceeds to be donated to the fund for the construction of the New London Cenotaph*. And at the bottom, in the smallest letters of all: *In memory of those we lost*.

Inside the folded invitation, a menu was listed along with various prizes that would be raffled off. Katie turned it over; on the back was a listing of the Daisy Club members. She scanned the list and there, second from the bottom, was Caroline Pierson.

"But I thought—you said that Caroline didn't ever want to talk about what happened," Katie said. "Why would she join this club? It looks like the sole purpose was to raise money for the memorial."

"Oh, no, that's not what the club was for. It was for the replacement babies."

"The what?"

"The babies that families had to replace the ones that died in the explosion." Scarlett looked at her curiously. "You didn't know that? Gomma was born like nine months after the disaster. Her birthday was December 28."

"The same year?"

"Yup, 1937. But actually, now that I think about it, Gomma didn't tell me that; I found out when my second-grade class went to the museum on a field trip. They had a little display of Daisy Club stuff, old photos and meeting minutes and attendance lists. There were eleven kids and their moms, and they kept meeting until the kids were in high school. I guess it started as a play group—they got together for luncheons and the maids would watch the kids, and then later when the kids were in school, it was just the moms who met."

"So you're saying that these women—the Daisy moms—they deliberately got pregnant after the school explosion to create *replacements?*" Katie repeated, fascinated. "That seems so, uh, wrong. Like a good way to really mess up a kid, knowing they only existed to make up for a dead sibling. I mean, did all the kids know? Was it like an acknowledged thing?"

"Things were a lot different then," Scarlett said. "Gomma said her mother never even told her about *sex,* so I kind of doubt they had a lot of heart-to-heart talks. She said Caroline wasn't very affectionate, that their maid did more to raise her than Caroline ever did."

Katie thought that over for a minute. "But if she wasn't all that into being a mother . . . why do you think she got pregnant the minute she lost her first child?"

"I don't know if she wasn't into being a mother, exactly," Scarlett said slowly. "Gomma said Caroline just had a hard time showing her emotions. I mean, Gomma's the same way. *Was* the same way. She kind of implied that's what made trouble between her and your mom. I mean, I'm sorry if that's too personal, Katie, it's none of my business—"

"No, no, not at all, this is . . . I mean, Georgina never talks about the past; it's like pulling teeth just to get her to tell me the most basic things." A thought occurred to her—had Georgina known about the Daisies? Something to ask her when they were sitting on the patio with a bottle of pinot gris, perhaps. "I think Georgina just sort of wrote Margaret off because she felt like she wasn't there for her when she got pregnant with me."

"That's sad."

"Yeah, I know. I'm just realizing that we're like the fourth generation of women in our family to have issues with their moms. It's like it's a genetic trait or something." She clapped her hand over her mouth. "Oh God, I'm so sorry, Scarlett, I didn't mean—I just didn't think. You and your mom were close, weren't you?"

Scarlett nodded vigorously, her eyes shiny. "Yes. She was my best friend. And you're going to be a great mom too, Katie."

Now it was Katie's turn to get a little teary.

"Thank you, but I don't . . . well, honestly, maybe it's for the best that it isn't happening. At least not now."

"Why not? I mean, you can't wait forever, right?"

Katie stopped herself from pointing out that she was hardly over the hill, but she'd forgotten that women had children a lot younger here than they did on the East Coast. "It's not that. It's just . . . things haven't been exactly great for me and Liam lately. I mean, I'm sure we'll work it out; it's just that he's incredibly busy at work, and he seems, well . . ."

Unenthusiastic. That was the word that came to mind, now that she gave it some thought. Sure, she was the one who had to track her ovulation, and consequently to initiate sex, but lately Liam seemed to anticipate their best days and be otherwise engaged: staying late at work, or taking his interns out for drinks, or playing basketball with Rex—any excuse, it sometimes seemed to Katie, would do.

But if she was *really* honest with herself, there were days when the app gave its encouraging chirp and she felt a sense of reluctance . . . almost dread. Not about the possibility of a baby— Katie longed for the miracle of a child growing inside her, the sweetness of an infant in her arms, more than ever. But sharing the experience with Liam—trying to convince him to go to childbirth classes, to talk to HR about paternity leave, to agree to move to a bigger place—maybe even a move to the suburbs that he scorned—would only lead to more arguments, more passive-aggressive sniping, more stony silence between them.

"Is he good to you, Katie?" Scarlett asked in a very small voice.

And suddenly Katie remembered the voice on the other end of the phone, yelling about ham and money. The fact that Scarlett couldn't even bring her home.

"Very good," she said. "Oh, we have problems like everyone else, but he's great. Wow, it's getting late—how about we get started on those errands so we make it to the attorney's on time?"

While Katie went to see about getting a new debit card at the bank branch in Harrison, Scarlett went off on a mysterious errand, promising to meet her in half an hour.

Katie was glad to be alone for this encounter, since she was afraid she might have to go all-out-bitch on the poor teller, something she wouldn't do if the situation weren't so desperate.

She gave the teller her brightest smile. "Hi! I've got kind of an unusual request." She described the mugging and trip across the country as succinctly as she could. "So what I was hoping was, since I've got my driver's license to prove it's me, that you could give me a cash advance on my Visa card account with this bank. I know I'm close to the limit, but I thought maybe you could bump me up temporarily, I mean, just until I get back home and have a chance to straighten this all out?"

"Why sure, honey, let's give it a try," the woman said. But after tapping on her keyboard for several agonizing minutes, she sighed. "I'm sorry, doll, it's just not coming up."

"Try under my husband's name. Liam Garrett."

More tapping. "Okay, yes, I do see a silver plus account for your husband. But unfortunately you're not on that account."

"What? But we're *married,* we share all of our accounts. I use my card all the time. Like literally *all* the time."

"Oh, I do understand, but it's *Mr.* Garrett's card. You're just on there as an authorized user. Without speaking to Mr. Garrett directly I can't increase the limit."

"Let me borrow your phone. I'll call him." As soon as the words were out Katie regretted her tone. "Please."

"I'm sorry, ma'am, I don't have a phone here." The woman looked pointedly past Katie, where the line had somehow doubled behind her.

"Okay," she said, already backing away, her face hot. "Fine. I understand. I'll go make the call and then I'll come back."

"Sure thing, hon."

Outside, Katie leaned against the unforgiving granite of the old bank building, taking deep breaths. She spotted Scarlett across the street, waiting for the light to change, hunched over her own phone, frowning. After a moment she held the phone away and looked at the screen, then slowly put it in her pocket.

Katie would bet that she'd just been hung up on. As the light changed and Scarlett started across the street, Katie slipped back into the entry to the building, then pretended to be coming out the door when Scarlett got to her side of the street.

"Oh, there you are," she said. "Did you get what you needed?"

Scarlett held up a little brown paper bag. "Hex bolts," she said. "Twenty-two cents each, so at least I can afford them. Only, I don't think they're the right ones. Merritt didn't say what size, and there's like six different ones."

Above the bank, there was an old-fashioned time and temperature sign. Eighty-six degrees at 12:54—and Katie's stomach was growling again. "Well, I didn't have any luck either. Do you think I could borrow your phone again?"

They sat down on a bench in front of the bank, and Katie tried Liam.

"Hey, Kate." This time Liam sounded like himself when he picked up.

"Liam," Katie said, all the stress of the morning

making her shrill. "I've just been at the bank. They won't advance me any cash on your card because apparently it's *your card*. Like I'm just some sort of secondary user. What the hell, Liam, you didn't trust me to have my own goddamn card?"

"Whoa, hey, slow down," he said. "You were there when we opened that account. You could have said something then."

"I didn't realize I had to say anything because I assumed that we were both adults!" This conversation wasn't going the way she'd intended.

"Look, Katie, I don't have time to sit here getting yelled at right now. Go check the front door. Rex said that Lolly overnighted you some cash. It was supposed to be there by three."

Katie felt a rush of gratitude—that was exactly something Lolly would do. She made a mental note to invite Lolly and Rex for dinner, with good wine and her wedding china.

"Well, it's not even one here, Liam. Time change, remember?" And also, why had Lolly sent it, and not him? "How much cash did she send?"

"I don't know . . . a couple hundred? And they're also supposed to be sending you a new debit card. It cost thirty-five bucks extra to rush it."

"Oh," Katie said shortly. "Well, gee, I hope you could spare it."

"Hey. Look. I'm sorry, okay? We're trying. *I* don't have any cash either, just so you know. I had to ask one of my interns to cover me at lunch. Also, I had to wait like seven hours for the cops to come, and I highly doubt they're actually going to do anything. The guy said they've had a lot of these lately."

"Huh," Katie said, picturing Liam holding court at lunch, spinning the story of their mugging into entertainment for his little band of interns. He'd emerge as a self-effacing hero—and the interns would probably fight over who got to pick up the tab.

"Right. Okay." Now he was pissed off too. "Well, you're welcome. Look, one of us is still working, okay, and this set me back for the rest of the week. I might have to miss Gavin's promotion thing."

"That's tonight?" Katie had never liked Liam's friend Gavin. "Wasn't that couples?"

"Well, yeah, but I am capable of holding a conversation on my own, Katie." Liam sounded even more pissed.

"No, I just meant—never mind. Tell him congratulations and I'm sorry to miss it."

"Yeah, okay." Katie could hear laughter in the background—she pictured the conference room she'd seen only once, when she'd accompanied Liam to his holiday party. There had been beanbag chairs in the corners of the room and a pair of foam antlers mounted over the door.

"Look, Kate—"

"I have to go," she said. "Tell Lolly thanks."

"I'll try you tonight."

"On what? I don't have a phone, remember? I'm using my cousin's."

"Yeah. Okay, right. Well, then you can try me, okay?"

"Uh-huh. Bye."

When Katie handed the phone back, Scarlett gave her a little smile. "Any luck?"

"Yeah, I guess my friend Lolly sent some cash. It's supposed to get to the house by three. I just hope he had the right address." Her stomach growled again, and she covered it with her hand, embarrassed. It was still two hours until their appointment with the lawyer. "Listen, Scarlett, I really hate to ask, but do you think I could borrow some money for lunch, and I'll pay you back tonight?"

"Um, yeah, but . . ." Scarlett stared down at her lap. "I've got cash at home, but Merritt's kind of . . . I don't think this is maybe the best time to meet him. He's, you know how guys are, he's been working on the retaining wall all morning. And I guess I got the wrong screws but he couldn't tell me what exact size he needed and . . . anyway, he'll be fine once he gets it done. So, like, tomorrow would be a good time, we could maybe sit out in the backyard or something. Hey, but listen!" She brightened, sitting up. "I know where we can get some lunch. It's Friday, right?"

Katie had to think about it for a minute. "Yes—"

"Well, come on! It's just down the street."

"Scarlett, we're not going to a soup kitchen or anything, are we?"

Scarlett laughed. "No. Friday's hog day."

Hogs, it turned out, meant motorcycles—and also pork ribs slow-cooked on a massive steel-drum smoker in a parking lot behind a garage with a half dozen bikes in various states of repair, refurbishment, and customization. A woman with short blue hair and dime-size holes in her ears emerged from the garage with a beer in her hand and gave Scarlett a hug.

"Wondered when you were going to show up," she said. "I heard a rumor you quit your job."

"Rumor's true!" Scarlett said. "Maude, this is my cousin Katie. Katie, I've been friends with Maude since kindergarten."

"So you're the prodigal cousin," Maude said. "It's nice to meet you, Katie." She wiped her free hand on her cutoff overalls before shaking Katie's hand.

"Is this your garage?"

"Me and my brother," Maude said. "He's around here somewhere—I sent him down to the market for more buns, but he should be back any minute."

"You guys got a good turnout today," Scarlett observed.

"Yeah, well, it's a good cause and all, right? We're raising money for Rover Ranch," Maude explained to Katie, pointing to a banner hung over one of the garage bays, which featured a silhouette of a dog leaping for a Frisbee. "They're a no-kill shelter. The puppies are pretty easy to place, but it's kind of hard to find people willing to take the older dogs, especially the ones they rescue from breeding operations. A lot of times they've lived their whole life in a cage and they've got a lot of behavior problems."

As if on cue, a chubby bulldog came trotting through the crowd with a package of buns hanging from its mouth. "Sadie!" Maude scolded, making a grab for the dog and managing to snag her collar. She dropped the bag of buns and collapsed at Maude's feet, rolling over on her back with her tongue hanging out.

"Sadie had eight litters before she was rescued," Maude said, bending to scratch her stomach. "Now she's our official shop dog. She likes to ride in my brother's sidecar."

"Eight litters? That's—that's awful," Katie gasped.

Scarlett shrugged. "These people just keep breeding them until they get too sick and then they put them down, unless someone turns them in. Come on, let's get something to eat."

Katie followed Scarlett through the crowd. Twenty-five or thirty people of all ages, some dressed for work, others in shorts and T-shirts, ate from paper plates. Manning the grill, half hidden behind a cloud of smoke, was a thirtyish man in a gray T-shirt stretched tight over well-developed muscles. His sun-bleached hair was cut short and he wore mirrored sunglasses and a scowl.

"Hey, now I can introduce you properly," Scarlett said. "Hi, Jam."

The man looked up just as Katie noticed that, under his cargo shorts, he had a prosthetic leg, a high-tech chrome assemblage that looked at odds with his well-worn, dingy sneakers.

"Scarlett," he said, in the same unfriendly tone Katie remembered from the night before.

"So I think you met my cousin," Scarlett said. "Katie's visiting all the way from Boston."

"Yeah, so you said." He glanced at Katie. "Burger or ribs?"

"What's your specialty?" Katie asked, determined to thaw his icy demeanor. "They both look delicious."

He merely shrugged. "Depends what you like, I guess."

"Have the ribs, Katie. Jam, give us a couple plates and pile 'em high. We're *starving*."

"Are you involved with the Rover Rescue?" Katie tried again.

"Rover Ranch," Jam corrected. "Yeah, I guess."

260

"He takes the tough cases," Scarlett said. "The ones that have so many behavior problems none of the other agencies will accept them."

Jam made a grunt that could have been agreement or disgust.

"That's admirable," Katie said, remembering the care with which he placed the food on the porch the night before, the wariness of the dog as it slunk past her.

"Not really. I'm already training my paying clients anyway," Jam said. "A few more don't make any difference."

He handed them each a plate piled with a mound of ribs glistening with sauce. The delicious aroma made Katie salivate. "Well, thank you," she said.

That earned her another grunt.

Scarlett led the way to a folding table with two empty seats. "Sadie was one of Jam's dogs," she said. "When he first took her in, she peed everywhere and she'd shake whenever anyone came close to her. She was so bad he kept her crate in his bedroom for a few months before he could bring her around any other people."

"How did you get to be friends with him?" Katie asked. "He doesn't seem especially, um, friendly."

Scarlett dug into the pile of ribs. "I mean, yeah, I guess if you don't know him—but he moved next door to Gomma with his mom when he was in high school. I was just a little kid, but he was always nice to me. In a kind of grumpy way. I used to sneak into their yard through the fence and he'd let me hang around until Gomma came and got me. I think he was my first big crush."

"And then after high school he went into the service?"

"Yeah, he went to college for a couple years but I don't think he liked it. He joined the marines—his mom had a fit. But he used to come home whenever he was on leave. When he got hurt, everyone thought he'd stay put, but he went to work at this military dog training school out in North Carolina instead. He only came home for good when his mom got married and moved to Oklahoma. He took over the mortgage." She shrugged. "He really is nice, when you get to know him. You should eat—they're best when they're hot."

Katie did as her cousin suggested and dug in. At first she tried to keep the sauce from getting all over her hands, but after a few bites of the delicious, smoky meat, she gave up and ate like everyone else at the table, with her elbows on the flowered tablecloth and big gulps of lemonade to wash it down.

It was only when she looked up and saw Jam staring thoughtfully at her, iron tongs idle in his hand, that she worried that she had sauce all over her face.

Chapter Eighteen

September 1963

Margaret stood very still while Lucille fastened the buttons of her cuffs: four each, tiny ebony balls pushed through black crape loops. Downstairs, Caroline was watching Georgina, who didn't understand a lick of what was going on, and had asked once too often why they couldn't go for ice cream.

When Margaret slapped her daughter's hand at breakfast after she nearly knocked over the syrup pitcher, Caroline had ordered her back to the apartment. Lucille had followed moments later.

"Miss Margaret, you know I'm a widow too," Lucille said, as she finished the cuffs and got to work on Margaret's hair. Margaret hadn't so much agreed to allow Lucille to arrange it as run out of energy to keep saying no. Her hands were hard and rough but she barely pulled, teasing out the tangles carefully with the metal comb.

"That can't be," Margaret said dully. "You're hardly old enough to be married."

"I'm twenty-four."

Through the haze of her grief, Margaret

263

was surprised—Lucille looked no older than seventeen or eighteen. She'd come to the family nearly two years earlier, when Alelia had a stroke.

"My Will, he was down to the sorghum plant helping a man load a truck," Lucille went on. "The axle broke and the truck ran him up against the wall. That was two years now. So I know what you're feeling, I do, and I can't say it'll ever get any better. But it do get easier."

Margaret peered at Lucille in the mirror with renewed interest. Dr. Galbo had given her some pills that he said would help her sleep; instead they had made her feel thick and sort of spongy, as though she was sitting next to herself and trying to speak around a mouthful of cotton.

"Easier?"

Lucille paused, meeting her eyes in the mirror, and appeared to genuinely consider the question. "Well, maybe not for you, since you have a child. Will and me, we never had time to. But the feeling like you wish you'd gone and died with 'em—that's the part that maybe doesn't last forever."

There was a knock at the doorframe. Caroline had come up the stairs without announcing herself, already dressed in her black suit. "If we might have a minute, Lucille."

"Sure, ma'am, I've just now finished up." Lucille left in a hurry, with a last glance at Margaret.

Caroline waited until she was gone and then lowered herself gingerly on the edge of the bed, the only other place to sit besides the single hardback chair. She looked around the room, sighing. "*Now* will you listen to reason and move back into the house? Georgina can have her own room, and so can you."

"Mother," Margaret said tensely. "My husband has been dead for five days. Do you think you could wait a little longer before you wash your hands of him?"

"I beg your pardon!" Caroline shot back. "I simply made a suggestion that would make you and your daughter—my granddaughter—much more comfortable. *Especially* because of what's happened. You'd be able to receive callers with a little bit of—of—*dignity*."

"Is that what this is about? I shouldn't be surprised. That's all you've ever cared about—the way people see you. See *us*."

"Margaret—"

"I'm sorry this happened, Mother, okay? I'm sorry I didn't marry someone who was worthy of you and Daddy. And I'm sorry that he's dead and left me with nothing and I'm a burden to you all over again."

"Sorry, sorry, sorry!" Caroline snapped. "Don't be so melodramatic."

She jumped up and began pacing the small room, her shoes tapping out a tense rhythm on the floor. Her mourning suit was trimmed with satin welting, the jacket fitting perfectly over an elegant, narrow skirt. Lucille had confided in Margaret that the suit had been purchased a year ago for the funeral of one of Hugh's business associates. So: her mother hadn't even bothered to buy something new for her son-in-law's funeral.

As she paced, Caroline seemed to grow angrier, and Margaret was thrown off course. She'd always managed her mother with her own displays of emotion: tantrums when she was a child, and as she grew, threats and demands and pleading. "She's a dramatic child," her mother would say in Daisy Club gatherings when the children were eight or ten or twelve and Margaret's outbursts took center stage. Some of the other Daisies had given almost as well as they'd gotten, and the other mothers would nod in chagrin: they too had treated their replacement babies with kid gloves, sparing not only the rod but any discipline at all.

The Daisies were undeniably spoiled, one more thing that bound them all together: Daisy mothers understood, and let their children's behavior pass without judgment.

Now, though, it was Caroline who appeared ready to fly into a rage. Which was all the more confusing, because she certainly hadn't lost anything she cared about. In the four years

266

of Margaret's marriage, Caroline—who after Georgina's birth had made an awkward truce, sending gifts and letters to Margaret, and many more for Georgina—had never, not once, acknowledged Hank. No birthday card, no Christmas gift, and certainly not a peep on their anniversary.

The memory hit Margaret in the gut. "It would have been our fifth anniversary next month," she snapped, seizing one of the folded, pressed handkerchiefs that Lucille had left on the table and dabbing her eyes. "And I'll never have another with him."

"So?" Caroline whirled around. "He was only a husband, Margaret. Even with the stunts you've pulled, you can probably find another one. Mark my words, you'll look back on this years from now and it will probably seem as though fate did you a favor."

Margaret leapt to her feet. "What did you say?"

But Caroline stared her down. "You heard me. Hank was a drunk. He was too busy burning through whatever money he made to take care of you and Georgina. People talked about it all the way back here in New London, Margaret. His parents would have died of shame."

All of the things that Hank had confided during his darkest moments—the dreams of Ralphie, memories of the fire raging in the rubble, his hands burning while he tried to free his brother—

how was it that Caroline could never understand? "I loved him!" Margaret cried, not caring that the windows were open, that all of the neighborhood could hear.

"You *loved* him!" Caroline echoed, her voice gone high and mocking. "You think so, truly? You think that love would have carried you through another year, a decade, the rest of your life? Do you really believe a man like that would have stayed with you? He already left one woman, Margaret. He'd have left you too. At least he had the courtesy to do it this way."

Margaret picked up the pitcher from the table and threw it across the room. It shattered against the wall, shards of pottery crashing to the floor.

Caroline merely shook her head in disgust. "You stupid girl. I blame myself. We expected much too little of you, we were always so concerned about protecting you. And look what you've become."

"What have I become, Mother?" Margaret asked, aiming for defiance, the waver in her voice giving her away.

"You want to know about real loss?" Caroline said, walking to the window and looking out on the garden. Last week, the gardener had stocked the pond with golden tench, and their scales glistened in the sun as they flicked through the water. The magnolia tree had just come into bloom, heavy blossoms weighing down the

268

branches and carpeting the lawn, but Caroline didn't appear to notice any of it, staring out at the treetops. "Real loss is feeling the floors shake before you even hear the boom, seeing the bricks fall from the walls. Hearing the windows shatter and seeing the smoke rise up, and all the mothers running like we've never run before, and getting outside only to see that it was—it was just gone, fire burning up what was left, and the screaming, and knowing—I knew, the minute I saw it I knew she was gone. But it doesn't stop there. I called her name for hours, until my throat was raw, I wanted to run into the broken buildings, they had to hold me back, some man I didn't recognize, I still don't know who he was, because the first of the volunteers didn't show up for half an hour, driving in from—well, you know that part of the story."

Say her name, Margaret willed her. She had grown up hearing versions of this story, over and over and over, from people who'd been there and those who'd learned it secondhand; from those who'd helped sift the rubble for the bodies and those who'd made sandwiches and coffee, those who'd laid out the little broken bodies—and parts—under donated blankets.

But never from her parents. And the other Daisies confirmed that it was so at their houses too: there might be photographs of the lost, carefully preserved reminders, favorite dolls and toys and art projects. Some parents kept shrines to their lost children; others preserved entire rooms just as they were the day when the children left for school.

But few of them could talk about the day. And her parents never had. Not until now.

"Saint Ruby," Margaret cried. "Why'd you even have me, when I could never measure up to her memory?"

"This isn't about you," Caroline shot back. "For once, please, just admit that you aren't the center of the universe. I'm telling you about grief. About *real* grief, not this—this romantic fantasy of yours."

"You want me to believe you loved her more than anything?" Margaret said. "I'll tell you what, I believe you loved her more than me. That's easy. There's never been room in your heart for me. But Alelia told me, *she* was the one who raised Ruby. You were too busy with your clubs and your committees, so intent on climbing the ladder, feeling like everyone was beneath you. You forget: I was your daughter too. Not once did you ever make me feel like I could take her place, that I was really yours."

And damn it, she was crying now, big messy gasping sobs and tears streaking down her face. She wouldn't have guessed there was room in her heart for more hurt, but it was almost as if she was a child again. Watching her mother put on her coat to go out while Alelia wiped away her tears and tried to console her. Lying in bed at night and wondering why her mother didn't ever come for a good-night kiss.

"At least Daddy tried," Margaret finished, miserably. "He always tried to keep me from seeing that his heart was broken, that he'd trade me for Ruby in a second. He—he—" But her voice broke, and she couldn't tell her mother that at least her father had swung her in the air as a toddler, had held her hand while she tossed stale bread for the ducks, that he'd bought her a bouquet of white roses for her twelfth birthday and a birthstone necklace for her sixteenth.

"Stop that ridiculous whining." Caroline's face was pinched. "Your father and I gave you everything. We did the best we could for you. It's never enough, is it?"

"I guess not."

Caroline went to the door, but at the last minute she turned around and looked back. Her eyes were dry and dull; her expression grim. "Well then, I guess we're even," she said. "Because you were never enough for me either."

CHAPTER NINETEEN

"You're sure we don't need to go home and change clothes?" Scarlett asked, after they'd finished their meal and helped Maude and her brother break down the tables and clean up the trash.

"I think we're fine," Katie said, as she took a last look around the parking lot. At some point, Jam had simply vanished, without saying goodbye to anyone. Katie found herself oddly disappointed.

She'd caught him watching her several times— but only because she couldn't seem to keep herself from staring at him. It wasn't that he was easy on the eyes—though he was, almost ridiculously so, with those Marine Corps abs and that gorgeous face that he did his very best to spoil by scowling. And it wasn't the leg, either; he moved so easily on his prosthetic that she barely registered its presence.

It was the riddle of all the kindness that he seemed so determined to hide. What kind of teenager lets the bratty kid next door hang out in his backyard? What kind of man chooses a career in the military after it nearly kills him, only to return to civilian life because his family needs him? What kind of man pretends that his work with helpless and abused animals is insignificant—then

272

spends his free time rehabilitating lost causes?

What kind of man had made a friend of the woman her own mother had described as a coldhearted monster?

A man very different from the one she had married, that was for sure. Liam wasn't a bad person—he had many great qualities, including keen intelligence, a sharp wit, a sense of humor. And he was good-looking, of course, though perhaps not as jaw-droppingly so as Jam.

But Liam looked out for Liam first. He'd landed the job at Boston's top ad agency by working his connections for all they were worth. With the exception of Rex, most of his friends seemed to have been chosen for the introductions they could make, the social circles in which they moved. Katie had known that when she married him, and she'd been happy to ride his coattails to the enviable life they'd built.

Here in New London, she was an outsider again. No one cared about her address, her wardrobe, the number of likes on her Instagram posts.

"Well, at least come fix up with me. The restroom's a two-seater," Scarlett said. "You can keep me company."

In the bathroom, Katie rinsed off her face and scrubbed the barbecue sauce from under her fingernails. Then she relinquished the mirror to Scarlett, taking a seat on a bench covered in fabric depicting pinup girls on roller skates, and watched as her cousin reapplied her makeup, from ebony eyeliner that winged out at the edges to a dab of gold shimmer on her already full lower lip

"Do you think I look okay?" Scarlett asked when she was finally finished.

"Honestly, you look beautiful, but I really don' think you need to worry about it. The lawyer's already been paid by Margaret. Uh, Grandma *Gomma.*" The name still felt a little strange on her lips. "He works for *us,* if you want to look a it that way."

"I guess," Scarlett mumbled. "I kind of wish we had time to run by the house, but it can be awful hard to find parking in downtown Tyler."

As Scarlett drove, Katie noticed the fuel gauge was hovering dangerously close to empty. She didn't mention it, because neither of them had any money to do anything about it. When they arrived at the lawyer's office, Katie had to stifle a laugh: unlike the near-impossible task of finding a free parking space in the Back Bay or Beacon Hill, a man in a cowboy hat actually stood in an empty parking space right in front of the building and waved them in, then tipped his hat and ambled away before they could thank him.

And parking was *free.*

Katie took the lead, hoping to calm her cousin's nerves. "We're here to see J. B. McNaughton," she told the receptionist, a young woman in a gauzy vintage-style dress and bright red glasses.

"Be right with you," she said, and hammered at her keyboard for a few seconds. "That'll show 'em. Okay. You must be Scarlett and Katie. Nice to meet you."

She stood up and offered her hand.

"Oh!" Katie said. "You're . . . J.B.?"

"Janice Beth," the young attorney said with a sly grin. "I use the initials to throw people off. Y'all go ahead, let's sit over here."

Now Katie realized that what she'd mistaken for a reception area was actually the entire office. A small round table with four chairs served as a conference table, and a glass-front cabinet kept books and files out of the way. The only ornamentation was a battered silk fern in a mauve ceramic pot, and half a dozen crayon drawings taped to the wall.

"My niece is the artist," J.B. said, following Katie's gaze. "She's a real pistol. Reminds me of me. Got to say, I've been real curious to meet you two after working for your grandmother-slash-cousin for the last few years." Noting Scarlett's look of surprise, she added, "I know I look young, but I promise I passed the bar. Margaret was one of my very first clients. She told me she wouldn't pay my full rate until I proved I could do the job. Never did give me a raise, either."

"Gomma was kind of cheap," Scarlett admitted.

J.B. chuckled and picked up a piece of paper from a manila folder she'd brought to the table. "You can say that again. When the appraiser she hired gave me this inventory of the contents of the house, he said he was pretty sure she hadn't bought anything new in years."

"Excuse me," Katie said. "You said *Margaret* hired an appraiser?"

"Oh, yes. She did it shortly after she had me revise her will, over a year before she had her stroke. She wanted every detail addressed, and I have to say, the man she hired was amazingly thorough." She glanced down at the list. " 'Seven pillowcases, various colors, standard size. Tissue box cover, crocheted.' And on and on for fourteen pages. I can only imagine what she put that poor man through. Unfortunately, it didn't really help the bottom line. He valued Margaret's possessions at six thousand, two hundred and sixty dollars, and most of that was for her jewelry, which she subsequently sold."

"Does it say there, did she sell her big jade ring?" Scarlett asked. "She always said I could have it when I got old enough not to lose it. The veins on it looked like a horse head."

J.B. shook her head politely. "I don't recall seeing a mention of that. I believe most of the value was in a wedding set that belonged to her mother."

"It doesn't matter," Scarlett said. "I don't think that ring was worth much. It just kind of reminded me of her."

J.B. regarded Scarlett thoughtfully. "Were you . . . close to Margaret?"

"Oh, yes, ma'am. I loved her."

"Well then," J.B. said gently. "I apologize. When Margaret said she was mostly estranged from family . . . and she was, er, very . . . matter-of-fact—"

"It's okay, you can say it," Scarlett said. "She was a grumpy old lady most of the time. But she meant well, she really did."

J.B. glanced at Katie as though for confirmation. "I, um, regret that I only met her once," Katie said.

J.B. cleared her throat. "Well, then. Let's get down to it. We can go over this in as much detail as you'd like, of course, but I'll begin by just covering the major points. Let's start with her checking, savings, and money market accounts, which totaled almost nine thousand dollars, and will be split equally between you."

"That's four and a half thousand dollars!" Scarlett exclaimed.

Katie said nothing: the share each of them would receive was less than the monthly mortgage on Rex and Lolly's town house, a fact that she was pretty sure would astound her cousin.

"Margaret left the house to you, Scarlett," J.B. continued, "and all of the contents of the house and garage to you, Katie. In addition, Margaret made a rather specific stipulation." She peered up at both of them, pushing her glasses up the bridge of her nose. "You have one week from this reading of the will to go through the house and decide what you want to keep, Katie, and then the rest of it is to be sold or otherwise disposed of, and the house delivered empty to Scarlett."

Scarlett blinked. "Well, that's ridiculous, why would Katie want to sell any of it? It was *Gomma's!*"

J.B. tapped her fingernails on the desk, stifling a smile. "You know, Margaret thought you might say that. I think that's why she had that appraisal done. She also had the house appraised. I've got that figure for you here."

She took another page out of the file and held it up for them to see the figure that followed a long paragraph of legalese.

124 Oliver St.—$154,600

"I have to say," Katie said carefully, after a long moment passed. "I would have expected a higher figure, given the, um, economic revival in the area. I looked online and they say the fulfillment center's going to bring almost a thousand new jobs. I thought . . ."

"Oh, real estate values are almost certainly going up," J.B. said. "Not at the rate you're probably used to in Boston, though. And now that they've moved the proposed site of the center, there isn't exactly a shortage of commercial space in New London. You could always hold on to the house and see if its value goes up, Scarlett, but there aren't any guarantees.

"And in your case, Katie, I obviously can't enforce your grandmother's wishes. If you tell me you're dumping everything without going through it, well, there's nothing I can do to stop you. I believe Margaret was hoping that you'd honor her wishes out of a sense of . . . affection, I suppose, and perhaps duty as well."

Katie was mystified. Her grandmother was a stranger to her, a thorn in her mother's side. From the way Georgina described her, she was stingy, selfish, and downright mean. But Margaret apparently had motives that were opaque to all of them, Scarlett included.

"Well," she said, attempting a game smile. "It should be an interesting week."

Scarlett was quiet on the drive back. She'd taken a call while Katie visited the ladies' room, and it hadn't improved her mood—when Katie asked if everything was all right, Scarlett had simply shrugged in a tight-lipped way that suggested she was trying to hold back tears.

As they passed the "Welcome to New London" sign, Katie couldn't keep quiet any longer. "Scarlett, that was a new experience for me too. I've never inherited anything before. I honestly don't know if I'll keep any of Margaret's stuff. So I guess I just wanted to say, if you want any of it—it's yours. And about the house, whether you end up selling it or not, I just wanted you to know that I'm ready to talk, or listen or whatever you need."

Scarlett glanced her way, hands tight on the steering wheel. "That's nice of you," she said. "The thing is, I know exactly what I'd do if it was just me. But Merritt—well, we don't really see eye to eye."

"How so?"

Scarlett sighed. "He thinks I should sell the house and invest the money. He's got this friend who's starting a business and if we get in on it now, before it takes off, we could make a lot of money. And the thing is, I kind of owe him. Merritt, I mean. I haven't always been able to pay my half of the rent this last year and so I just pay what I can, and . . . well, he says we're a team, we help each other out when we need it, and I agree with that, you know? I *want* to be fair."

Alarm bells were going off for Katie—she guessed that Scarlett didn't know the first thing about investing. Merritt might not be involved in the kind of high-stakes insider trading that landed people in jail, but given what she knew about him so far, she wasn't at all confident that he was looking out for Scarlett's best interests.

An idea was taking shape, one that didn't really fit into her plan to come down to Texas and wring every cent she could from Margaret's estate. What if she were to stay in New London a little longer, and help her cousin figure out if she could afford to keep the house and maybe even start her day care business? Katie had a business minor and had planned to get her MBA at some point, maybe even strike out on her own someday, and she knew enough, as Liam said, to be dangerous. But in this situation it seemed pretty obvious that Scarlett needed help.

"Listen, Scarlett, I know you're worried about owing Merritt money. But I'd hate for that to be a factor in your decision. What if I loan you the money to pay him back? That way you could take a little more time with this decision. I could help you make a business plan, if you want."

"Oh gosh, Katie, I don't know. It would take money to get started, and all I've got's the house."

"And the money from Gomma's accounts."

"Oh, right," Scarlett said, brightening. "It doesn't hardly seem real, does it?"

"It *is* real. And that money is yours, to do with what you want. Listen, how much do you owe Merritt right now?"

Scarlett thought for a moment. "Well, honestly, it's probably up to almost a thousand dollars at this point," she said. "I fell behind around the holidays. You know, buying Christmas presents."

Katie reached over impulsively and patted Scarlett's arm. "Then don't give it another thought. You'll easily be able to pay him back as soon as you get the money from the estate. And I can start doing a little research into the real estate market, to make sure J.B.'s estimate of the value of the house is accurate. If you need more cash—like for instance if you decide to open your day care business—we could look into a bank loan for start-up costs."

Scarlett's eyes went wide. "Wow, I never thought a bank would lend me money. It would be so great if you could help me," she said. "I'm so confused about what to do. It's been, well, this whole inheritance has caused some trouble between me and Merritt, I don't mind saying."

They had reached the end of Oliver Street, and Scarlett slowed the truck and coasted over to the curb. Up ahead, over the row of roofs of the other houses on the block, Katie could see the widow's walk perched at the top of her grandmother's old mansion, and the redbud trees blooming in the front yard.

"Just think, when Gomma was born this whole entire block was her family's land," Scarlett said. "The only other houses on the street were those big ones on the other side, but they didn't have near as much land as Gomma's family did. I know there's pictures—I think the historical society probably has them now, since Gomma gave them a bunch of her scrapbooks a while back. I wish you could see how it used to be before . . . I mean, in case I have to sell it."

"Listen, Scarlett, don't make up your mind

yet," Katie said. "We won't know what's possible until we look into it."

"Oh, it's okay. If I end up having to sell, well, that's just the way it is and I'll be fine with it. But I *do* want to make sure we go through all of Gomma's stuff so you can at least see it all. I know you need to get back to Boston, and what do you want all this old stuff for, anyway? It's like me and the house—it doesn't make any *sense* for me to have this big old thing when I don't even have a husband or kids. Or even a job. But still . . . I mean, it's *family,* you know?"

The little splinter of guilt Katie'd been wrestling turned into a giant spike. She'd known her cousin for two short days, and already she could tell that Scarlett was starving for family connections—and until this week, Katie had never even bothered to learn anything about her side of the family.

What if she did stay long enough to really get to know Scarlett, to help her figure out what to do with the house, to find a home for her grandmother's belongings instead of just carting them to a dump? Maybe the historical society and museum might want some of them, especially anything connected to the school explosion. They were an important part of local history, after all. And maybe she'd find other stuff—like the box of letters in the hall closet—that would shed some light on who her mother had been, and how she'd become the way she was. Maybe, just maybe, Katie might end up closer to Georgina.

Just like Scarlett, Katie had few real connections. She'd fought her way out of Texas and into Columbia, but once she got there she'd just drifted . . . through school and friendships and dating and even, if she was honest with herself, her marriage. She'd counted herself lucky to find Liam, everyone said they made a great couple, so just like the rest of her adult decisions—what job to take, where to vacation, when to have a baby—ending up with him simply seemed like a safe choice.

The truck was moving again, Scarlett inching along the street at a snail's pace, taking in the view. Katie wondered what she was remembering: coming here as a child, an adolescent, a teen; watching the once-grand neighborhood tumble further and further into disrepair.

Once they were parked in front of the house, Katie spotted a FedEx envelope propped against the front door, and felt a surge of relief. "Looks like the money my friend sent me came," she said. "How about we go get a drink to celebrate? My treat."

"I'd love to," Scarlett said, avoiding her gaze. "But maybe not tonight? I need to, um, get back."

"It's totally fine," Katie said. Another time,

she'd find a way to talk to Scarlett about Merritt's outsized influence on her decisions. "I'll keep myself busy. I think I'll start organizing things—that way we can both go through Margaret's stuff and figure out what each of us wants to keep. I mean, I know that technically she left me the contents of the house, but I want you to have anything that's special to you."

"That would be great," Scarlett said. "I'll come back in the morning, okay?"

Katie hopped out of the car, then leaned against the open window. "Thanks for everything today."

Only after Scarlett had driven away did Katie remember that she'd meant to give her some gas money from the cash Lolly had sent.

Katie wasn't a religious sort of person—her mother's Sunday traditions when she was growing up included bleaching her mustache and doing her nails—but a little prayer popped into her head, something one of her mother's boyfriends had taught her in a misguided effort to prove his suitability to Georgina.

> Bless my spirit as I roam
> Help me find my way back home
> Guide and guard me through the night
> And bless me in the morning's light.

"Safe home, Scarlett," Katie whispered as she let herself into the house.

CHAPTER TWENTY

November 1969

Margaret had been clutching the handles of her purse so hard that her fingers had gone numb.

"But surely—" she started, and then didn't have any idea what to say. The bank manager—Edward Forbus, who had been a knock-kneed runt of an adolescent when she'd left for college—peered at his desk blotter, which was covered with little curlicues and stars and other doodlings. He had flushed in a way that was similar to how her father had looked when embarrassed, which made Margaret a little teary, because Hugh Pierson had been gone nearly two years now and she missed him every day.

Although it was her father who'd put her in this jam. Oh, why hadn't he seen that his little ruse—to force her and her mother to get along, to ensure that Margaret took care of Caroline after he was gone—would never work? But that was how Hugh had always been: sweetly sentimental, ever hopeful, with an inextinguishable faith in other people. And for all those reasons, unable to help himself from loving the wife who married him for his money, and never loved him back.

It was too much to bear, at least for this hot, sticky afternoon that was sure to end in disappointment. But Margaret had to try:

"My father never meant for us to want for anything," she pleaded, hating the tremor in her voice. "His will was supposed to ensure that we were provided for."

"And so it has," Edward (she'd always known him as Eddie, but that was a lifetime ago) said a bit primly. "At the rate that Mrs. Pierson has been making withdrawals, you and she just might be able to live out your lives in comfort. And, of course, there's a nice nest egg for Georgina when she turns eighteen."

Margaret really didn't need to be reminded of that. When that day came, Georgina would inherit fifteen thousand dollars from her grandfather, who had adored her, naturally. Margaret was quite sure her father intended the money for Georgina's education, but he'd been careless enough not to specify that in the will. As she approached her tenth birthday, Georgina had turned out to be even more willful, defiant, and headstrong than she'd been as a child, and how was Margaret supposed to ensure that her father's wishes were honored if her daughter were allowed to squander the money?

And even though Margaret had understood

her father's wish to ensure that his wife and daughter's increasingly fractious relationship didn't disintegrate entirely by binding them together with money, it still galled that he'd left her nothing. The family's fortunes had dwindled as the oil field had played out and the wells dried up—and Hugh's increasing indifference hadn't helped—so there wasn't nearly the mountain of money she'd once assumed they'd always have.

The will specified that the money would pass to her when Caroline was gone, but that was cold comfort when Margaret had to ask her mother for money every time she went to buy groceries or put gas in the car she was forced to share with her. And heaven help her if she wanted to get her hair done or buy a lipstick or a ticket to the movies: her mother subjected her to a barrage of questions about whether she really *needed* whatever it was that she wanted the money for, if she'd shopped around and compared prices, if it would end up gathering dust in the attic *like some of your other foolhardy notions*.

"But all I'm asking is that you allow me to withdraw a little for myself. It won't affect the total amount, because then I won't have to bother my mother with these—these picayune details," Margaret said. "Mother is well over sixty"—an exaggeration; Caroline was barely sixty-two—"and I feel it is neither kind nor prudent to expect her to manage the finances for all three of us."

Edward sighed and stacked the papers on his desk, avoiding her gaze. "I do understand, and I'm not without sympathy, Mrs. Dial. But it's out of my hands. It would not only be against the bank's regulations, it would be against the *law* for me to violate the terms of your father's trust."

"Eddie," Margaret said, glaring at him. "You really needn't call me Mrs. Dial, considering that I once caught you and your friends trying to see into the girls' locker room at the club."

Edward turned an even more alarming shade of pink, and he ran his fingers through his hair. "Look, I *am* sorry. I can't do anything about changing the will. But I have to ask you—have you ever read through it?"

Margaret blinked. It had never occurred to her to try—the documents were stored in her mother's safety-deposit box, to which she alone had a key. "Can I?"

"Well, you'd have to ask your mother to show you, or talk to your father's attorney if she won't, but—yes, I believe that you'd be entitled. But the reason I ask is, it seems to me—that is, you've never mentioned, uh—"

"Spit it out, Eddie."

"Well, I just wondered if you know about your father's other bequests. To your cousins. Since it's never come up."

"My cousins?" Margaret was mystified—she'd seen Audrey last December, when she'd come for a brief visit with her family while on their way to her husband's mother's home for Christmas. She hadn't mentioned a word about it. "Levander and Audrey?"

"No, no, your, ah, cousins on your mother's side." He pulled a sheet from the pile and read: "Lassiter Wooley, Amy Wooley, and Pamela Wooley McGovney. Euda Wooley, their mother, was your mother's sister, I believe."

"My father left them money?"

More squinting and frowning, then Edward said, "Yes, two thousand dollars each. You seem surprised . . . ?"

Margaret kept her face impassive. She didn't know what to make of this information. Her mother hadn't mentioned the Wooleys in years, and none of them had attended her father's funeral.

"No, not at all," she lied. Suddenly she just wanted to get out of the hot little office, with Eddie/Edward's certifications and awards lining the walls. She stood up abruptly and gave him a stiff nod. "Well, then, thank you for your time."

She didn't wait to hear whatever namby-pamby response little Eddie Forbus came up with to finish dashing her hopes, but walked out of his office and through the echoing marble bank lobby with her head held high. She remembered coming here with her father when she was a little girl; back then, everyone from the doorman to the tellers to the other customers smiled and greeted her father. And not just because he was the richest man in town, but because those were the days when oil paid for everything in New London, and her father was the biggest oilman around. At one point, he employed nearly seventy-five percent of the men in town, and he treated his workers well.

That's what the old-timers told her, anyway. But the oil boom in East Texas had evaporated like the water in the bottom of a cattle trough, and with it, the town's fortunes. Margaret was a thirty-one-year-old widow in a town that had long ago given up on dreams of grandeur and now eked out an existence mostly from the dirt, just as the original settlers had in the days before the Spindletop gusher. Even the value of her parents' land had plummeted; if her parents had sold off the extra acreage years ago, before the field was played out, there would have been more than enough for her and her mother to live like royalty. As it was, her father had made some poor investments and worse decisions.

And for some reason, he'd squandered some of the money that was left on her mother's estranged relatives who seemed to have meant nothing to her. Six thousand dollars in total—not exactly a king's ransom, but certainly nothing to sneeze at.

If Margaret had been allowed to manage that money—which she was far more qualified to do than her mother (she had a bachelor's degree from the University of Texas, for heaven's sake, and her mother had only finished grammar school)—she would use it to buy stock in the Xerox Corporation. The stock market had become a recent interest of Margaret's, one she'd stumbled on in the periodical room at the library, having grown bored with *Vogue* and *Harper's Bazaar* and picked up the business section of the *Morning Telegraph* out of curiosity one day. As she read more and more, her interest grew, and she had even bought a few penny stocks, using money hoarded from her paltry allowance. Her stocks had earned a bit—she was up a total of almost thirty dollars—but she was certain she could do more, if only she had the chance! And instead, her dear father had given money to virtual strangers.

Margaret continued to fume all the way home, and it was with some surprise that she found herself at her own front porch, a bit out of breath and sweaty from the walk. She could hear the sound of her mother's voice through the screen door, Georgina's enthusiastic responses.

Margaret came into the kitchen and spied a box from the Levines department store on the table. Her mother was making lemonade, a pile of squeezed lemon halves on the counter, and Georgina was playing with a pile of red plastic hooks.

Margaret picked up one of the hooks and shook it. "*Another* new toy? Really, Mother? And what's this?"

She tossed the bit of plastic on the table, and Georgina snatched it up with an exclamation while Margaret pulled the ribbon off the box and lifted the lid. Nestled in tissue paper was a wide-collared middy blouse with rickrack trim and white sailor pants with four gaily stitched buttons on each side.

"Another new outfit? Mother, Georgina needs this like a hole in the head."

"I'm sitting right here," Georgina piped up. "You don't have to talk about me like I'm not."

"Fine," Margaret snapped, throwing the clothes back into the box. "You don't need more new clothes, Georgina Dial. And you certainly don't need—what on earth are those, anyway?"

"Monkeys!" Georgina held up a string of the hooks, which, on closer examination, did appear to be shaped like monkeys with their arms and tails dangling from each other. "Look, they're called '*Barrel* of Monkeys.' "

She shoved a red plastic barrel across the table, and Margaret picked it up and peered inside: nothing but more monkeys. "What are you supposed to do with them? Never mind, forget I asked. Just how much did these set your grandmother back, I wonder?"

"For your information," Caroline said coolly,

"the clerk said that he can barely keep these in stock. They're quite the sensation. We were lucky to get them."

"Oh, Mother," Margaret muttered. "You'd buy snow from an Eskimo in the middle of winter, as long as someone said it was in style."

"What was that?"

"Never mind. Tell me this instead—why on earth did Dad leave *your* sister's children money? And why didn't you ever bother to *tell* me?"

Caroline froze, her back going rigid. She set down the wooden spoon slowly and turned, a grim expression on her face. "I don't care to discuss that. Georgina, be a good girl and take your things to your room. Then you can help me get the sauce started."

Georgina glanced from her grandmother to her mother. She was as indifferent to their squabbling as she was accustomed to it.

"Do as your grandmother said," Margaret said automatically.

"I'm not going to discuss this, Margaret, I'm serious," Caroline repeated once Georgina left the room. "You can pester me all you like, but I'm not going to back down."

"Why ever . . . fine," Margaret said. She snatched the keys to the Chevy, her father's last car, which they were still driving almost ten years after he bought it, off the row of hooks by the back door. "I'll just go find out myself."

It took half an hour to drive to Archer, and another ten minutes for Margaret to park and find a telephone booth and look up her cousins' names in the book. Only Pamela (McGovney, Mr. and Mrs. Robert) were listed. Margaret went into the pharmacy and bought a pack of gum and asked for directions, which turned out to be complicated enough that the clerk drew a map on the back of a place mat from the soda counter, with a T extending out from the main road past a squiggle that was supposed to be a stand of trees.

"It's not really a proper road," the clerk said apologetically. "There ain't a sign or anything. The house is sort of green. Well, it was green, once, but . . . anyway, it's the third on the left. You taking your little one for the treatment?"

Margaret blinked. "Excuse me?"

"Oh, er, never mind," the clerk stammered. "I just thought . . ."

"Mrs. McGovney is my cousin," Margaret said primly. "I am paying an unannounced visit."

"Oh, I see. Good day, Miss, and stop in and see us again."

Margaret found her cousin's house, making frequent stops to consult the map, on the far edge of town on a dirt road that looked like a shantytown. The third house from the corner was green only in the sense that the paint that hadn't flaked off was a faded shade of mint. Its porch seemed to be hanging on for dear life, and the only things growing in the yard were cheatgrass and carpetweed and a leggy rosebush that hadn't received a proper pruning in years. Parked in front was a shiny newish Buick, looking quite out of place with its front tires sunk into the mud that had settled into the marshy low point in the street.

Margaret was almost to the steps when she noticed that there was someone sitting in the shade of the porch. A woman close to her own age, dressed in a bright cotton shift, her hair tied up in a fuchsia scarf, a paperback novel in her hand. At Margaret's approach she closed the book on her finger, marking her page, and sat up straighter.

"Hello," she said uncertainly.

"Hello . . . Pamela?"

"Excuse me?" The woman looked startled, setting the book down abruptly on an overturned bucket that apparently was used as an occasional table. She stood up, brushing off her skirt. "Oh, no no no, I'm just here . . . you know."

"Oh," Margaret said, confused. "Well, I'm Margaret Dial. Pamela is my, um, is who I've come to see." She couldn't quite bring herself to say *cousin* when the woman was practically a stranger.

"Are you here for—?" The woman made an odd little flapping-hand gesture, grimacing in the direction of the house. "I mean, I understand, that is, I've been told she's the best. And really, Timothy—that's my son, he's nine—of course it wasn't his fault. *At all.*" She leaned conspiratorially forward. "It's those Mexicans. My husband says that all greasers carry diseases. They can't help it, I suppose, but why must our children be made to suffer by going to school with them?"

"Oh," Margaret said, utterly mystified. She was aware, of course, that there were immigrant children at Georgina's school. Hank had served with a boy from Sonora, in the north, where he'd learned to play a little clay whistle that he carried with him everywhere—Hank would not allow any negative talk about Mexicans. Margaret was indifferent—back then, she'd been simply trying to keep her small family going, and she imagined that she understood what these miserable families had gone through.

But saying so was not going to win her a new friendship. Which worked just fine, because Margaret was not in the market for one anyway. "Well, I'll just go on in, I suppose," she said pleasantly. "It was so very nice to meet you."

"Oh, of course! Of course," the woman stammered, sitting abruptly back down. "It's just . . . do you have children?"

It seemed an odd question, but Margaret smiled gamely. "I do. My daughter, Georgina, is ten."

"Well, then you know how it is. I wonder . . . if I could ask you to keep this to yourself. Our chance meeting here." Her face twisted into an uncomfortable, strained smile. "It's just so awfully hard, you know, when certain people talk. I'm sure you understand."

Margaret wondered if the woman was a bit batty. "Of course," she said reassuringly. "I won't tell a soul."

She rapped on the door and then decided she might as well let herself in, twisting the old, tarnished knob—and finding herself in her cousin's living room.

She let the door close behind her. The house was a simple four-square style, with a front room that led directly to the kitchen, two bedrooms up the stairs with a bathroom between them. But the front room had been awkwardly bisected by a curtain fashioned from yards of muslin rigged on lengths of copper pipe suspended from the ceiling. On the right side of the curtain, two towheaded children sat at a small table, heads bent over their schoolbooks. On the other side, a miserable-looking little boy was hunched on a stool with a plastic shower curtain fastened around him like a cape. Bent over him was a haggard-looking woman in a man's chambray shirt with the sleeves rolled up, her thin hair twisted on top of her head.

And despite what she was wearing, despite the

ravages of time and poverty, there was something familiar about her, something that harkened all the way back to the reception for Hank's first wedding. Margaret thought of the five-piece combo, the trays laden with champagne flutes, Tansy's pretty little bouquet, which she was still clutching tightly when they left the reception.

The round table, the untouched hors d'oeuvres, her mother's discomfort—and her cousins, in their awkward homemade gowns.

Pammy looked up in surprise. She had aged—her skin had slackened, and her hair was streaked with silver threads—but she had the same shy, sweet smile and gentle brown eyes, and the simple blouse and skirt she was wearing did a lot more for her than the terrible blue party dress had.

"Hello," she said. "Are you here to book an appointment? I'm nearly done with Timothy here, if you could give me another ten minutes."

The boy scowled at her, and Margaret saw that half of his hair had been trimmed to a scant couple of inches, dark brown tufts of it lying on the floor. On a table draped with a plastic cloth were a variety of scissors and combs and a bowl of water.

"Oh, you give haircuts," she said.

Pammy gave her a curious look. "Well, only when it's real bad—when I can't be sure I get 'em all otherwise. I try not to cut any for the girls. Is that what you have? A daughter? Though it's best to bring all the kids in, once one of 'em's struck.'"

"Struck . . . ?"

Pammy stared. "With the lice? That's what you need, isn't it? Why you came to see me?"

Suddenly Margaret understood: the bowl of water on the table wasn't water at all, but oil, and now that she looked again, she could see the tiny black dots on its surface. Pammy was picking lice and nits from the little boy's hair: the lice were the dots, and oil was an effective way to kill them as she plucked them from his head and dropped them in the bowl.

"But why don't you just use the powders?" Margaret asked, for want of anything else to say. "Or shave it off?"

"Powders don't work as good anymore." Pammy picked up the fine-tooth metal comb. "Do you mind if I keep going while we talk? His mama's just real nervous about this, afraid someone's going to drive by and see her car. Though I tried to tell her, anyone comes down this road it's for the same thing as brought her."

Now the last of the pieces fell into place. The woman's strange behavior outside . . . the expensive car . . . the trouble Pammy was taking when simply shaving the boy's scalp would be less risky: all of this was meant to keep anyone from knowing that the boy had been afflicted.

When Margaret had been in grammar school,

lice infestations were rare, because of the availability of chemical treatments after the war. But every once in a while a child would come into the classroom scratching his scalp, and the mother would be called in to take him home. Usually it was one of the poor families, migrant workers and immigrants, and invariably there would be talk of "filth" and "trash" and worse, humiliation heaped on the children, strangers scolding women in the market to take them home.

No family wanted to be subject to the humiliation, so many kept a supply of DDT powder or pyrethrum on hand. But whenever there was an outbreak, Caroline had instructed Margaret to stay away from the poor kids and twice refused to let her attend school at all until the infestation was over. "No child of mine is going to come home with lice like common trash," she'd told Hugh when he'd questioned her decision.

"I didn't realize," Margaret said, abashed.

"Don't you worry now, I keep it real clean," Pammy said, as she pulled a strand of the boy's hair and examined it. "I hardly ever get a repeat. I can give you references."

"No—I meant, that's not why I'm here. I'm— do you remember me at all? I'm Margaret Pierson. Your, um, cousin."

Pammy looked up sharply. After a couple of seconds her expression changed to one of pleasant surprise. "Margaret? It *is* you! I'm sorry I didn't recognize you. But what on earth are you doing here? I've wanted . . ."

Her voice trailed away as her face clouded, and Margaret felt a surge of shame. "I'm sorry it's been so long," she said quickly. "I'm sorry I've never—that I didn't write, or, or, but . . ."

Now she had no idea how to bring up the subject of the money. She hadn't thought this through—hadn't imagined her cousin would be so happy to see her.

Pammy dropped the comb in a glass jar and went to the sink, picking up a bar of Lava soap and scrubbing furiously. "You just sit tight a minute, Timothy. I've got Pecan Sandies when we're all done. Margaret, I wish I'd known you were coming, I would have tidied up."

Despite the outside appearance of the house, the inside was neat as a pin, the counters sparkling and the dishes stacked neatly on the shelves, embroidered dish towels hanging from wooden pegs. The furniture was old but polished to a sheen, and there were crocheted doilies on the chair backs and a framed painting of a windmill on the wall. The children on the other side of the muslin curtain had been watching curiously, but when their mother looked their way, they immediately bent over their lessons.

"I'm terribly sorry to interrupt," Margaret said, her voice going stiff and formal the way it always did when she felt unsure of herself. "I just—you see, I just found out that when my father passed away—"

"I should have written," Pammy interrupted, her face flaming. "I can't believe I didn't. I just didn't know—wasn't sure—Amy and me, we talked about it and—well, we just thought maybe you'd rather not hear from us. And it was so unexpected! So generous. Lassiter and Bess were in a real fix before they got that money from your daddy; they almost lost their house. And Bob and me, we were able to buy a car. He was able to take a job in Tyler now that he's got a way to get there, and it pays so much better than around here."

Now Margaret felt even worse, knowing how much the money had meant to her cousins. "But I just, and I'm so sorry to ask, but there's been some, well, some uncertainty about—about some of his affairs, and I wondered—" Margaret broke off, stammering, wishing she'd just come out with it first thing.

But Pammy was bobbing her head in agreement. "We couldn't believe it ourselves. Why, none of us had talked to your family in ages, since Tansy's wedding. Other than your daddy's letters at Christmas, of course, and—"

"My father *wrote* to you?" Margaret couldn't remember her father writing a personal letter to anyone, ever—her mother kept the correspondence for the family. "What did he say?"

"Oh, just—you know, asking after how we all were, wishing us a merry Christmas. And, well, he always sent a check. For the children's gifts, he said. I'm sorry, I thought—we thought you knew. I'd have never cashed them if I thought— if you'd minded."

"No, no, of course not. I'm—I'm glad he stayed in touch. I just didn't know."

"Like I said, I just wish we'd written back. All those years . . . I used to wish you and I could— that we'd been, that I could have . . ." Pammy was so flustered she couldn't finish her thought. She put her hands to her cheeks and drew in a breath. "Oh, I'm so stupid. I haven't even offered you anything. Would you like lemonade? Or should I put coffee on?"

"No, no, I can't stay," Margaret said, already backing away. The little boy in the chair stared at her desultorily, playing with a folding knife that he must have been hiding in his pocket. "And I've interrupted your work. It was terribly rude of me. Please do give my best to your family."

"But won't you come back again? I'd love for you to meet Bob—and my kids, Sharon and Bobby, and hear all about your little one—but she's not even all that little anymore, is she?"

"Yes, yes, of course," Margaret said, wanting nothing more than to make her escape. "That will be lovely. Goodbye now."

She dashed out the door and pulled it firmly

closed behind her, forgetting that the boy's mother was waiting on the front porch.

"Oh—good afternoon," she said. "I must run now. In a hurry."

"But you won't tell anyone, right? That you saw me here?"

Margaret was already crossing the yard, relief seeping through her. This visit was a mistake she would not repeat. "Of course not," she said over her shoulder. "I don't even know you."

"Where are they?"

Georgina came bursting into Margaret's bedroom while she was brushing her hair the next morning. Though their bedrooms were next to each other, Margaret rarely went into her daughter's room unless she wasn't in it: Georgina had a finely developed sense of privacy and independence for a ten-year-old.

"Where are what?" Margaret asked innocently. She knew she was in for a tantrum, but she didn't plan to make it easy on Georgina.

"My monkeys! And my new clothes! I want to wear them today."

"They are going back to the store," Margaret said firmly. "We can't afford them, which your grandmother knows very well."

"It's her money," Georgina challenged, jutting out her chin. She was becoming increasingly difficult to handle with every passing day,

youthful tantrums giving way to crafty mischie
and dark moods. "Not yours. And she says
deserved a treat because I got such good marks."

Margaret rolled her eyes. "They weren't *tha*
good."

Georgina pouted. "They were third best, a
least for the girls. And Marabelle's mother gives
her a quarter whenever she has good marks
Mine are better than hers, and you don't give me
anything!"

"You want me to congratulate you every time
you do what your teacher tells you?" Margaret
said archly. "Listen, Georgie, don't get ahead of
yourself. You're a smart girl and you're going
to be pretty, but there are hundreds of girls just
like you in Texas. Thousands, probably. And you
know which ones are going to be the happiest
in life? The ones who don't get too big for their
britches, that's who."

"You always say that."

"Because it's true." Someday, Margaret
would have to tell Georgina about her own fall
from grace, about the dangers of growing up
believing you were above everyone around you.
Someday she would tell Georgina the truth about
her father—and about the wonderful life she'd
thrown away. Perhaps she'd show her the picture
from *Vanity Fair*, the one she'd clipped and kept
in a drawer in her dresser, of Tripp and his wife
at a party at the Millermore mansion in Dallas,

diamonds sparkling on her neck. "The sooner you realize that you're just like everyone else, the better. You have to work for what you get in life, you know. And going to school and getting good marks is your work."

"*You* don't work," Georgina pointed out stubbornly. "You don't do anything."

"I certainly do. You know very well that I volunteer at the VFW three afternoons a week. And who do you think organized the cakewalk at the school carnival?"

Georgina was unswayed. "I'll tell Grandma."

Margaret had been counting on this, a threat that Georgina made more and more often, testing how far she could push her grandmother's adoration for her. It wasn't without limits, and if necessary, Margaret knew she could prevail, shaming Caroline for her frivolous purchases. But she'd already come up with a counteroffer that might keep the peace with her mother.

"If you march downstairs right now, and eat your breakfast and help wash up without another word, you may keep the can of monkeys."

"*Barrel* of Monkeys," Georgina corrected. "Everyone knows that."

"Well, I'm not 'everyone,' and you shouldn't want to be either," Margaret said.

"*I'm not everyone,*" Georgina echoed in a singsong, mocking voice as she minced down the hall, making her escape.

Margaret didn't bother to go after her. She was already calculating how much money she might get in return for the outfit, to add to the small account she had opened at the bank. Caroline would not be pleased, but she felt guilty enough about spoiling Georgina so wretchedly that she wouldn't say anything.

It was a strange and difficult way to save money. But by the new year, if her mother's generosity continued, Margaret would have enough saved to buy five more shares of the American Telephone and Telegraph Company.

CHAPTER TWENTY-ONE

Lolly had wrapped the money—a thick stack of fifties and twenties—in wrinkled pink tissue paper. Katie counted it twice: five hundred beautiful dollars, enough for half a dozen mani-pedis . . . dinner for four at Auberge de la Nuit . . . a naughty weekend in Atlantic City.

Or . . . tantalizingly . . . a fresh start.

Where had that thought come from? Katie folded the wad of bills and tucked it into her pocket, and wondered what to do next. She was still full from their parking lot lunch, though she supposed she ought to buy a few staples for the fridge. And maybe one of those prepaid phones they sold in gas stations, the ones drug dealers used.

Or maybe a nice bottle of crisp white wine. She smiled at the thought, remembering the thin selection of bottles in the market the night before, their orange price tags. Why not? Bedtime was still hours away, and she didn't have a TV or computer to entertain herself. She'd buy the wine, lay in some snacks in case she got hungry later, and start going through her inheritance.

Katie locked up and walked down the street,

noticing how much lovelier the town looked when it was dappled by the gentle setting sunlight. She passed Jam's house and snuck a look into the front windows, but the shades were drawn. Maybe he was still out training dogs to kill people, or whatever it was he did to make money. Which reminded her—she'd have to buy a bone or something for the ridiculous mutt that her grandmother had been feeding. Eventually, the thing would get the hint and move on, but she supposed she owed it some interim measures.

The doors to the market swished open and there, manning the cash register, was not the charming young man from the night before but a woman Georgina's age with a hairdo at least a generation older. She set down her magazine and gave Katie a smile.

"Evenin', Miss. Kyle said to tell you he put some brisket by for you. It's in the cold case."

Katie stopped in her tracks. Last night she may have resembled a homeless person, but today she was clean and had made an effort with the makeup she borrowed from Scarlett, and while she was too old for the short shorts and platform sandals, they were hardly the clothes of a vagrant. "Thank you. But, um, what did Kyle tell you about me?"

"Oh, honey, he just said you were awfully pretty and skinny as a stick bug."

"Oh," Katie said, embarrassed. "I just—I didn't

have enough—I need to pay for last night's chicken."

"Don't give it a thought," the cashier said, returning to her magazine. "I'm sure you'll do someone else a good turn."

Katie headed down the liquor aisle just as another shopper headed up it, and they nearly collided. She started to stammer her excuses when she realized that the nicely built man she'd nearly run into was no other than Jam Mifflin.

"You stalking me?" he asked, without a trace of humor.

"No!"

Now she couldn't buy the bottle of wine without him knowing that she was planning to drink alone. But who did he think he was, wandering around the store at dinnertime while flexing those ridiculous muscles, distracting people who just wanted to pick up a few groceries?

Katie didn't want him to think she was staring at his leg, but she was so intent on not looking at it that she wound up staring at his stupidly attractive, glaring face instead. "I needed tampons," she snapped, which wasn't true but which might put an end to this awkward encounter.

"You're in the wrong aisle."

"And Pepto Bismol. Those ribs didn't agree with me."

"My ribs agree with everyone. They make

311

people cry. Guys on death row put their orders in for their last meal the minute they're sentenced."

Katie glared at Jam in consternation. He seemed to have no intention of moving out of her way. "That's a lot of words for you, isn't it?" she asked.

That got her a shrug.

"Look. I have a favor to ask you. It's a long story, but I don't have a phone right now, and I need to make a call. Would you mind . . . ? I'll just go outside for a minute and you can finish picking out your Hungry Man or whatever pathetic thing you're having for dinner."

"How do I know you're not going to run off and steal it?"

Was he serious? Katie couldn't tell. "Well, there's the fact that I don't have anywhere to hide out except next door to you."

His expression didn't change, but he handed over his phone.

"Yeah, well, thanks."

The cashier had made no secret of listening to the entire conversation, so Katie didn't bother to assure her that she'd be right back. Outside, a trio of adolescent boys zipped by on scooters, laughing and jeering at each other. The parking lot was nearly empty, the single streetlight flickering, and Katie shuddered at a memory of that other parking lot, almost two days ago.

Liam answered on the third ring. "Hello?"

"It's me."

"Yeah, I figured, from the area code. Did you get the money?"

"Where are you?" There were party sounds in the background, music and laughter, someone yelling indistinctly.

"Oh, I stopped by Rayburn's. I'm just having a drink with a few of the guys."

"Guys? What guys?"

"From the team," Liam said with a trace of impatience. "We had the big Axpense presentation today, remember?"

No, she hadn't remembered, because she'd been busy stumbling around East Texas with no money. And besides, Liam had made fun of the Axpence account before, calling it a Eurocanoe without a paddle, its principals "francofaux." Liam was always his cleverest when being disparaging.

But she hadn't called to pick a fight. "You went to the bank, though, right? To put me on the account?"

There was the briefest of pauses. "Yeah, see, the banks close at five, so . . ."

"Liam? Are you serious?"

"Look, I called. Just like you asked. And they said it had to be done in person, which I will, first thing tomorrow, but I can't exactly just drop everything the day we have a presentation for a major account. I mean, a lot of people flew in for this."

"And of course you had to get to Rayburn's. Wouldn't want to be late for that," Katie said.

"Jesus, Katie, didn't you get Lolly's package? I mean, even for you, that ought to be enough to last you a few days."

Even for you—said the man in the two-hundred-forty-dollar trousers. Katie fumed.

Anger—that was good. Maybe her hormones were settling down, since she didn't feel like crying, for the first time in days.

She felt like punching something.

"I'll be sure to thank Lolly for the cash," she said coldly. "But I have to have the bank card to buy a phone. And I don't have any clothes."

"I thought you borrowed some from your cousin."

Katie looked down at herself. As the evening cooled, she'd dug a sweater from the bag that Scarlett had left, a short pink acrylic shrug that didn't cover her midriff. "I went to see the lawyer today in Payless sandals with glue-on crystals, Liam."

"Oh, hey—so what happened with that?"

"I inherited a houseful of junk. Oh, and about four thousand dollars, which is probably what it'll cost to haul it away."

Liam didn't say anything for a minute. "Okay. Well, look, can your mom come? It's only a few hours' drive, and she can help with the bank stuff as well as I can. And then you can ride back with her, since you're going to visit anyway."

Katie let that sit for a moment. Liam had just managed to excuse himself from doing anything at all to help her—and a part of her wasn't even surprised. The distance that had grown between them over the past few months felt like it might be permanent. Here she was, dealing with what was probably the most significant thing ever to happen in her family, and rather than offering to come and help, her husband had chosen to go to some noisy, crowded happy hour with people he claimed he didn't even like that much.

"There's a guy living next door," she said for some reason. "Former marine. Nice guy, probably around thirty, in awesome shape. He's come over a couple of times and offered to help, since he's really good with tools. Maybe I can ask him to help me clear out the house."

"Yeah, that sounds good," Liam said distractedly. "You can probably hire people cheap down there."

Katie closed her eyes and fumed. She'd just implied that she was spending time with a hot single man, and Liam hadn't even noticed.

"Actually, I think I'll stay here awhile longer," she said tightly. "I'll deal with the house and give Scarlett a hand with things. We'll probably miss my fertile days this month, but I'm starting to think you don't care about that anyway."

"Jesus, Katie. Look, I'm sorry if I'm not reacting the way you want me to. I know you're disappointed about not being pregnant."

"But you're not," she said dully.

"Not like you are. I mean . . . you have to admit, the timing isn't really right."

"You're the one who wanted to start trying last January!"

"Yeah, I know we talked about it then, but—"

"I asked you like fifty times if you were sure. Remember? When we were in Aruba?"

"It's not my fault things change," Liam shot back. "I had no way to know I'd be up for a promotion. Or that you'd get so . . . never mind. This is stupid. All I was saying is let's try to chill with what's right in front of us for a while, okay? Revisit this when things calm down."

"That's just great," Katie said. "Because what's in front of *you* is a bar full of BU girls and an open tab. And I'm standing in a parking lot wearing plastic shoes and talking on a phone I had to borrow from a stranger."

"Then come home," Liam said. "Or stay there and deal with it. Either way, I don't care. Look, I don't know what else I can say to you that isn't going to piss you off more."

Katie opened her mouth, then closed it on her retort. What difference would it make? Liam had been perfectly clear—he didn't want a baby anymore, he didn't care enough to come to Texas, he literally didn't care if she came home or not.

And the worst part was that none of that surprised her. Coming to Texas had somehow forced her to face a few things that she'd been pretending not to know. The truth was, her job performance *hadn't* been all that great lately, because she just couldn't seem to care about her work. And she'd been putting off her friends, even dear Lolly, who was always so generous, because she couldn't bear to keep pretending that everything was just fine with her and Liam.

Her life had somehow taken a wrong turn, and she'd had no idea how to get it back on track—and then her grandmother's death had forced the issue.

"You're right," she said to Liam, suddenly tired of talking to him. "There's nothing you can do for me. Just the bank, okay? Just swear to me you'll get that done. Do it first thing in the morning, before you go to work. Text my cousin when it's done."

"Anything else, boss?" Liam said sarcastically.

"No, I think that's it," Katie said tersely. "Go back to your little celebration."

She ended the call without saying goodbye.

Back inside, Jam had paid for his groceries and was reading the notices on the bulletin board.

"Listen," Katie said, making a split-second decision as she handed back the phone. "I haven't had a real drink in weeks. I think tonight's the night. If you promise to keep that mutt from attacking me, we can sit on my grandmother's back porch and you can tell me what I missed out on, not knowing her."

Jam Mifflin considered her offer. "I'm not sleeping with you, just to be clear," he said. "That isn't part of the deal."

"I wasn't asking," Katie said, aiming for outrage and missing the mark. "I'm married."

"And I don't talk about this, either." He pointed to the prosthesis.

"That's fine," Katie said. "You hear one how-I-lost-my-leg story, you've heard them all, am I right?"

Where this flippant bravado was coming from, Katie had no idea, but she willed herself not to blink and held her ground through yet another Jam Mifflin staring contest.

"I guess you're the black sheep in the family," he finally said. "Margaret did warn me, so I've got only myself to blame."

Katie plucked a bottle of vodka off the shelf, the expensive stuff. She usually didn't drink hard liquor, but the way the evening was shaping up, she figured she'd need something a little stronger than chardonnay. "What exactly did she warn you about?" she asked.

"She said the women in her family have the kind of sense that shows up too late to do any good."

"Maybe," Katie said, remembering her first glimpse of her cousin, driving all that way to pick up a virtual stranger. She thought of Liam, buying rounds and soaking up his coworkers' attention. And she thought of that hot afternoon so many years ago when she'd passed through her grandmother's life, never expecting to return. "But maybe not."

"You sure you're okay to climb up here?" Katie called down through the trapdoor in the attic floor. A cobweb brushed against her cheek, making her flinch and flail until she realized it was actually the chain of a lightbulb.

She gave it a tug and flooded the attic with light. Jam was climbing nimbly up the ladder. "I've done a triathlon with just this one leg," he said. "So yeah, I think I can handle it."

He stepped into the attic, ducking under the sloped roof, and looked around. For a moment neither of them said anything.

"Huh," Katie finally ventured.

"You know, I could have told you," Jam said. "I've been up here a few times helping her clear out stuff."

"Well, why didn't you, then?" The attic was bare, save for a thick layer of dust and a single old chair with a broken leg.

"Didn't want to crush your dream. You were acting like you thought she'd stashed a fortune up here. Besides, Margaret could be unpredictable. For all I knew she'd changed her mind after we got it all cleaned out."

They'd spent the last hour drinking vodka out of juice glasses and wandering through the house, Katie opening cabinets and drawers and peering into closets, Jam following without comment. The clutter that had greeted her when she'd first toured the house turned out to be deceptive: for all the furniture jammed into the house, the paintings and curios and teacups and umbrella stands and multiple sets of crystal in the breakfront, there were surprisingly few personal mementos. The few clothes in the closets seemed relatively new. The books on the shelves were mostly recent paperbacks. The rolltop desk in the wood-paneled den was empty save for a roll of stamps and a few pens.

"I guess she wasn't very sentimental," Katie said forlornly. The attic was the last place she'd thought to look for clues to who Margaret had been.

"That's true, but she also got it in her head to get everything organized a couple years ago," Jam said. He was standing close, by necessity. He smelled like sawdust and liquor, and up close she could see tiny lines around his eyes. "She didn't want anyone to have to clean up after her. But there's one more thing you should see."

In Katie's memory of her long-ago visit, the backyard had been a veritable maze of exciting possibilities. Weeds and flowers competed along a stone path, and a rabbit had peered at her through an overgrown hedge, its nose twitching before it dashed away through a hole in the fence. The ground under a stand of fruit trees had been littered with yellow lemons, and there had been a gazebo whose peeling trim was carved into intricate patterns.

But her favorite thing had been a little pond that was covered with a thick green layer of algae, from which a loud croaking emanated. She'd taken a stick and skimmed the surface, stirring up a few jewel-winged dragonflies. She crouched down to touch the back of a little turtle sunning on a rock and felt a thrill of bravery.

She didn't remember there being a garage at the back of the lot, much less an apartment above it, but Jam said that a fair number of trees had been cut down over the years, so maybe the garage had been hidden behind them. Now, as they picked their way across the yard under the bright moon, she saw that the stately two-story garage matched the house, with its stained and flaking stucco and tiled roof—and it was easily as large as any of the newer homes that had been built on the sold-off land.

As they drew closer, Katie heard the movement of an animal in the bushes and instinctively drew closer to Jam. But the next moment, the mutt appeared, slinking in a cautious circle around them, keeping his distance.

"Oh, hey there, Royal," Katie said. "I meant to get you a bone at the market."

"He shouldn't have those," Jam said. "They can splinter and damage his stomach or intestines. I'll bring some kibble over when we're done here."

"You heard him," Katie told the dog. "Don't blame me."

Royal sat on his bony haunches, watching her, his head cocked to the side. From this angle, she thought she could see a little border collie in him. She held out her hand, keeping enough distance that she could retreat if he lunged. Royal sniffed delicately, then gave her a heavy-lidded gaze of indifference.

"Oh, you're warming up to me, aren't you?"

"I wouldn't be so sure," Jam warned her. "Don't approach him."

"They have dogs in Massachusetts. I know how they work."

Slowly, Katie bent down until she was crouching, hands on her knees. She willed Royal to come closer, if only to prove Jam wrong, but he merely watched her with an expression of exquisite boredom. Scarlett's tight shorts cut into her thighs, and she was pretty sure that a good portion of her butt cheeks was exposed. "Okay, your loss," she said, trying to stand up as gracefully as she could.

Meanwhile, Jam had gotten the door open and turned on the lights. A narrow wooden staircase led up to the second floor; to the right was the cavernous, empty garage. A few rusting tools hung from pegs over a wooden bench near the back, and an overturned stool lay on the floor. The air inside smelled of oil and tobacco and dirt.

Katie followed Jam into the landing at the base of the stairs, but he turned, blocking her from going up.

"Listen, if you don't mind my asking . . . what exactly are you hoping to find?"

"I don't have any family besides my mom. I mean, and Scarlett's side, I guess, but I never knew any of them. And my mom never talks about the past."

"So you're hoping to find the answers to all your questions here. Skeletons in the family closet and all that."

Katie shrugged. "I guess. Maybe. I don't know."

"Because I don't think your mom and Margaret were very close."

"That's not exactly a news flash."

"I just didn't want you to expect . . . anything."

"Okay, well, Mr. Feelings, thanks for looking out for me but I think I can handle it."

"Thank God!" a voice called behind Katie, making her jump. She whipped around, backing into Jam, and shone her flashlight on someone crossing the backyard.

"Scarlett?"

"Yes! It's me!" Her voice was bright—unnaturally so, and when she got close enough for Katie to see, her eyes looked bloodshot and puffy, like she had been crying and was doing her best to hide it. "I looked all over the house, and the lights are on and the front door's unlocked and I thought you'd been kidnapped. What on earth are . . . *Jam?*"

"He was going to show me the apartment," Katie said defensively. "Also, there's a dog."

A low, throaty growl came from behind Scarlett. Royal was trying to back into the bushes, but the brambly low branches blocked him.

"Who's that?" Scarlett asked, backing away hurriedly.

"That's Katie's new dog," Jam said.

"It is not!"

"Finders keepers." Jam gave her what she was pretty sure was the first smile she'd seen on his face, and she had to admit, it was a nice one.

"I didn't find him, I just—"

"I know. *He* found *you.*"

"Well, *well!*" Scarlett said, as Royal slunk back toward the house and started nosing around the porch. "What else have you been doing while I was gone? You guys kind of smell like you've been drinking."

"Yeah, okay, maybe a little."

"I was just heading home," Jam said. "You two enjoy your evening."

"Jeez, Jam, I didn't mean to run you off—"

"You didn't. I've got gun trials in the morning. Moving the girls up to the rifle tomorrow."

"All girls this time?"

"Yeah, three of 'em. Two are sisters—difficult little bitches, so I need a clear head." He jogged off, slapping Scarlett on the shoulder hard enough to knock her sideways as he passed, and vaulted over the dried-up pond, landing nimbly before letting himself through a gap in the fence.

"Um, did he just say . . ."

"Hmm? Oh, that. Can I have some of whatever you're drinking?"

Katie handed her the glass she'd carried with her, and Scarlett drained the last inch in one gulp, then burped delicately. "Is there more?" she said hopefully.

"Sure," Katie said, "only I'm already kind of drunk here, and I'll come right out and say I think you've been crying, and if you need me to sober up so I can do a good job of listening I probably need to take a quick shower or something, which I totally will, if—"

"You can be drunk and still listen," Scarlett said. "I don't mind. In fact, it might make it easier."

"Okay then," Katie said. She grabbed her cousin's hand. "We have to go by the man-eating brute, though, so come around this way so he doesn't get you by the throat."

"Didn't you feed him? He's just hungry," Scarlett said as they skirted the porch. "All Gomma's strays are spoiled."

Katie went to the bathroom and, when she was washing up, took a good look at herself. She definitely looked tipsy. But also, the humidity and lack of styling tools had left her hair in soft, cascading waves, and her skin had a faint sheen of sweat that was weirdly flattering.

Had Jam noticed?

Back in the kitchen, Scarlett had mixed two tall tumblers of vodka and the generic ginger ale that Katie had seen in the fridge and was filling a bowl with kibble.

"Where'd you get that?"

"Gomma's stash, down there." Scarlett pointed to a corner cabinet, and sure enough, she'd missed several bags of dog and cat food and a huge bag of birdseed when she'd been poking around earlier. "Her secret shame. Jam was just her enabler."

"I guess Royal wasn't her first . . . ?"

"Oh hell no. When Jam came back home the second time, after his mom got married and moved away, he was planning to sell the place. Gomma wanted him to stay, so she found a stray that she said she needed his help with. Oh, and by the way, that whole bitches thing—he meant dogs."

"I figured that out, Scarlett," Katie said drily. "Give me a little credit. But what's a gun trial?"

"That's where, if a puppy's going to hunt, they have to get it used to the sound of a gun going off.

They start with a pistol and move up to a twenty-two, then a shotgun. A skittish dog can't handle it, but at least they find out early on before they make the problem worse."

"But then what happens to the dog?"

"Every once in a while you get a hunter that returns the dog. Most breeders will take them back. But most of them, well, you can guess how it goes, people get attached. It becomes the house dog and never has to work a day in its life."

Katie thought of the dog in her backyard, slinking along the edges of the yard, baring its teeth at the slightest provocation. That was not a dog that had wormed its way into anyone's heart.

But it was also not Royal's fault.

She grabbed her drink. "Can I do it? Feed him?"

"Be my guest," Scarlett said. "That actually sounds kind of entertaining. And I can drive you to the emergency room after he bites your hand off."

Scarlett had kicked off her shoes, and Katie did the same before following her out onto the back porch. She turned out the light so that the only light came from the moon, and the glow from the windows of the neighboring houses. One of which belonged to Jam, so it was a good thing she wasn't the least bit attracted to him or anything.

Scarlett grabbed a threadbare lawn chair from under a tree and dragged it over, plopping down in it a safe distance from the porch to watch. Katie took a sip of her drink and sat on the porch with her back against the house and the bowl of kibble between her feet. She picked up a nugget and chucked it in Royal's direction. He seemed to debate with himself for a moment before slinking forward and retrieving the bit of food.

"So," Katie said casually, tossing a second chunk to the dog, "what happened? And remember, I'm drunk, so you can tell me the truth. I mean, I've already figured out that Merritt isn't exactly boyfriend of the year."

Scarlett didn't say anything for a long moment. Then she let out an aggrieved sigh.

"Okay, look. I don't need a lecture. Merritt's got his issues, but he's not, like, *abusive*. I do know the difference, okay? My bio-dad put my mom in the hospital after he knocked her up, when she was only sixteen."

"That seems like kind of a low bar," Katie said after a moment had passed.

"But it's fucking hard, you know? We haven't been getting along all that well, but I don't exactly have all kinds of alternatives lined up. Before Mom died, I thought— I always knew I could go back and live with her. But . . . see, I went straight from our trailer to Merritt's place. I've never lived on my own, or even with a roommate. I guess— I just feel like I haven't had any practice. And Merritt doesn't like any of my friends, so they don't really come around like they used to, and I'd feel stupid calling them. And besides, sometimes he can be so sweet. I mean, really sweet, not like he's faking it." She tapped her forehead. "He's got a few issues, right? But I feel like, all of us do, at some level. And I know that doesn't mean he gets to treat me bad or whatever. But most of the time he's fine."

Katie was biting her lip to keep herself from saying anything. This was real; this was important—and she was half in the bag and slurring her words.

How many times had she tried to talk to her mother about the ridiculous choices she made in men? Her last husband—Gil, the doctor—had been at turns desperately dull and officious, and about as attractive as a fresh cow pie. But when Katie pointed out that Georgina didn't love him, her mother quit speaking to her for over a month.

She tossed some kibble to the dog, but her aim was off and the nuggets fell short, fanning out on the porch. Royal stared balefully at her over the gulf of the old, weathered boards.

"Suit yourself," she said. "I thought you were hungry."

The dog's eyelid twitched and he gave her a long, assessing look. Then he loped up the stairs and hoovered up the food before retreating again.

"Aha," Katie said. "I think he's starting to trust me."

"Yeah, right up until he sinks his teeth in your neck," Scarlett scoffed. "So tell me, were you and Jam up there doing the nasty when I got here? 'Cause you both looked like you got caught with your hands in the cookie jar."

"No! We were doing exactly what I said we were doing—going up there to look around."

"It's okay with me," Scarlett said. "I'm fine with it."

"Scarlett, you do understand that I'm married, right?"

"I mean, yeah . . . that's what you said. Only, it doesn't take a genius to figure out you and him are having trouble."

Great. "It's not like that," Katie said. Then she hiccupped.

"See?"

"See what?" Another hiccup—this one louder. She covered her mouth with her hand. "Excuse me! I don't usually drink like this."

"Well, okay. But you wouldn't be hiccupping like that unless you were lying to yourself."

"What? That's ridiculous."

"No, it's not," Scarlett said earnestly. "My mom always said if you start hiccupping and you can't stop, you're trying to talk yourself into something. Or out of something. Or you're just generally in denial."

"Scarlett . . ." Katie took a small, dainty sip of her drink. Really, it would be a good idea to slow

330

down. "All couples go through difficult times." But wait—she was supposed to be guiding her cousin *away* from her terrible boyfriend. "I mean, sometimes it's because they shouldn't be together at all, or the guy is . . . is . . . um." She took another sip, a bigger one, to give herself time to focus.

"The guy is?" Scarlett prompted helpfully.

"The guy is *selfish,*" Katie said, enunciating carefully, wiping her mouth on her forearm. "He says he wants to start a family, right? And you think you're both on the same page? But all he does is work and . . . and . . ."

Her eyes were blurry, and she dabbed at them experimentally. Huh. She seemed to be crying.

"Hang on," Scarlett said, setting down her drink. She disappeared into the kitchen and came back with a paper towel, ignoring Royal's warning growls, plopped down next to Katie and dabbed gently at her face. "You had a little, um. Eyeliner, or something. Do you love him?"

"Liam? Well, of course I do."

"You sure about that? Look, I saw how you were with Jam. There were practically flames coming out of the two of you. Does Liam do *that* to you?"

Katie snorted just as she hiccupped again, which made her giggle. "Oops."

"You know what this makes me think of? When I was thirteen, a boy at school said I had a big ass. I still had some baby fat on me, I guess, and anyway it just about killed me because I *liked* this boy. So I decided to go on this diet one of my friends told me about where you pick one thing and just eat that, only that. And my thing was popcorn because I *loved* popcorn. I made a big batch in the morning and I ate it all day long. The first day was great, and after three days I was kind of tired of popcorn but I thought my ass looked a little smaller so I just kept going. But after about a week I was so sick of popcorn that even the thought of it disgusted me."

"I think I see what you're doing here," Katie mumbled.

"I'm not saying Liam's popcorn."

"But you're not . . . not saying . . . not popcorn. That he *is* popcorn."

"Yeah, sweetie, something like that." Scarlett smiled wistfully. "Although what do I know? I'm not exactly good at relationships."

"I just thought . . . I mean, we never used to fight. Everything was the way it was supposed to be, you know? But maybe we were both just trying to fit in these . . . these *templates* our families and friends had of us. Like Liam was a *successful advertising executive,* right, and I had a job at this branding firm that everyone wants to work at. Seriously, all my friends were so jealous, but by the second month I was there I was so stressed out my hair started to fall out.

"And then all of our friends started having babies. And I mean it was like a baby blizzard—I was going to one baby shower after another. And it just kind of seemed like it was time. Plus I always thought I'd be good at it. Being a mom. I mean . . . I couldn't do any worse than Georgina." Katie realized that she'd been tossing the kibble shorter and shorter distances, until the pieces were falling only inches from her feet. Royal didn't look happy about it—his ears were flattened against his skull and his eyes rolled up when he lapped at the food—but he had inched forward on his belly until he was almost close enough to touch.

Not that she was about to try. She valued her hands too much.

"I think you'd be a good mom," Scarlett said quietly. She put her arm around Katie and held her, which was both awkward and comforting, and after a while Katie blew her nose in the paper towel and sat up straighter.

"God, I'm sorry," she said. "We were supposed to be talking about your problems. I swear I'm not always this selfish. Or—or maybe I am, but—"

"Look," Scarlett exclaimed softly, pointing.

Royal was watching her with what looked like canine concern. Scarlett toed the bowl of kibble toward him over the splintery boards, and after hesitating a moment, he ate the rest in a few bites. After a final furtive glance, he retreated at a trot, disappearing through the same break in the fence that Jam had used.

"I told you he liked me," Katie said.

"Nah, you're just a free meal," Scarlett said. "You could be Jack the Ripper, but if you smeared some raw hamburger on your skin he'd probably follow you anywhere. Now, with Jam, on the other hand, you might want to play a little harder to get."

"Stop!" Katie shrieked, scrambling to her feet. "Watching Royal eat makes me realize I never had any dinner. There's fish sticks and a package of mixed vegetables in the freezer—how about we pretend they didn't expire months ago?"

"Mmmm," Scarlett said. "My favorite—how'd you know?"

Chapter Twenty-Two

March 1977

Margaret set the basket of folded laundry on the papasan chair, practically the only surface in the old coachman's apartment that wasn't already burdened with clutter. Georgina liked to sit in the chair and talk on her princess phone for hours at a time—all night long for all Margaret knew, since Georgina had moved into the apartment when she was fifteen, nearly three years ago.

Both the chair and the telephone had been gifts from Caroline, whose generosity had ratcheted up sharply since her diagnosis last year. At the time, her doctor had predicted that she wouldn't last six months, but until last week she'd still been feeling well enough to climb the stairs to her room. Now there was a hospital bed in the living room, delivered two days ago, and Margaret couldn't get a moment's rest unless she escaped to do an errand or sneak up to the apartment.

At fifteen, Georgina had hung a hand-lettered sign on the door that read "Keep OUT that means YOU Mom!!!" Now the sign was gone, but Georgina was just as fierce in her insistence on privacy. Nevertheless, she made an exception for the delivery of laundry—otherwise, she would have had to do it herself.

Margaret leaned against the doorjamb, exhausted. She'd been up no fewer than four times last night when she heard Caroline's moans traveling up the stairs and through the open door of her room. It was as if her hearing had grown preternaturally strong, stronger even than it had been when Hank used to stay out late at night and she lay awake waiting for the turning of the key in the door.

She let her gaze travel the room, looking, as always, for evidence of what went on in her daughter's head and heart. Georgina was aloof and often hostile to Margaret; she was grudgingly polite to Caroline, effusive with her girlfriends, and positively seductive with boys, a precocious siren. Since the arrival of the hospital bed, however, Georgina had gone silent and unreadable, gliding around the house in stocking feet, barely eating. Just yesterday Margaret had caught her sitting on the old sofa in the last light of day, watching her grandmother sleep.

One might think that the impending death of the child's grandmother might sweeten her up a little. But instead it seemed to have rendered her numb. It was as though she wasn't entirely there—as though a piece of her was flying high above, where Margaret could not follow; as though she'd taken refuge in the searing blue skies of the travel poster depicting a Grecian seaside village that was pinned to the wall over Georgina's bed.

The bed. It had been a plain, worn iron bed when Margaret had lived there so long ago, with baby Georgina nestled next to her on the sagging mattress. Now the iron frame had been painted a brilliant lime green (and not very tidily; there were spots of paint on the old plank floor that Georgina hadn't bothered to clean up) and a pile of secondhand quilts was mounded on the mattress Caroline had insisted on buying when Georgina moved into the apartment. A large pillow that Georgina had bought from a street market (actually, Margaret was nearly certain that she had stolen it, which would be unsurprising behavior from the band of hippies and punks she was hanging around with) was silk-screened with a lush pink large-petaled flower that looked so like a woman's private parts that Margaret couldn't bear to look at it.

The entire bedroom was a riot of color and clutter. It hurt Margaret's eyes—or rather, the place behind her eyes where her headaches were born. These days, a bad one could keep her in bed for the entire afternoon, and Margaret had to resist the urge to flee. She was here looking for clues, and she meant to find them while Georgina was safely gone for the weekend at some outdoor concert in, of all things, a fallow field off Highway 243. (If that's where she had really gone: Georgina had refused Margaret's offer of a perfectly good suitcase and stuffed a dress and a peasant blouse into an old canvas bag she found hanging on a nail in the garage, something that Hugh had probably used for rags. She'd added a paper bag full of foul-smelling tea bags and two lipsticks and a blush compact, a hand mirror and her hairbrush. Margaret, for her part, couldn't imagine how one would get through two whole days in the outdoors with such meager provisions, and suspected that Georgina was actually planning to spend the weekend in some boy's house while his parents were away.)

Somewhere in this apocalypse of a room there was a diary—the one habit Georgina seemed to have inherited from her. She often spotted it tucked furtively under her daughter's arm or wedged between the papasan chair's frame and cushion. It was a pink vinyl-covered thing, bursting with dog-eared pages and all kinds of ephemera that served as bookmarks—strips of photographs from the carnival photo booth and torn dollar bills and cocktail napkins and bus tickets. In it, Margaret suspected, were, if not the secrets to her daughter's soul, at least answers to some of the questions that plagued her: Namely, what did Georgina think about when she was sitting sullenly at the dinner table waiting to be excused? What on earth did she see in that horrible boy with the grotesque sideburns?

And—the most pressing question of all—why did Georgina *despise* her so?

Hands on hips, Margaret tried to decide where to search first. She would have to be careful—as random as the clutter appeared to Margaret, she knew that there was a kind of strange order known only to her daughter, and that if she was careless when searching the stack of her drawings or the pile of library books or even the overflowing wastebasket in the corner, she'd be found out for sure.

She decided to start in the part of the room that had once served as a kitchenette. Georgina used the old pine cupboards to store all kinds of things, mostly memorabilia from her childhood—the red plastic monkeys were strung like Christmas lights from the knobs, and the shelves were full of board games and cigar boxes full of Barbie clothes and Lite-Brite pegs and troll dolls.

She threaded her way gingerly through the mess on the floor, unable to stop herself from picking up several dishes and bowls as well as two empty Big Red bottles. Then she noticed something sitting on the narrow strip of counter. Between a shoe box filled with makeup (some unopened, no doubt more evidence of her daughter's shoplifting with her hoodlum girlfriends) and two of Caroline's old handbags and a bottle of eau de toilette that had gone missing from Margaret's dressing table was a letter. Its crisp white ordinariness stood out in the cacophonous tableau, and when Margaret saw the return address, she caught her breath.

Setting down the dishes and bottles, she seized the letter and made a break for it, holding it against her skirt until she was in the house and up the stairs with her bedroom door closed and locked. Her daughter might be forty miles away in a field getting bitten by chiggers and serenaded by hippies, or she might be five blocks away getting stoned in Duke Sauer's parents' lanai, but either way, she would have a fit if she knew what her mother had stumbled on.

Georgina had been telling the truth after all, judging by the dirt on her skirt and the sunburn that was already peeling on her shoulders. She came through the door as twilight was dappling the kitchen with gold and Margaret was peering over her reading glasses at the *Joy of Cooking* propped up against the toaster, attempting a Mornay sauce for chicken divan.

"What's for dinner?" Georgina asked by way of greeting, dumping the canvas bag—even more misshapen now, with bits of grass and twigs stuck to it—in the hallway. Something clanked inside, some new "treasure" that Georgina had picked up somewhere. She looked lovely despite her slightly stale odor and the knotted tangles of her hair.

Margaret had been preparing for this moment all day. She was glad her mother was asleep in the other room; she didn't need Caroline to hear. She removed her glasses and set them on the counter with trembling fingers, and untied her apron and folded it over a chair before plucking the envelope from behind the coffee canister, where she'd concealed it earlier. She slapped the envelope onto the kitchen table and, in a high-pitched voice that didn't sound like her own at all, demanded "Do you want to explain this to me?"

Georgina glanced at it, then scowled. "I assume you read it, so what's there to explain?"

"How about starting with why you've been telling me you hadn't heard back from UT yet? That you were pretty sure you hadn't gotten in, since other people had already gotten their acceptance letters?"

Georgina slumped in a chair and rested her arms on the table. *No elbows on the table,* Margaret thought automatically.

"Okay, Mother, you're right. I was accepted. But—"

"Accepted? Accepted, with a *scholarship!*" Margaret interrupted. "Do you understand what that means? You can save some of your college money for something else. For when you get married."

"Huh," Georgina said in a bored voice. "That money's mine now, to do whatever I want with. Grandpa never said I had to use it for school. All I have to do is walk down to the bank and ask for it, that's what Grandma said."

Oh, the perfidy. Margaret had thought she'd convinced her mother to collude with her, to help ensure that her headstrong daughter didn't throw away her future.

"Georgina! Your grandfather intended for you to use that money for your education. He believed very strongly that you should attend college."

"Why? You went, and it didn't help you at all. I bet I could marry a drunk and get knocked up without taking a single class."

Margaret slapped her.

She hadn't meant to—she was standing above her daughter and she'd started out intending to shake her by the shoulder, to force her to listen to reason—and then her palm had bounced off Georgina's smooth, freckled cheek.

Immediately she thought of that day almost two decades ago back in the Vandeveer Hotel, her own mother staring at her in horror but also a strange kind of satisfaction after hitting her. She wondered if this moment had been inevitable, passed down in the blood, along with the propensity to fall vastly short of one's potential.

"I wanted better for you," she said hollowly. "I wanted you to get to do the things I never did."

Georgina laughed. "Oh, you can count on that, Mother. I plan to do *everything* you never did."

Then she stretched, taking her time to get up from the table—it was as if she was made of melting caramel, she moved so languidly—and picked up her bag and pushed past Margaret to the back screen door, letting it slam behind her, and leaving her mother holding the envelope in the empty kitchen.

The next morning she was gone. Margaret realized, standing in the door of the apartment that had finally been restored to a sort of order, the clothes Georgina had left behind stuffed into the dresser and nearly everything else mounded in a trash heap in the middle of the room, that in her heart of hearts she had seen this coming.

Georgina, who'd come into the world on the crest of the wave of her parents' tumultuous union, had now slipped out to the vast sea of her future, leaving Margaret forgotten and emptied on the shore.

Chapter Twenty-Three

Katie woke with the sun warming her back, a lovely sensation that was distinctly at odds with the cottony feeling of her mouth.

A hangover! The more ambitious part of her brain announced. She blinked several times, her eyelids feeling dry and sandy, and saw that she'd made it into bed—but not alone. Scarlett was curled up with her back to Katie, cradling the covers bunched in her arms like a teddy bear.

The end of the evening came back to Katie: they'd eaten their freezer-burned supper at the dining room table by the flickering glow of several candle stubs stuck in tarnished silver candlesticks, drinking a fresh round of vodka and ginger ale, and Scarlett had tried to explain a promise that Merritt had extracted from her concerning the inheritance, which Katie did her best to reassure her she was not obligated to keep. Then Scarlett had told Katie a story about Jam that was hard to follow, involving Scarlett getting her period for the very first time at school while her mother was pulling a double shift at the restaurant where she waited tables, and Jam being the only person who could pick her up and go to the drugstore for her and then sit in the living room watching *Jeopardy* and calling out encouragement while Scarlett wrestled with a maxi pad in the bathroom.

"It's funny," Scarlett had said. "He knew exactly where the tampons were in the store. I mean, not that it's important, but . . . what if it's, you know, *important?*"

Katie let her eyelids drift closed. Maybe she could manage to fall asleep again and spend the morning drifting in and out of dreams, and then they could wake up and go for more of those delicious breakfast burritos.

Something crinkled underneath her. She leaned up on her elbow and pulled a small piece of paper from the sheets, and it came back to her: searching for a cookie sheet on which to bake the fish sticks, she'd discovered a cigar box behind a Bundt pan in the pantry. Inside, bound with a rubber band that snapped in her hands, was a stack of mourning cards for the children who had perished in the school explosion.

She and Scarlett had pored over the cards, examining the photographs and reading the names aloud. There were almost three dozen of them. Had Margaret's parents gone to all of those funerals? There was no card for Ruby in the stack; could they not bear to keep one, to see their daughter's name engraved above the dates of her birth and death? It was almost impossible to imagine, all those children buried in the space of days or weeks, an entire generation simply vanished.

Had Caroline gotten the box down from the shelf from time to time, remembering the children who'd once run gaily through the halls of the school, who'd squirmed on the church pews and played baseball in the park and gone door to door to collect metal for the war? The card she had taken upstairs to bed was for a little girl named Tabitha Coates, who'd been eleven, just like Ruby, with a shy smile and a smattering of freckles across her nose.

Had Tabitha and Ruby been friends? Had she played in this very house? Sipped lemonade in the backyard?

How had Tabitha's parents endured without her?

Someone was knocking on the front door. Was that what had woken her? Whoever it was paused, and then started up again, an annoyingly insistent rapping.

Maybe it was Jam. Katie's heart quickened at the thought, and she extricated herself from the tangle of blankets and got out of bed, Scarlett sighing in her sleep and tugging the sheets up under her chin.

Katie padded down the stairs. She was still in the same clothes she'd been wearing yesterday, and the shorts hadn't gotten any longer overnight.

Giving them a hard yank, she opened the door.

A man was standing there, holding a bouquet of flowers. Maybe Liam had come through after all—a thought that wasn't entirely welcome.

"They're lovely," she said perfunctorily. "I'm so sorry I didn't hear you. I was, uh, upstairs."

But what was she going to do for a tip? All she had was the thick stack of twenties from Lolly. Though, what the heck, why not? After all, she'd made the guy stand there for who knows how long.

She accepted the flowers and inhaled their scent, which was disappointingly like the inside of a refrigerator. "Stay right here," she said, "I just need to grab my purse."

"Hey, whoa, hold on. Those flowers aren't for you," the man said. "They're for Scarlett. She's here, right?"

Katie took another look and realized that he wasn't a deliveryman at all. He was dressed in brown polyester pants and a shirt with a Chem-Kleen logo stitched on the pocket . . . right above his name.

Which was "Merritt."

She thrust the flowers back at him like they were on fire. "She doesn't want these. She doesn't want to see you. You'd better go."

The friendly smile disappeared from his face like a light turned off. Now that she took a good look, she realized that Merritt wasn't at all what she'd been expecting. He was clean-cut and handsome, with nice teeth and an expensive pair of Ray-Bans.

"You're her cousin from Boston," he said accusatorily. "I know about you. You never gave a shit about her until your grandmother left her the house. Scarlett told me you weren't getting any of it, so why don't you go the fuck back there, hey?"

Katie felt her face color with rage and embarrassment. "Leave, or I'm calling the cops."

Merritt raised his eyebrows and then burst into laughter. "Yeah, huh, good idea. They'll *love* that. What exactly are you going to tell them? That I brought my girlfriend flowers? Listen, tell Scarlett to call me. Or don't—she will anyway."

He turned and sauntered back to his truck, a white van with the Chem-Kleen logo on the side and the words "No Mess Is Too Big For US!" emblazoned in purple letters. He got in and peeled away from the curb, tapping the horn and flipping her off.

Katie's heart was pounding as she went back inside. She dropped the flowers into the garbage and washed her hands. Then she twisted her hair into a knot, grabbed a trash bag, and got to work.

"Morning," Scarlett said from the doorway of the parlor half an hour later.

Katie hadn't heard her come downstairs. She

was kneeling in front of a built-in cupboard in the dining room, feeling around in back. After she'd taken out a tureen and a cake stand and a few other items that likely hadn't seen any use in years, she'd discovered a small wooden box carved with Greek letters of the Alpha Chi Omega sorority. Inside were a little gold pin shaped like a harp studded with tiny pearls and enameled with the same tiny Greek letters, a larger gold pin in the shape of a leaf set with red stones, and a folded page torn from the February 1968 issue of *Vanity Fair* with a photograph of guests at a black-tie gathering hosted by a Dallas socialite, a couple identified as Mr. and Mrs. Robert Withnall III.

"Hi there. Do you have any idea who these people are?"

Scarlett took the page and squinted, then turned it over. "Nope. But there's a Hoover vacuum cleaner ad on the back. Maybe Gomma was thinking of buying one."

She handed back the page and Katie carefully folded it and put it back in the wooden box. She stood up slowly, her legs cramping from being on her knees so long, and set the box on the dining room table.

"Wow, look at you!"

Katie glanced down at her outfit, a lavender polyester skort and matching floral top that she had taken from her grandmother's closet. They fit surprisingly well, and the elastic waist was a bonus, given all the bending and reaching she'd been doing.

"Oh God, I know. Please don't ever tell anyone. No offense, but I was getting chafing on my inner thighs from those shorts."

Scarlett made a zipping-her-lips gesture. "Is there anything left to eat? I'm starving."

"I think we cleaned the place out last night. I thought we could go get some groceries. My treat. Only before we go . . . um, Merritt came by about an hour ago."

"He did?" The change in Scarlett was instantaneous, all humor vanishing from her eyes. "What did he say?"

"He, uh, he wanted to talk to you and I told him you didn't want to see him."

"You really told him that?"

"He brought flowers, as if that was going to change—I mean, Scarlett, you aren't seriously doubting you did the right thing, are you? By coming here last night?"

"I mean, he needed some time to cool off," Scarlett said, twisting her hands anxiously. "But I never said— I mean, the thing is, he cools off almost as quick as he heats up. He just overreacts, is all. He doesn't mean any of the things he says when he's stirred up."

"But last night you said—"

"Last night we were drinking, Katie. I said a lot

of things—you did too. But this is a *relationship* we're talking about here. I've been with Merritt for almost three years. He got me through when my mom died and I didn't have anyone else. I mean, he wants me to be his *business* partner. I can't just—"

As much as Katie wanted to grab her cousin and shake some sense into her, she knew that anything more she said against Merritt was just going to make Scarlett dig her heels in further.

"Look, Scarlett, I'm sorry I didn't ask you first. It's just that you were sleeping and—and he said some things to me—but that doesn't matter, I know we were all . . . that you're hoping to work things out. I just—please don't go back there alone, okay? Let me come with you."

"He isn't going to want to see you," Scarlett said. "Not after you sent him off like that."

"Okay, I'll stay in the car. He doesn't even have to know I'm there. And if, I mean, after you talk to him, and you don't need me, I'll go."

Scarlett took a deep breath and looked up at the ceiling. "Okay," she finally said. "You really don't have to, though, because I mean, I *live* there. And I know how to handle him. But if you feel like you have to or whatever . . ."

"Good," Katie said, relief flooding through her. At least she'd bought some time. "He won't even be back from work until tonight, right? So we can, you know, get something to eat, work on the house a little—I haven't even seen the apartment yet! You can show me."

"Yeah. Okay."

"Just let me go get changed. My standards may have fallen quite a bit, but I don't think I can stand for anyone to see me in this."

"There was a cute sundress in the clothes I brought you," Scarlett said, softening. "It's a real pretty pale yellow, it'll look great with your hair."

"Perfect. And do you mind if I rinse off real quick? I've stirred up so much dust I feel like I've been rolling in it."

"Yeah, go ahead. I'll keep going through this stuff."

Katie hurried through her shower, combing out her wet hair to let it dry naturally and picking through the cosmetics Scarlett had brought her. A bit of coppery eye shadow, navy-blue mascara, an intense fuchsia lip gloss that softened to a flattering shade once she'd applied it—when she was done, Katie was surprised at how good she looked. She put on the sundress and tried to adjust the straps over her bra for a few moments before giving up.

"Ready or not," she called as she came down the stairs. "Here I . . ."

But Scarlett wasn't in the dining room. Puzzled, Katie made the circuit of the downstairs, through the dining room to the parlor, the front hall, the den, the morning room, and back to the kitchen. She raced back upstairs and checked every bedroom. She leaned out the windows and scanned the street, then ran to the back of the house and checked the backyard.

"No, no, *no,*" she mumbled.

But it was no use. Scarlett was gone.

Katie pounded on Jam's front door, which was painted a moody sea blue and adorned with a brass knocker in the shape of a dog's head. When Jam didn't answer, she tried the knob, but it was locked. She was about to go when she heard a chorus of barking . . . from the backyard.

She let herself through the side gate and around the side of the house. On her right was the overgrown hedge separating Jam's house from Margaret's; on the other side of it would be the broken-down fence through which he'd made his escape last night. On this side, the hedge was trimmed neatly and restrained by white pickets and a flower bed filled with asters and snapdragons.

Katie rounded the corner and nearly ran into a lineup of dogs, nearly a dozen of them, each with a child holding its leash. The dogs were small and large and in between, and the children ranged from a little boy of six or seven holding on to a fat, panting pug to a girl in her early teens who was having a tug-of-war with what looked like a cross between a beagle and a dachshund.

Standing on the other side of the circle, toward the back of the yard, was Jam. He was wearing a baseball cap and a wrinkled Hawaiian shirt, over an even more decrepit and baggy pair of shorts than usual.

"Hey kids, look—a stranger has somehow broken into my backyard," Jam called. "I think she's about to approach your dogs. Quick, what do you do?"

All the children but the owner of the beagle mix, who had somehow managed to trip over the leash and ended up on the ground in a tangle with the dog, stepped between Katie and their dogs. "Please stay where you are," they all chorused in unison, before ordering their dogs to sit. Only two of the dogs sat right away; the rest required pleading and cajoling and, in one case, a little boy trying to sit *on* his spaniel. During the commotion, Jam watched Katie with his arms folded and the hint of a smile at his lips.

"May I have a word?" Katie asked. Something in her tone must have alerted him, because his smile disappeared.

"Good job, kids, see how long you can maintain the sit. This stranger looks like she doesn't know much about dogs, so I'm going to go teach her about the safe way to approach unfamiliar animals for a few minutes."

He jogged over and took Katie's arm, guiding her out of earshot on the side of the house.

"I need a ride," Katie said. "Scarlett's boyfriend is way out of line. I don't think she's safe with him. He came by the house this morning and I sent him away and I went to take a shower and—and I just *know* she went back there. I'm worried about her. What if he does something?"

Jam raised an eyebrow. "What would you do to stop him?"

"I—I don't know, call the cops! Or just get her to come with me. Help her pack up her stuff—"

"Katie," Jam said patiently. "Does Scarlett look like a child to you?"

"No, but—"

"And do you have any proof that she's in danger? Or that she was forced to go with him?"

"No! But what do you want me to do, just stand by and let him *hurt* her?"

Jam looked off in the distance, his expression grim. When he spoke again, he sounded tired. "Scarlett's been dating that asshole for three years. I've gone to talk to him twice. He's no idiot, Katie. He knows his rights and he stops short of anything that would get him in trouble. Buddy of mine looked him up for me—he's got a track record. Last girl he was with, she had him arrested, but she ended up dropping the charges."

"He *beat* her?"

"Not clear. Hear me out. Merritt King can be very charming. He'll probably roll out the red carpet today, just to prove you wrong. My guess is he'll be careful for a few months. And I'll tell you something else—my bet is he *is* genuinely sorry. He's probably convinced *himself* he'll never threaten her again—that's how he's able to convince *her*."

"Oh my God," Katie said, outraged. "So he could be pounding the crap out of her for all you know, but you want to do *nothing?* You almost sound like you're on his side!"

"No, I'm not. I'm just telling you to think for a minute. If Scarlett left, it's because she wants to go back, and neither you nor I are going to change her mind. Don't you think I'd like to see that worthless piece of humanity squashed like a bug? Don't you think I'd like to be the guy who does it? Scarlett . . . she's like a little sister to me. But that's why I'm playing the long game here. Whatever it takes, you know? I've let him know that the minute he makes a mistake—and he will—he answers to me. But the last time I went to see him, he called the cops after I left and said I'd threatened *him,* and I almost had a restraining order put on me. And I'm no good to her if I get locked up."

"That's . . . that's so unfair."

Jam regarded her steadily. "Seems to me you should have figured out by now that life isn't fair. Look, this class is over in another half hour. Go on home, and when I'm done talking to the parents and the kids are all picked up, I'll come get you. We can go to Scarlett's place so you can see she's safe—but then we leave. Got it?"

"Got it," Katie said in a small voice. "And thank you."

She watched him jog back toward the kids; nearly all of the dogs had gotten bored with sitting and were now sniffing at each other's butts and rolling on the grass.

"Place!" he commanded. Most of the dogs snapped to attention and sat up, with the exception of the beagle mix, who was now straining to drag his child toward a butterfly that had settled on a nearby bush.

Jam walked over to the beagle and stopped a few feet away. He dug something from his pocket and held it at his side. "Place," he said again, and this time the beagle sat down, sniffing the air, and Jam palmed him the treat as though he was bribing a maître d'.

Whatever it takes.

"I got your note," Jam said, holding out the only piece of paper Katie'd been able to find, a decades-old diner menu she'd unearthed under a stack of cookie sheets that featured a Deluxe Salisbury Steak Dinner for $1.99. She'd written "I'm in the garage" on the back and jammed it in the front doorframe. "I wasn't sure it was meant for me."

"And yet here you are."

357

That got her a ghost of a smile. "I'd say I liked your outfit—except I don't think it quite fits you."

"No?" Katie smoothed her hands over the hot pink belted minidress that barely covered her butt and gapped across the bust. "Maybe I could get it tailored."

"Did you make this mess all by yourself?"

Katie looked around the room. As she removed things from the cabinets and dresser drawers, she'd been sorting them into piles on the bed and chair, trying on a few of the more outrageous outfits. Originally she'd planned to have a "keep" pile for the things that someone might buy at the garage sale, and a "trash" pile for everything else, but she'd begun to realize that she'd stumbled on a veritable fashion time capsule that spanned the fifties, sixties, and seventies.

"This is so weird," she said, holding up a pair of orange Dacron pants that flared out at the hems. "Most of this stuff had to be my mom's, right? I mean, I can't imagine that Margaret would have worn something like this in the seventies. She would have been—what, forty-something?"

"Is that the sort of thing your mom would wear?"

"Back then? Who knows? I mean, she's definitely a clotheshorse. She's got accounts at Neiman Marcus and Nordstrom and half a dozen boutiques in Dallas." She shrugged. "It's kind of hard to explain my mom's style. She puts out a bit of a cougar vibe, but deep down she's kind of . . . sweet." Was she really defending Georgina? "Did you ever watch the TV show *Dynasty*?"

Jam snorted. "I'm a *guy*. But yeah, I know what it was."

"It was my mom's favorite show. We used to watch reruns together when I was in middle school. And she identified so hard with Krystle Carrington. Remember, she was the blond one? And Georgina did her hair the same way, and every once in a while people would tell her she looked like Krystle . . . and that made her so happy, because Krystle was gorgeous and glamorous and rich. But she was also *nice*. She was like the opposite of Alexis Carrington, who everyone loved to hate."

"And was she? . . . Nice, I mean."

Katie laughed. "Not really. Not unless you were a rich guy who wanted to take her out. Then she bent over backward. She could make a man feel like he was on top of the world." She paused, remembering those evenings when her mother started preparing for her dates hours in advance, telling Katie to go to her room and watch TV when the man arrived. "And it worked. I mean, we never wanted for anything, even though she only worked part-time—and the last guy she married left her enough money that she'll never have to worry."

"She sounds like . . . like she's not like you."

"Yeah. I guess. What about you?"

"Ah, you know, pretty much the same story—single mom, doing what it takes, raising a kid on her own. Only, my mom wasn't all that good at it. She . . . well, we're not really close."

"I'm sorry, I shouldn't have pried."

"You didn't." Jam picked up a brown and gold maxi dress with gauzy printed bell sleeves. "So, what are you going to do with all of this stuff?"

"I don't know, actually. I think some of it might be valuable. Like, look at these—they're practically mint condition." She went to the kitchenette counter, where she'd stacked the board games and puzzles, and boxes full of Barbie dolls and clothes. "Check this out, there's even a Barbie VW Camper. And you've got to see this—still in its original packaging."

She offered him the pink box reverently: a Barbie "Dream Furniture Collection Bath Chest and Commode"—complete with tiny pink towels.

"That's a pretty swell-looking pink toilet," Jam commented, handing back the box. "I wonder what the 'real water action' is."

"Well, that's the dilemma, isn't it? It might be worth thousands of dollars as long as we never open it."

"So that's what was up here this whole time? Just your mom's old clothes and toys and stuff? Margaret never brought me up here."

Katie sat down on the bed, in between a stack of furry ponchos and crocheted afghans, and a box of old costume jewelry, strings of plastic beads and medallions and mood rings. Suddenly she felt tired and a little defeated. "Yeah. I guess I was hoping . . . I mean, I thought my mom might have left more of herself behind. She never really talks about what it was like for her, living here with Margaret and her grandmother, just that she hated it and couldn't wait for the day when she could leave."

Jam cleared his throat. "I can relate."

"But you moved back here!"

Jam stared out the window, which looked out onto his own yard. In fact, Katie had covertly watched him say goodbye to the kids and dogs, shake the dads' hands, chat with the moms. Several of the moms seemed to be in no hurry to leave.

"Yeah, well. Sometimes the best way to deal with the past is to beat it into submission."

His gaze locked with hers, and for a moment they just looked at each other, inhaling the scent of old clothes.

"So," Jam finally said. "You want to head over to check on Scarlett now?"

"I was thinking about what you said. That you're probably right. I thought . . . I don't want her not to trust me, you know? I thought maybe we could wait until tonight and kind of drop in and see, like, casually ask if she wanted to get some dinner or something. And you could glare at Merritt and flex your muscles and look terrifying or whatever." A thought occurred to her: it was Saturday night, and judging from the moms' reactions, Jam had no shortage of admirers. "Unless you're busy, of course. I didn't mean to presume—"

"I'm not. But I'm not playing games with Scarlett. We make sure she's okay, let her know she can call anytime, leave. And then you can buy me dinner. There's a good Burmese place right outside of town."

"What—are you serious?"

"About which part?"

"Burmese. Back when I lived in Texas, the most exotic place I ever ate was El Fenix—and that was in *Dallas*."

"Well, little girl, things have changed since you left." That gaze again . . . and the room was feeling warmer and warmer. "So, pick you up later?"

"Um, sure. Unless—I mean, you don't have to go. If you don't want to. I could use some company."

Jam looked around dubiously. "You want me to help you go through these clothes?"

"No, I need a break from it," Katie said, picking up a box from the stack of games. "I was actually thinking we could hang out in the backyard and play Battleship."

. . .

They found an old iron table on its side in the garage, pulled it out, and placed it under the cedar elm tree. Low branches drooped almost all the way to the ground, making a sun-dappled, shady cave. Jam went next door and brought back a six-pack of beer and a container of bright green olives and a box of Triscuits, and warned her that he had never lost a game of Battleship while they set up the plastic pegboards.

"I'll be red," Katie said. "It's my lucky color."

"Red, blue, it doesn't matter—I'm going to crush you either way."

But as they drank beer and nibbled at the olives, Katie sunk two of his ships in quick succession.

"You're cheating," Jam accused.

"You just can't admit you're being beaten by a girl, even when it's obvious you're outplayed," Katie said, twisting the cap off her second beer. It was delicious in the heat of the day, the icy condensation dripping on her thighs. "Story of my life."

"You always have trouble with men?"

"Ha. Funny." She considered. "Although I did just get fired by one man, mugged by another, and . . ."

And then there was Liam.

"And?"

"Nothing. I was just thinking how nice it was to take a break from my life, actually."

"Yeah? Is that what you're doing?" Jam had been tilting back in his lawn chair, but now he lowered it to the ground and leaned forward, his knees brushing against hers. "Seriously, why have you stayed away from Texas so long?"

Katie shrugged. "I mean . . . my mom likes to travel, and she comes to visit a few times a year. And . . . and we moved around a lot in Dallas, switched schools every year or two, and Mom had all these relationships—I didn't ever live anywhere long enough to make friends."

"It's too bad you weren't closer to Margaret and Scarlett. And Heather—Scarlett's mom—she was kind of a mess, but she meant well."

"You know more about my family than I do," Katie said wistfully.

"Yeah, well." Jam stared at the ground, which was carpeted with leaves and moss and weeds. "I didn't really have one of my own. When I joined the marines, that's the first time I ever really felt like I was . . . part of something."

"Why did you—"

"Still not talking about that." Jam cut her off. "My bad, I shouldn't have mentioned it."

"Ouch," Katie said. "You know about my messy and embarrassing past. Fair's fair—if you don't want to tell me about the marines, tell me what you did before."

"Smoked a lot of weed," Jam said. "Started a few community college classes and dropped 'em.

Worked on the line at the processing plant long enough to earn a thirty-five-cent-an-hour raise and an aversion to chicken. Got my nose broken by a girl's boyfriend."

"So you're a rogue," Katie said. "A bad boy."

"Only when the situation calls for it." Jam reached for a stray curl that had sprung free from her headband and gently tucked it behind her ear, sending a bolt of desire rocketing through her.

Katie caught her breath. "Jam . . ."

"I know you're married. I also can't help noticing that he couldn't be bothered to come here with you, and that he doesn't much care how you're doing. Yeah, Scarlett told me."

"She . . . shouldn't have."

"Don't take it out on her. I asked. I texted her that first night. I told her I wanted to know about you."

"I was sure you thought I was an idiot."

"But that's how I like my women," Jam said, closing his hand around hers. "Helpless, messy— oh, and rude."

Katie stared down at her hand in his. She ought to pull away—but she didn't. "Is this like summer camp or something?" she asked. "Doesn't count because I'm thousands of miles away from home?"

"Oh, it counts, all right," Jam said.

Then he kissed her.

Or she might have kissed him first—Katie

wasn't sure of the order of things, and it didn't really matter because she was pretty sure this was the best kiss of her life. Jam's muscles were hard and his lips were soft and he smelled like dog and soap and leather, but in a good way, and he was doing something with his hand on the nape of her neck that seemed to have a direct connection to the commotion in her lady parts, and if she didn't stop soon she was going to drag him into the house and make love to him on her grandmother's bed.

There was a rustling in the branches. The leafy curtain parted, and there, panting from exertion, was Georgina. She stared at Katie and Jam as they hastily tried to disentangle from each other, and gasped.

"Katherine Jennifer Dial, what on earth are you doing in my dress?"

Chapter Twenty-Four

May 1977

"Stop moping," Margaret snapped.

Caroline had been clutching an embroidered napkin—one that Margaret had laid on her tray next to the gruel that she was tasked with getting her mother to eat each morning by the home aide, who would arrive soon, but not soon enough—letting her bony wrist flutter languidly. Her sighs were long-suffering, and it didn't help as much as it might have that she actually *was* suffering, as her expiration was taking too long in the opinion of everyone but the doctor and aide who seemed bent on squeezing a few more weeks of life out of her.

"I'm terribly sorry," Caroline wheezed, "but in my condition, there are few options left to me. Sleep and stare out the window, except when you force me to eat that disgusting swill. I wish God would realize that I'm ready to go."

Immediately Margaret's irritation drained away, and she set down the dust rag she'd been using to tidy for the aide and came to sit next to her mother. The folding chair was too low, or perhaps the bed was too high, but either way, she was at a distinct conversational disadvantage to her mother, who reclined on a mound of pillows arranged to keep her more or less upright.

"Maybe," Margaret began, and then had to stop while she collected herself. She cleared her throat. "Maybe *I'm* not ready. For you to, you know."

Caroline tsked. "Now, now, enough of that. You're just put out because Georgie hasn't written you back yet."

Instantly the ire was back. "*Written?* I told her she could call collect. I offered to send her things. The only address I have for her is this—this *hotel.*" A note had come from Georgie two weeks after she'd left home, on cheap notepaper printed with "Elizabeth Ann Mercer Hotel for Women." In all of four sentences, Georgina had communicated that she planned to be a fashion model and also an artist or poet, that everyone in Manhattan was *super nice,* and that Caroline and Margaret should not worry about her. That last bit was underlined three times above Georgina's sloppy signature. "I mean, it sounds like a house for unwed mothers." A thought stopped Margaret in her tracks. "You don't—you don't think she . . ."

Caroline laughed, a dry, papery rasp that ended in a series of gasping coughs. "And wouldn't that be rich," she wheezed. "A taste of your own medicine. But no, our Georgie's too smart for that."

Something in her mother's voice caught Margaret's attention. "What do you mean, Mother?"

Caroline managed a coy shrug. "Girls have resources these days that you and I never had."

Suspicion turned to certainty. "Mother! Did you—is she on *birth control?*"

"Oh, calm yourself. It was just a box of rubbers. And if I didn't buy them for her, she probably would have just stolen them. Besides, you should be glad. One less thing to worry about."

"Glad?" Years of hurt that Margaret had kept carefully buried threatened to spill over the levee of her heart. "Glad? I should be glad that my mother and my daughter have been sneaking around behind my back—you probably had a big laugh at my expense too, didn't you?"

She burst into tears.

Not dainty ones, either, not the silent rolling kind that she'd usually been able, whenever she argued with Caroline or Georgina, to conceal with a cough and a quick swipe at her cheek. No, these were gusty, loud sobs, and despite snatching the napkin from her mother's hand and blotting for all she was worth, she couldn't stop.

"Margaret," Caroline said in alarm. "What on earth has gotten into you?"

"She's gone," Margaret wailed. "She didn't love me, and she's been waiting her whole life to leave me. I tried. You *know* I tried. But no matter what I did, I could not make that child love me."

"Oh, nonsense," Caroline said, but in a gentler tone. "Margaret . . . oh heavens, come up here."

Margaret wiped her nose on the hanky and blinked. "Up where?"

Caroline patted the bed next to her. "Up here, obviously. It's not like I can come to you."

"But . . . is there room?" Margaret asked. Only, that wasn't the question at all; the question was why, three months before the seventieth birthday she would not live to see, her mother was finally offering an embrace.

For a moment, Margaret wondered if Caroline was about to die. As in, right now, right in front of her. Then she pushed the thought away and climbed carefully into the bed.

The hospital linens were cool and smooth and perfectly white. The aide had changed them before she left the night before, and she'd tucked and turned them more perfectly than Margaret ever could, and her mother somehow still managed to look elegant in her satin pajamas with her hands folded on the turned-back picot edge of the sheet.

As Margaret lay back gingerly against the pillows, Caroline put her thin arm around her daughter's shoulders and let out a sigh.

For a moment Margaret didn't dare even breathe. She closed her eyes and allowed herself to slowly absorb the novelty of the moment. Her *mother* had her *arm* around her. Not only that, but she was murmuring the sorts of things that . . . that mothers are meant to murmur.

"Sweetheart," Caroline whispered. "My poor, poor baby girl. You're going to be fine, you know."

Margaret allowed herself to breathe again. She smelled her mother's rosewater scent over the earthy, sour notes of illness; there was the sharpness of the bleach from the laundry, and the sun on the marigolds from the garden. Moments went by, her mother gently stroking her hair. Margaret's tears slowed, but she didn't dare break the spell by pulling away to wipe her face.

"Mother," she finally whispered. "Why couldn't you ever love me like you loved her?"

The stroking stopped for a moment. She could sense her mother considering. There was no doubt in Margaret's mind that Caroline knew exactly what she was asking.

Margaret was not at all sure she was ready to hear the answer. But if not now—when? In a day, a week, her mother would be dead. Margaret had never gotten to ask her father the same question. It was now or never.

"You weren't like that with Georgina," Margaret pressed. "You always told her . . . told her that she was pretty, and smart, and funny. You held her when she was little, I had to pry her out of your arms. It was you she ran to when she came home from school. It was you she wanted to go with her when she got her tonsils out. But you never . . . never . . ." The words trailed away. "Was it because I was a replacement baby?"

There—she'd named it, her greatest fear. She'd first heard the term used casually at one of the early Remembrance Days. She couldn't have been more than five or six, and she didn't know what the word *replacement* meant, but she was quite sure that the two ladies at the punch table were talking about her and the other children. "We are not," she said stoutly. "We're *Daisies*."

But it wasn't very many more years before she understood the term and all the implications it carried with it. She and Helene and Clara and Eileen and Rosalee and Nell, Tim and Gordon and Johnny and Lorenzo—none of them had been wanted, not really. Not for themselves, for who they really were. Their families had been complete, until the terrible tragedy that ripped the best-beloved children from their parents, leaving a gaping hole that they were desperate to fill. And then the term became a curse, one so unbearable that no Daisy ever uttered it to another.

Two of the families had seemed to recover: the Cains, who lost a daughter, carried on with their second "only" child with a cheery, brisk can-do attitude. Margaret couldn't imagine Mr. Cain hunched over his workbench, the way she'd found her father that day, but maybe it was because he now had a boy to throw a baseball with and take fishing. Maybe it had even seemed like a fair trade.

And then there were the Bakers, Margaret's least favorite Daisy family. They had had six children and had lost four, then had Lorenzo and then they did what no other Daisy family had done and had two *more* children. So Lorenzo was folded into the pious melee of a pastor's family too busy not just with their own affairs but with those of their entire congregation to continue endlessly mourning their loss.

Two relatively unscathed families out of eleven. The rest, if you looked at all closely, never really recovered. And more meetings of the Daisies than not ended in a sort of solemn gloom that even the most elaborate luncheons and ambitious Remembrance Day plans could never extinguish.

"I guess I can sort of understand," Margaret said softly. "She was perfect."

Caroline pushed herself up with great effort so that she could stare down into Margaret's face. Margaret tried to burrow into the covers, feeling ridiculous—she was a grown woman, for heaven's sake, not a toddler at naptime—but Caroline took her chin in her hand and forced her to look at her.

"She was *not* perfect," she said. "Ruby was clingy and fearful and lazy. Your father thought she'd never catch up to the other children in her class and was threatening to send her to private school. She fed her dinners to the dog—"

There had been a dog?

"—under the table and thought I didn't know and if I caught her she would just excuse herself and put it in the toilet. She copied from the other children and got terrible marks."

Margaret was aghast. She couldn't have been more shocked if Caroline had said that Ruby had actually been a goblin. "But—but the poster," she said. "The pictures—you couldn't even bear to look at them."

"Your sister wasn't perfect. Good heavens. But that doesn't mean that we didn't love her. We did, with all our hearts. I loved her much more than I ever loved your father and the same was true for him, even if we never spoke of it."

"But why . . . why couldn't you love me like that too?"

Margaret had imagined this moment for her entire life: why, she imagined asking, and she fully expected the answer to be that the love of her parents had been all used up, smashed, destroyed, before she came along. But she also could never escape the knowledge that she had not been a very lovable child.

"I know I was spoiled," she said in a rush, scrabbling to sit up. Suddenly it seemed very urgent to get the words out. "I sassed back and I was unkind and selfish and never appreciated everything you gave me. No matter how bad Ruby was, I know I was worse. But it was just that—I always felt like you were . . . I don't know. Looking past me. Looking through me. Like I wasn't there—like it was *her* you were always wishing for."

When Margaret had imagined saying this dangerous truth, she'd assumed that her mother would protest that it wasn't true, that she'd try to spare Margaret's feelings with hasty assurances that it was all in her head, that she'd been loved just as much as Ruby was.

Instead, Caroline looked at her thoughtfully for a long time. Her face, ravaged by her illness, was still except for the bright intensity of her gray eyes. Finally she cupped her hand around Margaret's cheek and took a breath.

"I'm so sorry, my darling. I wish it had been different."

So it was all true. Ruby was the best-loved, and Margaret had never been enough. She felt her heart give way, felt it flatten in defeat. The years that had taken her beauty, her sass, her once-famous wit, had turned her into this morose, lumpen thing, looking for crumbs at her mother's knee.

"But you don't know the whole story," Caroline said. "And if I may, I'd like to tell you the rest."

CHAPTER TWENTY-FIVE

Georgina couldn't stay. She had a date (an *appointment,* she called it, but eventually admitted she was meeting a gentleman with whom she'd been conducting a monthlong OkCupid campaign) in Tyler, one that, she coyly announced, might well extend into Sunday.

"I only came to make sure you hadn't fallen into the well or gotten trapped in the basement," she explained. "When I didn't hear from you, I thought something dreadful had happened. Well, not that dreadful, obviously, or I would have made a beeline!"

"So instead you made more of a fire ant line," Jam suggested. He was standing at the counter mixing drinks, at Georgina's request, and using the provisions she'd brought in the tiny trunk of her little red Miata convertible.

"Ha! You're so funny, darling! Now fill it up the rest of the way with Sprite and grenadine—more Sprite than grenadine."

Jam did as he was told and then presented Georgina with the drink, something she called a Bend Over Shirley, which included at least two fingers of raspberry vodka.

"Georgina, are you going to be able to drive?" Katie asked. She had stayed in her seat while her mother flirted shamelessly with Jam and ordered him around the kitchen she had grown up in—and hadn't said one word about the fact that she'd discovered them kissing.

Georgina clucked and shook her head. "Katie, Katie, always my little worrywart! I'm just pregaming a little."

"Don't!" Katie moaned. Georgina had a mortifying habit of picking up slang from the girls at her health club.

"Do you want something to eat with that?" Jam suggested. "I could go back to my house—"

"I'm *fine*."

"Georgina, is there anything here that you want me to save for you?" Katie asked, to change the subject. She'd given her mother a brief summary of the events since she'd arrived. Georgina took it all in stride, including the disappointingly small inheritance. "Do you want to go up to the apartment and look through your old things?"

Georgina shuddered. "Hell no. Everything here is just the way I remembered it, which is to say, depressing. And please don't start telling me I need therapy again. I'm working with the HOA board to plant a memorial tree for Margaret by the pond near the golf course, and we'll have a nice little ceremony in the spring when it's in bloom. Jam, would you like to come for that?"

"Mother!" Katie rebuked her. "Please."

"Actually, Mrs. Dial, I need to head back to my place. I've got a few things to do before we head over to Archer."

"Well, it was very nice to meet you, Jam. And please give my regards to Scarlett. Next time, I'm going to *pry* it out of you!" Georgina wagged her finger playfully at him, as though her efforts to get him to tell her about losing his leg were a merry little game they both enjoyed.

"I'll, uh, look forward to that," Jam said. "See you in a couple hours, Katie."

Neither woman spoke until the front door closed behind him. Then Georgina practically threw herself across the table. "What on earth is going on, Katie-Bear? Is this because of the baby thing? Is it hormones?"

"It's—it's nothing. I mean, it just happened—I don't know, it's been a really weird few days."

"Well, in case you want my opinion, I'm not very impressed with how Liam's handling all of this," Georgina sniffed. "I must have called him half a dozen times. And in return I get what—a single text? Here, look!"

She dug her phone out of her handbag and showed Katie. "See, it starts with the day you left."

Katie isn't answering my calls. Everything OK?

"Then he answered that night, after he got a new phone."

> We were mugged. We are both fine. Mugger got our phones and wallets. He let her keep license so OK to fly. Will send her money and cards tomorrow.

> Oh no! Poor you and poor Katie!

"Next day."

> Has she called you? Does she have a new phone yet?
> Do you have a number for her cousin?
> Liam, please check in and let me know everything is okay. Tell Katie to call me please!!!!!!
> LIAM GODDAMNIT

"—and that's when I just got in the car and came here. When did *you* last talk to him?"

"Um, yesterday, I guess. I asked him to overnight me some cash, but he had Lolly do it, and he was supposed to go to the bank this morning and change the account so I can get a new card."

"He didn't do it?" Georgina demanded angrily. "Doesn't he realize that you need *money?* I mean, look at you!"

Katie rolled her eyes. "Thanks, Mom. I *have* money; Lolly sent me like five hundred bucks. And I have higher priorities than going shopping for new clothes, believe it or not."

"Like concealer," Georgina suggested. "And I'm not sure what's going on with those shoes."

"They're Scarlett's," Katie said tiredly. "Look, I'm sure Liam did go to the bank, and he's probably been trying to call me on Scarlett's phone too, but I don't have a way to get in touch with her." It was a transparent fib, but it didn't seem to occur to Georgina to ask why Katie couldn't just call Scarlett from Jam's phone.

"Honey . . ." Georgina said, and then she held up a finger and took a long, deep draw on her drink, emptying half of it. "Ahh. That boy can mix a drink. Anyway, I know I'm probably the last person in the world who should be giving romantic advice. But if what you're doing here"—she pointed vaguely in the direction of Jam's house—"is about getting back at Liam—for not wanting to have a baby as bad as you do, for spending so much time at work, for any reason at all—then you're going to have to deal with it sooner or later. Putting on a Band-Aid, even a Band-Aid as attractive as Jam, is just going to make you feel worse eventually. I can't even count how many times I went from one man to the next because I didn't want to work on what I had. Just imagine what I've missed out on."

Katie closed her eyes and focused on her breathing. In . . . out. In . . . out. "Georgina. I'm calling bullshit. Name one man you wish you'd gone back to."

She opened her eyes to find her mother staring at her, openmouthed with surprise. "Well, but that's me," she said. "I mean . . . yeah, I wouldn't—but I'm just an awful person when it comes to men. Remember?"

"Wait one damn minute," Katie said. She certainly did remember—those were the very same words she flung at her mother her freshman year when, after telling all the girls in her new sorority that her mother was bringing her boyfriend the investment banker to parents' weekend, Georgina had showed up with Katie's high school boyfriend's *father,* with whom she had kindled an affair after rear-ending him in a Burger King drive-through—and begged Katie not to say anything until the poor man had left his wife. Which he proceeded to do—only to have Georgina go back to the banker.

"I know what you're thinking," Georgina said. "I'm not trying to dredge up anything, really, sweetie. I'm trying to tell you that I was wrong. *Am* wrong. I'm awful. And you're not. You're a hundred times better than me. A thousand! Oh, oh—"

She started flapping her hands and Katie leapt up and grabbed a paper napkin off the counter.

Crying, in their household, had always been treated as an emergency, since it led to ruined mascara and red eyes and puffy skin and nose blowing, all unacceptable before a date.

"It's okay, Mom," Katie said. "Here, let me do it."

"Watch the eyeliner! If you knew how long it took me—"

And so Katie dabbed around the artful ebony wings at the outer edges of her mother's eyelid.

"But what if I'm really not so different from you?" she asked quietly. "I mean, would that be so terrible?"

Her mother snuffled a couple more times, then swatted Katie's hands away. "I know what I *don't* want," she said fiercely. "I don't ever want to lose you. I don't want to end up like my own mother, alone at the end of her life, bitter and sad and having driven away everyone she loved."

"Oh, Mom." Katie sank into a chair next to her mother. "In the first place, you'll never drive me away. I *love* you, okay? And in the second place, I think you might have been a little bit wrong about Gomma. I mean Margaret," she added hastily. "I'm not saying this to make you feel bad, and I know you had your own reasons, and I'm sure they were good ones, for staying away. But she *wasn't* alone. If that helps. She had Scarlett and Jam and—and a dog and a lawyer who was pretty cool and probably other people too. So you don't need to feel guilty."

"Hmm," Georgina said. "I'll need to think about that one."

"Well, think about it on your drive, okay? And after you get home from your dirty weekend, let's talk about my visit. I have a feeling I'm not going back to Boston for a while."

When Jam came back, he was wearing a pair of khakis that was barely frayed at all, and a button-down shirt in a nice blue and white stripe. His hair was still damp and he'd shaved—he'd cut himself and there was a tiny spot of blood—and he looked altogether delicious.

"You're distracting me," Katie said.

"Well, let's get this fool errand over with, then."

He drove a very tidy white truck with a big toolbox bolted to the bed. He held her hand while he drove.

"Can I ask you a question?" she asked after a while.

"I can drive just fine. It comes in handy that it was the left leg."

"Oh. That's not what I was going to ask," Katie lied. "I just wondered if you could stop at the Walmart so I could buy a phone."

Jam told her he'd meet her out front, and when she emerged a while later, after buying a phone and a six-pack of underwear and shampoo and conditioner and the same Maybelline mascara she'd worn as a teenager, he was waiting with a shopping bag of his own.

"Whoppers," he explained, holding up the bag, "and pink Peeps. Scarlett's favorites."

"Aww."

"Don't."

It took most of the rest of the drive for Katie to get the phone set up and charged. They had passed the Archer town limit before it had enough power for her to make a call.

"Pull over," she said. "I just—I need to make one call before we, you know."

Jam did as she asked, pulling into a Dairy Queen parking lot. He stared straight ahead as Katie jumped out of the car, his jaw twitching fiercely.

Oh dear, this was complicated. She dialed Liam's number, then waited patiently until it went into voice mail. "Liam," she said. "I still don't have my phone, so I don't know if you've been trying to call me, and I'm hoping, I guess you probably went to the bank today, but to be honest I haven't had a chance to go check and—well, this is my number now, at least until I get a real phone, so—call me?"

She hesitated for a moment, then ended the call.

Then she called Lolly.

"Hello?"

"Hey, Lolls, it's me, Katie."

"Katie! Oh my God! Uh—have you talked to Liam?"

Her voice sounded strange. The skin along Katie's arms prickled. "No, why?"

"Oh! Because! Because . . . how *are* you, anyway? Find any treasures yet? How's your cousin?"

"Lolly," Katie said.

"Oh God, okay, you dragged it out of me. Shit. I didn't want to have to—you sure you want me to tell you?"

"Lolly, I swear if you don't—"

"Okay look. I think it's some weird thing about, you know, you guys trying to get pregnant and then you going to Texas and having this whole, like, finding a whole other *life* that you never had before, because you know how Liam is, he can be such a child about being left out . . ."

"What did he do?"

She could hear Lolly take a breath. "Okay. Well, I guess he had some thing at work, like a happy hour or something, and he got really drunk, and he called Rex and asked him to drive him home and he was going to leave his car at work and then go get it. Right? But then this morning, he's such an idiot, he was so drunk he forgot that he left his car downtown and he called Rex up and, I mean, get this, he thought it had been *stolen*."

"What?"

"Yeah. Like somehow the mugger had your keys from your purse and he—I mean, it didn't make any sense, but Liam was freaking out so

Rex went over there and—and I'll just say it, there was a girl there."

"A . . . girl?"

"Yeah, from work. I don't know, I guess she'd been at the same bar. Her clothes were all over the living room. And she was in the bathroom, throwing up—I mean, this is the next morning, which gives you some idea of how bad off she was, and Liam *obviously* wasn't expecting that; he figured Rex would pick him up and she'd hide in the bathroom and they'd get the car and—well, you get the picture."

"Liam fucked an intern in my bed," Katie gasped. "Is that what you're telling me?"

"I don't know if she was an intern—"

"And while they were going at it, my mother was texting him! I was leaving him *messages!* God*damn* him!" She gasped for air. "I could have been dead in a ditch somewhere for all he knew! In *Texas!*"

"Well," Lolly said carefully. "I don't know about that part. But yeah, he's a dick. Did I ever tell you that I never liked him? I take it back if you get back together with him. Do you want me to come there? I can probably get a flight tonight."

Katie realized she'd started pacing. She looked over at the truck; Jam was watching her, still glowering. She gave him a little wave. "You'd do that? For real? I mean, you're not just offering because you know I'll say no . . . are you?"

386

"I'm offended," Lolly said. "I'm your best friend."

You are? Katie almost asked—and then she stopped herself.

"I kissed someone," she said. "And you're my best friend too."

"Everything okay?" Jam asked, his jaw so tight it looked like it could break glass.

"Uh . . . I think so," Katie said. "My husband slept with an intern from work."

"Oh," Jam said. "Huh."

"Can we talk about it later?"

"Sure. This is it, by the way. Their house."

"You only drove a half a block!"

"You said to pull over . . ."

"You pulled over half a block from their *house?*"

"Women are complicated," Jam said somberly. "I've learned it's best to accommodate them where possible."

"Well—are we going in?"

"Give me a second."

He jumped out of the car and came around to her side. Opened it, and offered his hand.

"Why so formal?"

"Because, if the thing we're not talking about is true, then it puts things in a different light, maybe. Not that I'm making any assumptions."

Katie accepted his hand and jumped down,

feeling like Cinderella alighting from a pumpkin coach. And also like Linda Hamilton in *Terminator*. "Let me at him," she said.

"I think I'll handle this. Walk behind me, like a good girlfriend."

The house was a slapdash tract house in a row of a half dozen others just like it, each with a thin strip of lawn and a tiny front porch trimmed in raw lumber painted white. Jam knocked on the door. After a few moments, it opened, and there was Scarlett. She was dressed in a halter top and short skirt and tortuously high heels, her hair blown out stick straight and huge hoops in her ears.

"Damn it, Jam," she said. Then she saw Katie, and sighed.

"Who is it?" a male voice called from inside the house.

"It's Brittany," she called back. "I got to get my stuff out of her car. I'll just be a few minutes."

She shut the door behind her and grabbed each of their arms.

"Come on," she said, dragging them down the street and around the corner, where they were out of sight.

"Look, I'm sorry I took off like that," she said, not meeting Katie's gaze. "But I think everything got way overblown. I was . . . it was just the heat of the moment, you know?"

"Sounds about like what you said last time," Jam said mildly.

"You have no right to—"

"I know, I know," Jam said. "And I tried to tell her that. But she's excitable, as you've probably noticed. She just wanted to see for herself that you're okay, and now we'll go."

Scarlett's expression softened and she finally looked at Katie. "Look, I know it seems bad," she said. "But it's going to be different now. We're going in on this together—partners. Merritt's going to make a contract and everything."

"You're selling the house?" Katie asked in dismay.

"Well, I mean, what am I going to do with it? And we can have a lot better return on our investment this way."

"Scarlett—please. I'm only here for a few more days. Couldn't you—can't you just come back with me? I promise I won't say anything more about you and Merritt. Or if not tonight, tomorrow? I . . . we're *family*," she finished, miserably. "And we just got started getting to know each other."

"Katie, don't be like that," Scarlett said hoarsely. "Don't make this worse. Look, I'll try, tomorrow, okay? Only it's Sunday, and that's his day off, so . . . it's just harder. Monday for sure, because he'll be back at work. Listen, Katie. You're my cousin and I love you. But you don't understand this."

"You're right," Katie said, tearing up. "I don't."

Scarlett grabbed her in a fierce, fast hug. Then she punched Jam on the shoulder.

"Bye, assholes," she said, and jogged back around the corner in her towering heels, every step a feat of unlikely grace.

Jam put his arms around Katie, and she leaned into his hard, broad chest. "My mom would have a fit," she said. "She always said you should never, ever cry in front of a man unless there's a sure-thing payout."

"Well, I'm a pretty sure thing," Jam said. "As long as we're still talking about you getting into my pants."

Despite herself, Katie snickered. "Okay," she said. "Guess I better strike while the iron's hot."

Jam led her up to his own front door without asking, and Katie didn't object. Halfway across his living room he picked her up and carried her the rest of the way. He took off his leg, and she took off the dress her mother wore before she was even born, and then they looked at each other in the moonlight for a moment.

"This isn't a mistake," Katie said. "I promise."

"I hope you're not trying to talk yourself into this." Jam put his hands on either side of her face. "You're the most beautiful thing I've ever seen."

"My goodness," Katie said, laughter bubbling up from the deepest part of her heart, until he silenced it with a kiss.

CHAPTER TWENTY-SIX

Ruby shouldn't even have still been at school that afternoon," Caroline said, as Margaret poured her a glass of water from the pitcher the aide had left on the nightstand, and helped her take a sip.

On Friday afternoons, she used to take piano classes at Miss McFarland's house. But some of the children from her class had been invited to perform for the mothers at the PTA meeting, and Ruby was selected to be part of a Mexican hat dance. She had a darling little dress with a ruffled petticoat, and I had done up her hair in braids—she was just bursting with excitement.

Because there were so many of us, the mothers and the children who were going to perform, they moved the PTA meeting that afternoon. We usually met in the high school auditorium, but that day we were to hold our meeting in the gymnasium, which was a separate building out back of the elementary school classrooms.

There were maybe fifty of us, sitting

in folding chairs. The children were adorable; they'd been rehearsing for weeks. Some of them were dressed up like little Indians, and there was a performance by the rhythm band, and we clapped and clapped for them when they took their bows. After the performances, there were just a few more orders of business—I don't remember what anymore—and the children went back to their classrooms to get their things and then everyone was going to go home.

The last time I ever saw Ruby, she was walking out with the others in her class. At the last minute she turned around and looked right at me, and gave me this little wave. Her teacher was trying to get everyone to keep moving, so it was quick—she smiled at me and then she was gone.

I had a book that I had promised to loan to Marilyn Beard, and I had seen her come in but lost track of her, so I was looking around the room trying to find her. Everyone was getting their things and starting to go, when there was this—this roar, like the earth was splitting open. No one knew what was happening. The building shook and suddenly bricks and glass were falling in on the floor, like some giant was squashing the building from above, and we all just ran. There was no sense to it, no rational thought—in a moment like that I suppose your instincts take over and your feet carry you.

My ears were ringing with the explosion and the air was filled with dust—there was a gray cloud, a huge chunk of concrete on the walk. Someone yelled that we'd been bombed, and none of us had any reason not to believe it. As the dust began to settle you could see that the elementary school building had collapsed—the roof had been blown clear off of it. But I didn't trust my eyes—how could my child's classroom simply be gone? And I turned around in a circle and I saw that the only thing still standing besides the auditorium was part of the junior high school building. But as my eyes adjusted to the sight, I saw something I'll never forget—a child was caught on the jagged top of the wall, slumped over with blood pouring from his side, just hanging there.

I started running—and I wasn't the only one. It was a stampede, all of us mothers running toward their children's classrooms, or what was left of them. Everywhere there were unspeakable horrors, children who'd been thrown clear only to die when they hit the ground, pieces . . . oh God, you couldn't believe what you were seeing, the little arms and hands and bits, a shoe lying in the dirt, a bloody dress with part of a body in it. Still it didn't occur to me that Ruby might be one of those children, not really—my mind couldn't accept the possibility.

Everyone was screaming and as we ran into the rubble I realized I was screaming too. There was a beam that had fallen where the doorway stood and I was trying to lift it, I never had a chance of lifting it by myself but you stop thinking straight in a moment like that. I was pulling and pulling when one of the fifth-grade mothers came staggering toward me, crying out, "They're all dead, our children are dead!" and another mother just fell on her and started hitting her, screaming at her to stop saying it.

People were running toward the building from every direction. Later we learned that for miles around, people heard the explosion and saw the smoke go up and dropped what they were doing and came. Farmers left their tractors in the field and drivers left their cars, shopkeepers ran out without locking up their stores. I had gotten disoriented and I couldn't tell where her classroom should have been, and a man—I never did find out who it was—put his arms around me and picked me up and carried me out. I fought him—I could see the dead children, some of them slumped over their desks like they'd just gone to sleep, and I thought maybe there's a chance, there has to be a chance that somehow she escaped. So I kicked and screamed but it was no use, he carried me out into the yard, where already the first of the firemen had arrived and were trying to help the survivors.

There were children who were buried, some of them still alive, and there was a sort of bucket line of people pulling off the debris. But us—we mothers who could not find our children—of course we were no help. The teachers who survived the blast, and some of the other parents, they tried to help us. Already they were starting to lay the bodies out in rows, and we just stepped over them—looked to see that our own children were not among them and just stepped over them.

It wasn't very long at all before the men started coming in from the oil fields, bringing whatever tools they had at hand. Torches and pickaxes and shovels. They drove in some trucks and used their winches to drag the huge pieces of the walls and roof. And by then there were parents who were finding their children lying dead on the ground. Everywhere, the screaming just went on and on. Mothers were trying to breathe life back into their children, pleading with them, yelling at them to live, to just live.

I saw children dying. Later on I wouldn't be able to stop thinking back about what I saw and heard—all those little voices calling for their mothers, begging for help, for water. But at the time I didn't care. I was angry at them because they were still alive, and I ran back and forth, I didn't have a plan, I was just calling and calling for Ruby.

Your father came in one of the rig trucks—he wasn't driving; one of his men brought him. He told me that night that he knew when he first saw the school in the distance, what was left of it, that she was gone. He said they were driving behind a truck carrying a load of peach baskets, and that truck pulled over and the driver started pulling the baskets off and handing them out to the rescuers. He grabbed a basket without thinking about it and ran into the wreckage.

Before long there were more trucks—

dozens of them. Some of them emptied their loads right on the ground so they could take the hurt children to the hospital. By the end of it there were children in hospitals in Tyler and Henderson and Overton and other towns too. I remember seeing dozens of loaves of bread on the ground, just lying there in the dirt, and someone said they'd been headed to Kilgore when the driver saw the explosion.

There was a rig man who'd worked as a welder, and he started cutting through the beams with his torch, and I thought—I was out of my mind, and I was begging him to dig Ruby out. Because you see, I hadn't seen any sign of her yet, so I thought she must be buried underneath. He was trying to work and I was pulling at his shirt and begging him to find her when your father found me. He said my name and I went to him and when I saw his face, how broken he looked, I knew it was true, that we had lost our child.

After that I had no hope left. We waited in the gymnasium, where they had set up a morgue. A lot of us parents stayed there so we could see when they brought the bodies in. Whenever someone identified their child it would start all over again, the wailing. I saw a father pick up his dead son and leave with him. He was out of his mind—he took him home. Some of the Mexican families just took the bodies of their children and left that night; they'd come here with nothing and they left with nothing, it was like they were never here at all.

The last child they found alive, he'd been buried under a desk and that had kept him alive, because there was a space that held air for him to breathe. When they brought him out he was dazed and weak but he could talk a little. But when they carried him past the rest of us, one of the mothers ran out and started yelling at him, because her child had been in the same classroom but had died. She kept saying, "Why did it have to be you? Why are you still alive?"

Those peach baskets that had come off the truck, they ended up being used to carry out the bricks and plaster and pieces of wood as they dug farther and farther in. They worked all night, two thousand volunteers by the end of it. The blast had thrown pieces of the building hundreds of yards in every direction. Sometime toward morning a man came to your father and asked him to come along. He told me it was all right, that I should stay where I was. The school librarian, she had been walking between buildings when the explosion happened, and she survived—she stayed with me and held my hand and kept me calm. It seemed to take forever, but when your father came back he had tears streaming down his face, and he just shook his head. She had her little petticoats on, but he identified her by her shoes, that he'd helped her buckle that morning.

After that there was no reason for us to stay, so we went home. I don't think we said a word between us. Your father opened the front door and we stood there looking through it but it was like neither of us wanted to go in. Once we went in the house, somehow that would make it real—that she would never be there with us again, that house where she grew up. We were so proud of that house, but I remember standing there thinking that it might as well fall to ruins too. Because without Ruby there was nothing for me in the world.

I said to your father, "I don't think I will." He turned me around and put his hands on my shoulders and made me look at him.

"Come in now, darling," he said, and again I told him no. So he put his arms around me and we just stood there for the longest time. I could smell the smoke on him and the dust. He was shaking from exhaustion and shock and the effort of holding me up, and when he asked me again, I felt sorry for him and so I said all right, and I went in with him.

We went up the stairs and your father led me to our bed and told me to lie down. I didn't take off any of my clothes, not even my shoes. He went out into the hall for a moment and when he came back he said he'd gone to check in her room. He lay down beside me and we were like two little children, curled up with our foreheads touching.

He said he had to make sure that she hadn't somehow found her way home and into her bed. That maybe the shoes he'd seen hadn't been hers—the petticoats. But her room was empty. I told him I understood and we held each other until it was light outside.

Alelia came late that day, she had gone to look for us at the school when she heard. By the time she got there, your father had finally fallen asleep and I had gotten up and washed and dressed and I was downstairs at the table. I could tell that Alelia had been crying, though she was trying to pretend she hadn't, and she started up again when she saw me. I told her, *Stop that now*, because we had a funeral to plan.

By the time Caroline finished, Margaret was crying again. So much pain . . . so much grief.

"I don't—I don't even know how you and Daddy survived," she whispered. "If I lost Georgina—"

"But wait," Caroline said. "I'm not quite done."

CHAPTER TWENTY-SEVEN

Seven days after she arrived in Texas, and ten minutes before the garage sale was officially supposed to start, Katie called J.B. Already there was a horde of early-rising lookie-loos checking out the goods, many of them with shopping bags over their arms, one older lady with an honest-to-God change maker fastened to her belt, ready to haggle.

"Today's the day, huh?" J.B. said.

"Yes. I'm upstairs in Margaret's bedroom, looking down at them—I swear it's like a scene from *The Walking Dead*."

"It's not a good garage sale unless a fight breaks out," J.B. cautioned. "So, any word from our girl?"

"No," Katie said glumly. "She won't return my calls, but she did text to tell me she hopes it goes well today."

"That sucks."

"I've been wondering, J.B.—do you think this whole thing was just Margaret's way of trying to get me to help Scarlett? You know, to force her to confront a bad relationship?"

"I don't know," J.B. said dubiously. "I mean, that's a lot of moving parts right there."

"Yeah, I guess you're right."

"Well, good luck today. I hope you make piles and piles of cash, and then on Monday you can come in and we'll get the final numbers and have you guys sign everything. You headed back to Boston right after?"

"Actually, I'm going to go visit my mom in Dallas for a while. I—I'm between jobs, so I thought I'd take a little time."

"Awesome. Okay, I won't keep you from your customers."

"Thanks for everything, J.B."

Katie hung up and took a last look around the empty room. Yesterday, Jam had come over with a couple of friends to move all of the furniture into the driveway while Katie set out the racks of clothes and boxes of dishes and folding tables piled with china and crystal and knickknacks. Afterward, they'd had pizza and beer and told stories from their high school years that embarrassed Jam no end, until he finally told them it was time to go and he'd kick their ass if they didn't.

"I like this one," one of the guys said as he was leaving.

"Don't fuck this up, Jam," the other added.

Jam locked the door behind them.

He'd had to go to Kilgore for the day, to give a training session for the Sheriff's Department K-9 unit. Katie was almost relieved: there was no way she'd be able to concentrate on making change and haggling with Jam standing around distracting her.

She was almost out the front door before she realized that she didn't have a cash box. She raced to the back door, out through the backyard to the garage. She'd emptied half a dozen cigar boxes in the last week, and they were all still up in the apartment, awaiting the cleaning crew she'd scheduled for next week, a last gift to Scarlett before she had to deal with selling Margaret's house.

Katie stepped into the apartment and slowly turned around, forgetting for a moment the chaos outside. She'd cleaned the cobwebs and dirt while she worked, and wiped down the cabinets and counters and swept the floors. The walls were a soft shade of creamy white, and the old wavy glass in the windows did something lovely to the light.

Georgina had lived here once, and before her, Margaret. They'd dreamed and wished and raged, regretted and planned and hoped. There, where she'd pulled the bed away from the wall to sweep up the dust bunnies, they'd . . .

A little spot of pink poked out of the baseboard. Katie nudged it with her toe: a scrap of ribbon, maybe, or a bow from a dress—but it didn't budge. She got down on her knees and tugged at it with her hands: it was the hard plastic corner of something, a book or a case. But how had it gotten stuck behind the wall?

Katie felt along the baseboards until her fingernails met with a gap in the baseboard—and the pink object shifted. Just a little, but enough to dig her fingers in farther, and work out a piece of baseboard that was about a foot long. It had been carefully cut and replaced like a puzzle piece, forming a little hidey hole.

It *was* a book, of sorts—a diary. The year 1975 was printed on the cover in fancy gold. Inside, her mother's handwriting—page after page of it, in different colors of ink, with little scribbles and drawings in the margins. Katie flipped back to the first page:

Thursday, February 6

I know I am supposed to say "Dear Diary" or something like that, but who talks to a book? I just need to write down my thoughts somewhere because I am going CRAZY. Two years, two months, and twenty-two days before I turn 18 and I can finally LEAVE.

Katie snapped the book shut. She was breathing hard, feeling like she'd stolen something. She got down on her hands and knees and peered into the hole, but it was too dark to see anything. Praying that rats weren't nesting behind the wall, eager to bite her and give her rabies, she pushed her hand in and felt around.

There was an envelope, a thick one. Katie tugged it carefully from the hiding place. It was a plain manila envelope, brittle and yellowed and tied with a string. She opened the envelope carefully and slid out a stack of stiff papers.

On top was some sort of document, with an official-looking seal with the year 1963 in its center. "American Telephone and Telegraph" was emblazoned across the top in heavy ink. In smaller letters, with typewritten words filling in the blanks, it went on:

THIS CERTIFIES THAT <u>MARGARET ANNE DIAL</u> IS THE OWNER OF FOUR FULL-VALUE AND NON-ASSESSABLE SHARES, WITHOUT PAR VALUE, OF THE COMMON STOCK OF AMERICAN TELEPHONE AND TELEGRAPH COMPANY (HEREIN CALLED THE CORPORATION). . . .

A stock certificate! Her grandmother had somehow come to possess four shares of—could it really be AT&T? Or, more likely, some other company that had long ago shuttered its doors and disappeared into obscurity?

Katie flipped to the next piece of paper. Another

just like the first, dated 1964, this one for eleven shares of the American Telephone and Telegraph Company. The one after that was stamped 1965 and its ornate border was printed in blue ink; it was for sixteen shares in the Executone company.

"Executone?" Katie said out loud. Her heard was pounding, but this was silly; her grandmother had dabbled in stocks of companies that, in all probability, were all defunct, the value of the certificates having evaporated before she was ever born. But it was another facet of the woman that she could have—should have—known, and that knowledge felt heavy on her heart.

She continued going through the stack of certificates, setting each carefully in a pile after she'd looked at it. There were probably fifty or sixty of them, and she shuffled ahead and saw that the last one was dated 2005, for fifty shares of Nvidia, a company she'd never heard of.

Katie went back to the middle of the stack. Some of the companies were familiar, like Hewlett-Packard and IBM, and others were not, like Mohawk Data and Walter Kidde. There seemed to be a lot of computer and technology stocks, which was confounding: Katie hadn't found a single shred of evidence that her grandmother had owned a computer, or even a cell phone. Had Margaret invested in a future that she didn't intend to participate in? Was she a believer in the inevitable march of progress, content to rattle around with the ghosts of the past?

Then she got to 1987.

One hundred forty shares of Apple Computer Inc.

"No way," Katie gasped. "Are you kidding me, Gomma?"

Scarcely breathing, she turned to the next: 1988—three hundred shares of Apple. Then thirty-five more. And on and on over the next several years, until—Katie went back and added up all the shares—she had amassed almost three thousand shares of Apple over a six-year period.

That had to be worth some serious money, didn't it?

Katie stood up, her head swimming. This changed things. It had to! Somehow her grand-mother had found the money to invest in stocks without anyone knowing and, through either shrewdness or pure dumb luck, had possibly managed to amass a fortune. Maybe. Katie didn't know a whole lot about investing, but she was pretty sure that these were the real thing. What she needed was someone who knew what they were doing, who—

"Excuse me," a voice called up the stairs. "Anyone up there?"

Katie stuffed the certificates back into the envelope and pressed it to her chest, hurrying to the top of the stairs. Standing at the bottom was a woman with thick gray braids and a fishing hat.

"Oh, hello," Katie said.

"Are you the one running the sale?"

"I—yes, ma'am."

"Would you take twenty bucks for this?"

She held up a silver teapot covered with tarnish. Katie had no idea if it was sterling or merely plated, and no inclination to find out. "Yeah, okay. Just—I just need to find something to put the money in. Here."

She grabbed a cigar box off the counter and came down the stairs. The woman dropped a wadded bill inside. "Thanks," she said. "Real shame to see Mrs. Dial's things sold off. We'd all hoped someone from her family would come in and take care of this place. Now it's probably going to go to some tech exec, I imagine."

"Oh," Katie said.

"You know she was one of the replacement babies, don't you? From the school disaster?"

"I—I did, actually."

"Well, they're all dying off, now. I guess that's just the way it goes. History don't stand a chance when big business comes into a place. You take care, now."

She ambled back across the yard, stopping to examine a moss-covered ceramic urn. Katie watched her go, her mind reeling.

She dug her phone out of her pocket and hit redial.

"J. B. McNaughton, attorney at law."

"J.B., this is Katie again. Can I hire you on an emergency basis today? Like, pay you time and a half or whatever?"

"What's this about?"

Katie took a deep breath. "I need you to take a look at some documents I found. And . . . I need to borrow your car. Oh—and I need you to run a garage sale."

Katie arrived at the ugly little tract house a few minutes after nine. The smell of bacon wafted through the air, and two little girls were playing on the sidewalk, blowing bubbles with homemade bubble soap in a Big Gulp cup.

"Who are you?" one of them asked.

"I'm—I'm Katie. I'm here to see my cousin."

"Who's your cousin?"

"Scarlett. She lives here. Do you know her?"

Both girls laughed.

"Of course we know her!"

"I'll get her for you!"

They barreled toward Scarlett's house, abandoning the bubbles, and pounded on the door. A few minutes later Scarlett appeared, her hair tumbling around her shoulders, wearing a thin tank top and no bra and shorts with dinosaurs printed on them. "My goodness, girls, did you forget to look at the clock? What's the Sunday rule?"

"Not before eleven!"

"But your *cousin* is here! We *had* to!"

"Can we play with Stinky?"

Scarlett glanced at Katie, her expression unreadable.

"Tell you what, sugar pies. Stinky needs a little more beauty sleep in her cage. Come back tonight after dinner, okay?"

"Aw—"

"We can make mug cakes."

"Yay!"

"But right now I need to talk to my cousin, so you two run along, okay?"

" 'Kay!"

" 'Bye!"

"They're adorable," Katie said.

"Yes," Scarlett said, sighing. "They are. What happened, did you sell everything already?"

"No. Although I think the entire town is there right now. Listen, Scarlett . . . what if there was a way for you to invest in this partnership with Merritt, *and* keep the house, just for yourself? To do what you want with? You wouldn't even have to live in it, at least for now. You could fix it up and rent it out—you'd probably make tons of money on it, with all the jobs the fulfillment center's going to create. You could do anything you wanted."

Scarlett narrowed her eyes suspiciously and folded her arms over her chest. "Yeah, with what money?"

Katie took a deep breath. "That's going to take a little explaining. Any chance I could take you out for breakfast?"

They ate their Taco Bueno bacon and egg quesadillas in the parking lot, because J.B. drove a Lexus CT so new that it still smelled like the showroom floor.

"No offense," Scarlett said, "but I want to hear this directly from J.B. I don't want to get all excited and then find out those certificates aren't worth anything."

"Okay," Katie said. "Well, we're paying her for today, so I think we can go ask her right now."

"It's like we have an entourage!" Scarlett smiled for the first time that day.

"Kind of, I guess. Listen, Scarlett—I know I can't tell you what to do with the money. I would just, I mean, I think it would be the smart thing, before you tell Merritt about any of this, please hire J.B. to take care of the, um, details, okay? Or if you don't want to hire her, we can get some recommendations for other attorneys and—"

"J.B.'s fine," Scarlett said dully, the smile disappearing from her face. "I'll hire her."

"Is everything okay?"

"Yeah, it's— Look, I don't really want to talk about it. It's just, the thing with Merritt's friend, well, now they're talking about using *all* of Gomma's money for like start-up costs and whatnot."

Katie said nothing for a moment as her blood simmered with red-hot rage. "What kind of business is it?" she asked casually.

"I don't want to talk about it."

"Okay, sorry. So, yeah! J.B.! This is going to be great!"

Impulsively, she threw her arms around Scarlett, who stood stiffly for a moment before tentatively hugging back. Katie pressed her face against Scarlett's neck and smelled sleep and hairspray and stale perfume and ersatz Mexican food. *I love you,* she thought, but she wasn't really an *I love you* kind of person and she wasn't a hugger and all of this was difficult and uncomfortable and messy.

Scarlett squeezed harder.

"I love you," Katie whispered.

It just slipped out.

There were cars up and down the block and they had to park J.B.'s car in Jam's driveway ("Of course he won't mind!" Scarlett said, and "Who cares if he does?"). Many of the big pieces of furniture were gone, and the racks of clothes and tables of junk looked decidedly picked over.

"Oh gosh," Scarlett said. As soon as Katie turned off the ignition, she hurtled out of the car and ran toward the house. "This garage sale is *over!* Everybody out! *Shoo!*"

Katie took a moment to watch, standing next to the beautiful Lexus. Scarlett stopped at the card table behind which J.B.—in mirrored sunglasses and a baseball cap and a tank top emblazoned with the words "Pussy Grabs Back"—was minding the till, and they exchanged a few words. Then Scarlett ran up to a woman whose arms were full of clothes and snatched them out of her hands.

"Oh dear," Katie sighed.

It took twenty minutes before they were able to get everyone to leave. Katie called the market and got Kyle's number and called him up and told him that it was an emergency, and he and his brother rode their bikes over and they started moving the furniture back into the house.

"Thank God nobody got the chafing dishes," Scarlett said. "That stock better be worth something."

"I wouldn't worry about that." J.B. smirked. "You'll be buying me lunch on Monday. Lobster and martinis and maybe even cigars, like the ballers we are."

"And you can always have another garage sale if it doesn't work out," Katie said hastily. Somebody had to be the voice of reason, after all, and she'd had a lifetime of practice.

"Oh, I almost forgot," J.B. said. "The woman who bought the rolltop desk—she and her husband took the drawers out to load it up in their pickup, and this fell out of the back."

She handed Scarlett a sheaf of letters, tied with a faded rose-colored ribbon. Scarlett carefully untied the ribbon and handed half the packet to Katie. She examined the one on top. In a spidery, careful hand, someone had written "Mrs. Hugh Pierson, 124 Oliver Street, New London." The return address was "Mrs. Paul Wooley, Archer." The postmark date was March 1937.

"These are from Gomma's aunt Euda to her mom," Scarlett exclaimed, flipping through the stack. "They're all from 1937."

"And 1938," Katie said.

"They had a big falling-out before Gomma was born," Scarlett said. "She said they never spoke again. Want to read these together?"

"Sure," Katie said. "Good thing nobody bought that ugly-ass kitchen table."

Chapter Twenty-Eight

September 1986

In the weeks that followed, Margaret would find the fork that she had been polishing that afternoon right on the windowsill where she'd set it down, its tines still dark with tarnish and its stem bright as a nickel in the sun. She would pick it up and stare at it for a minute, puzzled, before remembering that she'd pulled her chair close to the window so that she could enjoy the breezes that still stirred as the sun was rising on another sweltering August morning.

The bigger mystery was why it took her nearly two weeks to discover the fork there. Margaret had offered to host the fund-raising committee of the Library Society for lunch and had experienced a brief burst of, if not enthusiasm exactly, at least a mild determination to outdo Harriet Barber, who'd served pimento cheese sandwiches without even cutting off the crusts the month before. Margaret had in mind something on the order of the long-ago Daisy Club luncheons, scaled down to the more modest appetites of the ladies of the committee, who were all on diets.

She'd dug the old lace-trimmed napkins out of the breakfront and ordered iced petits fours from a bakery in Tyler and made a quiche bursting with flecks of bright green broccoli and cheese that she would insist was low-fat.

She'd gone ahead with the luncheon, but by that time she was still so distraught about the events of that morning that she must have passed the fork on the windowsill a hundred times and never even noticed it. Who could blame her?

What happened was this: she'd been up early the day before the luncheon, unable to sleep, and decided to get a jump on her chores. She was polishing the salad forks one by one, setting them in a neat row on the kitchen table as she finished them, when there was a knock at the door. At seven-thirty in the morning! Margaret (having set the fork down, it seems) got up with a sense of indignation, mixed with apprehension. Had someone died? But who?

It never even crossed her mind to worry that it might be Georgina.

When she opened the door, she saw a lovely young woman dressed in soiled and wrinkled clothing with what looked like pillow creases on her face. Her hair was a brassy shade of yellow with the beginning of soft strawberry blond roots. Her fingernails had traces of shimmering pink polish, but most of it had chipped away and they were bitten to the quick.

She was also enormously pregnant. *About to pop!*—was what Margaret thought, and she even wondered if the poor thing had gone into labor right in front of her house when she happened to notice the girl's bracelet, a filigreed gold bangle that resembled one that had been missing from her jewelry box forever.

And then she thought: *oh.*

A thousand times she'd imagined what this moment might be like, but she'd never imagined this. She'd tried on many different emotions and written a dozen speeches in her head, all of them variations on a theme of wounded aloofness, but they all vanished and she grabbed Georgina's sun-browned wrists and pulled her into the house.

After eating the toast and bacon that Margaret set in front of her, and drinking all the orange juice in the carton, and after she had taken so long in the bathroom that Margaret was considering forcing the lock and going in after her, Georgina emerged an entirely different version of herself.

While Margaret had been cooking, casting worried glances over her shoulder from the stove, Georgina had slumped over the table with her head on her arms, apparently asleep. She perked up when the food was set in front of her, but when Margaret asked her questions she held up her finger and—after swallowing and dabbing at the corners of her mouth—had said only, "In a minute, Mother, I haven't eaten since Philly," a frustratingly cryptic response. She'd asked for a bath and accepted a clean towel with barely a thank-you and disappeared again.

When she came back down the stairs, she was wearing the towel wrapped around her breasts, and a pair of tiny bikini underwear over which her stomach swelled like a zeppelin. "God, that felt good!" she exclaimed, plopping in the same chair. "Thanks for breakfast, by the way."

Margaret had so many questions, but Georgina gave her clipped, impatient answers:

Paris, most recently, but most of the time in Geneva, with a stretch in Chamonix.

Working, of course—how did Margaret think she'd survived?

—oh, modeling for a well-known artist, working as a waitress and chef, selling paintings in a gallery.

Didn't Margaret receive her letters? Only six? Surely there'd been more than six—she was quite certain she'd written twice a year at least, on her mother's birthday and at Christmastime. Well, then, they must have gotten lost in the mail.

Just this morning, actually—she'd had a layover in Philadelphia and then there'd been a mix-up that would take too long to explain and she'd been on a bus for nearly (she checked her wrist, where there was a pale band of skin, but no watch)—well, for over a day, that was for sure.

"But, Mom, we can talk about all that later."

Good, thought Margaret, because of course what she really wanted to talk about was the one thing neither of them had mentioned.

"All right. Will you be . . . staying . . . for long?" Instantly she regretted the words: she should have said something more along the lines of *You're welcome to stay as long as you like, you and the baby's father, of course.* But Georgina only glanced away, up at the wall where, when she'd last lived at home, a stern black-rimmed clock had hung. One day it had simply stopped working, and rather than take it down to the repair shop Margaret had ordered a new electric model from the Montgomery Ward catalog, with gold numbers and a showy red dial. Georgina stared at it in what seemed like consternation and Margaret remembered how she herself had resented every little detail that had changed in the time she'd been away before Hank died.

"Look, Mom." Georgina turned her attention back to Margaret with obvious effort. "I'm sorry to have to ask, and I wouldn't, if it wasn't for Button. The baby, that's what I call him. I mean, obviously I'll choose a real name, but I want to wait until he's born to get a look at him before I decide. But the thing is, I haven't been able to work since my fourth month. They're funny about it over there, you know? And I've gone through all my savings and . . . well, I just need some to tide me over for a few months, until I can find a place and someone to watch him. And get a job."

Margaret felt the warm glow of impending grandparenthood, the possibility of reconnecting with her long-missing daughter, evaporate like the mist on Lake Tyler on October mornings. Georgina wasn't here because she wanted to be— she was here because she *had* to be. Which was a very different thing, as Margaret knew better than nearly anyone.

But that wasn't fair!—because while Caroline had all but banished Margaret after she'd chosen to marry the man she loved, and refused to even talk to her on the telephone until the baby (that baby being the pregnant woman in front of her, how strange was that?) came along, and been cold and distant after that . . . while that had been Caroline's response to Margaret wanting some small life of her own, Georgina had ignored every single one of her mother's wishes and desires and snuck out in the dead of night and even stolen that bracelet that she was wearing brazenly on her wrist.

And even after all of that, Margaret had tried. She wrote to Georgina every other month, long letters at first, apologies and entreaties, news from home and carefully worded questions (*don't pry too much,* Margaret had reminded herself as she squeezed the pen until her fingers ached)—

then later simply cards, since she'd run out of new things to say, but always closing with *your loving mother always*.

And yet here was Georgina, who had practically disappeared without a trace, with the audacity to demand money while in the same breath lying to her face. Georgina had sent four letters, and two were postcards, so they hardly counted, and the last—which had come over a year ago—had hinted strongly that "anything you might care to send" would be welcome. That was the only letter that had a detailed return address both on the envelope and on the airmail paper itself.

"What happened to the money that your grandfather left you?" Margaret asked in a cold, prim voice.

"What? You're not serious, Mother—that was gone almost by the time I got to Europe. New York is *expensive*," she added, "and my modeling agency held on to my checks. I should have sued, but I just needed to be *out* of there at that point, you know?"

This was too much. Georgina had a tell—when she was lying, the right corner of her mouth somehow managed to twist down while the other side twisted up. It had done so since she was a little girl, but back then her prodigious lies had been easy to identify by their sheer fabulousness. At first, Margaret had flattered herself that Georgina took after her—that somehow her youthful talent for spying had carried in the blood to a new generation, one who might actually turn it into something useful or lucrative or glamorous, rather than squandering it on something as ordinary and unremarkable as *love,* as she had done.

But as the years went by, instead of branching out in some exciting direction, Georgina merely grew craftier and more careful. She lied to get out of trouble and she lied to get what she couldn't convince her mother to give her (Caroline had been her willing dupe practically since her birth) and she lied, Margaret was convinced, for no reason at all other than habit.

"Where on earth is the father of this baby, Georgina?" Margaret asked, knowing she'd never get the truth, and feeling like the walls of the kitchen were closing in around her. Her daughter had come home, the answer to the single prayer she whispered in secret every night, begging God to forgive her failure to hold on tight enough, to be a good enough mother. And instead of feeling joy, the joy she saw on her friends' faces as they chattered on about their children's weddings and babies and new houses and fancy jobs, she felt . . . furious.

Georgina shrugged. "If I knew who he was, I might be able to answer that."

Margaret burned. That was her daughter's other trick: a shock offensive, rendering people speechless. But Margaret hadn't exactly been living in a convent for the nine years that her daughter had been gone. She'd read Dworkin, she'd read Steinem, she'd even read Marilyn French and Erica Jong. She could play her daughter's game.

"Tell me the possibilities," she said calmly. "That is, if you remember them all. Did you keep a list, by any chance? I rely on lists quite a bit, myself."

Georgina goggled at her, and Margaret felt a spark of satisfaction that her barb had hit the mark. But then her daughter's features rearranged themselves. She was as crafty as ever, reading her mother so easily.

"Well, I suppose if it's the black one, we'll know right away. Probably not my landlord, since he always used a rubber—though I guess I'm proof that accidents do happen," Georgina said in a bored tone. "And the painter was probably too old to produce viable sperm. I certainly hope it wasn't the guy from the Metro—he wasn't attractive at all. More like *jolie-laide*—are you familiar with that term?"

As a matter of fact, Margaret was. She'd learned it in a history class at the University of Texas that seemed like it had taken place in another century, on another planet. But she had grown weary of this little sparring match, especially because Georgina's mouth had given her away, again.

It hurt: her daughter probably knew very well who the baby's father was, but she wasn't going to tell. The fact that Georgina had come home alone and broke was a good indicator of heartbreak—but her daughter hadn't come to her for comfort.

Margaret's hands itched to hold her. What would happen if she . . . but no, no, no, Georgina didn't want that, didn't want her. Even now the girl was yawning, maneuvering her enormous belly out of the chair. Standing, favoring the small of her back the way pregnant women will.

"You're carrying just like I did." The words tumbled out of Margaret's mouth like pennies from a jar. "It's going to be a girl."

Georgina snorted a haughty little laugh. "So now you're a shaman, Mother? Well, maybe you're right."

"Move back in," Margaret pleaded, despite herself. "I can't give you money, but I'll give you a place to stay—your old room in the house, if you want, and we can make a little nursery for the baby. You won't want the apartment—trust me, it felt very small when the two of us lived there." She was talking faster and faster, as though she could outrun her daughter's wariness with words. "We can go see Dr. Morris; he's got a very nice partner now, a young Italian from New York of all places, he's delivered a dozen babies since he got here. And when you're up for it, when she's a little older, and you're recovered, well, *then* you can find a job."

But Georgina was already shaking her head. "It'll never work, Mother. We'd kill each other. We never got along before, remember? What makes you think a squalling little brat's going to help? It's not like it made you and Grandma closer; all you ever did was argue."

Oh, but it did, Margaret thought, but that wasn't a story she was prepared to tell. If only Georgina had given her a little notice—a month, a week, even a few hours. But showing up like this, finding her at her worst—she hadn't even had a bath and she was wearing an old poplin housedress that she didn't mind getting silver polish on—it wasn't fair.

"Things *are* different," she said, but she had a feeling that her words hadn't come out the way she meant.

"Look." Suddenly Georgina seemed tired, as though she was feeling every extra pound the baby had piled on, weighing on her bladder and her spine. "Just a few hundred dollars, Mother, that's all I'm asking for. I'd say I'd pay it back, but . . . well, I guess we both know I probably won't. I'll try, though. Give me this, please, and I'll try to be better. To . . . not let it stay like this between us again."

Margaret inhaled the air between them, let her eyes drift closed. She could *have* this. She could have this unexpected bounty, this treasure she had stopped daring to dream about back when Georgina was still a child who was even then running as hard as she could away from her. All she had to do was . . . give a little. Let down her guard a little. Offer a little more than she could expect to get back. Her mother's dying words were stored away in a tight little pocket of her heart, and she'd somehow let all these years pass without acting on them. *Be better than I was,* Caroline had rasped, the death rattle between her teeth.

"There's . . . there's a cute little apartment above the travel agency," she said carefully, her mouth dry. "Joe Stoffel converted it for his son when he got back from Vietnam, but he ended up getting married and . . . well, I imagine that Joe would let it go for a song."

Georgina's eyebrows rose in alarm. *"Here?* In New London? Thanks but no thanks. Time to break the cycle. I want this child to see more than this dusty little shit hole, no offense. I mean, I'm sorry. Look, if you want— I mean, I guess we could stay a few months or something. Give you some time to bond with him and all."

But as Georgina went on, offering bits and slivers of herself, Margaret saw through to the smoke-and-mirrors sleight of hand that her daughter was practicing, as slick as any Vegas dealer.

"No," she cut in. "I'm not asking for your *pity*. You don't see it now, but I could be a *help*. You've already deprived your child of a father—"

"Oh, right," Georgina said, slamming down the water glass she'd been holding. "I'm selfish, right? I don't deserve to ask for more than I'm given? I know how it goes, remember? I had to hear it often enough."

She grabbed her bag off the floor, slinging it over her shoulder and clomping awkwardly through the front room.

"Wait—" Margaret gasped, but then the front door slammed.

She could have run after Georgina, could have begged, could have asked for another chance. But she did none of these things, because they would have only delayed the inevitable.

Georgina had never been hers. She was a wild one, meant to carve her own path. She'd come with her bag of tricks and Margaret knew that she should be relieved that she'd resisted.

But she didn't feel relief. All she felt was . . . empty.

CHAPTER TWENTY-NINE

March 24, 1937

Dear Caroline,

I hardly know where to begin. I have begun this letter over and over and I don't know what to say that could be a comfort to you. Today when I saw you and Hugh sitting up in the front pew, my heart broke in pieces. You were with that other family and how the tears flowed in that church, those two tiny caskets and all those flowers.

I wanted to tell you why we didn't stay and why we didn't come after to greet you, though Pastor Maddrell was kind as could be especially when I told him we are sisters. He made us feel very welcome but we had our three with us and it didn't seem right, not with all those families who lost their little ones, especially Lassiter because he was the same age as so many who perished. And with Amy and Pammy not old enough to sit quiet and behave. So

I said to Paul this is not the time or place, we will go home and pray for Ruby there.

Caroline, I know that I only got to see your Ruby a few times but she was a beautiful little girl. If there was any way in this world that I could bring her back to you I would. May the Lord comfort you in this time of grief.

Your loving Sister,
Euda

May 22, 1937

Dear Caroline,

I hope you got the cards from the Women's Ministry. We had a quiet afternoon together writing them because in addition to your dear Ruby there were six others among us who were related to families who lost children.

Lassiter asked me on Tuesday if he could send his money to the families to help them feel better. Caroline, he has seventy cents he has saved up and he wanted me to put it in this envelope and I couldn't find a way to explain to him. That to a mother there is nothing more valuable than her own children and nothing that can ever make up for their loss. I pray for you every day and I wish so often that we had never quarreled. I know it was a hard thing for you being older and all the responsibilities when Mam and Pappa died and you had to go to work while I stayed in school. Sometimes I think there is too much sadness in life and you have endured so much already.

Caroline, there is something that has been heavy on my heart. I wanted to tell you in person but I got your letter last week saying you were not ready yet to receive visitors. I am expecting again, this child will be born at Christmas or early in the new year. Paul and I were surprised because we thought that after the difficulties with Pammy we could not have any more. I have been sick with this one and worry something might not be right, but that is in God's hands and not ours.

I hope this news is not hard for you to hear. I have been fretting over it all week. I hope you take comfort in prayer during these hard times. Reverend Mayhew reminded me last Sunday to read Revelation again. "He will wipe away every tear from their eyes."

Your loving sister,
Euda

June 2, 1937

Dear Caroline,

You and Hugh left four hours ago and I have been sitting in this chair almost the whole time while the laundry is still on the line and supper never got started. Paul took the children to visit with his mother but he will be back soon and I know he will want an answer from me. At first, after you left, he told me he would never allow it but I begged him to remember that you and Hugh are a mother and father who have lost their only dear child.

It is a very hard thing that you have asked of us. I wish you had told me all these years the suffering you had been through with all the babies that didn't take. I had no idea. You have always had so many friends, but it should have been your sister who was by your side.

I keep thinking about what you have asked us to do. Paul says it would be impossible to keep people from finding out, but I think mostly he cannot conceive of a child of his not being raised by us. He says he could not bear even to look at it if we are not to keep it. I think when we almost lost Pammy, something changed in him, and he became fearful of things that might come to pass. But he says it is my decision and if I ask him to do this he will never tell another soul.

I did not want to say this in front of Hugh but we cannot accept money as he suggested. Hugh is a very kind man and I know he meant no insult but Paul went out to the shed after he left like he does when things are heavy on his mind. Please understand, the only way Paul and I could ever give you this child is out of love for you and Hugh and never for money.

I know that you have a plan which you explained in some detail but I confess I didn't pay attention as well as I should have. I still don't understand how you would convince your neighbors and friends that you are pregnant. For me it would be easier. No one will question if we say we lost this one, since we came so close last time.

I want to say I need more time to think about it but as I read what I have written, it seems I have already made up my mind. I expect I'll feel more certain in the morning. It's just a shock, that's all.

Do you remember when we used to talk

late into the night? You always said I was all elbows and knees, but I remember all the times you fell asleep first. I used to like to hold the hem of your nightgown in my hand. You didn't know it, but I always held on until I fell asleep too, and sometimes I woke up still holding on.

Please tell Hugh that Paul didn't mean anything when he didn't come back to say goodbye.

Your loving sister,
Euda

October 2, 1937

Dear Caroline,

I am enclosing the children's thank-you notes. I helped Amy and Pammy write their names, otherwise you'd never know what their chicken scratches mean! Lassiter hasn't wanted to part with his slingshot for a moment. Yesterday his teacher threatened to take it away from him and so today he left it at home, but I know when he gets back from school he'll be at it again with the acorns. And the dolls that you sent for the girls are beautiful, but I fear they are much too fine for children that age. I let the girls play with them for a little bit each day but mostly they are up on a shelf where they will stay nice.

I know it is hard for you to travel right now but you really shouldn't send gifts, especially because Lassiter was asking me whose birthday is it? Also it must be very hard to keep up this ruse day after day. You did make me laugh with your description of your maid finding the pillow in the bedclothes and having to hide in the dressing room until she went away so you could tie it back on. It seems like an eternity since we used to play those silly pranks on Mam but how amazed she would be to know what we have got ourselves up to this time.

Caroline, do you ever wonder if we are doing the right thing? I wonder if you ever wish we hadn't made this decision. If you do, please tell me, because I have a feeling this one isn't going to wait like the others did. And after it comes it will be too late.

You were kind to inquire after my health. I'm big as I always get, but this one is carrying low. She likes to tap-dance in the afternoons, and I'm up every other minute to visit the toilet! The doctor says I should be eating more, but by the time

I'm done seeing to the children's supper I hardly have an appetite.

Your loving sister,
Euda

December 26, 1937

Dear Caroline,

I'm sorry I never sent the Christmas letter I promised. It has been a whirlwind here, Lassiter was hopping up and down all week waiting for Saint Nick to visit and the girls were cross because he kept teasing them that they were only getting lumps of coal. Paul's mother still hasn't recovered from that fall she took and the doctor is worried about her lungs. She stayed with us for Christmas but of course she can't help with anything and also she needs someone to go with her to the bathroom, so I didn't get the roast out of the oven until almost six o'clock.

I'm sorry to keep complaining, I must sound terribly ungrateful. Everyone enjoyed the package that you sent. Lassiter says he could eat oranges at every meal for the rest of his life and not get tired of them. The girls love the nutcracker and they fight over who gets to pull the crank and none of the rest of us ever have to shell any because they're like a couple of little squirrels.

You asked if the doctor had changed his mind about when the baby is coming but he still says middle of January. I asked him twice.

Your loving sister,
Euda

CERTIFICATE OF LIVE BIRTH

PLACE OF BIRTH—STATE OF TEXAS—COUNTY OF HARRISON

Full Name of Child—MARGARET ANNE PIERSON

Father Full Name—HUGH TRACE PIERSON

Residence at Time of This Birth— NEW LONDON TEXAS

Race/Color—WHITE

Age at Time of This Birth—43

Mother Maiden Name—CAROLINE FAY WILLEMS

Residence at Time of This Birth— NEW LONDON TEXAS

Race/Color—WHITE

Age at Time of This Birth—30

NUMBER OF CHILDREN BORN TO THIS MOTHER INCLUDING THIS BIRTH—2

NUMBER OF CHILDREN BORN
TO THIS MOTHER AND NOW
LIVING—1

ATTENDANT'S SIGNATURE—
This is to certify that this is a true
and correct copy of the official
record which is in my custody.
—M. A. Selmond, December 28, 1937

CHAPTER THIRTY

March 1998

Margaret flicked the dust rag at the crevice of the window frame, wishing she'd been able to find that clever little attachment that had come with the vacuum cleaner, the one that could be used in tight spots. But lately she was forgetting the oddest things. Nothing to worry about, according to Dr. Pancioni—he did her the favor of including himself in their conversations: "at our age," he'd say, though Margaret knew for a fact that he was almost ten years younger than her sixty years.

He'd prescribed her verapamil at her last visit and Margaret had been dutifully taking it, though it interfered with her digestion and she wished she'd thought to skip a few doses so that she could manage to get down more than a few bites of lunch. She'd planned to make Georgina's favorite, a dish called Thrifty Tetrazzini that she'd discovered long ago in *Family Circle* and copied onto a recipe card that was now so worn that it was almost impossible to read her handwriting, which didn't matter because she knew it by heart.

(Maybe she should tell Dr. Pancioni that the next time she saw him.)

But yesterday in the supermarket, as she held a can of pimentos in her hand, she was beset with worry. *What eleven-year-old child eats pimentos nowadays?* The kids she saw around town were always snacking on chips and pizza. The more processed the better, which had given her an idea—cruising the prepared foods, she discovered a packet of seasonings for sloppy joes and added it to her cart. Ground beef, soft white buns, iceberg lettuce for a salad none of them would eat, a box of baker's chocolate with the foolproof brownie recipe on the back.

Now, at eleven forty-five on the appointed Saturday morning, the brownies were cooling on the counter, the sloppy joe mixture was slowly congealing in its greasy orange sauce on the stove, and the salad—she'd added a chopped tomato and slices of cucumber—was in a bowl in the fridge with plastic wrap on top.

The table was set with a cloth that Margaret was very much hoping Georgina would recognize, because it was the olive branch in the tableau she'd spent all week preparing. At seventeen, Georgina had brought it home from one of her mysterious haunts, claiming it had been imported from India. And indeed, its pattern of jewel-tone paisley swirls was plenty exotic. Margaret suspected its provenance was considerably more ordinary, based on the "easy-care" tag she'd found sewn into the seam when she threw it into the wash, but what mattered was that years ago Margaret had thrown it out because she had found a nest of spiders in its skunky folds, and Georgina had retrieved it from the trash and stuffed it into a drawer, where it had languished all these years.

Margaret had experimented with several different table settings, using Caroline's several sets of china, but in the end settled for her trusty "Spice of Life" Corelle, which didn't fight with the tablecloth. She added sunny yellow napkins she'd bought at the Walmart in Harrison and a bouquet of flowers from the garden.

In recent years Margaret had become considerably more relaxed about housekeeping. Why it had seemed so important to keep the unused bedrooms dusted, she could no longer even remember. For several years running, she'd made a halfhearted effort to clear out the clutter for the Ladies Auxiliary tag sale, but then she'd had a falling-out with the president and quit going to club meetings. She'd considered calling an appraiser to look at some of her mother's things, which she suspected might be valuable, but every time she picked up a crystal stem or opened one of the drawers in Caroline's old silver chest, she was overcome with emotions that she didn't care to sort through: it was easier to leave all of it undisturbed.

This idea of hers, to invite the grandchild she'd never met to lunch, had actually sprung from a chance afternoon when she'd been searching for her mother's scrapbook. The New London History Guild was mounting a retrospective on the disaster, and they'd put out a call for memorabilia to fill the display cases in the public library. Some of the members of the Society remembered Caroline's scrapbook, which her mother had kept with obsessive care. Many other families had done the same, but the Piersons' wealth and connections had allowed her to amass and preserve a bigger trove than most.

Margaret continued to receive far more communication than she would have preferred from the New London History Guild: not just the photocopied and stapled quarterly newsletter, but regular announcements of events and the occasional invitation to speak or participate in school lessons. She turned them all down, suggesting, without coming out and saying it, that her mother's passing had made the past too painful for her. The members of the Guild— the former Daisy Club had renamed itself ages ago, now mostly a group of descendants and busybodies and people with nothing better to do—claimed to have adored her mother, which Margaret also found suspect.

The decade since Caroline's death had passed at a pace that seemed both eternal and lightning quick, depending on the day and Margaret's mood, but one thing that had remained constant was her unease with her association with the disaster that had taken place before she was even born. The other ten Daisy children seemed to feel the same way; a majority had moved away, and the few who remained seemed no more interested in the past than she did.

Ever since her mother's deathbed confession and plea, Margaret had preferred not to think about it at all. Because, of course, it wasn't as simple as her mother believed: How could she atone for a wrong of such magnitude, committed so long ago? And why should she have to? Especially because she was as much a victim, in her own way, as the rest of them.

It didn't help that Pammy McGovney now sent her a Christmas card every year, chatty photo-copied missives full of misspellings and news about her two children, relentlessly optimistic despite all the trouble they seemed headed for. The older one had given up after a year at community college and was working at the cannery; the younger, the girl, had had a baby out of wedlock before she was even out of high school. Margaret threw these letters away as soon as she read them.

If there was one thing that life had taught Margaret *not* to do, it was to wallow in the past, wasting time and energy on things that had happened an eternity ago.

That was why she had been searching for the scrapbook, planning to donate it and then never look at it again. Instead she'd stumbled on the photograph, the one her father had been holding the day she'd found him crying in the garage. She'd never seen it after that day and assumed it was lost—but there it was in the attic, wrapped in tissue and tucked into a silver-plated tureen.

Ruby Pierson, 11 years. The passage of time had faded the photograph, but the lively spark in the little girl's eyes was unmistakable, the slight gap between her teeth adorable as ever. Margaret had touched the photograph with her fingertip and thought: *my sister.* It was the first time she'd ever allowed herself the thought.

The photograph had ignited a curiosity—well, it was more than that; a longing—to see the granddaughter who was now the same age as her sister had been when she died. There was a sense of everything coming full circle. Margaret was reasonably healthy and didn't anticipate her demise anytime soon, but seeing the lines in her face in the mirror, feeling the aches in her knees and wrists in the morning—well, it had added a sort of urgency to the notion of reconnecting with her child and grandchild. She didn't let herself think about it too hard—she dashed off a succinct note and when the reply came (a piece of typing paper with her daughter's handwritten response as stiff as her own: *Dear Mother, Thank you for the invitation, Katie and I will see you at noon on the 22nd*—no *Love,* just *Georgina*) she was surprised.

There was a knock at the door. Panicked, Margaret looked at the clock. Still ten minutes before noon! But that was Georgina for you, always on her own schedule. Margaret stuffed the rag under a seat cushion and wiped her hands on her skirt as she went to the door, whispering, "Okay, okay."

She opened the door and there was her daughter, her hair dyed streaky blond and cut like that TV star, wearing white pants and a slinky emerald-green blouse and a guarded expression but otherwise utterly unchanged. Her hands were on the shoulders of a little girl so innocently beautiful that Margaret gasped, and Georgina gave her a little shove and she held out her hand and politely said, "It's very nice to meet you, I'm Katie."

The lunch was eaten (though not much of it, as it appeared Margaret had guessed wrong about the appetites of her guests) and the coffee perking when Georgina touched her daughter's hand and said, "Katie, why don't you go see Grandma's garden and let us visit for a few minutes."

"Oh, the garden's not—I haven't—all right," Margaret stuttered, catching her daughter's frown. She hadn't done a thing back there in

445

years—the only efforts she made were in the front yard, where passersby still stopped to sniff the hedge roses.

"I'm sure it's fine," Georgina said. "Now, scoot."

Katie, who'd been perfectly polite all through lunch but obviously bored and only pretending to be interested in Margaret's attempts at conversation, made her escape gratefully, letting the screen door slam just like her mother always had.

"Okay, I'm going to make this fast," Georgina said. Now she sounded nervous, like she'd practiced for this moment. Her hands twisted tightly in her lap, and Margaret noticed for the first time the nest of fine lines at the corners of her eyes, the ones all that makeup didn't quite conceal. "I came today because I thought Katie had a right to at least meet you. But I'm not interested in a relationship, Mother. The emotional damage you caused me is too great and I need to look forward instead of backward and honor my own journey."

Margaret blinked. "I beg your pardon?"

But Georgina was shaking her head. "I'm sure you never thought I'd survive a day after you threw me out."

"I didn't—"

"Stop!" Georgina slammed her hand down on the table. "*I'm* talking. I'm entitled to be heard.

I came to you, about to have a *baby,* hungry and having just escaped an abusive relationship, not that you were interested in my problems, and you wouldn't give me a dime."

"What? You never said one thing about being abused. You sat right there in that chair throwing it in my face about all the men you'd been having sex with."

"That was a cry for help! *God!* This was stupid." Georgina got up with a clatter, her face flushed with anger. "My therapist warned me not to come. I should have listened to her. But I won't let the damage you did to me in my childhood affect my daughter."

She went to the back door and called for Katie, who came running with dirty knees and twigs in her hair. "There you are," she said brightly, ignoring Margaret, who was gasping like a gutted fish. *Damage? Abuse?*

"Wait," she stammered. "I have— I wanted to give— Katie, dear, I have a present for you."

Katie looked to her mother pleadingly and Georgina hesitated, then let out an aggrieved sigh. "All right. But make it quick. We're already running late."

Margaret led the way numbly into the living room, her hopes for the afternoon splintering. She had planned to make a presentation of sorts, had practiced the words she would say. *Your great-great-grandmother Griseldis Willems brought only one treasure from the old country,* she would begin, and then explain how Griseldis had scrimped and saved to add a second delicate porcelain teacup to the collection before passing it on to her own daughter; how Hugh had taken to giving Caroline cups to mark their wedding anniversaries, until there were nine cups hanging from the polished walnut rack he'd had made for her. Margaret had planned to offer Katie the newest of them today, reasoning that if it broke it wouldn't be the end of the world, and then each year on Katie's birthday she'd receive another until, on her twentieth birthday, Margaret would present her with the most precious, the original delicate blue and white Mosa Maastricht all the way from Holland.

But Georgina seemed on the verge of bolting, so Margaret grabbed the cup off the end and pressed it into Katie's hands.

"Someday," she began, but at the same second Katie said, "Thank you very much," and Georgina gave her hand an impatient tug, and then—

And then they were gone.

CHAPTER THIRTY-ONE

Katie and Scarlett had been taking turns with the letters, passing them back and forth across the table. Scarlett had read each first, and so when she exclaimed "Holy *fuck!*" Katie had to wait her turn to read for herself.

In those moments, a parade of possibilities galloped through her mind. Murder, betrayal, intrigue . . . but when Scarlett wordlessly handed over the brittle folded paper, watching her as she read, Katie realized that somewhere deep inside her she'd already considered this possibility—if not in this precise outline, at least in some rough and unexamined form.

She read the letter twice and then set it down. It took her a moment to comprehend it. "So Gomma was really Euda's daughter," she said slowly. "And Caroline took her and raised her as her own."

"And no one ever knew!"

"But we don't know that," Katie said. "I mean, these were in Margaret's desk. *Someone* put them there."

"It must have been Caroline," Scarlett said. "Caroline hid them there and they've been there ever since. She might even have wondered what happened to them—maybe she forgot and thought she threw them out."

"I don't know," Katie said. "How could you forget something like that? I mean, this is the biggest secret I can imagine. Caroline faked a pregnancy! She basically bought Euda's baby!"

"No, it said in the letter, Euda didn't want any money."

"But she wanted *something,*" Katie said. "I mean, it was in every letter, between the lines. She wanted her sister back."

"And Caroline wouldn't have anything to do with her," Scarlett said. "Gomma always said her mother thought our side of the family was trash. Gomma only met her cousins one time, at a wedding. And she never met the rest of us until she just decided to drive over to Archer when I was five. She didn't call or anything. She told me she was afraid my mom would shut the door in her face."

"But . . . there has to be more to it than that," Katie said. "Don't you think it's strange she just showed up at your door one day for no reason? I bet you anything she found those letters and realized that—that she was actually Pammy and Amy and Lassiter's *sister,* and her parents were actually her aunt and uncle. God, this is confusing!"

"But she would have told me!" Scarlett said. "I

mean, Katie, we talked about *everything*. Things I never even told my mom."

"Maybe she figured it was too late," Katie said. "That too much time had passed—that it was better not to stir things up."

For a while neither of them spoke, rereading the letters. Then a thought occurred to Katie.

"What if . . ." she said slowly. "I mean, think about her will. About her wanting us to take a week to clear out that house. You have to admit that's kind of strange, right? What if this was her way of forcing us to get to know each other—"

"—and leaving us a treasure hunt so we'd find the letters?"

"Not just the letters, but the stock certificates." Katie snapped her fingers. "And my mom's letters! Remember the very first night—"

"In that box, in the hall closet," Scarlett said excitedly. "Like she *wanted* you to find them."

"Because there wasn't any other way to tell her side of the story," Katie said. "My mom refused to even talk to her on the phone."

"And my mom never even had a chance to know," Scarlett said wistfully.

"Do you think you should tell your grandmother?"

"Grandma Sharon?" Scarlett did the calculations. "So her mom was Pammy, who really . . . Margaret's *sister*."

"Wow," Katie said. "That's . . . that would be

hard to process. All this time they lived thirty miles from each other and never even spoke. Just like Caroline and Euda."

"So what does this make *us?*" Scarlett said. "Gomma told me you were my second cousin, once removed. But if we were actually . . . let's see. Your grandmother was my great-grandmother's sister. Her child was . . . this is so confusing."

Katie shrugged. "Then don't think about it. Let's just be cousins. I mean, does it really even matter?"

Scarlett grinned. "I don't guess it does." She lifted her glass of lemonade. "Here's to family."

As they clinked glasses, the breeze coming through the window lifted one of the sheets of paper and swept it to the floor and under the old stove, so that only a corner peeked out. Katie dove to the floor and retrieved it. "That was close. Just imagine, the truth could have been buried for another eighty years!"

"This is the story we'll tell our own children. Oh!" Scarlett exclaimed, her eyes shining. "You'll be my kids' auntie! Aunt Katie. You know, if you end up marrying Jam, then I'll be related to him for real."

"Hold on there, Scarlett, you're out of control," Katie protested. "In the past two weeks, I've lost the grandmother I never knew, made out with a man who isn't my husband, and discovered a shocking family secret. Don't you think that's enough for a while?"

Scarlett gazed at her happily. "Maybe not. I mean, isn't that the point of all this? Caroline did this unthinkable thing and lived with the secret her whole life. Margaret never even got to know her own family. Shouldn't we learn from that? Seize the day, or something like that?"

"Close enough," Katie laughed. "Seize the day, indeed."

CHAPTER THIRTY-TWO

March 1998

A week later Margaret drove the thirty miles to Archer, to the house she'd visited once before. It had been painted a cheery yellow, and there was now a neat square of lawn edged in a flower bed bursting with marigolds and zinnias. She walked up to the door, trembling with nerves. Before she even had time to knock, a little girl opened the door and looked up at her with wide brown eyes set in the most beautiful heart-shaped caramel-colored face that Margaret had ever seen.

"You must be Scarlett," Margaret said, her heart knocking around her chest like a bug in a jar. "I'm very pleased to meet you."

EPILOGUE

The weeks following the garage sale were marked with record rains. Indian Creek rose up in its banks and flooded the construction site, and work on the fulfillment center was stalled as engineers reviewed their calculations. Civic groups from both Rusk and Harrison Counties took advantage of the opportunity to stage protests and, since it was a slow news week, got their faces on TV, at least in the local markets.

On the day that the sun burst through the clouds and lit the entire town with streaks of gold, drying up the puddles and bringing everyone out of doors with faces upturned to the sun, Katie was on her knees in the upstairs bathroom of her grandmother's house using a Q-Tip to scour the grime from the seam where the baseboards met the beautiful old tiny hexagon floor tiles, when suddenly the light was blocked by someone standing in the doorway.

"Please, please tell me the pizza's here," she said, backing awkwardly around the toilet on all fours. "Because I'm about to faint from hunger."

But it wasn't Jam standing in the doorway. At eye level were a long and lacy yellow skirt and crimson gladiator sandals and three silver toe rings, one with a jet stone. On one ankle, a familiar tattoo of a moth.

"Lolly!" Katie stood up so fast that she knocked her head against the sink, but it didn't matter, because Lolly wrapped her arms around her and hugged her so hard she lifted Katie clean off the floor. "I can't believe you came!"

"Of course I did, you ninny." They were both laughing and crying at the same time, Katie breathing in Lolly's familiar peony perfume. "Do you think we could get out of the bathroom? I mean, I love you madly, but there's barely room for both of us. What are you doing in here, anyway?"

Katie led her across the hall and into Margaret's old room, which Scarlett had painted a soft powder pink and filled with furniture she'd rescued from elsewhere in the house. On the bed were a stuffed hippo and a headless doll that she'd found up in the cupboards of the garage apartment.

"I'm *helping,* Lolls," she said, taking armloads of laundry off the settee and tossing them on the bed so they could sit down. "It turns out I'm a helpful person! Who knew?"

"Not Nickell, March, obviously," Lolly said, wrinkling her nose. "They never recognized your potential. I heard they're into a second round of layoffs, by the way."

"Yeah, I saw that." Katie allowed herself a

smirk. "How'd you get in the house, anyway?"

"Uh, the door was wide open? Plus the Lyft driver apparently knew your grandmother."

"Trust me, *everyone* knew Gomma," Katie said, rolling her eyes. "I have to admit this small-town stuff takes a little getting used to."

"But you really are liking it, right?"

There was the faintest trace of uncertainty in Lolly's voice. Katie grabbed her hands and squeezed. "That's why you're here, isn't it? You didn't believe me?"

Lolly squeezed back. "I mean, yeah, I *believed* you, I guess, except every time I talk to you there's a dog barking or power tools in the background or a man's voice yelling for you to come back to bed . . ."

Katie felt her face redden. "That only happened one time. And I told you I'd be back in Boston for your birthday!"

"Which isn't for three more months." Lolly tossed her impossible hair. "You know I've got no talent for deferred gratification. Besides, I have some gossip that's too good to share over the phone."

"What!"

"Let's just say . . ." Lolly cocked her head and regarded her with an expression of great gravity. "A certain unnamed ex of yours got trapped in the elevator after work and the janitor had to get the security guy, who ended up calling the fire department, because he apparently did something to the controls that caused it to get jammed between floors and then couldn't get it going again. They were in there for *hours*."

A tiny beat passed. "They . . . ?"

Lolly nodded triumphantly. "A different intern this time, I think from HR? Which, I mean, not great for her career prospects, right? But here's the *good* part: Liam didn't have any pants. Like, nowhere in the elevator. Nowhere to be found!"

Katie felt a wave of dizziness not unlike the time she rode the Poltergeist at Six Flags, the sense of the car chugging up the roller coaster's tracks to the top, the horror and thrill of the steep pitch that would follow. "Okay, I'll bite," she said faintly. "Where were his pants?"

"Well, Rex had to pour like half a bottle of scotch down him—and by the way, Rex says to tell you he and Liam are getting a divorce and can he please come home, and don't worry, I told him he needs to grovel a little longer—but anyway, Liam finally admitted he'd left the pants on the floor of his boss's corner office because he and the intern were playing *truth or dare*." Her good humor gave way to a look of disgust. "Like a couple of fucking thirteen-year-olds. Honestly, I think that was the last straw for Rex. Although, now that I think of it, there's probably at least a thirteen-year age difference between them, so—hey, honey, you okay? God, should I not have told you?"

Katie brushed impatiently at her eyes. "No, no, I'm fine. I'm *good*. That just confirms everything I said to him the other night."

"So you *did* call him!"

"Yeah . . . I mean, I got to thinking, and this is going to sound stupid because of everything I've ever told you about my mom, but—well, I thought, *What would Georgina do?*"

"No!" Lolly gasped.

Katie nodded. "And so I called him up and I gave him a chewing-out he'll never forget. I didn't let him get a word in until I'd let him know every single way he didn't measure up. Including in the sack." Katie smiled at the memory. "*That* part was pure Mom."

Lolly shook her head, grinning. "Look at you . . . all grown up."

The door was flung open and there was Jam, his powerful arms glistening with sweat, tool belt slung low on his hips, two large pizza boxes balanced on one hand.

"My, my, my," Lolly said under her breath. "You sure do know how to bury the lede, honey."

Several months later, the morning of the grand opening of Daisy Day Care dawned bright and clear and filled with the delicious aroma of cinnamon as Jam and Kyle came walking into the house carrying trays of rolls and fruit.

"I'm so nervous!" Scarlett fretted, as the guys

went out back to make a final check on the play structure, which they'd only finished installing the day before. "What if no one comes?"

"Um, didn't you tell me yesterday that the waiting list just topped ten?"

"Yeah, but—"

"But nothing."

Georgina walked into the kitchen, dressed in tight white pants and a daring V-neck navy pullover, silver bangles jingling at her wrist, her makeup perfect. "Where's the coffee?"

"Nice of you to join us, Mom," Katie said. "Sorry you didn't get to help with any of the setup."

"I needed my beauty sleep," Georgina said mildly, kissing Katie on the cheek. She gave Scarlett's hand a squeeze and helped herself to a strawberry. "Your office is just a darling little hideaway. So romantic!"

"So help me, Mother, you'd better not sneak Darryl up there and have your way with him on my desk," Katie warned.

Her mother wrinkled her nose. "About that," she said. "Darryl won't be joining us."

"Oh dear," Scarlett said.

Katie rolled her eyes. "What happened, did you poison him in his sleep and make off with his Jaguar?"

"It turns out it was *leased,*" her mother said with a shudder of distaste.

"That's terrible," Katie said drily. "Well, maybe you can lure one of Scarlett's new clients into your lair. All those young dads—one of them's bound to have a Mrs. Robinson thing."

"Hmmph," Georgina said, taking another strawberry. "I'll be out back. Maybe Jam and Kyle will be a little more grateful for my company."

"You never know," Katie said cheerfully. "Hey, Mom?"

"Yes?"

"I'm glad you came."

"I wouldn't miss it, darling!"

Once she was safely out of earshot, Scarlett refilled their coffee cups. "So you were going to tell me," she said.

"There's nothing to tell! We had a very nice dinner at the Grub House. I can see why it's a local legend."

"All-you-can-eat crawdads, and free bibs too!" Scarlett crowed. "Not bad for your six-month anniversary."

"It's not an anniversary if we're not dating," Katie said. "Which we aren't. I'm still technically married, remember?"

"Only because J.B.'s been too busy with your business stuff to get around to filing," Scarlett shot back. "Seems to me I've heard you come in the door when the sun's coming up a few times."

"It seems to *me* someone recently reminded me

that we're grown-ass women," Katie said. "If I want to do the walk of shame every day of the week, well, I don't guess anyone can stop me."

The "someone" was none other than J.B. herself. In the months since Margaret's death, while Katie and Scarlett had overseen repairs to the old house, J.B. had handled the inheritance, the incorporation of Katie's new branding business that she ran out of the old groundskeeper's apartment, and the dissolution of the contract Scarlett had unwisely signed with Merritt. The latter had taken a healthy chunk of change, but since Scarlett waited until the papers were filed to inform Merritt that she was worth well over a million dollars, he had no recourse but to get fantastically drunk, drive across their front lawn, and stand on the porch yelling a colorful variety of threats and curses— which gave Jam the opportunity he'd been waiting for for years. His ass well and truly whipped, Merritt had slunk away and not been heard from again.

"You know," Scarlett said, "you're sounding more like a Texan every day."

"I guess there's worse things," Katie said.

She went out into the foyer, which was now lined with colorful cubbies for the children's belongings. In a matter of days, the downstairs rooms would ring with the sound of their voices. Occasionally, Katie still had a pang of sadness when she saw the colorful mobiles over the cribs or the stack of diapers in the dining room built-ins, but she was ready to accept that her chance to be a mother would come again when it was the right time.

Eighty years ago, a child had run through this house, the apple of her parents' eyes, as beloved as any who had died that warm afternoon in March 1937.

The following winter a new child arrived, a replacement for the one who was lost.

Nothing in life seemed to turn out the way it was planned. People loved as best they could, made fortunes and lost them, chased dreams that were ever out of reach, and hid their pain out of sight. Katie thought she'd left the messiness of her family behind, never realizing that she was every bit the creature of all who'd come before.

This was home—for now. Technically she rented a room and leased an office, but Scarlett was family, and so it went much deeper than a place to live and work. The new business had scored a couple of clients from back in Boston, and next week she'd sign her first local client—a mobile massage business.

"Hey, good-lookin'." Jam appeared in the doorway. "Your mother just ordered me to fix her a screwdriver."

"Let her fix it herself," Katie said, throwing her arms around his neck. "She's resourceful. What do you say we go back to your place and check on the dog?"

"If 'check on the dog' is still a euphemism for what we did the last time your mom came to visit, I'm in," Jam growled, nuzzling a spot under her ear.

"Quick—the coast is clear," Katie said, and hand in hand they ran, laughing, through a beautiful East Texas morning toward the rest of their lives.

Center Point Large Print
600 Brooks Road / PO Box 1
Thorndike, ME 04986-0001 USA

(207) 568-3717

US & Canada:
1 800 929-9108
www.centerpointlargeprint.com